# WHAT THE LADY WANTS

## Nika Rhone

Booktrope Editions
Seattle WA 2015

Cover Design by Greg Simanson
Edited by Pam Harris

This is a work of fiction. Names, characters, places, brands, media, and incidents are either the product of the author's imagination or are used fictitiously. Any resemblance to similarly named places or to persons living or deceased is unintentional.

Print ISBN 978-1-5137-0466-1
EPUB ISBN 978-1-5137-0516-3
Library of Congress Control Number: 2015918193

# ACKNOWLEDGMENTS

While writing is, by nature, a solitary endeavor, no writer is ever truly alone on their journey, and I have found myself extraordinarily lucky in the people who have shared this trip with me. My undying gratitude goes to my LIRW friends and mentors Jeannie Moon, Jolyse Barnett, Jennifer Gracen, Patty Blount, Meara Platt, and Maggie Van Well, who helped drag me kicking and screaming to the next level, and Elena Parish, who never laughed at my many stupid questions about how to do anything even remotely related to technology.

A thousand thanks to my editor, Pam Harris, who had some fantastic ideas that made the story better, and to Greg Simanson for giving me a totally gorgeous cover when I had absolutely no idea what I wanted. And thanks and hugs to the rest of my dynamite team, Melody Barber, Samantha Williams, and Karen Alcaide. You all rock.

My father may have instilled his love of books in me, but it's my husband, Danny, who has allowed me to spread my wings and explore my writing obsession despite the time-suck that it can so often be. He's never once complained about hot dogs for dinner or Jurassic-sized dust bunnies when deadlines loom. Thank you for believing in me, babe. You're my best hero.

*To all the dreamers: yes, you can.*

# CHAPTER 1

"SO, HOW MUCH LONGER do you have to put up with your shadow?"

*Too long.*

Staring morosely into her coffee, Cynthia Fordham sighed. "At least until my parents get home from their trip." Which was another three long weeks away.

She hadn't wanted or accepted a bodyguard in years, but Thea had grudgingly agreed that for now, considering the circumstances, she'd have to have one with her whenever she left the family estate. Her mother wouldn't have agreed to get on that plane otherwise, and there was no way in the world Thea would have ruined her father's extravagant plans to give her mom the mental and physical vacation that she so desperately needed.

Not even if it meant giving up some of her own hard-won independence.

Truthfully, for the most part, she didn't really mind her shadows. She liked most of them, and they knew her well enough to make the situation, if not enjoyable, then at least bearable. No, it was just Simon Poole who felt like a splinter under her fingernail, always making his presence known in painful little ways. Now, if *Doyle* had still been one of her bodyguards instead of having become their boss, she wouldn't mind the close attention one little bit.

Not that she'd ever managed to get Doyle to give her the kind of attention she actually craved from him. Not yet, anyway.

"Are they still in Kenya?" Amelia Westlake asked, her light green eyes dancing with avid interest. "I am *so* going to bug your mom for pictures when they get back."

"They're on safari until the end of the week," Thea confirmed, "and you know she'll keep you captive for a whole day once she starts showing you her ten-thousand shot photo album." She chewed her lower lip. "Maybe if I call my dad when they get back to civilization and ask really nicely, he'll agree to let Doyle give me a little more breathing room."

Or not. Frank Fordham tended to be a little crazy when it came to protecting "his girls," as he called her and her mother. It was one of the reasons Thea had insisted on going out of state to attend college. Sometimes her father's brand of love could be more than a little overwhelming.

"He wouldn't have wanted you protected if he didn't feel there was a need," Lillian Beaumont pointed out, tearing a bite off of the monstrous double chocolate chip muffin she'd been steadily consuming with her mocha latte. Thea had no idea where all the calories went, but as much as her petite friend ate, she never seemed to gain an ounce. Which was so totally unfair, since just looking at the thing had probably slapped a good half-inch onto her own waistline.

"It's not that big a deal," she muttered and then sighed in resignation when Lillian gave her "the look." "Okay, okay. I know, every threat is bad," Thea conceded. "I just really hate knowing there's someone watching me all the time." She knew they'd understand, since they'd both made the same complaints over the years. Fighting the urge to steal a piece of the muffin, which looked so much better than her plain biscotti and smelled like chocolate heaven, she groaned pathetically. "I could put up with it for now if only he just wasn't so…Simon."

Three sets of accusing eyes peered over at the man sitting with his back to the wall of the coffeehouse, his body angled so he could view both the patrons coming in the door and the dozen or so already clustered around the various tables and booths sipping their cappuccinos and lattes. *Like someone is going to jump me in the middle of Pot and Kettle,* Thea thought with a disgusted mental snort.

But that was Simon. He was all about the job. A little too much so, if her opinion counted for anything, which it seemed it didn't since he'd been assigned to her again today despite her previous objections.

"He does look a little…intense," Amelia conceded.

"There's a definite Clint Eastwood complex going on there." Seated across the round bistro-style table from her two friends, Lillian flicked a finger at the spiky bangs edging her narrowed brown eyes as she scowled at Simon. With her elfin features and pixie haircut, she looked like an annoyed fairy. "Doesn't he realize how ridiculous he looks?"

"I was thinking more *Men in Black* myself," Amelia disagreed. "I mean, come on, the suit, the sunglasses? Definite Will Smith wannabe." The grin on her face slid away when it seemed like Simon's gaze zeroed in on her. "I hate it when he does that," she muttered into her mug, blushing violently. "It's creepy."

Thea agreed wholeheartedly. It wasn't that Simon was a bad guy, really. He was just a little too into the whole bodyguard persona. If only he could at least *try* to blend in, maybe having him around wouldn't be such a royal pain in her butt. Even Daryl Raintree didn't stand out as badly, and that was saying a lot, considering Daryl was a six-foot-four, half-blooded Sioux. Daryl wore normal clothes. And smiled. And he wasn't a jerk.

"Why don't you just ask Doyle not to put him on your detail?" Lillian asked.

As always, thoughts of her father's head of security sent mixed signals of frustration and warmth through Thea. She forced herself to ignore both. "I did."

"And?"

Thea sighed again, giving her stirrer a brisk turn around her cup in agitation. "He feels I have an unreasonable dislike of Simon, and basically told me that if I couldn't give him a legitimate reason to remove him, then I should just pull up my big-girl panties and deal with it."

Amelia's eyes widened. "Wow."

"Ouch," Lillian agreed.

Thea didn't offer her own feelings on the matter. The memory of that conversation still chafed. All she'd done was make what was, to her, a simple and reasonable request. She didn't need movie-star level protection. She normally didn't require *any*, despite her father's wealth, especially not here in Boulder, where she'd grown up and had always felt extremely comfortable and safe. So safe, in fact, that all three of them had managed to wriggle free of that constrictive net once they'd turned eighteen and gotten a say in the matter. Now they only had to deal with security for special occasions and if there was some kind of credible threat.

Like now.

And, as Doyle had reminded her, since a large chunk of his team was currently half a world away with her parents, there were only so many people he could spare to accompany her when she decided to "flit around town" with her friends. That had actually hurt. Thea knew she could be accused of doing a lot of things, but "flitting" wasn't one of them. She just couldn't stand to stay locked in at the family estate 24/7. It would drive her insane.

Especially since Doyle was there.

Shoving away the shaft of pain that unfair accusation had jabbed into her, she determined to put both Doyle and Simon out of her mind and enjoy her time out with her friends. "So, how goes the wedding plans?"

Amelia had surprised them both by getting engaged the previous month. She and Charles Davenport had only been dating for a few months and mostly long distance at that. Since she'd spent the first sixteen years of her life being trotted out for display at one political function or another by her senator father and hating every minute of it, her engagement to an up-and-coming young politician had come as something of a shock to her friends.

But since Amelia seemed to genuinely love her fiancé, and so far it seemed that he returned the sentiment, they were trying hard to be supportive of her decision. Although privately, Thea thought Charles was a bit of an arrogant ass.

"Oh, things are going fine." Amelia toyed with her mug, not meeting anyone's eyes. "Mother and Mrs. Davenport assure me that they have everything well in hand."

Thea glanced at Lillian, who met her gaze with an answering frown of concern.

"Mellie, honey," Lillian said gently, "you're not letting them take over everything, are you?"

The way Amelia shifted in her seat was answer enough. Her quiet nature tended to allow people to walk all over her. Her mother certainly did. The woman was a human pit bull. With the addition of Mrs. Davenport, the two political *grand dames* were likely to steamroll right over Amelia's—and probably Charles's—wishes without giving either the bride or groom a second thought.

Poor Amelia would end up lucky to get an invitation to her own wedding.

"Oh, Mellie," Lillian started. Amelia shook her head, her cheeks reddening again, something the fair skin she'd inherited along with her pale blond hair tended to do with great frequency.

"No, it's okay, really," she said quickly. "They know how to plan an event like this. I don't." She smiled weakly. "I wouldn't want to embarrass Charles."

Judging from the strained condition of Amelia's smile, Thea was fairly sure she was repeating a sentiment she'd been hearing a lot lately. She put a comforting hand on her friend's arm. "Honey, you couldn't embarrass Charles if you tried."

The strained quality softened, but the smile remained more wan than happy.

"He's at the most important stage of his career, when everyone's eyes are going to be on him. Everything has to be perfect for him." Amelia refocused on Thea and asked determinedly, "So, how goes the job hunt?"

Leave it to Amelia to find the one topic Thea was excited enough about to allow the blatant use of her own tactics against her. She beamed with delight. "I think I might have actually gotten it."

"Which one is this?" Lillian asked.

"Timberlake Interiors," Thea answered with no little amount of pride. It was one of the most prestigious firms in the state and, best of all, based right there in Boulder. "I interviewed with Janice Timberlake herself last Friday, and I think I made a good impression. She seemed to like my portfolio, and we got along really well." That was as important to Thea as salary or benefits. More, actually. She just couldn't see herself working for someone she didn't like.

"What about…the other thing?"

"The other thing" was what had kept Thea from taking the other half dozen jobs she'd already interviewed for in the months since returning home from college. Never mind that her grades had been top notch. Forget the letters of recommendation from both her teachers and the firm she had interned with during her senior year. All that had mattered to her prospective employers had been the name Fordham on her résumé. As in Fordham Electronics. As in Money, with a very capital M.

"Did this one have any sons that 'just dropped by' while you were there?" Lillian asked with a barely concealed grin. She ducked the wadded up napkin Thea tossed at her.

"No." Thankfully, that had only happened once, which had been more than enough. She'd barely escaped without having to be rude to the woman who was so certain that Thea and her thirty-year-old, twice-divorced son made the "absolutely perfect" couple.

Not.

By the time she'd gotten to the Timberlake interview, Thea had known to address all of the important issues in the first five minutes. With a determination that would have done even Mrs. Westlake proud, she had assured and reassured Janice Timberlake that as far as she was concerned, the name Fordham didn't make her any better—or worse—than anyone else. If she was hired, her job would in no way be influenced by her family's wealth or social standing.

"I think I managed to put that behind me this time," Thea said, mentally crossing her fingers. She really wanted this job. She didn't need it, of course, but she *did* need to have something to do with her life that didn't include living off her trust fund or taking a position in her father's company. She loved her father dearly, but she wanted her own life. A nine-to-five job in an office just wasn't for her.

Interior design intrigued her on a visceral level. She loved playing with color and texture, and matching the feel of a room to the person who would be using it. Madison Helmsworth, the owner of the firm she'd interned with, had told her she had a natural eye. She'd also only half-jokingly predicted that Thea would have her own design firm within five years.

While starting her own business appealed to her, especially after the difficulties she was currently having finding the right fit in someone else's company, Thea still felt she needed some practical experience first to establish her credentials. That was why she was so excited about the possibility of getting the Timberlake job. If she did, she knew it would be because she was considered an asset rather than a trophy.

Most of all, though, getting the Timberlake job meant she would stay in Boulder, although she wouldn't admit to anyone that it wasn't staying close to her family that fueled that desire. She'd spent the four years away at college trying to squash her feelings for Brennan Doyle. He'd dealt her eighteen-year-old ego a huge blow before she'd left for California, and she had been determined to get over him once and for all. Unrequited love was hell on a person's self-confidence.

But after less than a week back home, she'd known that nothing had changed. She still loved the big jerk as much as ever.

Now she just had to decide what she was going to do about it.

"When will you know?" Amelia asked.

"She's supposed to get back to me by the end of the week." Which meant every day until then would be spent on pins and needles waiting for the phone to ring.

As they discussed which shops they wanted to browse through that afternoon, they cleared the small table, dumped their trash, and headed for the restroom. Before Thea could touch the door, however, a hand appeared to block her. She tensed, knowing who it belonged to and what he wanted, and bit back a hiss of displeasure.

She waved at the door with a flourish. "Go ahead. Be my guest." Scowling at Simon's back wasn't satisfying enough, so she added sweetly, "Could you make sure there's paper in all the stalls while you're in there, too?"

Lillian stifled a snort, but Thea was feeling far from amused. There was being a good bodyguard, and then there was being an anal-retentive jerk that couldn't see the line between necessary and excessive. Yes, both Francine and Kirsten would have gone into the restroom with her if they'd been on duty, but they would have made it feel natural. Low-key. Unlike Simon, who managed to push all of her mad buttons without even trying.

Ignoring him when he came out and gave the all-clear, Thea pushed through the door, followed by Lillian and Amelia. Her friends tactfully continued their discussion of their shopping plans as they touched up their makeup, but Thea found her joy in the day had been soured. Her feelings must have shown because Lillian gave her a hip bump and grinned into the mirror at her.

"We can always do a fire drill and lose the loser."

A fire drill. Thea grinned. They hadn't pulled that stunt since their senior prom, when they hadn't wanted their respective shadows tagging along to the after-prom party and ruining their fun. All three of them had bolted from their limo at a red light, dates in tow. By the time the light had changed and the cars with their security details had broken free of traffic, they'd been in a friend's borrowed SUV and on their way to the party. Calls home had assured everyone they hadn't been kidnapped, but there had still been hell to pay come morning.

Thea sighed. As good as the idea sounded in the abstract, in reality she knew ditching her bodyguard would be the height of stupidity. Even though she felt the threats that had been made against her family were very unlikely to come to anything, she'd made a promise and she'd keep it.

That didn't mean she wouldn't keep trying to get Doyle to see reason about him axing Simon from her detail, though. She was doing her best to be reasonable and adult in her war of wills with him over that, but he was making it tough. The fact that she got distracted by that panty-wetting belly tingle every time she was alone with him didn't help, either.

Not that she was willing to admit that little factoid to anyone, not even her best friends. As far as they were concerned, her unrequited teenage longings for Brennan Doyle had been discarded along with her penchant for M&M binges and midnight skinny-dipping.

If only Doyle were as easy to give up as the chocolate.

Forcing her thoughts away from the too-sexy-for-her-peace-of-mind Doyle, Thea said, "As much as the idea appeals, I think I'll just have to put up with him for today." Her sense of humor reemerged as she added, "Besides, I kind of like the idea of dragging him through every dress shop in town. It should bore him stupid."

Lillian had just opened her mouth to comment when a sharply raised voice outside the restroom door caught everyone's attention. All three stared at the door as the words "You have no right!" rang clearly through the wood. Some woman was not a happy camper, and Thea knew exactly who was to blame. She swore under her breath.

"You'll both testify that it was justifiable homicide, right?" she muttered through clenched teeth as she reached for the door. "Because I'm going to kill him." Steeling herself, she yanked it open.

At first, all she saw was a lot of back, since Simon was standing directly in front of the opening doing his Secret Service impersonation. Then he shifted to the side to let her out—after she poked a hard finger into his ribs—and Thea saw the very angry woman who had evidently been denied entry to the restroom while her oh-so-special personage was using it.

Janice Timberlake.

Of course.

Thea smiled a weak apology at the woman, but somehow she knew she wasn't going to be getting that happy phone call she'd been expecting. In fact, she might as well forget about applying to any other design firms in the state of Colorado once Mrs. Timberlake got through with her.

Oh yes, her humiliation was quite complete.

And she knew just who she was going to share it with.

* * *

There had been many times in Brennan Doyle's thirty-four years that his sharply tuned instincts had saved his ass.

They'd made him ditch his cigarette down the toilet just seconds ahead of the principal's arrival back in his St. Cyril's High School days. They'd let him slip unnoticed from Mary Jane Kelly's bedroom window right before her mother did a surprise post-midnight bed check. They'd even kept him and his men alive during more than one mission in the Middle East and other hot-spots around the globe.

Several of his Marine Recon buddies had laughingly referred to it as "Doyle's Spidey Sense," but to a man they had respected it. If Doyle said jump, they didn't ask why, they just asked which way.

Doyle's instincts had never let him down yet. And those instincts were telling him that something was about to screw up his day. Big time.

Not five minutes after the troublesome feeling began, the door to his office in the security bungalow slammed open, and that something stalked in and stood in front of his desk, practically spitting fire at him.

"You have to do something about him." The words sounded as though they were being yanked through clenched teeth, which, on closer inspection, Doyle saw they were. Everything about the rigid line of Cynthia Fordham's body screamed restrained fury. *Barely* restrained. Her fists were clenched so tightly at her sides that her fingers had gone white, and her entire body practically quivered like a live wire.

There was only one thing he could think of that would drive her to such a state. What the hell had Poole done now?

Adopting his professional tone and expression, Doyle said calmly, "Why don't you—"

"I don't want to sit down, Doyle," Thea interrupted, anticipating his opening salvo. There wasn't much room in the small office, packed as it was by a desk, credenza, filing cabinets, and two chairs, but she began to pace in tight, quick steps in the only floor space available, right in front of his desk. It was as though she had to expend the tension in her body or explode from it.

"I don't want to calm down. I don't want to discuss this rationally. And I don't want to hear how he's a professional and I should just let him do his job." Thea stopped and leaned on the front of the desk with both hands, bringing her eye-to-eye with Doyle. "I just want him gone."

With great difficulty, Doyle ignored the way her silk blouse gaped as she leaned over, revealing creamy skin that he definitely shouldn't have been noticing. Harder was not inhaling the intoxicatingly sweet scent of vanilla and honey that seemed to surround her like a delicious cloud.

"We've had this discussion before," he said, willfully maintaining eye contact. "Several times, in fact. I'm not going to remove one of my people from a detail just because you don't get along with him. He's there as your bodyguard, not as your friend."

"What he *is* is a pain in my—"

"Thea," Doyle warned.

Drawing herself upright, for which Doyle was eternally grateful, Thea glared down at him with narrowed eyes. "He's embarrassed me for the last time, Doyle. He's supposed to be a nice, invisible shadow. Everyone else is a shadow. Francine is a shadow. Daryl is a shadow. But Simon..."

"Not a shadow?" Doyle ventured, half-amused despite himself.

"Worse. He's...he's an attention-seeking Secret Service wannabe. Or a *Men in Black* wannabe. We haven't quite decided which."

Doyle didn't need to ask who the "we" was. The Royal Court, as the trio of friends had been dubbed for their combined wealth and family power as much as for the way people always seemed to gravitate toward them and try to ingratiate themselves into their inner circle.

Their security code names had even been derived from the teasing appellation: Lillian Beaumont was the Queen or Queen Bee, the one who led them on most of their outrageous stunts; Amelia Westlake was the Princess, the one born with a silver spoon in her mouth and a dragon of a mother to guard the castle gates; and Thea was the Lady, the calming influence and voice of reason.

Usually.

Swiping a hand through the air as if to wipe away what she'd been saying as unimportant, Thea continued her tirade. "Whatever he is, today he went too far, Doyle. He humiliated me, and he cost me the job I wanted. A job I worked damn hard to get, by the way. One I would have been really good at, too, if anyone would give me half a chance to prove it." She drew an unsteady breath. "So I'm not asking anymore, Doyle. I'm telling you. Get Simon off my detail. Today. Right now. This second."

Doyle frowned slightly. "What do you mean he cost you a job?"

"Mrs. Timberlake." Her voice wobbled slightly, making his gut tighten at that obvious sign of true distress. "Timberlake Interiors. She was there, at the coffeehouse, and he wouldn't let her in, and I could tell. I could just tell from the look on her face, she was thinking everything that I told her was a lie. That I really was this spoiled little rich bitch, and there's no way on earth she's going to hire me now, and she'll tell everybody what happened and no one else will, either. And I'm going to end up decorating tacky little motel rooms in the middle of nowhere for the rest of my life, and it's all his fault." She ended in an almost-wail.

Since Thea wasn't usually so verbally challenged, it took Doyle a few long seconds to make sense of her convoluted explanation. "He wouldn't let her in to get coffee?"

"The *bathroom,* Doyle. He wouldn't let her into the bathroom." Thea rolled her eyes in disgust. "Don't you get it? He stood there like…like…"

"Like a bodyguard?"

"Like a jerk," Thea said, shooting him a scathing look, "and refused to let her in. To a *public* restroom, Doyle. What part of public didn't he get?"

"It stopped being public the minute you went into it."

"Damn it, Doyle!" Thea exploded. "How many times do we have to have the same argument? I don't care how much money my father has. I'm not going to spend my life surrounded by bodyguards and handlers. I managed on my own for four years while I was away at college, and there's no reason I can't manage something as simple as going to the bathroom on my own now that I'm back home!"

There was, of course. A big, fat, dangerous reason, only not the one she thought. Not that Doyle was going to tell her that any more than he was going to tell her that she hadn't been quite as alone during those four years away as she liked to think.

No. Right now his main concern was getting her calmed down before she did something impulsive or stupid. Thea was usually neither, but Doyle had sensed a change in her since she'd returned home two months earlier. There was a sense of dissatisfaction that hadn't been there before, an edgy restlessness that made him wonder who or what had put it there and what Thea might end up doing because of it. To do his job, he needed her happy and contained.

And if happy wasn't possible, well, then he'd settle for just contained.

"Your father's takeover of Zephyr Industries made a lot of people very unhappy," he reminded her, drawing on the cover story Frank Fordham had insisted upon when the need to increase the security surrounding Thea had first arisen. "There were more than a few ugly threats made."

"By a bunch of overpaid executives who were pissed at losing their cushy jobs and golden parachutes, both of which were why the company was failing and ripe to be bought out by Dad in the first place," Thea replied with dismissive disgust.

Doyle stifled a grin. She might say she didn't want to work for her dad, but she was definitely her father's daughter. "All the more reason for them to want a little revenge. You saw the letters."

Thea sighed. "I know."

"They threatened to hurt him and his family as payback."

"I know."

"Your mother only agreed to go ahead with the trip your father had planned for them if you promised to accept as much security as I deemed necessary to keep you safe from any possible danger those threats might present."

"Damn it, Doyle, I *know*."

Invoking her mother's concerns had been a little low, but Doyle refused to feel guilty. He needed Thea's complete cooperation. If he had to push some buttons to get it, he would. Still, there was an undertone of sadness in Thea's voice that reminded him that this wasn't the first time she'd had to be concerned with being the target for any nut job with a grudge or a get-rich-quick scheme in his pocket.

Clearly, growing up an heiress wasn't always the sunshine and roses people seemed to expect it to be. The threat of kidnapping had been a very real and present danger from the day her father had made his first million.

"I would have promised just about anything to keep her from cancelling their trip," Thea said, reminding Doyle of how his boss's wife had cornered him the morning they'd left for the airport to drag a personal promise from him to keep her daughter safe. She'd been given the cover story as well, which Frank Fordham had deemed the lesser evil when given the truth of the real threat to their only offspring.

Even if he hadn't been following orders, Doyle would have also promised whatever it took to get Evie Fordham on that plane. The month-long trip had been planned as a way for her to finally de-stress after the health scare she had struggled through earlier in the year. The last thing she needed was to worry about the fact that Thea had acquired a stalker.

He might have had to lie about the reason, but he hadn't had to lie about his promise. He had every intention of keeping Thea safe. He just wondered if either he or Frank would be once Evie found out that they'd withheld the truth from her as well as from Thea. Doyle knew exactly which side of her parentage Thea got her magnificent temper from.

"It won't be forever," he reminded her.

"It'll only feel like it," came the muttered reply. Thea sighed. "Fine. I've accepted that I have to have someone with me whenever I leave home. For now," she added pointedly, seeming to need to reassert her stand on her right to be a Normal Person, an argument that had lasted her entire senior year of high school and ended with her winning the right to go away to college.

Her and a very clever security detail she'd thankfully never caught on to.

"For now," Doyle agreed, saving that particular argument for another day.

"What about Simon?"

This time it was Doyle who sighed. "Do you think he really cost you that job?"

To her credit, Thea didn't launch into another emotional tirade. Instead, she pushed her hand through her thick, chestnut hair and blew out a long breath. "I don't know, Doyle. I really think he did. The look on her face…" She shook her head sadly.

Doyle felt his mouth dry up as the motion of Thea's arm pushed her breasts snugly up against her silk blouse. Her nipples, hardened by the air conditioning, dimpled the soft material as they stood at pert attention. Roughly, Doyle jerked his attention away from the sight. He cleared his throat. Then cleared it again. "I'll talk to Simon."

"You've talked to him before," Thea reminded him. She looked at him with pleading eyes. "*Please,* Doyle."

Staring into those blue, blue eyes, Doyle knew he was already beaten. He'd never been able to say no to Thea when she looked at him like that. Well, except once. But that time, saying no had been a matter of honor, not to mention self-preservation, and had been the hardest damn thing he'd ever had to do.

"I'll take him off your detail." It was a reluctant acceptance of the inevitable. Simon and Thea had clashed from their first meeting. Some people enjoyed the whole "look at me, I'm important enough to rate a bodyguard" thing, but Thea wasn't one of them. Simon just hadn't seemed to be able to get that through his thick head, no matter how many times Doyle explained it to him. Well, maybe now he would.

Thea blinded him with a dazzling smile. "You're the best, Doyle!"

Watching Thea's exit was a trial, since her crisp linen slacks gave him a perfect view of her firm rear. Doyle slumped back in his chair. The best? Hell no, he was the worst. The worst kind of bastard, checking out his employer's daughter's assets. No matter that her breasts were full and looked to be just enough to overflow his hands, or that her ass was tight and round, or her long legs would wrap just nicely around his waist while he…

Viciously, Doyle snapped a leash on those thoughts and brought them to heel. This was Thea, for chrissake. *Thea.* He had no business thinking of her in terms of her assets, full, tight, or otherwise. He worked for her father. The man trusted him to keep her safe. Even from himself. Especially from himself. She was a child, a mere twenty-two to his thirty-four. He was old enough to be her…well, her older brother. And here he was, practically drooling over her lovely, young breasts.

God, he was disgusting.

Doyle picked up the phone and asked to have Simon sent to his office. After that, he called and left a message on Margo's cell phone asking if she was free for dinner the following night. If he was paying attention to little Thea's assets, that meant he wasn't availing himself of Margo's generous charms as often as he should.

Yes, that was it. He was a healthy man in his sexual prime, and he'd been depriving himself of his needs for too long. It made perfect sense.

But it still didn't explain why his palms itched when he thought again of little Thea and her perky assets.

# Chapter 2

**THEA GLARED AT** the phone on the corner of her sleek mahogany desk.

*Come on, ring.*

Her lips pressed into a grim line as she turned her chair and ignored the phone, staring instead at the still unfinished sketch of the bedroom her mother's friend had asked her to redesign. It was slow going. Not because it was a difficult task—the room had great bones and Mrs. Butler had wonderful taste and an openness to trying things out of the box, which gave Thea a lot of freedom to find the perfect look—but because her mind just wouldn't stay focused.

Usually, the atmosphere of the home office she'd created in one of the spare bedrooms was perfect for blocking out all distractions and letting her focus solely on her work. But today was Friday, and that just wasn't going to happen.

*Ring, damn it!*

Since neither glaring nor ignoring had produced the desired effect, Thea resorted to something she hadn't done since she was eight years old and wanted a pony for Christmas, even though her parents had said that they had no room in their two-bedroom house in Durango to keep one. She closed her eyes, crossed her fingers, and wished as hard as she could.

*Please let the phone ring. Please, please, please, please…*

After a few minutes of silent chanting, Thea groaned and dropped her head onto the desk. It was no use. Wishing wouldn't get Janice Timberlake to call any more than it had gotten her that stupid pony. It was almost three o'clock. If the call was going to come, it would have come by now. Her job at Timberlake Interiors was history. His-to-ry.

The pity party was intense but short. Never one to wallow—not for too long, anyway—Thea pushed herself upright and took stock. Sure, she'd lost her best shot with Timberlake thanks to the Bathroom Incident, as Lillian was now calling it. And, yes, she'd pretty much exhausted all the other interior design firms in the greater Boulder area. That didn't mean she was going to quit now.

There were still dozens of firms out there. Just not as close to home. Which might help in trying to distance herself from her name and all the attendant pitfalls that went with it but would also mean removing herself from the one place she most wanted to be.

Near Doyle.

Ridiculous, really, since the man didn't have a clue. He either treated her as a museum piece to be safely guarded and surrounded in bubble wrap whenever a tiny bump loomed on the road of life, or he treated her the same way he had when he'd first come to work for her father: like a big brother. A very domineering, overprotective big brother.

*Ugh!*

Thinking of Doyle in the big brother role had been all well and good when she was thirteen, but she'd grown up in the nine years since then. Too bad Doyle seemed to have missed that little fact. When she looked at him now, she didn't see the guy who taught her to hold her breath so she could swim underwater for two whole minutes, or who had sat up with her all night while she cried her eyes out after her dog had dug under the fence and then been hit by a car.

No, when she looked at Brennan Doyle, she saw a tall, darkly tanned man whose military training showed in every disciplined line of his well-toned body, whose intelligence and wit shone from twinkling hazel eyes that could stop a girl dead with one look, whose very presence in a room could start her heart tripping in a triple-time beat no salsa could match. She'd racked up more sweaty dreams about the man than she cared to count, starting when she was sixteen and didn't even understand what sweaty dreams were all about.

Doyle, her big brother? Not in a million years.

But knowing how she felt didn't change a thing about how *he* felt. Or didn't feel. That was the part that made her the craziest. She didn't know if that spark of something she sometimes thought she saw in his gaze meant anything or if she was just pathetically projecting what she wanted to see into those beautiful, see-into-your-soul eyes.

Thea sighed, putting aside the sketch pad and turning on her laptop. It wouldn't hurt to do an Internet search for interior design firms based in Denver, Pueblo, and maybe even Colorado Springs. At least it would help to keep her mind off of the what-ifs and maybes that surrounded her turbulent feelings regarding what to do about Doyle.

Attracting men was not something she'd ever really gotten the hang of. Rebuffing them, now *that* she had gotten down to a science by her second semester at college, right after the Dave Disaster. He had been her first, and only, lover and it had been, well, a disaster. She'd caught him cheating. He'd accused her of being frigid and needy, and she'd lost whatever small amount of self-confidence she'd started with. After that, it had been easier, and safer, just to avoid relationships altogether.

Attracting men was more Lillian's tour de force. If only Thea could ask for Lil's help. But that would mean admitting to her friend that she was still hung up on Doyle after four years of silent denial. Maybe she should write to Dr. Phil. *Dear Dr. Phil; There's a sexy ex-Marine living in the guest house on my parents' estate, and I dream about him every night in enough detail to make Hugh Heffner blush, but I don't know how to tell him I want to tear his clothes off and have wild monkey sex with him until neither of us can walk straight. What do I do?*

A faint shudder ran through her. Okay, what she definitely *shouldn't* do was think of Doyle and wild monkey sex in the same sentence. The same paragraph. The same time zone.

With a groan, Thea saved her search results and shut down the computer. She needed help all right, and it was time to swallow her pride and ask for it. The hardest part was going to be finally confessing the truth to her friends.

\* \* \*

"What do you mean, you know?"

Ignoring Thea's stunned exclamation, Lillian plucked a brownie from the plate on the kitchen table between them and took a huge bite. She rolled her eyes and gave an appreciative moan. "Rosa has *got* to give up her recipe for these someday. They're just too decadent to keep a secret." As if to prove it, she shoved the rest of it into her mouth and continued to make yummy noises as she chewed.

"What do you mean you know?" Thea demanded a second time. She slid the plate of treats she'd brought with her as a bribe out of reach. "Lil, I'm holding the chocolate hostage until I get an answer."

After taking a large swallow of milk to wash down the gooey brownie, Lillian gave her friend a slightly exasperated look. "I mean, I know. I've always known. Just because you stopped whining about unrequited love and drowning yourself in chocolate binges every Saturday night when he disappeared into town to shack up with his bimbo of the month doesn't mean it isn't still perfectly obvious that you're in love with the guy."

Heat flooded Thea's cheeks. Was she that transparent? God, was she that *pathetic*?

"I didn't whine," she mumbled defensively. Her shoulders slumped. "Okay, I whined. A little. But that was then. This is now. *Then* I was eighteen, a kid. He was thirty. I get that. *Now* I'm twenty-two. I'm a woman, damn it, and he still doesn't notice me. So, give it to me straight, Lil. What's wrong with me?" Thea shoved a bite of brownie into her mouth before sliding the plate back toward the center of the table.

She ran a finger absently over the indentations marking the distressed oak surface as she chewed, unconsciously enjoying the tactile feature. The table had been the only hard sell when Mrs. Beaumont had let Thea convince her to redo the kitchen, but it was the perfect complement to the French country cabinets Mrs. Beaumont had fallen in love with. The new style was a much better fit with the family's overall tastes than the miles of stainless steel and glass it had replaced. Every time she saw the Beaumonts using and enjoying the room, Thea got a small thrill of satisfaction. She really was good at her job, darn it.

Realizing her friend had grown silent, Thea looked up to find Lillian staring at her with the same level of assessment Thea had been giving the table. It was uncomfortable being the singular focus of that intense brown gaze. Lillian might be the least serious one of their group, jumping from job to job and interest to interest with frenetic abandon, but she was also the one who read people the best. Thea barely resisted the urge to squirm.

Finally, Lillian picked up another brownie and nibbled on it as she shrugged. "There's nothing wrong with you."

Thea snorted, but she bit back her retort as Lillian's twin brother, Peter, walked into the kitchen. At a few inches over six feet, he was a commanding presence in his crisp, black police uniform, complete with gun belt, handcuffs, and nightstick. The only thing missing was the gun, which Thea knew had been safely stored in his gun safe the minute he'd come home.

This was not a man anyone in their right mind would want to come up against, all brawny muscle and intimidating stares. Until he smiled and two huge dimples at the sides of his mouth turned his stern expression into boyish glee.

"Brownies!"

"Good to see you, too, Pete," Thea said dryly as he swooped down and stole a half dozen of the gooey cakes.

Having the decency to look sheepish, he dropped a kiss on her cheek. "Sorry." The spicy scent of recently applied body spray touched her nose. Not a fashion statement, Thea knew, but a necessity to counter the amount of perspiration generated after wearing a bulletproof vest for eight hours in the early summer heat. That subtle reminder of the very dangerous and grown-up job he did never failed to sober her and make her thankful that he could still be the big goof she knew and loved.

Which was why she waved away the apology, knowing he didn't mean it. "I understand. Food must come before the niceties. You're a growing boy, after all."

This time it was Lillian who snorted. "Like he needs to grow anymore. He's already a walking mountain."

"So says the molehill." He went to one of the glass-fronted cabinets for a glass.

Just to be perverse, Lillian emptied the rest of the milk into her glass as her brother's back was turned, leaving only a dribble behind in the container. Thea hid a smile behind her own glass and watched as Lillian pasted an angelic expression on her face when her brother came back to pour his drink.

Predictably, when Pete went to pour his milk and found the container empty, he leveled his best cop-face at Lillian and shook his head solemnly.

"Childish, Lil. Very childish." He sighed as if in deep disappointment and walked to the fridge.

"No, childish would be entering your baby pictures in that amateur photo contest *The Boulder Gazette* is holding this month. You know the ones I mean, don't you? The ones with you wearing your toy police hat and holster and nothing else? And I do mean *nothing* else."

Thea nearly choked on her suppressed laughter at the horror on Pete's face as he spun around. "Mom said she burned those," he gulped. "She swore."

Lillian shrugged. "She may have missed a few." In an aside to Thea she said, "He really looks adorable, you know. Three years old and proud as can be, holding his toy gun and his—"

"Lil!"

She turned an innocent look on her brother. "Hmm?"

Beginning to take on the air of a trapped animal, Pete dragged a hand through his hair, a few shades lighter than his sister's, standing the short strands on end. "What do you want?"

"I'm sure I don't know what you mean."

"Damn it, Lil," he growled, "do you have any idea what something like that could do to me down at the station? They'd never let me live it down!"

"Imagine that." There was an edge of humor to Lillian's otherwise cool voice. Thea could tell her friend was seconds away from bursting into laughter. The teasing might have seemed cruel if Thea didn't have a pretty good idea of what had prompted it. If she was right, then Pete deserved every moment of agony he was getting.

"Name your price."

Lillian smirked, probably at the desperation in her brother's voice. "Swear that you'll never, *ever* follow me again when I'm on a date. Or have one of your buddies follow me," she added, closing that loophole. Pete's mouth set in a mulish line.

"The guy had a record, Lil. Five speeding tickets. Five!"

"And we did forty-five all the way to Denver and back thanks to the squad car that sat on our bumper the whole night."

Pete saluted her with his milk. "Mission accomplished, then."

"First prize gets their pictures published in the *Gazette*," Lillian warned. "And all the entries will be available to be viewed on the paper's website. For weeks. Do you know how many hits that website can get in weeks?"

Pete glared at her.

Lillian smiled sweetly. "Swear it."

"Damn it, Lil…"

"Swear it."

His brow drawn into a fierce scowl, Pete was silent. Finally, seeming to realize that he'd been neatly boxed in, he sighed in defeat. "Fine," he grumbled, "no more following you on dates. But I want those pictures back."

"Deal."

Thea shook her head. Sometimes she felt like she was missing out on something by being an only child. At times like this, she knew she was. Lillian and her brother might snipe at each other with deadly accuracy, but let someone else threaten either one and there would be hell to pay.

"Well, as much as I enjoy watching you eviscerate your baby brother—"

"Only by ten minutes!" Pete protested.

"—maybe we can get back to my, um, difficulty with, um, you know."

"And that's because she was pushy even in the womb."

"I just wanted out because you were taking up all the room, Gigantor." Untrue, since they'd weighed within six ounces of each other at birth, regardless of their disparate sizes now, but Lillian always made the claim anyway.

Thea waved a hand in her friend's face. "Hello, remember me, the needy friend?"

Lillian blinked and then looked from Thea to her brother thoughtfully. "Pete, you're a guy."

A wary look crossed his face. "No good has ever come from those words passing a woman's lips. Especially yours."

Lillian waved an impatient hand for him to shut up. "Do you think there's anything wrong with Thea?"

"Lil!" Thea objected. Oh God, this was so *not* what she needed right now! Bad enough for Lillian to know how pathetic she was, but Pete! That would be blackmail material to last him a lifetime, and she didn't have any potentially damaging photos she could drag out as protection. "I really don't think—"

"You won't take my word for it, so maybe you'll listen to a member of the sex in question," Lillian interrupted. She waved a vague hand in Pete's direction. "Poor specimen that he is, he's still the best we have at the moment. So, go on. Make use of him."

Coloring up, Thea shoved a brownie in her mouth instead and shook her head.

Undeterred, Lillian asked her brother, "Well, do you? Think there's anything wrong with her?"

"Wrong?" Pete's face scrunched, as if he sensed a trap. "Wrong, how?"

"Do you think there's anything about her that would prevent her from attracting a man?"

With a mortified groan, Thea sunk lower in her chair, wondering if either of them would notice if she just slid onto the floor and crawled out of the room. Silently, she plotted evil ways to get even with her former best friend.

"Ah." Peter offered Thea a knowing nod. "Doyle's still doing the won't-look, can't-touch thing, huh?"

For the second time in less than an hour, Thea gaped like a dead trout.

"Does *everybody* know about me and Doyle?" Realizing that she'd just confirmed what Pete might have only been assuming, she let out another groan. "Please, just shoot me now and put me out of my misery."

Pete gave her shoulder a sympathetic pat. "I wouldn't say *everyone*. Just me and Lil. And Richard and Theo, of course," he added, naming their other two brothers. "Although Mom probably figured it out, too. You know how good she is at noticing things like that. But Dad is probably still oblivious, though, unless Mom told him, which she might have, but I'm not sure he'd care even if she did. Oh, and Amelia probably knows, too, since what one of you three knows the other two always do, too, but I don't think her mother would even care about—"

"And this would be why they'll never let him become a hostage negotiator," Lillian said, shaking her head.

Pete gave her a blank look. "What'd I say?"

Ignoring him, she turned to Thea, who had sunk even lower in her chair, with only her nose and eyes—which were closed in mortification—visible above the table. "Forget who knows and who doesn't. The only two people who matter are you and Doyle."

With a sad laugh, Thea opened her eyes. "Too bad that one of those two is the only person who apparently *doesn't* seem to know how I feel. Or how he feels, for that matter."

"Maybe, maybe not." Pete rubbed his chin as he sunk into deep thought. "Doyle came to work for your father when you were what, ten, twelve?"

"Thirteen." A very young, immature, tomboyish thirteen, who had tripped and fallen straight into hero-worship at Brennan Doyle's boot-clad feet the second she'd laid eyes on him. "So?"

"So first impressions are hard to shake."

"But I was a kid!" Thea protested.

"Exactly."

Thea's shoulders slumped in defeat. "So basically I could strip in the middle of his office and dance a naked Macarena on his desk, and he'd still never see me as anything other than a kid."

Pete made a small choking sound, although Thea wasn't quite sure if it was a laugh or not. "I didn't say that," he finally managed to get out. "But that would definitely do the trick."

"What trick?"

"Of shaking up that first impression," Lillian said, catching on to her brother's train of thought. She beamed at him. "Maybe you're not such a rock-head, after all."

"And maybe *I* am," Thea said, "because I have no idea what you're talking about."

Lillian turned her smile on Thea. "We're talking about giving Mr. Brennan Doyle a hard enough shake to make him see the real you. All of the real you."

Thea felt herself pale. "I was kidding about the naked Macarena thing."

"We'll save it as a last resort."

Thea gulped. "Maybe I should just go with plan B."

"And what's plan B?"

"I move to South America and start decorating huts in the Amazon."

With another of those dismissive waves that she seemed so darn good at, Lillian said, "You'd hate it. The constant humidity would make your skin peel like a snake."

Well…eww. "Alaska, then."

"Frostbite. You'll walk funny when you start losing toes, and I don't think Manolo Blahnik makes an orthopedic pump."

Hmm. No Doyle, no skin, no toes, no clothes. Eeny, meeny, miny…

"Guess it's moe," Thea muttered. She forced herself upright in the chair, dreading her next question. "So, what do I need to shake, and how hard do I have to shake it?"

\* \* \*

"Kiss off from a woman or a summons to a tax audit?"

Doyle's head jerked up at the voice, annoyed with himself that he hadn't heard the other man come into his office. He'd been too deeply sunk in rage as he read the note in his hands. "What?"

With a tip of his head, Charlie "Red" Fields, Doyle's second-in-command on the Fordham security team, indicated the paper clutched violently in Doyle's hand. "From the way you were scowling at that, I figured it had to be one or the other."

Doyle sighed. He dropped the paper onto his desk, disgust and anger still roiling together in his stomach, and fought the desire to go wash his hands despite the latex gloves he wore. "I'd have preferred either."

The other man's weathered face tightened in sudden comprehension. "Shit."

"That about sums it up." Doyle watched as Red took a latex glove from the box on the corner of the desk before picking up the paper by its edge and scanning it. He knew exactly when Red got to the worst part by the way his mouth tightened into a thin, bloodless rope; he knew it because the words still churned his own guts into a tight knot over the picture they'd painted in his mind.

Love and devotion laced with anger and madness, all wrapped into a disgusting mélange of pain and sexual violence. Try as he might, he knew it would take quite some time before he could push those unwanted images away.

"Same son of a bitch," Red pronounced in a flat voice.

Doyle nodded. There was little doubt. Even if the tone of the letter hadn't been the same as the others, the small, cramped handwriting that filled the page was unmistakable.

"Damn it." Red let the paper flutter back to the desk. "How did this one come?"

"With a box of chocolates that mysteriously found its way into the groceries that were delivered this morning. It's on its way to the lab," he added, knowing it would be Red's next question. Red grunted. "I already sent Sam and Kirsten to question the staff at the grocers, but I'm not expecting much. Whatever else this guy is, he's not stupid."

"It would make me feel better if he was."

Silently seconding the sentiment, Doyle put the offending missive into a plastic sheet protector with its envelope and locked them away in his desk. The sender had been careful to keep fingerprints or any other identifying marks from the six previous notes and letters, so there was little hope that he would have screwed up this time, but he'd still send it to the police lab and have it checked out. Sometimes one dumb mistake and a little blind luck were all you got. At this point, he'd gladly take either.

Disposing of the gloves he'd worn to handle the letter, Doyle poured two cups of coffee from the machine on the credenza behind his desk. There was a bottomless communal pot always brewing in the kitchen area of the small bungalow that served as the security office. But, in a concession to the grumblings about the strength at which he preferred his coffee—sludge was one of the kinder phrases used — Doyle had installed his own personal coffee maker. Everyone had been happier since.

Except Red, who as a former Navy SEAL preferred the sludge.

"That's two in a week, both with gifts." Red propped his ass on the corner of the desk rather than take one of the straight-backed chairs facing it. He took his coffee and swallowed a mouthful of the steaming black brew as if it were ice water. "He's escalating."

Doyle nodded, his expression dark and brooding as he sank back into his own chair, inhaling the comfortingly familiar aroma of the dark roast. The letters had been arriving by mail over the past two months, starting not long after Thea had arrived home from college. The fifth had arrived just over a week ago. But it was these last two that had Doyle worried.

The one before this had come pinned to a bouquet of flowers delivered by a local florist. The order had been taken over their website. So far, tracing the computer that had been used to do it and the account the payment had been wired from had proven fruitless.

The note that had been mailed to the florist to be sent with the flowers had had a California postmark, but that had been of little help since each of the other notes had been postmarked from different places around the country. No two were the same, and they followed no pattern that anyone had been able to discern. For now, the postmarks were a dead end.

It was this latest gift, though, that had Doyle concerned. Not only was it Thea's favorite brand of chocolate, it was her favorite collection as well, loaded with the brand's signature burnt caramel. Definitely not something you picked up at the corner drug store.

That inferred a very intimate knowledge of Thea's likes and habits, something their anonymous letter sender shouldn't have. That alone made Doyle uneasy. The fact that the accompanying letter had been more detailed and graphic than any of the others made him angry. Add that to the fact that the "gift" would have had to have been slipped into the Fordhams' groceries in person, and he was downright disturbed.

"I still think we should tell her there have been more," Red said, scowling. More after the first letter, he meant, which she'd gotten and read. Thankfully, that one hadn't been as sexually explicit as the ones that had followed. It had been more of an overture, an introduction, letting her know she had an admirer. It had creeped her out enough that she'd brought it straight to Doyle, despite her embarrassment over the content.

Stubborn she might be, but Thea definitely wasn't stupid.

Doyle shook his head. "Her father doesn't want her exposed to the garbage in those letters." Neither did he, but that didn't mean he agreed with

Frank Fordham's decision. They'd had one hell of a disagreement over it, actually, and Doyle knew he'd come very close to losing his job. Only the thought that he wouldn't be around to help protect Thea if that happened had made him shut his mouth and agree to go along with Frank's lie.

"I didn't say let her read them. Just let her know the basics. Some creep has fixated on her, and she needs to be more cautious when she goes out."

"She already knows she needs to be careful, and she's got someone with her whenever she's off the grounds."

"And she's never ditched a bodyguard before?"

"She won't. She promised."

Red looked surprised before an understanding glint lit his eye. "So that's why Poole's been sulking the past few days. She bargained him off her detail."

"Something like that."

Running a hand through his distinctive brush-cut hair, Red let out a long breath. "You're probably right. Still, I know if it was me, I'd like to know there was a reason to watch my six. She'll be pretty ticked about being kept in the dark when she finds out."

Ticked didn't begin to cover the wrath Thea would pour on everyone's heads if she ever found out that the amorphous threat against the family he was using to keep her in line was in truth a very real threat against her personally. If there was one thing she didn't tolerate, it was lying. "With luck, she'll never know anything about it."

# CHAPTER 3

**WHEN DOYLE DEPARTED** the security cottage a short while later, it was with Red's words still ringing in his ears.

The agent at the camera console had told him that Thea had left a message that she wanted to speak with him when it was convenient. A quick check told him he could find her with the other two members of the Royal Court at the swimming pool behind the house, so he headed in that direction as he mulled over the situation.

He knew Red was right. The more Thea knew, the safer she would be. And while Frank had been appalled by the letters that had arrived before he'd left—hence his gag order—he would no doubt be even more crazed by the letters and gifts that had arrived while he'd been in the middle of the African wilderness and out of touch for all but the direst of emergencies. A man smart enough to build a multimillion dollar empire in ten short years was smart enough to know that no situation remained static.

And this one hadn't.

The appearance of gifts as well as the sender's now likely presence in Boulder, as implied by the chocolates, changed things considerably. The creep had gone from admiring from afar to courting with flowers and candy, at least in his own sick little mind, and that made him a thousand times more dangerous than he had been before. Surely Frank would agree that as things sat now, his edict was no longer the safest possible choice.

The sound of laughter and splashing brought him out of his musings. Stepping out of the shadows of the graveled path and onto the polished flagstones of the pool surround, Doyle paused to slip his sunglasses on while his eyes made an unconscious circuit of the area.

Amelia Westlake sat on a chaise in the sun, her pale skin gleaming with sunscreen. Lillian Beaumont was sprawled in the hot tub, her short hair spiked up in front from the steam, her hands flying as she held a boisterous conversation with Thea, who was treading water in the middle of the free-formed pool. Thea laughed at whatever her friend said, throwing her head back as the throaty sound echoed between the waterfall and the tiled walls.

Entranced as much by the sound as the sight, Doyle found himself unable to look away from Thea as she splashed a wave at Lillian, who screeched as the cooler pool water rained over her. Avoiding retribution, Thea dove smoothly under the surface. Doyle watched as her long strokes brought her to the end of the pool, where she broke the surface and laughed again. With her thick chestnut hair slicked back from her face and the wide grin she wore, she reminded Doyle of a mischievous otter.

Damn. How could he tell her the truth now? She looked happier than she had in weeks. Months, actually. The specter of fear and uncertainty over her mother's surgery had weighed on her heavily, especially when she'd found out her mother had known about the tumor for several months and not said anything to her until right before the operation.

Even after the biopsies had come back negative, Thea had remained a bit too solemn, a little too cautious around her parents, as though she'd felt guilty for being away when her mother got sick. It had been one of the reasons Evelyn had agreed to the trip, not just for her own benefit, but to give Thea the chance to accept that everything was fine and that life could go back to normal for everyone.

Did he have the right to take that away from her? No. He couldn't do it. Not right now, anyway. Not until he knew something for sure. Depending on what Sam and Kirsten learned at the grocer, he'd reconsider defying her father's orders. But for now, he'd keep his silence. Thea was too happy. She was enjoying herself. She was...she was...

She was practically naked!

Fighting to draw breath into lungs that had suddenly seized, Doyle stared at the expanse of honey-gold skin that was exposed as Thea made her way up the steps out of the pool. His first thought was that she'd lost her bikini bottoms somewhere during her swim, since her toned, taut buttocks were right there for the world to see, water glistening on the delicious globes like diamonds on silk.

No, not delicious. Doyle shoved the word away, but he was less successful in dragging his gaze from Thea's body, which on some dim level he now realized was encased in a thong bikini. A very small, very indecent thong bikini. Pale gold, just a few shades off of her skin tone. God, what was she thinking wearing something like that? And what was he thinking, looking at her while she was wearing something like that? It was...

Doyle bit back a groan as Thea started toweling herself dry. It was too much, that's what it was. Once more he tried to look away, but his eyes seemed to have abdicated from his brain and refused to come to heel, staying greedily on Thea's unconsciously erotic motions as she dried first her barely concealed breasts and then her firm, tanned stomach, and her long, long legs, first one and then the other, from hip to knee to ankle, down the front and then up the back.

By the time she was done, Doyle was certain that every drop of blood in his body had headed south of the border and planned to make camp. Indefinitely.

The fact that he'd just gotten a hard-on from watching little Thea Fordham run a towel over her tight young body was exactly the thought he needed to drag his wayward libido back under control. Guilt rolled through him, dampening his ardor, even though his erection was evidently going to take a bit longer to tame. Thankful for his loose-fitting khakis, Doyle mentally wiped the drool from his chin and resumed walking.

Thea spotted him first. She smiled and called out a greeting but didn't pause in her application of sunscreen. Afraid that any smile he attempted might come out as a leer, Doyle settled for a nod in return, trying hard to ignore the sensuous movement of her hand.

"You left a message you wanted to see me. Is anything wrong?"

"No, nothing's wrong. I didn't mean for you to rush right over. Anytime would have been fine."

Ignoring for the moment the realization that he *had* rushed right over when he'd heard she wanted to speak to him, Doyle simply shrugged. "What's up?"

"We," Thea vaguely waved her hand to indicate her two friends, "decided we want to do a girl trip before Mellie gets too bogged down in her wedding plans, but I wanted to check with you about it before we made too many plans, seeing as how I'm pretty much under house arrest and everything."

The sweet scent of coconut filled the air, making Doyle think of piña coladas. "You're not under house arrest and you know it, so stop making it sound worse than it is." Behind his sunglasses, Doyle had to struggle to keep his eyes on Thea's face rather than her hand, which was now diligently applying a layer of the scented lotion to her stomach. "What kind of trip did you have in mind?"

"We haven't reached a consensus yet," Thea admitted. "Lil wants to spend a week in New York, seeing sights by day, hitting some shows and clubs by night at her usual run-till-you-drop vacation pace."

"There's nothing wrong with making the most of your time," Lillian called from the hot tub.

Already mentally tallying the security nightmare a trip to New York City would create, Doyle asked, "What are your other choices?"

"I'm leaning toward a week in the Caribbean somewhere," Thea replied. "Someplace warm and slow paced, where all you have to do is lay on the beach and catch up on your daydreaming." A dreamy look crossed her face. "A morning swim in turquoise water as warm as a bath, an afternoon nap on sun-warmed sand, dinner on an outdoor patio with the sea breeze kissing the air…" Thea sighed. "That's the perfect vacation."

Try as he might, Doyle couldn't stop watching the slow circles her hand was making as it passed over her ribcage and dipped down toward her waist and the almost-there bikini bottom, her movements taking on the slow, dreamy cadence of her voice.

"Perfect," Doyle murmured, surprised to find his voice slightly hoarse. He cleared his throat. "That sounds like a nice vacation to me."

"Put like that, I may have to change my vote," Lillian said, appearing at the chaise next to Amelia and grabbing her towel. "Although you did leave out the best part." She gave a gamine grin. "Lots of buff, sun-drenched men in Speedos."

Okay, maybe not so nice.

"Or we could even hit one of those clothing-optional resorts and get the full monty," Lillian added.

Okay, definitely not so nice. In fact, New York was looking better and better, logistical nightmare and all.

"I'm not so sure I'd be at all comfortable with a place like that," Amelia said tentatively.

*Good girl.* Doyle waited for Thea to second that sensible opinion. Instead, she looked a bit thoughtful, as if she were mulling over all the possibilities.

Damn the girl! What was she playing at? Those kind of resorts usually catered to a more worldly crowd than the Royal Court, and while they didn't exactly offer Bacchanalian orgies as evening entertainment, things were apt to get a little wilder than any of these three innocents were prepared to handle.

"Amelia's right," Thea said finally. "We shouldn't do anything that would make her uncomfortable."

Make *her* uncomfortable? Meaning she, Thea, wouldn't be? Doyle almost opened his mouth to say something when Thea spoke again.

"We could always find one that has a separate clothing-optional beach. I'm sure I read about a few of those, where those who want to go au naturel can be private from the rest of the guests, and everybody's happy."

*Not everyone,* Doyle muttered to himself. His hope that Amelia would offer another objection was dashed when she grinned and nodded. "Then you two can go off and be adventurous and leave me safe in the bosom of the fully clothed. Works for me."

"That's two votes for fun in the sun. Lil?"

Lillian plopped down on her chaise and slipped on her sunglasses. "Count me in."

"The islands it is." Thea looked at Doyle expectantly.

He gritted his teeth. "When would you want to go?" It was tough, but he managed to keep all of his aggravation out of his tone. Or, at least he thought he did. When Thea cocked her head slightly as if to question him, he wondered how well he'd succeeded after all.

"The next few weeks, maybe," Thea said. "It's really up to Mellie, since I'm still unemployed and Lil makes her own hours at the gallery when there aren't any showings scheduled."

The woman in question shrugged. "Anytime is fine with me, as long as it keeps me from having to hear the words 'poll results' and 'strategic positioning' ten times a day."

Doyle winced inwardly in sympathy for her, but it didn't surprise him that Senator Davenport was planning to use the wedding to push his son's political ambitions into the news. Amelia and Charles made an attractive couple. The magazines and tabloids were sure to be splashed cover-to-cover with "exclusive" photos of the event. Thea had mentioned that one of the top fashion magazines had already contacted Amelia about showcasing her wedding trousseau, and a travel magazine wanted to send a photographer with them on their honeymoon for some "candid" shots.

All of this when the happy couple still hadn't officially announced their engagement yet.

Yeah, he could see where Amelia would need some breathing room. Still, he found he couldn't like this idea of theirs. At all. Thea and naked beaches. That just wasn't going to happen. So, he fell back on what was, essentially, the truth.

"You know that our security concerns are high right now."

"Yeah, but—"

"It would be better if you put your trip off for a while."

"But—"

"At least until after your parents are home and they give the okay."

Thea raised her eyebrows. "Finished?"

"Think so."

"Then you don't have a problem with the trip itself?"

He had a dozen problems with it, but he'd cut his own tongue out before he admitted to any of them. "Nope."

Thea studied his face for a few long seconds and then sighed, her shoulders seeming to sag slightly, as if she'd tensed for a fight that hadn't come. "Well, okay then. Good." She smiled brightly. "It'll be a blast."

"With you three unleashed on the unsuspecting population of the Caribbean, without a doubt." He looked at his watch, desperate for any excuse to get away before he lost the battle with his dick and let his eyes stray below Thea's chin again. "I have to make some calls. Did you need anything else before I go?"

The devilish turn of her lips should have warned him, but it was too late to call the words back. Thea held out the bottle of sunscreen, her eyes sparkling with mischief. "If you don't mind smelling like coconuts all afternoon, my back still needs to be done."

Only self-preservation gave him the strength the step back when his hands practically itched to reach out for what was offered. "I have to go."

Without bothering to say good-bye to any of them, Doyle spun on his heel and retreated as gracefully as he could back toward the security cottage, his long legs putting as much distance as possible between his rebellious body and the half-naked siren that was tempting him beyond all reason.

*  *  *

Thea collapsed onto her chaise with a groan. "Oh, God!"

"Well, that was certainly interesting." Amelia sipped her iced tea and stared after Doyle thoughtfully.

"Oh, God!"

Lillian, who had followed Doyle's hasty retreat with her sunglasses pulled low for a better view, pushed them back in place and grinned. "Most informative."

"Oh, *God!*"

"When you're done being tragically overdramatic, we can discuss our next plan of attack."

Thea shot up into a sitting position. "No. No next plan. No attack. This was mortifying enough. I'm not about to make a fool out of myself a second time."

Lillian grinned. "Sweetie, you didn't make a fool out of yourself. You were *brilliant!*" Amelia enthusiastically nodded her agreement.

Thea scowled at them both. "*Brilliant?* In case you missed it, he didn't even blink twice at any of it!" She glanced down at the teeny thong bikini Lillian had talked her into buying and had practically had to forcibly put on her earlier and groaned again. "I feel like an idiot."

"Well, you don't look like an idiot. You look hot," Amelia told her.

"Didn't notice you?" Lillian snorted. "Girl, he damn near swallowed his tongue when he saw you!"

That got Thea's attention. "He did?" It was hard to believe Doyle would ever have that much of a reaction to her, bikini or not, but it was certainly an ego-soothing thought. "Really?"

"Oh, please! Behind those shiny Oakleys, Doyle's eyes were bugging out a mile trying *not* to look at the dish that is you."

A small thrill of success trickled down Thea's spine. "So he got shook after all, huh?"

"Like an earthquake."

"He sure didn't sound happy about our trip plans, did he?" Amelia asked. She frowned. "But he didn't say you couldn't go, either."

"Well, he can't come right out and say 'Thea, I don't want you exposing yourself to other men on a nude beach in the Caribbean,' can he?" Lillian replied. "But he was thinking it. Oh yes, he was most definitely thinking it."

"But he could have been thinking it in a big brotherly way," Thea said, her brief moment of confidence already waning.

"Trust me, T, any thoughts that man had while you were rubbing sunscreen on yourself were definitely not of the big brother variety."

Thea flushed, remembering how embarrassed she'd felt doing that. Oiling up her arms had been the only easy part, and that had been accomplished before Doyle had closed the distance between them. Doing her upper chest had been unnerving, and by the time she'd gotten to her belly, she'd been practically shaking with a combination of nerves and unexpected arousal.

Looking at Doyle as she stroked her own skin in long, lazy circles had been a disturbingly erotic experience. For her, at least. But for Doyle? She hadn't thought it had affected him at all, but maybe Lillian was right. Maybe he'd been able to hide a lot behind those mirrored glasses. He was definitely the king of the controlled expression. The controlled everything, actually.

She'd been sorely tempted to take a quick peek at the fly of his trousers to see if he was controlling *that*, too, but she hadn't been able to work up the nerve.

Remembering that the trip hadn't been entirely a fabrication, Thea grimaced at Amelia. "Sorry my dad's business problems are going to delay things. I know you really wanted to get away."

Amelia just shrugged away the apology. "I'm sure I'll be in even more need of the escape after the engagement party as before it. Besides," she added, a gleam entering her eyes, "I think watching you torment Doyle will be more than enough to distract me for the time being."

"Speaking of distracting, who do you think Doyle will send with us?" Lillian rubbed her hands together in anticipation. "I hope Daryl makes the team."

Thea rolled her eyes. "You're obsessed with the man's shoulders."

"His shoulders, his arms, his long, strong legs." Lillian sighed and feigned a swoon back into her chaise. "The man is definitely made right." She flicked her sunglasses up and waggled her eyebrows, one of which was currently sporting a dainty little diamond barbell. "I wonder how *he* feels about nude beaches."

Thea laughed at her friend's outrageous expression but felt a tingle run through her as she thought of not Daryl but Doyle lounging on the beach under a tropical sun, his skin glistening with sunscreen as he toasted to a golden brown. All over.

She shivered. Doyle in all his naked glory would certainly be a sight to behold. And she planned to behold it, somehow, someway, or hurt herself trying. Some goals were worth all the trouble in the world, and, for her, convincing Doyle that they would be good together was at the top of the list.

"I don't think Richard would appreciate you drooling all over Daryl's anything," Amelia said, raising a censuring eyebrow.

Lillian made a *pfft* sound and flicked her hand. "Richard is over, so he doesn't get a say."

"Wow, that was quick." Thea tried to do a quick count in her head. "What was that, three weeks, or two?"

"More like one and a half, I think," Amelia replied. "So, Lil, what was wrong with this one?"

"There wasn't anything wrong with him," Lillian said, dropping her sunglasses back over her eyes to hide them. "There just wasn't anything particularly *right*." She shrugged as though it meant nothing, but Thea knew better. There had been a lot of *not right* guys drifting in and out of Lillian's life in the past year, and she could tell that her friend was starting to worry that the problem wasn't with them but with her.

"Who knows," Lillian said, squaring her shoulders, her body language screaming *done talking about it*. "Maybe I'll find Mr. Right playing naked beach volleyball."

"Great. Thanks for that mental picture," Thea groaned.

"You wouldn't actually go to a nude beach, would you?" Amelia asked hesitantly. "I thought we were just saying that to get a reaction from Doyle."

Thea considered it. "I don't know," she finally answered, shrugging. "I might go to see what it was like, but I'm not sure I could really take off my clothes for the whole world to see." For Doyle, though, maybe. In private. In the dark. Well, twilight, at least. Maybe candlelight.

"It's not some sordid place where people go to ogle each other, you know," Lillian said, sounding a bit superior. "To Europeans, it's just a natural way to sunbathe. Since practically everyone is naked, no one notices."

"Oh, been to one, have you?" Thea asked, raising a questioning brow.

"As a matter of fact, when we were in Cannes last year, we spent a few days at the beach there."

"And?" Thea was gratified to see a flush creep up Lillian's neck that had nothing to do with the sun.

"And...I noticed." After blurting the admission, she shoved her straw in her mouth and gulped iced tea in an effort to dissuade further questions. Only Thea wasn't letting her friend off that easily. She still needed payback for the thong bikini.

"And did you join in this oh-so natural way of sunbathing?"

Lillian choked on her tea. Coughing, she looked at Thea in disbelief.

"Are you nuts? I was with my *parents*!"

Amelia looked horrified. "*They* didn't...?"

"*No!*" Lillian dropped back against the chaise, plucked off her sunglasses, and flung an arm over her eyes. "But they wanted to. At least, my mother did. But she wouldn't because I was there and she wasn't sure how I would feel about it."

"Embarrassed," Thea murmured, grinning as much at her friend's discomfort as her theatrics. She had said more than once that Lillian had missed her calling when she'd majored in business instead of acting. Her present job as part-time manager of one of the local art galleries was much more suited to her artistic personality than being a forensic accountant for her father's investment firm.

"Mortified," Lillian corrected.

"So, they didn't, you know...?" Amelia waved her hand vaguely.

"Strip?" Thea offered helpfully.

"No. Not that day, anyway," Lillian added, removing her arm and blinking owlishly in the suddenly bright light before slipping her shades back in place. "But I spent the next day out sightseeing with Peter and Theo, and when we came back to the hotel to meet my parents for dinner, they were a bit more sunburned than they'd been the day before." She smiled weakly. "And judging by the way they squirmed all through the meal, it was in some very, ah, unusual places."

The idea of Lillian's somewhat staid parents sneaking off for an afternoon of nude sunbathing was just too much for Thea to take. Fight as she might, she couldn't hold back the wellspring of giggles that bubbled up out of her, filling the air with their merry sound. Even Amelia, usually too repressed to find such things amusing, let loose with a few timid giggles of her own.

Lillian, however, merely sniffed indignantly and said, "Go ahead and laugh, T. But my parents are going back again this fall, and they're talking about asking your parents to go with them."

As intended, that brought Thea's amusement to an abrupt halt. "No."

A wicked smile curved the edges of Lillian's lips. "Oh, definitely yes."

Groaning, Thea buried her face in her hands. "That would be so wrong. So very, very wrong." It was one thing to laugh over someone else's parents doing something as crazy as going to a nude beach but *her* parents? Thea shuddered. No. That was so not an image she wanted in her brain. Ever.

"What about Doyle?" Amelia asked after several minutes of silence had passed.

"What about him?"

"Well, what's next? I'm assuming there was more to the plan than just you buying a new wardrobe."

"Well, yeah, actually, there is." Thea squinted at Lillian. "What do you think? Is it time for stage two?"

With a shake of her head, Lillian said, "Oh no, we're definitely not done with stage one yet."

Amelia looked first at Lillian and then Thea. "What's stage two? And what's stage one, for that matter?" She scowled. "You obviously left out some important parts when you told me about Operation Shakeup."

Ignoring Thea's bemused expression at her naming of their campaign against Doyle's frustrating reticence, Lillian told Amelia, "Stage one is making Doyle notice Thea in the most basic way—her body. It's the best way to grab his attention in the shortest amount of time. Short of taking a big stick to the side of his head, anyway," she added with a smirk.

"Hence the new bikini," Amelia said, nodding.

"And the new jogging clothes. And the new dresses, shoes, tops, pants..."

"There was nothing wrong with my old clothes," Thea contended defensively.

"And most especially lingerie," Lillian continued as if she hadn't spoken.

"Not that he's going to be seeing my lingerie," Thea muttered. Her face was suddenly burning, and it had nothing to do with the sun.

"Not until at least stage three, anyway."

"Which is?" Amelia prodded.

Lillian sighed and ticked off her fingers. "Stage one is noticing her body, acknowledging she's a woman, not a little girl."

"Right, got that."

"Stage two is getting him into a social situation—a movie, dinner, something normal that any normal couple might do to spend time together. That puts them on equal footing as man and woman, instead of as employee and employer."

"Daughter of employer," Thea corrected. It was a small point but an important one.

Amelia nodded. "Check. And stage three?"

The look that crossed Lillian's face reminded Thea of a cat that had just found the canary cage wide open. This was the part of the plan that worried Thea the most and she knew that Lillian knew it. "Stage three is contact."

"Contact?" A small wrinkle of confusion appeared between Amelia's eyebrows. "What kind of contact?"

"Any kind she can get. Lips, tongues, hands…"

"Okay, I think she gets the picture," Thea said hurriedly. She was dying to jump in the pool just to get away from Lillian's smirking presence, but she was afraid she'd send up a steam cloud if she did. She rolled her iced tea glass over her cheeks instead, blessing the cool trickle of condensation she found there.

"Hence the lingerie," Amelia said knowingly.

"Exactly."

Thea gritted her teeth. "I'm returning it tomorrow."

"Can't," Lillian chirped sweetly. "It's illegal to return lingerie to the store. Health codes or something."

"Then I'll give it away." Not that she would. She loved the beautiful silk and lace garments she'd picked out, and she was looking forward to seeing if they felt as good as they looked. But daydreaming about Doyle seeing her in them and speculating about it out loud were two totally different things. In fact, it embarrassed the hell out of her.

Huh. She frowned over the unhappy possibility that maybe she wasn't as grown-up and sophisticated as she thought she was after all.

"Oh, stop pouting," Lillian said, misinterpreting Thea's pensive expression. "I won't tease you anymore about your sexy new undies. Sheesh, what a baby."

The offhanded tease pricked at her confidence even more. "I'm not pouting," she said stiffly. "I just don't want to talk about my underwear. It's…it's stupid."

"I was just teasing," Lillian muttered, doing a little pouting of her own.

"I can understand why you're nervous about your, ah, about stage three," Amelia said. "It's a big step. Possibly an irrevocable one. You need to be sure you really want to do this before you go ahead with it."

"Oh, I really want to do it," Thea said quickly and then grimaced. "I'm just not entirely sure I *can*. What if I make a fool out of myself?" She'd already done that once before. Caught by Doyle on her eighteenth birthday during one of her midnight skinny-dipping escapades, she'd taken a chance and asked him if he wanted to join her. He hadn't even declined. He'd just turned and walked away without a word.

It had been the most mortifying experience of her life, and it had been almost a year before she'd felt comfortable in Doyle's presence again. She didn't think she could bear a repeat.

Her voice dropped to a horrified whisper as she considered a worse alternative to Doyle's disapproving silence. "What if he *laughs* at me?" She shuddered, the mere thought sending tendrils of cold fear into her stomach. She would die if he laughed at her, she just knew she would.

"First off, Doyle would never laugh at you," Amelia said. "He's too much of a gentleman. Second, if and when you actually get to stage three and whatever comes with it, it'll be because stages one and two have already been a success, which means Doyle will already see you as a woman and as someone he wants to be with. It's not like you're going to bonk him over the head, tie him up, and stash him in the pool house so you can have your way with him whenever you want to."

That surprised a laugh out of Thea, as she guessed it was meant to. "Yeah, but—"

"And lastly," Amelia cut her off, giving her a quelling look worthy of her mother, "I don't think Doyle is nearly as oblivious to you as you think. I think once you get him past the hurdles of stages one and two, he might just take stage three right out of your hands."

Thea shuddered again, but this time it was a different kind of feeling that moved through her. Heat at the thought of Doyle taking the initiative in advancing their relationship into the physical seared away all of her earlier nervous chill. It would be magical, she knew, to have Doyle take her in his arms, lay his lips to hers, put his strong hands on her...

"Earth to Thea!"

With a start, Thea realized both her friends were watching her with identical amused expressions. She blushed and then laughed at herself. Lifting her glass in a salute, she said with a broad smile, "To sexy lingerie."

# CHAPTER 4

**SHE WAS DRIVING** him crazy.

Barricaded in his office with a hefty pile of paperwork as a bulwark between him and whoever came through the door, Doyle applied himself to the task of not thinking about Thea Fordham. Not thinking about her long legs and the incredible ass they were attached to as she'd sashayed out of the pool three days before; not thinking about her taut, tan tummy slicked with oil that reflected the sun like diamond dust; not thinking about the way her nipples had tightened under that tiny scrap of a bathing suit as he'd watched her stroking herself—

*Damn!* He was going to have to do a better job of not thinking than that or he was going to be trapped behind his desk for the rest of the day hiding the erection that was threatening to tent his pants. Again. What he needed to do was think about all the reasons he shouldn't be thinking about Thea's many glorious body parts. Her many glorious *off-limits* body parts. There were lots of reasons. Dozens. Hundreds. If he could just come up with one of them. Soon.

She was too young. There, that was one. True, there were only twelve years between them, but they were like dog years when it came to experience. He'd traveled the world, been a member of one of the most elite units in the Corps, seen and done things that no one his age outside of the military or possibly law enforcement would ever understand. Or accept. No, compared to him, Thea was no more than a baby.

The baby of a millionaire. Couldn't forget that one. Doyle might bring in a more than comfortable salary, but he was still a working man. Thea was an heiress. He *had* to work, whereas she simply *wanted* to. For all Frank Fordham treated him like a member of the family, it wasn't hard to imagine how the man would react if he ever actually aspired to the real thing.

As if he'd conjured her, the object of his chaotic thoughts suddenly appeared through his door with a perfunctory knock. One look and Doyle suddenly couldn't remember a single one of those reasons he shouldn't be thinking about Thea and all her parts. He also knew he wouldn't be getting up from his desk any time soon.

"Good morning!" Thea's smile collapsed into a frown. "You're not ready for our run." She looked at her watch. "Am I early?"

"No, I, uh, forgot to call up to the house to tell you I couldn't make it today." Which, in hindsight, might have been an easier way to decline joining her on her daily run. At least then he wouldn't have had to see her in another one of those shiny, stretchy outfits she'd suddenly taken to wearing instead of her usual sweat shorts and baggy T-shirt. It was blue today. A deep cobalt blue that almost matched the color of her eyes, which were right now looking at him expectantly, reminding him that he hadn't given her a reason why he was backing out of their usual twice weekly run.

"Work," he said abruptly, gesturing at the papers in front of him as if to provide proof for his claim. "I have to catch up." It sounded like exactly what it was—an excuse rather than a reason, and a rather lame one at that. He braced himself for Thea's objections, her arguments, her gentle cajoling, all her usual tactics when he didn't fall into line with her plans. But she surprised him.

"No problem," Thea said with a shrug. Just when Doyle was congratulating himself for having dodged a dangerous bullet, even as a small part of him was hurt by the ease with which Thea had accepted his withdrawal, she blindsided him by adding, "I can get one of the other guys to go with me instead."

One of the other guys? One of *his* men? Jogging with Thea while she was encased in that spandex outfit that hugged every curve like a lover's touch? Smelling like a combination of ripe strawberries and a hint of something spicy?

Something flared inside Doyle's gut, hot and angry. Although he refused to put a name or reason to the sudden feeling, he knew he didn't like it. Not the feeling, and not the reason he'd had it.

More gruffly than he'd intended, Doyle said, "There's enough security around the property. You don't need anyone to go with you." It was true, since he had never accompanied her in any capacity other than fellow runner, and yet it was a lie as well. There were several wooded areas on the estate grounds that would put her out of sight for long minutes at a time, and with the letter sender very possibly in the area—something they still hadn't been able to verify, damn it—those blind spots constituted danger areas. So, of course, she needed someone with her. What had made him say that she didn't?

*Jealousy.*

The ugly word popped into his head without warning or invitation and was immediately turned away. Jealous? No. Protective. That was the better word. Not jealous. Definitely not. He was feeling protective of her, just as he always had, simply more so because of this sudden fascination she'd developed for inappropriate clothing. Inappropriate *tight* clothing that revealed way too much of her womanly curves.

Womanly? No, no, no. Girlish. Girlish curves. Because if Thea had womanly curves, that would mean he could think of her as a woman, and he most definitely didn't want to think of her as that. So, girlish curves it was. Lush ones, to be sure, but not womanly. Curves in all the right places for a man to grab hold of and hang onto while he was—

"Doyle, are you even listening to me?"

Jerked from a train of thought he was grateful to leave behind, Doyle realized that he hadn't a clue as to what Thea had been saying. The expression on his face must have revealed that fact because she heaved a very put-upon sigh and crossed her arms, something Doyle wished mightily she hadn't done, since it made her full spandex-encased breasts plump even fuller.

"I said I wasn't planning to run on the estate today since it rained last night and the trails are probably muddy. I was going to use the indoor track at Fit. If that's okay with you," she added grudgingly

An upscale gym on the edge of the downtown area, Fit was a strictly members-only establishment. There was little chance of their letter writer sneaking in, which was good. Even better, being early morning on a weekday, the gym would most likely be on the empty side. He told himself that made him feel better because it made guarding Thea easier than if there was the usual afternoon or weekend crowd, but he finally had to admit that it wasn't the whole truth. Part of him was just glad there wouldn't be too many young gym studs around to see her in that outfit.

Mentally reviewing the roster, Doyle said, "Sam is supposed to be your outside escort today." He frowned slightly. Sam Britten was one of the younger members of the security staff, only a few years older than Thea at twenty-six. He was sharp-witted, cool-headed, and had instincts that would have made him a top-flight law enforcement agent had his color blindness not disqualified him from almost all work in that line.

He was also blond, blue-eyed, and had a face that made even the usually immovable Francine sit up and take notice when he came into a room.

Suddenly, sending Sam out with Thea didn't seem like the best of ideas. If the kid could put Francine on point, how would he be able to keep a proper watch on Thea while at the same time fighting off the gym bunnies that were sure to swarm him like bears to honey? Doyle absolutely refused to consider the possibility that his sudden concern might be for more than Thea's safety. In no way was the sudden tightening in his gut personal. He was a professional. He acted professionally.

So he was entirely motivated by his professionalism when he said, "Take Kirsten with you instead." Was that disappointment that flashed across her face? For some reason, the possibility that Thea had wanted to spend time with Sam bothered Doyle immensely. "Sam can't follow you into the locker room," he pointed out, although he wasn't entirely sure if that bit of justification was for Thea or himself.

"And Kirsten can't run yet on her twisted ankle." The pucker of Thea's brow said that Doyle, of all people, should have known that. And he did, damn it. He'd just forgotten. He never forgot, especially important things. What was it about this girl that made him act so brainless sometimes? Maybe he was allergic to spandex. Maybe it was sucking all the brain cells right out of his head.

Maybe he was avoiding giving her an answer.

His reason for sending Kirsten in place of Sam was valid. A male bodyguard wouldn't be able to follow Thea into certain parts of the gym. Members only or not, it was a risk that, under current circumstances, he wasn't willing to take. But he also knew that while she enjoyed her daily run, Thea preferred to do it with a partner, a habit left over from her high school track days. He'd already disqualified himself from going with her with his claims of having too much work. The only other female not away with the senior Fordhams was Francine and she was off duty. Switching Sam with one of the other men would make it seem as though he had a problem with Sam accompanying her and doing his job. And he didn't.

Really.

"I'm sure you'll find yourself a run buddy when you and Kirsten get there." Realizing from the surprised look on Thea's face that he must have sounded more dismissive than he'd meant to, Doyle tried to soften his words with a smile. It didn't seem to help.

"I'm sure I will. There are lots of men who don't find the idea of spending time with me such a trial." Without a goodbye, Thea spun on her heel and stalked out of the office. Actually stalked. Doyle sighed to himself. A trial? God, yes, the girl was that and more. She was a thorn in his side. She was trouble with a big, fat T.

She was also on her way to the gym wearing an R-rated outfit to seek out the company of men who wouldn't mind spending a few hours getting winded and sweaty with her.

Doyle shook away the unwanted image that thought brought with it. She was going for a run. In a public place. With lots of people around. It wasn't like she was going to a bar to get picked up.

Although Fit was where he'd first met Celeste.

And Trina.

And Margo.

Well, hell, there was a trend he didn't want to examine too closely. Anyway, Thea wasn't like Margo and the others. She was only looking for a run buddy, not a fuck buddy. And Kirsten would be there just in case anyone got the two confused.

So why did the idea still bother him so much?

Damn whoever it was that had convinced her to wear those damned outfits!

*   *   *

Damn Lillian for convincing her to wear this stupid outfit!

Nothing was going the way it was supposed to. First Doyle had backed out of their run. Okay, she could live with that. In fact, she'd pretty much seen it coming over the past few days, ever since she'd adopted her new wardrobe and consigned her comfy sweats to the back of the closet.

His growing discomfort had been a sure sign that he was seeing her as more than his boss's young daughter. That he was—finally, thank you, God!—seeing her as a woman. *Although in these outfits,* she thought wryly, *it would be almost impossible to not see her as a woman, since every womanly part she owned was out on display.*

Three cheers for spandex.

No, backing out of their run was an almost predictable retreat for Doyle. It gave her hope. As had his snap decision to yank Sam from escort duty in favor of Kirsten. For a second there, just a second, he had actually looked *jealous.* How much better did it get than that? Okay, she had hoped that he was going to relent and substitute himself for Sam, which would have been way better, but she knew Doyle well enough to be happy with baby-steps of progress.

But then he had totally blown all her good feelings out of the water by blithely telling her to go find herself a run buddy at the gym. Any run buddy. Any tight-abbed, muscle-bound run buddy she wanted. Damn him! Did he care, or didn't he? Had he thought that having Kirsten in tow would keep her choices benign, scare off anybody who was looking for more than a few laps around the track, or did he think she couldn't attract anyone worth him worrying about?

Or was she just projecting too much into his responses to her, seeing what she wanted to see, and he really didn't give a damn about who she cozied up to? Worse, was he *encouraging* her to attract someone else? Was he subtly trying to scrape her off himself like some unwanted and annoying clinging vine?

Thea wanted to groan out loud. This had all sounded a lot easier than it was turning out to be. Wear sexy clothes, get Doyle's attention, have sex, make him fall in love, and live happily ever after. Okay, maybe that was an over-simplification of the plan as she saw it, but, still, things weren't even coming close. She'd worn sexy clothes, gotten Doyle's attention, and twice now sent him running in the other direction. So *not* the way it was supposed to go.

Was it her? Was she so repulsive? Or boring? Or...or...what?

Finishing her final lap on Fit's indoor track, Thea slowed to a cool-down walk, but her mind was still going full gallop. What was it about her that was holding Doyle back? She didn't think he was totally disinterested, not after the way he'd nearly tripped over his own feet the first day she'd shown up for their run in one of her new outfits.

The look on his face had been one of such pure male admiration that she'd barely been able to keep from doing the happy dance right there in his office. But then, as was to be expected, he'd packed away whatever he was feeling along with the expression showing it and become stoic Doyle again, his eyes as unreadable as if he were wearing his trusty, all-concealing mirrored Oakleys.

So, she knew she could attract his attention. But how could she keep it?

Thea chewed her bottom lip as she thought on that. This was Lillian's area of expertise, not hers, but running to her friend every two days to ask for advice was starting to make her feel even more inadequate than she already did. Sure, Lillian had a new boy-toy in tow every other week. She was cuteness personified with a personality that attracted people, men and women both.

Well, so what if Lil could always draw so many into her orbit without even trying? That didn't make her an expert on relationships. In fact, the fact that she *had* so many people flitting in and out of her love life meant she had very little personal experience with long-term relationships. She'd held onto Richard for less than two weeks, and the guy before that hadn't lasted much longer. And Thea was going to *her* for advice?

Just as quickly as it had risen, her annoyance with Lillian faded. Maybe Lil didn't have experience with long-term relationships, but at least she had experience with short-term ones and that was still more than Thea had herself. A few dates and one steady boyfriend scattered over her high school and college years didn't really add up to much more than a sadly deficient love life and a somewhat depressed sense of self-worth.

Of course, those long lonely years had been mostly her own doing, much as she hated to admit it. Even as far back as her teens, she'd held onto the fantasy of Doyle suddenly confessing his undying love for her and demanding her hand in marriage from her father, before sweeping her off her feet and taking her off to his private bungalow, closing the door with his foot as the music swelled to a resounding crescendo around them.

That was where the fantasy had ended when she was sixteen, like some old Cary Grant movie. Now she knew what came next. She *wanted* what came next, and she wanted it with Doyle.

Too bad Doyle wasn't cooperating.

But she wasn't giving up yet. Not by a long shot. She just needed to find the right way to crack that shell he was so damned good at wrapping around himself, the one that held his emotions in and everyone else out.

But how?

# CHAPTER 5

"SEX."

Caught in the middle of swallowing, Thea choked on her peach iced tea. Fighting to catch her breath, she left it to Amelia to murmur, "Isn't that, like, skipping a few stages?"

Thea nodded emphatically, tears streaming down her face as she wrestled her lungs into compliance and dragged in a shuddery breath. "Yes," she managed to croak. She held up two fingers when further words proved impossible.

With a sigh and a roll of her eyes, Lillian tossed her napkin over the patio table to her choking friend, who gratefully used it to mop up her face. "Not sex with Doyle, you dope." When Thea's eyes widened in alarm, Lillian snorted and rolled her eyes again. "And not sex with anyone else, either. God, get a grip, will you?"

"Well, you could have been a little more specific," Amelia pointed out. Again, Thea nodded her agreement. Then, when Lillian remained silent, Thea made a "give me" gesture with her free hand, beginning to feel as though she were participating in some bizarre game of charades.

"Sex. Appeal." Lillian enunciated each word clearly and slowly, as though teaching two incredibly slow children. And perhaps she was, because both Thea and Amelia wore identically confused expressions, causing Lillian to mutter something unpleasant under her breath. "Sex appeal, you know, when you strut your stuff, shake your booty, jiggle your—"

"Lil!" Amelia squeaked.

"—assets," Lillian finished with a smirk as Amelia's face turned bright pink. To Thea she said, "You've been wearing the clothes, but you haven't been *wearing* the clothes, if you know what I mean."

Stupefied, Thea gave her head a slow shake and then cleared her throat. "'Fraid not." Good. Her voice only sounded like she'd been swallowing broken glass instead of gargling razor blades.

With a very put-upon sigh, Lillian slumped back in her chair. "You do know that you're totally hopeless, don't you?"

Knowing her friend as well as she did, Thea knew that far from being as exasperated as she looked and sounded, Lillian was enjoying the hell out of herself. It wasn't often that she, out of the three of them, had the upper hand in social situations.

"So, help me be *un*hopeless." Out of habit, Thea neatly folded the linen napkin she'd used and placed it back on the glass and iron table. The existence of a paper napkin was *verboten* in the Westlake household. It was strictly linen and fine china, even when snacking on iced tea and lemon sherbet on the patio. "Or at least less hopeless. I'm in serious trouble here, Lil. I can't lose him before I ever really get him."

"Not a chance. You said he nearly tripped over his tongue the first day you showed up in your yummy new workout clothes, right?"

Thea squirmed slightly. "I never said *tripped*."

"And he acted jealous of sending cutie-pie Sam with you to the gym, didn't he?"

"Well, I thought maybe…"

"So you've got his attention. Now you just have to hold onto it."

"That much I'd already figured out for myself, oh-so knowledgeable one," Thea said with a slight smirk. Then it faded. "But how?"

"This is where the shaking and jiggling comes in, isn't it?" Amelia merely grinned into her drink when Thea shot her a dirty look.

"Don't forget strutting."

"I don't strut," Thea said, folding her arms in rebellion. "Or shake, or jiggle, or…or anything else that makes me sound like a bowl of Jell-O. I want to get Doyle's attention, not make him think of dessert."

"Oh, sweetie," Lillian sputtered as she collapsed into laughter, "that's *exactly* what you want him to do!"

Feeling her face turn hot, Thea gulped the rest of her drink. Images that Lillian's words had conjured up flashed through her mind. Doyle laying her on the huge mahogany table in the formal dining room. Doyle stripping her of her clothes under candlelight. Doyle selecting carefully from a large tray of condiments, choosing a small jar of warmed honey, which he then drizzled over her breasts and proceeded to remove with his tongue…

She grabbed up the napkin again and used it to blot the sudden sheen of perspiration from her face. Good God, where had *that* come from?

Smirking as if she somehow knew what Thea had been thinking, Lillian refilled Thea's empty glass from the insulated carafe on the table. "You look a little warm, hon. Have some more. It'll cool you down."

"The sun is a little strong," Amelia said, missing the byplay. "Maybe we shouldn't have taken down the umbrella."

"I'm fine," Thea said, answering both of them at once. "I just…" *Just what? Had an erotic daydream that nearly singed my eyebrows off? Took my obsession with Doyle to a whole new—not to mention disturbing—level?* She cleared her throat. "I'm fine."

"Mm-hmm," Lillian murmured knowingly, but, thankfully, she let the matter drop. "What I meant by strut, shake, etcetera, is that there are certain mannerisms that go with the clothes. A flip of the hair here, a turn of the ankle there…"

"I'm not turning into some brainless, hair-twisting bimbo," Thea said vehemently. "Not for Doyle, not for anyone."

"Brainless, hair-twisting bimbo?" Amelia repeated, amusement dancing in her eyes.

"You know." Thea jumped to her feet and struck a pose, one hip out, one hand catching the end of her chestnut locks and turning them around and around her fingers as she pursed her lips into an exaggerated pout.

"Hi, Mister Studly-man," she cooed in a breathy Marilynesque voice. "I may not have two brain cells to rub together, but I certainly have two of something else you might be interested in." She did an exaggerated jiggle of said somethings. "So hows about buying me some sparkly jewelry because girls like me just *love* anything shiny, and then you can take me someplace expensive to eat, and then we can go back to your place and hump like bunnies."

Even over the hysterical laughter of her two friends, Thea heard the small gasp from a few feet behind her. Without even turning around, she knew who it was just by the heavy aroma of hideously expensive perfume that overtook the fresh air like a floral miasma. It was just the way her luck was running lately.

She closed her eyes, as if blocking out reality would let her disappear down a rabbit hole somewhere—with or without humping bunnies—but, sadly, it didn't work, so she pasted on her best smile and turned. "Good afternoon, Mrs. Westlake." Belatedly, she remembered to drop her hand from her hair and the other from her hip, which she quickly tucked back into its proper, demure position.

Mrs. Westlake did not look upset. She didn't look surprised. In fact, she didn't look like much more than a perfectly smooth bit of cool marble, thanks to her recent conversion to the religion of Botox. Judging by the total lack of movement on a face that Thea knew would normally be scowling in vivid displeasure, Amelia's mother had been praying (or was that paying?) at the altar of her plastic surgeon that very morning.

"Cynthia." Only one word and Thea felt the need to check for frostbite.

"Excuse my language, ma'am," she said as contritely as she could. "We were just joking around."

Even without a wrinkle of expression, Mrs. Westlake's snapping eyes were enough to warn Thea that she hadn't found anything amusing about what she'd overheard.

"A true lady never uses vulgarity, no matter the cause."

"Yes, ma'am."

"That sort of humor can only betray a lack of breeding, as you well know."

*Said the old money to the new.* Thea forced herself to remain as expressionless as the older woman was. "Yes, ma'am."

"In a few short weeks, there are going to be hundreds of very important people here for the engagement party. You are a member of the bridal party." Thea heard the unspoken "unfortunately" at the end of that reminder and barely contained a flinch. "Just think how poorly it would reflect on us if you were to use such language within earshot of one of our guests."

"Mother!" Amelia gasped in embarrassment.

Mrs. Westlake paid her daughter no mind. Instead, she narrowed her eyes as best she could—which was to say, minimally—and delivered her *coup de grace.* "Even if you don't care about your own reputation, you could at least be concerned for Amelia's. Her position as a future senator's wife will depend on how well she's received by the Washington elite. Alienate them now, and she might as well not get married at all."

"Mother, that's totally unfair!" Amelia was now bright red with mingled indignation and mortification. "You know Thea isn't like that. We were just goofing around. There was no one else around to hear."

"I heard, didn't I? And it only takes offending one person to destroy everything we've worked for."

"People who eavesdrop rarely hear anything good," Lillian muttered so low under her breath that Thea wasn't entirely sure she'd meant to say it out loud. As aggravated as she was by Mrs. Westlake's reprimand, it wasn't the first time the society matron had taken her to task for her lack of breeding and social graces, nor would it be the last, she knew.

Still, it rankled that she always managed to take the one moment out of a thousand that showed Thea at her less than best and use it to beat Thea over the head to drive home the point that she wasn't one of *them.* She couldn't trace her money back five generations, couldn't pick up a who's who and point out a half dozen family connections, and would never be able to claim a proper place in High Society.

Which was all fine with Thea, because as far as she was concerned, High Society sucked. She was much happier with her middle-class beginnings and values, thank you very much, and would happily slit her own wrists before she ever shoved a silver spoon down her own children's throats.

"I would never do anything to hurt Amelia," Thea said, striving to keep any trace of resentment from her voice. And she wouldn't. She'd glue her lips shut first. Which might be the only way she'd get through an entire evening without Mrs. Westlake finding her at fault for some social infraction or another.

With a disdainful sniff that said she'd love to differ but was too much a lady to do so, Mrs. Westlake turned her attention to her daughter, who had sunk so low in her chair that she was in danger of sliding completely under the table. That fast, she found a new direction in which to vent her scorn.

"Amelia Ann! Dear Lord, what kind of posture is that? Sit up straight, girl. And why are you sitting in the sun? You know you get spots. You can't afford to look anything but your best for the photographers. Your engagement pictures have to be perfect. Do you *want* to embarrass poor Charles? What on Earth were you thinking?" She snapped a look at Thea, as if she'd forced her daughter into the sun at gunpoint.

"I get freckles, Mother, not spots, and *I'm* not trying to embarrass anyone." *Unlike you.* The unspoken words hovered in the air like a grenade waiting to go off.

"Well!" The word came out in a rush of haughty indignation. "That's the thanks I get for trying to do my best for my only daughter, who would rather cavort with her uncultured friends than help with her own wedding plans!"

"Cavort?" Thea mouthed to Lillian with comically raised eyebrows.

"Uncultured?" Lillian mouthed back, looking equally amused.

They'd heard Mrs. Westlake's "That's the thanks I get" speech too many times to really take the words to heart. It was Amelia who would end up wounded. Her mother was never satisfied until she'd drawn blood.

"The last time I tried to help with my own wedding plans, I was told there was nothing for me to do. You and Mrs. Davenport hired a wedding planner to handle all the details, remember?"

"Well, of course, we did." She sounded shocked at the mere idea that they wouldn't. "It's what one does for a Society wedding."

Amelia made a small strangling noise. "You can't have it both ways, Mother. You can't hire someone to plan my wedding and then complain when I'm not doing what you're already paying her to do."

"You should be overseeing the details."

"I would be, except for the little fact that every time I've spoken to her, it seems that you and Mrs. Davenport have already overseen everything to death."

"Well, what else can we do? *You* never showed an interest, and things needed to be done. At least with Constance and myself handling things, we can be assured that everything will be done the right way. With class."

*There it was,* Thea thought with an inward cringe. The blade had just been unsheathed.

"Meaning that if I were to handle it myself, I wouldn't know how to do it with class?" Amelia's voice was tight but steady.

"Well, I would never be so tactless as to say such a thing, dear." But she wouldn't dispute it when it fell from Amelia's lips. With that deft thrust of the verbal knife, all of Amelia's bravado evaporated, leaving her vulnerable to whatever other jabs her mother might be inclined to make. Thea and Lillian quickly stepped into the breach before the woman could bring her daughter to tears.

"Is the president invited to the wedding?" Lillian asked.

Momentarily nonplused by the unexpected question, Mrs. Westlake gave Lillian a quizzical look.

"Yes, of course." Her gaze went back to her silent daughter. "That's why it's so very important that everything—"

"You're good friends with his wife, aren't you?" Lillian persisted, drawing attention back to herself.

"Well, yes, yes I am," Mrs. Westlake preened despite the fact that she'd been interrupted. It seemed rudeness could be overlooked for at least some reasons. "We were sorority sisters. Then when both our husbands entered politics, we were brought back together again. It's good to have allies."

Not friends. Allies. *What a sad life politicians' wives must lead,* Thea mused and wondered again how Amelia was ever going to survive it. She didn't have the requisite backbone of steel or rhinoceros hide for skin. Even now, she saw her friend's hand surreptitiously clutching at a stomach that was probably mere months away from blossoming into a full-blown ulcer. But she loved Charles and was willing to brave the dragons of Washington for him. Thea just hoped Amelia had time to toughen up before one of those dragons gutted her like a kitten.

"It'll be fun to meet him," Lillian said, slanting Thea a sly look. "I mean, how often does one get to sit down to dinner with the leader of the free world?"

"Right," Thea added, picking up her cue, "this will probably be the only time we get to have a nice long chat with him. At least, until Charles goes to Washington and we come for a visit."

As hoped, Mrs. Westlake forgot all about Amelia in light of this new dilemma. "Meet?" she repeated. "Chat?" Her mouth managed to purse into a pinched line despite the Botox, a sure sign of her extreme agitation. "One does not *chat* with the president. One acknowledges him with the deference due his position and replies if, and only if, he speaks to you first, and even then you do not *chat*." She seemed horrified by the thought.

"Okay, no chatting," Thea said obligingly. Too obligingly. That, along with the sweet smile she bestowed on Mrs. Westlake was enough to convince the woman that she was up to no good. The woman drew herself to her full regal height and glared down her surgically narrowed patrician nose at her.

"I know you're plotting something in that devious little mind of yours, Cynthia Fordham, but you can be sure that you won't have the opportunity to do whatever it is you're thinking of doing. This wedding will be the event of the year, and I won't allow you to ruin it for me." After a final glare, she stalked her way back into the house. Unfortunately, the heavy smell of roses didn't depart as quickly. Thea escaped it by retaking her seat.

"She's probably going to sic the Secret Service on you, you know," Lillian said to Thea. "You won't get within a mile of the president now."

"Gee, color me disappointed." Thea looked at Amelia and felt a rush of sympathy for her friend. "You okay?" She nodded meaningfully at the roll of antacids Amelia had withdrawn from her pocket.

"Peachy." She grimaced as she chewed two of the chalky tablets and then rinsed her mouth with the last of her iced tea. "Sorry about that," she said with a vague wave of her hand. "The closer the engagement party gets, the worse she is, barking out orders and biting off everyone's head if everything isn't *perfect*." She said the last word like it was a curse. Fiddling with the roll of antacids, she said, "If you're wondering what to give me for an engagement present, a few cases of these wouldn't go to waste." It was supposed to be a joke, but there was a slight tremor in her voice that said it wasn't that far from the truth.

"You could always elope," Lillian suggested.

Amelia gave a harsh laugh. "You heard my mother. My wedding is going to be the event of the year. She'd never forgive me if I took that away from her."

"It's your wedding," Thea reminded her gently, "not hers. And it's supposed to make you happy, not insane. Just tell your mother you want something smaller, more intimate." But even as she spoke, Amelia was shaking her head.

"But it's not just my wedding, though. I have to think of Charles. His career is just getting started. Between his father and mine, he's got a foot in the door, but if he can make a good impression on even half the people who are invited, his political future is almost guaranteed. With the right support, he'll be able to bypass the lower, local offices and go right for a seat in Washington. It could put him on the fast track to the White House."

Those sounded an awful lot like William Westlake's words coming from his daughter's mouth, but Thea knew better than to point it out. It was no secret that the former senator, recently retired from politics due to a bad heart, had long planned a run for the White House himself. Now that that dream had been taken away from him, Thea wouldn't put it past him to be a driving force behind putting his future son-in-law into the Oval Office in his place.

"So Charles gets exposure and a boost to his career by letting the dragons plan the wedding of the century," Lillian remarked in a sour tone. "What do you get out of it?"

Thea's heart broke a tiny bit when Amelia stared off at some unseen spot and answered simply, "Someone to love me."

"Does he?" Thea couldn't keep herself from asking. "Really?"

"He really does." Amelia smiled, and the happiness of it actually reached her eyes for a change. "I know you don't see it, but he's actually very romantic and sweet. Since he's been on the road with his father so much since the engagement, he's been sending me little notes to let me know he misses me." Her smile turned very cat-ate-the-canary. "Love notes."

"*Sexy* love notes?" Lillian asked, sitting forward in sudden interest.

Amelia's cheeks got pinker. "Maybe just a little."

"Wow. Way to go, Charles." Lillian toasted the absent groom-to-be with her glass.

Thea was surprised. She never would have guessed that Charles had a romantic streak. From her few encounters with him over the past few months, she'd always thought he was a bit of an emotionless jerk. It was good to know she'd been so wrong.

"I'm happy you're happy, Mellie," she said, "but you still should put your foot down about not getting a say in your own wedding plans."

The sparkle in Amelia's eyes dimmed and her smile grew tight. "It's okay. All I have to do is keep from going into a homicidal rage for the next nine months. After twenty-two years, nine months is a piece of cake. Once the wedding is over and done with, and Charles and I are settled into our lives in Connecticut and his parents are back in Washington, aside from missing you guys, everything will be perfect. You'll see." She tapped her finger against her glass in an agitated staccato. "Anyway, enough about my issues. We're supposed to be helping you on your manhunt."

Somehow Thea doubted it was going to be quite that simple to dislodge Amelia's mother and mother-in-law from her life. But she could tell that

Amelia was desperate to turn the subject away from herself, so she swallowed her protest.

"Right." Thea looked to Lillian and grimaced. "So? We're back to strut, shake and...jiggle." She practically had to choke the word out. "I suppose you're going to teach me how?"

The wicked smile on Lillian's face should have served as warning. "Oh, no, not me. But I know just the person who can."

# CHAPTER 6

"THEA, *DARLING!*"

Enfolded in an enthusiastic hug that made her wince, Thea had to wait until she was released to draw enough breath for a reply.

"Good to see you, too, Des." She grinned as the same rib-crushing greeting drew a surprised squeak out of Amelia. What Des lacked in height and bulk—he only topped Thea and Amelia by a few inches, keeping him just shy of that six-foot mark most men seemed to strive for—he always made up for in exuberance.

Des turned to Sam Britten, who had insisted in his quiet but firm way that he'd have to come inside with them, old friend of Lillian's or not. Des's lips kicked up into a pleased half-smile. "And who is this you've brought along, kittens?"

"My shadow for the day, Sam Britten," Thea told him. "Sam, this is Desmond Finkle."

"Just Des is fine," Des said, smoothly taking the bodyguard's hand in a lingering shake. Thea groaned to herself. She'd forgotten Des's penchant for blond-haired, blued-eyed men. He laughingly said that aesthetically they were the perfect counterpoint to his own mixed-Mediterranean skin tone and dark hair, but Thea thought it had more to do with the man he'd loved and lost and still hadn't quite gotten over. Not that she'd ever say as much. For all his flamboyance, Des was one of the most private people she knew.

When Des flashed her a quick, questioning look, Thea shook her head. Nope, Sam was as straight as the days were long, more's the pity for Des's hopes. Des pursed his lips slightly and sighed.

"Ah, well," he murmured before sweeping them all toward the duplex's large living room with a courtly gesture. Thea wasn't sure if Sam had caught or understood the byplay, but, wise man that he was, if so he had chosen to ignore it.

Des settled the women onto the comfortable, overstuffed furniture that filled the oblong room, which was tastefully decorated (thanks to Thea's talent) but filled with enough kitschy tchotchkes to feel homey and lived-in (thanks to Des's eclectic taste).

"So, to what do I owe the pleasure, loveys?"

Both Thea and Amelia glanced at Lillian, who in turn threw a glance at Sam, who had habitually moved to the far side of the room, doing his potted plant impersonation. With a glint of understanding lighting his dark eyes, Des jumped back to his feet like a large cat.

"Wait, where are my manners! Let me get some cool drinks, and then we can have a nice coze." That fast, he was gone from the room.

"How are we supposed to talk to Des about...*things* with Sam in the room?" Amelia whispered nervously. Lillian gave her a knowing smirk.

"Trust me. Des will take care of it."

Sure enough, Des returned a few minutes later with not only a pitcher of lemonade and glasses, but with his roommate, Sheila, as well. The petite redhead was dressed in snug jeans and a cropped baby blue T-shirt that teased at her pierced navel and carried a dish of sugar cookies that smelled as though they had just come out of the oven. Thea had to bite her lip to keep from smiling at the sudden look of interest on Sam's face. Food and sex. Trust Des to use a two-pronged attack to go right for a man's greatest weaknesses.

"You three all remember Sheila, yes?" Des said, knowing full well that they did. He turned to Sam with a wicked smile. "Mister Britten, allow me to introduce you to my roommate and dear, dear friend, Miss Sheila Anderson."

"My pleasure, Miss Anderson."

"Sheila, please." Her voice held the soft lilt of Ireland, which seemed to fascinate Sam as he took her offered hand.

"A pleasure, Sheila."

Jumping at the golden opportunity Des had handed her, Thea said, "Sam, didn't you come inside so you could check out the rest of the apartment?"

"Oh, I'd be happy to give you a tour of the place." Thea wasn't sure if Sheila had volunteered because Des had primed her to her role as a distraction or because the look of interest she was giving Sam was as real as the one she was receiving in return. Either one suited her purpose, but Thea still felt a pang of conscience. She liked Sam. She didn't want his feelings toyed with just to get him out of earshot.

"Be sure to show him what you have in the kitchen, love," Des encouraged with a wink.

"What does she have in the kitchen?" Thea couldn't resist asking when Sam and his escort had left the room. Sheila was a pastry chef for one of the local upscale restaurants and spent most of her spare time coming up with new and exotic desserts to tempt the palate and dazzle the eye. Amelia had wanted to hire her to make her wedding cake, but the dragons had both vetoed the idea. No mere *local* pastry chef could possibly be up to the task of such an important event. They were flying someone in from Paris or somewhere to do the deed, even though Thea had no doubt that Sheila could do the job twice as well for a fraction the cost, not to mention the huge boost it would have given her career.

Yet another loss for Amelia on the wedding war front.

"She's working on a commission for a bachelorette party this weekend. They wanted her to design something appropriate to the occasion, but she's having a little trouble getting the desired results." The twinkle in Des's dark, Mediterranean eyes spoke volumes of forewarning, but poor Amelia fell right into his trap.

"What kind of results?"

With gales of laughter in his look but a mere faint smile on his full lips, Des replied, "It seems the centerpiece to the whole design is having trouble holding its erection. It keeps wilting after mere minutes." This, he illustrated with his hand. "Hopefully, it's not a portent of the upcoming wedding night."

Amelia colored bright red and took refuge in her lemonade.

Choking back laughter even while trying to picture the malfunctioning bit of pastry, Thea shook her head. "You're too bad, Des."

"Yes, I know. A fatal flaw, I'm afraid." He sighed dramatically and then recovered. "So. While Sheila still has sumptuous Sam occupied, why don't you tell me what's brought you to my door." With a shrewd look at Thea, he asked, "Are you in some kind of trouble, sweet? You don't usually have a watchdog on your heels."

"No, no trouble," Thea assured him, although that wasn't strictly true. "Sam's more of a precaution than anything else. Doyle's orders until my father gets back," she added with a moue of distaste.

As usual, Des saw too much. "Ah, yes, Mister Doyle," he purred. "And how is the dear man?" Thea merely shrugged, but Lillian wasn't nearly so reticent.

"He's stubborn and blind, especially where Thea is concerned, and we need your help teaching her how to make the most of her assets so he'll stop being an idiot and notice her. She's got self-confidence issues," she added in a confiding-a-secret tone.

Des looked mildly shocked. "Whatever for?"

"Bad boyfriend experience."

"Ah." Des nodded sympathetically. "Once bitten, twice shy. Understandable. But definitely something we can overcome."

Rather than crawling under her chair, which was her initial inclination, Thea muttered, "You didn't have to just blurt it all out like that. I sound pathetic."

"Yes, I did, and no, you're not. We just don't have time to beat around the bush. The house is only so big, and Sheila can't keep Sam occupied forever." Lillian looked at Des, who was looking at Thea with a speculative gleam in his eye. "So, do you think you can help her stand out in a crowd?"

Des laughed. "Oh, kitten, standing out in a crowd is what I do best!" He sobered and motioned for Thea to stand up, which she did. Reluctantly. But really, what other choice did she have? She needed to do *something* to make Doyle take notice of her as a woman, and clearly the clothes alone weren't cutting it.

She couldn't go on this way forever, living on wishes and hopes and maybes. She needed to find out, one way or another, if Doyle might possibly want her or if she was simply flogging a much-dead horse. Her feelings for him seemed to grow stronger every day, but she kept getting nothing in return. How was it possible to love somebody so much that it hurt and yet have them be so absolutely oblivious?

Still, she was a little nervous about what Des meant, exactly, by standing out in a crowd. She might want Doyle to notice her, but she didn't want to make a spectacle of herself, either.

"The clothes are good," Des mused, almost to himself as he studied Thea's new teal sundress and matching Jimmy Choo sandals, both of which highlighted her long, tanned legs. "Not that they were ever bad," he added quickly at Thea's frown, "but it's all about the presentation. The body language," he clarified at her confused look. "Right now, you aren't saying 'look at me, I'm a beautiful woman.' You're saying 'I feel awkward and I'm not quite sure what to do with my hands.'"

Embarrassed, Thea tucked the offending appendages behind her back.

"Well, I do feel awkward," she said, thrusting her chin up. "I don't like being on display."

"Sweetheart, the mating dance is all *about* being on display." Des stood and walked over to her, gently pulling her hands from behind her and holding them in his own. "Your body is the best marketing tool in the world. You can be the most amazing, wonderful woman ever to draw breath, but if you can't get your man to take notice of that fact, then you're sunk."

"I don't want it to be all about sex." Because that was all she'd had with Dave. She'd thought there was more between them—friendship, at the very least, if not true affection—but he'd quickly disabused her of that notion when he'd cheated on her and then dumped her with brutal indifference right after the midwinter break for a perky transfer student with a double-D cup and a mind-boggling amount of flexibility.

"Sex is the lure," Des assured her, "but not the bottom line. You don't hand out samples; you merely entice." When she still looked skeptical, he sighed and released her hands, taking a step back and indicating her body, which had gone stiff and defensive from her remembered humiliation. "If you're looking to grab hold of a man's attention, you need to think of yourself as a display window in a sweet shop. Let him get a glimpse of what treats await within, and he'll be coming through your door in no time."

Not entirely certain whether he had meant it to sound quite that blatantly sexual, Thea blushed anyway.

"Well, he has looked," she admitted, "but he certainly hasn't, um, wanted to come inside." She blushed even harder.

"Hasn't wanted to, or wanted to and didn't?"

"Um…"

"Oh, he definitely wanted to," Lillian offered. "He nearly died right there at her feet when he got an eyeful of her new bikini."

"String?" Des asked, raising an eyebrow.

"Thong."

Des's grin widened. "Thea, you naughty puss."

Feeling as though her face was bright enough to light a runway at Boulder Municipal Airport, Thea wondered what she'd ever done to deserve friends like these.

"Not that it helped any," she pointed out. "He hasn't been back near the pool since." She couldn't help but wonder if Lillian had been wrong, that it hadn't been lust in his expression but disgust. Had she totally turned him off by the way she'd acted that afternoon? Maybe he was thinking that she was a total slut, coming on to him the way she had, and *that* was why he'd made excuses to get out of their run. Oh God, had she screwed up her one chance at getting him to notice her by throwing herself at him? Again?

"Stop it."

Thea looked up at Lillian's sharp command. "What?"

"Stop thinking whatever it is you're thinking. That look on your face says it's not anything good."

"I was just thinking—"

"Don't! Don't think you did anything wrong and don't think he wasn't interested because he was, in a very definite I'd-kill-to-see-you-naked kind of way." Lillian grinned at Thea's shocked look. "I've known you a lot of years, T. You're not that hard to read."

"So he's interested in the sweets, but he's trying to resist the temptation they present," Des said, tapping his chin thoughtfully. "We can definitely work with that."

"But now he's avoiding her," Amelia interjected. "How do we get him to want the sweets when he won't even look in the window anymore?"

"I'm getting a little tired of being referred to as food," Thea grumbled, but Amelia had come right to the heart of the matter. She might be as tempting as a double-fudge chocolate cake, which she knew was one of Doyle's favorite desserts, but if Doyle wouldn't stay in a room with her for more than five seconds, she was just going to sit there on the shelf going stale.

She groaned inwardly. Great. Now they had her doing it, too.

"Simple," Des replied, obviously choosing to ignore Thea's complaint. "If the customer won't come to the sweet shop, then the sweet shop will just have to use a little hard-sell advertising to change his mind."

"Hard-sell advertising?" Thea wasn't sure she liked the sound of that.

"Strut, shake, and jiggle," Amelia murmured helpfully.

Nope, she was right. She didn't like it. Not at all. Especially with the way Des was grinning at her, like he'd just been handed a present he couldn't wait to unwrap.

Thea sighed.

"I'll take whatever help you can give," she said, "but I draw the line at jiggling."

\*    \*    \*

"This is a really bad idea."

"No, it isn't."

"A really, really bad idea."

"Stop complaining so much and smile."

"I am smiling."

"No, you're grimacing. God, Thea, are you *trying* to scare everyone away?"

"Don't I wish," Thea muttered, but she did her best to rearrange her face into something she hoped more closely resembled the flirtatious smile that graced Lillian's elfin face. "Better?"

"Oh, much," Lillian drawled. "Now you only look like you're only attending an execution rather than taking part in one."

Thea sighed heavily. "I can't do this."

"Yes, you can." A bit of sympathy softened Lillian's expression. "Des wouldn't have said you were ready to try out your new talents if he didn't believe you could pull it off."

"I know, but…" *But* it was different to be in a bar full of strangers instead of the raucous but cozy dressing room at Club Platinum where Des had taken her for her "lessons" in body language. *But* these were men out look-ing for a woman and as good a time as she was willing to provide, not Des's performer friends playing at being the victims of her newly acquired flirting skills. *But* she was terrified of making a fool out of herself, or worse, getting herself into trouble by choosing the wrong person to flirt with. But, but, but. "But…they're not Doyle," she finished lamely.

"Exactly." At Thea's confused look, Lillian said patiently, "This is practice, T. This is where you get to make your mistakes, refine your technique, and, hopefully, have a little fun while you're doing it. Most people get this part out of the way in high school. You're just a little behind the curve is all."

"Wonderful. Remedial flirting one-oh-one."

"Plus," Lillian added with a sly grin, "your every conquest tonight will be witnessed firsthand by one of Doyle's loyal staff."

Following her friend's gaze toward where Daryl Raintree sat at a table sipping what she knew to be either ginger ale or Perrier with lime, Thea felt a real smile start to curl her lips for the first time all night. True, Daryl wasn't happy with her right now. He would never openly question her on her choice of evening entertainment, but she knew him well enough to have read the mild censure in his dark gaze when they'd entered the bar.

Farraday's wasn't exactly one of her usual hangouts, catering to a slightly older, less affluent crowd than, say, H2O or Misto. That had been the point. To get outside her comfort zone, away from her usual friends and acquain-tances. To have a fresh slate to see if she had managed to retain any of the self-assurance and body language magic Des had worked so hard to drum into her. Threatening letters to her father notwithstanding, she felt perfectly safe with Daryl there, observing from a discrete distance.

She smiled because she knew he would also be filing a report about the evening's events when they got home. A report that Doyle would read. A report that would include how she was besieged by dozens of adoring men who didn't have a problem with seeing her as a desirable woman even if Doyle did.

Well, okay maybe besieged was a little too fanciful. And adoring might be a bit of a stretch. Most likely not dozens, either. Maybe a few. One or two. But even if she had only one or two really nice-looking men—not boys, but *men*—paying her a bit of attention, talking, flirting, buying her drinks, that would show Doyle that she wasn't at all the child he seemed to insist on seeing her as.

Wouldn't it?

Sighing inwardly, Thea attempted to apply herself to the task at hand. Sipping her rum and coke, she took stock of the men that didn't already have a woman or two hovering at their sides. From that group she mentally tossed out the ones who were too old, too drunk, or too obviously checking out the waitresses or, worse, the women already with other men. An evening spent dodging the leers and grabs of a lecher on the make was not what she had in mind at all.

With her list of possible flirts winnowed down to a mere handful, Thea felt her doubts begin to creep back in again. Could she do this? *Should* she do this?

"What about him?"

Resolutely shoving her reservations into a tiny corner and chaining them there, Thea glanced at the man Lillian nodded toward. Standing alone by the blaring jukebox, she could just make out his profile. Tall. Older than she was, but not as old as Doyle, maybe late twenties or even thirty, the bar lighting made it hard to tell. The rosy hues thrown up by the neon in the jukebox cast his features into stark lines and shadows, but he seemed good-looking in a Russell Crowe rather than a Tom Cruise sort of way. Jeans, worn but neat, and a white shirt, sleeves rolled past his elbows gave him a slightly more sophisticated air than the beer-logo T-shirts and biker boots sported by many of those around him.

Neat, cute, and apparently alone and sober. He would do.

"He's looked over here at least a half dozen times already," Lillian said with a smirk. "Your fish is already half-hooked. Now all you have to do is reel him in." With that, she sat back in her chair, settling in as though getting ready to watch a performance. Which, Thea thought wryly, she was. Mister Jukebox might turn out to be pure gold, but for her, he'd never be anything more than a practice flirt.

"I can do this," Thea muttered under her breath. She repeated it to herself like a mantra. *I can do this. I can do this. I can —*

"Uh, T? You have to actually get out of the chair first."

Fighting down the flush that burned her cheeks, Thea shot her friend a sheepish look and, through a sheer force of will, got to her feet. One step toward the jukebox. Two. See, she could do this. She *was* doing this. Five steps. Almost there. Three more steps. Two. Just one last step…

And she was there. Next to him. Close enough to feel the heat of his body. Close enough to smell the slightly spicy cologne he was wearing. Close enough to see that he wasn't just good-looking, he was positively *gorgeous*. She stared blindly down at the song selections, frantically rummaging through her suddenly blank mind for what the heck she was supposed to do first. Smile? Flutter her lashes? Ask him if he wanted her to have his babies?

"Hello."

That was it! She was supposed to say hello! Only he'd beaten her to it. That was good, right? It was much better if he was the one to say something first. Less chance of him thinking of her as too forward. Or easy. But what was she supposed to do now? Oh, right…

"Hi." She managed a small smile. Polite, friendly, yet rife with possibility. Either that or she looked like the fish she'd had for dinner hadn't agreed with her. She wasn't quite sure which.

"Good selection." Mr. Jukebox tapped a finger on the glass. "Lots of oldies mixed with the newer stuff."

Gladly grabbing onto the conversational gambit, Thea quickly scanned the listing. "Maroon Five. I like them." Did that sound stupid? And what was she supposed to do with her hands? Maybe she should have brought her drink with her.

Mr. Jukebox grinned. "A pretty lady with good taste in music. My luck must finally be changing."

"Oh, and has it been so bad? Your luck, I mean?"

With a grimace, he replied, "Well, there were the two canceled flights, the missed connection in San Francisco, the lost luggage that is probably right now doing a world tour without me, the hotel room from hell with a/c that only has two settings—Death Valley and North Pole—the rental car that got a flat before I'd even left the airport…"

"Okay, okay," Thea laughed, waving her hands in mock surrender. "Definitely bad. Worse than bad. You've got your own personal black cloud following you around."

"Well, you know what they say. Every black cloud has a silver lining. And I'm thinking that maybe you're mine."

Thea blinked. Well, that was…lame.

Evidently Mr. Jukebox thought so, too, because he winced and shot her a sheepish grin. "I'm a little out of practice, but even for me that was a lousy line. Sorry."

It hit her then. He was as nervous as she was. For the first time since walking through the front door of the bar, Thea relaxed a little. "No worries. Everyone's entitled to at least one bad cliché per night."

That earned a small grin. "Are you going to use yours now, or were you planning to save it until later?"

"I think I'll hang onto it," Thea teased back. "You never know when the urge to cliché might strike." Maybe this flirting stuff wasn't so hard after all.

Mister Jukebox's face lit up as he laughed. It was a deep, pleasant sound, but it didn't make her tingle way down inside the way Doyle's laugh did. Pity, that.

He stuck his hand out. "Nick Hastings."

"Thea Fordham." Inwardly, Thea winced at the gaffe as she shook his hand. How many times had Doyle warned her about giving her name to strangers? But there was no flicker of recognition in Nick's handsome face, so she shrugged the worry aside. It wasn't as if Nick was going to toss her over his shoulder and kidnap her right out of Farraday's or anything. And anyway, Daryl was somewhere nearby, just in case.

"So," Nick drawled with a wicked grin, hooking his thumbs in his front pockets, "come here often?"

Yes, this flirting stuff might actually be fun. But it would be even more fun with the right man. If only she got the chance.

# CHAPTER 7

**THEA DIDN'T WANT** to admit it, but the evening wasn't turning out half as bad as she'd expected it to be.

After leaving Farraday's and the cute but not-for-her Nick behind, they'd ventured even further out of their usual comfort zone and into The Hole, where Thea had drinks bought for her by several very nice men who didn't seem to think she was inept or awkward or any of the things that she always felt every time she tried to get Doyle to notice her the way *they* were noticing her. In fact, the only awkward moment had come when the guy with the amazing collection of tattoos on his arms had asked for her number and she'd had to say no. Not that it had stopped him from giving her *his* number, though.

That was when she'd started to feel guilty about possibly misleading any of the men she'd been flirting with, but Lillian had quickly disabused her of that worry. She'd pointed out that everybody bar-flirted and that flirting in no way implied actual intent. Unless you came right out and said yes to someone, they had no reason to expect more.

Thea had been ready to call it a night after that, but Lillian had badgered her into making one more stop, this time at a dance club rather than a bar.

"For variety's sake," Lillian had joked as they paid the cover and joined the very large crowd straining toward the dance floor at the center of the converted warehouse.

"But I won't be able to have a conversation with anyone here," Thea had pointed out, raising her voice to be heard over the music.

"Exactly! That means it's going to have to be all about the body language."

*That* had almost had her turning and heading right back out the door, but Thea had let herself get pulled out onto the dance floor and quickly lost herself in the music, happy to not have to think about anything more important than not stepping on anyone's toes.

Now, sweaty and out of breath, they found that Daryl had worked some of his bodyguard ninja magic and procured a table for them, one situated close to the wall where the crowd wasn't as thick and the music not quite as obnoxiously loud. Two unopened bottles of water even sat waiting for them.

Thea scanned the immediate vicinity until she found Daryl standing a few yards away against the wall, his height giving him an unobstructed view of the table despite the crowd. Cracking the seal on the bottle, she saluted him in thanks before taking a long drink, once again having to repress the pinch of guilt at making him tag along on her evening out. She knew it was his job, but that didn't mean she wanted to make that job harder than it had to be, and going clubbing definitely did that.

*All for a good cause,* she reminded herself. If all of this practice did what it was supposed to and helped her finally have a real shot at getting Doyle to see her for herself and not some idealized junior version of herself, it would have all been worth it.

"Hello, beautiful ladies. Would you like to dance?"

Thea glanced up at the two men who had stopped at their table. Both dark-haired and dark-eyed, they looked enough alike to be brothers. It wasn't until they both grinned that she realized they were twins. Very good-looking twins.

Who sadly did absolutely nothing for her.

"Sure," Lillian answered for the both of them, bumping Thea as she got out of her chair.

"Love to," Thea answered after the prompt. Right. Focus. Practice.

After Carlos and Miguel, there were Kevin, Leon, and a few others she didn't even bother to trade names with. That was the beauty of the dance floor. People switched partners at will, no words or names exchanged, just a willingness to share the beat.

Finally, though, Thea tapped out, needing a respite. Lillian was still going strong, so Thea just made sure her friend knew where she was heading before she wormed her way through the crowd and back over to the table, which through some miracle of miracles—or maybe it was just the miracle of Daryl—hadn't been claimed by anyone else.

A plastic bucket of ice with new, unopened bottles of water sat in the middle of the small table, and Thea gratefully cracked one open and chugged half without stopping. She'd forgotten how tiring dancing could be. Not that she'd ever been much of a clubber. Even when she'd been away at college, most of her weekends had been spent in her dorm room working on design projects to help her hone her skills. She'd wanted to be ready to take on any job that came her way once she graduated.

Fat lot of good that had done her so far.

"Hey, fancy meeting you here!"

Thea looked up at the half-shouted words of the man who slid into the seat next to her. His easy smile brought out her own, but the look in his eyes made her immediately suspicious. "Peter, hey!" She leaned into the hug Lillian's brother offered. "I didn't know you hung out at Blaze."

"Oh, yeah, sure, sure, all the time." Peter kept his arm slung around the back of her chair and looked across the table to the other man who had sat down with him rather than meet her gaze. "You remember Seth, right?"

*Oh, damn.*

She slapped a friendly smile on and said, "Of course, I do. Nice to see you again, Seth."

"Yeah, it's good to see you, too!" Seth Reed was still one of the most solidly built men Thea had ever met. The bulk had served him well back on the high school wrestling team. Now, though, it just made him look like he was living in a world that was built two sizes too small for him. His white-blond hair, always short, was now shorn down into a brutal crew cut. Not his best look. The lack of hair somehow made his head seem even more out of proportion with the rest of his body.

"I didn't realize you and Seth were friends," Thea said to Peter. She could tell by the way he still wouldn't look at her that something was up, and she meant to get to the bottom of it.

"Oh, sure, sure," Peter said. His fingers were drumming a nervous beat on the back of her chair. She didn't think he realized she could feel it. "He just joined the force, actually, and I thought hey, we should go out and do something to celebrate, and then we saw you sitting here and I remembered that you and Seth used to date back in the day, so we thought we'd come over and say hello, and then, well, here we are." He cleared his throat and reached for one of the bottles of water. "Man, it's a little warm in here, huh?"

Thea wasn't sure which part of that rambling explanation surprised her the most. That Seth had become a cop; that he and Peter were apparently friends; or that Peter actually thought that she and Seth had dated back in high school. They'd gone out a grand total of twice. Neither date had been anything worth repeating, which was why there had never been a third, despite Seth's dogged persistence otherwise. Graduation had been a godsend if for no other reason than it finally got her away from having to see him every day.

And here he was, four years later, sitting across the table and grinning at her like he'd just been handed his fondest wish. *Double damn.*

"So, you're a police officer," Thea said, using the body language and smile that Des and his friends had taught her sent the "back down, back off, back away" message loud and clear. Either she wasn't doing it right or Seth was immune because his smile just got wider.

"Yeah, I just graduated from the Academy last month. I reconnected with Pete here during one of the ride-alongs we cadets have to do. That was a helluva night, wasn't it?" he asked Peter, slapping the table with one large hand and making the bottles jump.

Peter made a noncommittal noise that might have been agreement.

"We might not have had a lot in common growing up, but once you wear the badge all that changes," Seth continued, sounding more like a ten-year veteran than an untried rookie. "At the end of the day, we all bleed blue."

Thea wondered if he had any idea how ridiculous he sounded.

"What have you been doing with yourself since high school?" Thea asked before she could stop herself when silence lapsed over the table once again. Stupid manners.

"Well, you know that after graduation I went into serious training to make the Olympic wrestling team, but, well, things just didn't fall into place for me on that, so I kind of drifted through a few things here and there, trying to find the right fit, you know?"

Since she'd always known that she wanted to study design, Thea didn't know, but it did make her feel a little sorry for him.

"I was over in California for a while to see if I could get anything going for me there, but nothing panned out there like I'd hoped, so I moved on up to Oregon, until I finally decided last year to just come on back to Boulder and see what my hometown could do for me."

The news that he'd been in California at the same time she'd been attending college there made her doubly glad that a rash of middle-of-the-night hang ups right after high school graduation had forced her to change her phone number. Not that she would have caved and gone out with him even if he had managed to contact her but still. She'd been going through enough crap trying to get over Doyle and dealing with the Dave Disaster and all its emotional fallout. More drama would not have been welcome.

"I thought about going with the State Patrol at first," Seth went on, not needing any prompting to keep talking about himself, "but, well, that didn't feel like the best fit, you know? So I ended up with the Boulder P.D., and here I am." His gesture strained the material of his shirt, making Thea wonder idly if he had to have his uniforms custom-made to actually fit him. It was either that or wonder how fast she could make an escape out one of the bathroom windows.

"And here you are," Thea repeated, hanging onto her smile by a thread. She looked at Pete in desperation. "Want to dance?" She accompanied the suggestion with a pinch to his side that said he'd better say yes. Before he could reply, though, Seth was already on his feet holding one beefy hand in her direction.

"Great idea!"

Thea stared at the hand for a long second as she tried to come up with a polite way to refuse, but there was just no way to correct Seth's misunderstanding without embarrassing him. She shouldn't care about that, but she did, darn it. Seth hadn't had many friends in high school, and she got the feeling that might still be the case, seeing as how his somewhat abrasive personality hadn't really changed much since then. Telling him she didn't want to dance with him would be like kicking a puppy.

A really large, incredibly annoying puppy.

Damning her manners a second time, Thea got up and stepped past Pete, glaring down at him with promised retribution as she did. Naked baby pictures wouldn't be nearly enough. No, for this, she was going to have to come up with something truly evil.

As she was tugged along to the dance floor like a dingy in the wake of a tugboat, Thea had the time to wonder if it really *had* been a misunderstanding on Seth's part that had gotten her there or just a willful end run to get what he wanted. Seth had always been good at making the dumb jock image work in his favor, but she'd always gotten the impression there was a much more devious brain at work underneath all of that muscle.

Thea had to admit that for a large man, Seth danced surprisingly well. And if he hadn't taken every opportunity to get into her personal space, she might have actually enjoyed dancing with him. The crowd kept them close, but every time Thea found a few inches of space to retreat into, Seth was right there, closing the distance again, smiling down at her like there was no place on earth he'd rather be.

Thea could think of about a dozen other places *she'd* rather be at the moment. Several of them involved tearing a strip off of Pete's butt for bringing Seth to the club to "run into" her. No way did she buy that it was just coincidence.

The beat slowed, the crowd shifted, and Seth stepped right up into her personal space again, his hands going to her shoulders as though he was going to pull her up against him in a full-frontal press. Thea stiffened and shot her hand against his chest to hold him away, anger burning away the manners that had gotten her into this mess in the first place.

"Look," she started sharply, only to be cut off when Pete appeared at her side.

"My dance," he said, giving Seth a look that wasn't entirely friendly as he claimed both of Thea's hands and danced her into a turn that put her out of the other man's reach.

There was a second where Thea thought Seth would try to snatch her back, but thankfully after giving her a final covetous look, he turned and bulled his way through the dancers and off the dance floor. The tension that had risen in her washed out with a relived sigh. She took a second to get her emotions back in check then looked up at Pete, who was watching her with serious eyes. Cop eyes.

"Thank you," she said.

"You shouldn't be thanking me. I should be apologizing. If I'd known he was going to be such a douche—uh, dumbass, I would have never agreed to bring him tonight." He glared off in the direction Seth had disappeared.

"Was that your idea or Lillian's?" Thea asked innocently.

"Mine. I thought—" His gaze swung down to hers in surprise.

"I'm not entirely dimwitted, you know," she said with a smile, enjoying the way he squirmed at being caught out.

"I was only trying to help," he said quickly. "Swear to God."

"How, exactly, is throwing me in the path of someone I haven't seen since high school—by choice, mind you—supposed to help me? Help me what?"

He mumbled something that the music drowned out.

"What?"

With a sigh, Pete repeated louder, "Make sure that you're not so totally focused on Doyle that you miss out on someone else who might be a better fit."

Thea's eyes widened in disbelief. "And you thought that person might be *Seth*?"

Pete had the decency to look embarrassed.

"Well, we got to talking about high school one day, and he remembered that Lil and you were friends, and that kind of led to talking about you and him. He made it sound like you two were really tight before you went off to college."

"Do you *remember* me being tight with him?"

"I didn't exactly pay attention to your love life back then," he replied with a roll of his eyes. "Do *you* remember who *I* was dating senior year?"

"It was a cheerleader." Thea tried to dredge up the vague memory. "Buffy something. No, Bitsy. Betty?" She huffed. "Okay, I see your point. But the truth is, no matter what he might have told you, we had a grand total of two dates, and we were done way before I left for California. End. Of. Story."

"I guess he remembers things a little differently."

Revisionist history at its finest. Something else she was just now remembering that Seth had always been good at.

"You wouldn't have any reason to think he was exaggerating," Thea sighed, although lying through his teeth might have been a more accurate description, "so you're forgiven for bringing him tonight. But your *reason* for bringing him was way out of line."

"Hey." Peter gave up even pretending they were dancing and tugged her off the dance floor on the side of the club opposite where their table was and over toward the wall away from the giant speakers.

Thea allowed herself to be pulled along because she had a few things she wanted to say to him about his sticking his nose into her personal business, and shouting at him over the music in the middle of the dance floor wasn't how she wanted to do it.

"Look," Pete said when he finally parked them in a relatively private spot, "I get that you're probably a little pissed at me for tonight, but you don't have your own big brother to watch out for you, so I feel that I kind of have to step up and take on that role whenever the time comes that you need one. And I kind of felt that time was now. So I did."

He couldn't have said anything better designed to puncture her anger at him.

"You've been all starry-eyed about Doyle for years, and after listening to you talking with Lil the other day about how hard you're willing to work to get him to notice you, I gotta admit, I was a little worried. I just didn't want you to get sucked into this tunnel vision with him as the only guy who exists for you."

He shook his head and scowled. "If you want my opinion, if Doyle is still so blind to all you have to offer after all these years, then he doesn't deserve you. You can do better. There are guys out there who would worship the ground you walk on. I'm not kidding," he insisted when she snorted and rolled her eyes. "I think you're really selling yourself short if you think Doyle is all there is."

Wow. Pete was far from stupid, but he *was* a guy, which meant he didn't usually think about things like feelings and relationships the same way women did. For him, that statement had actually been quite eloquent.

Unfortunately, it had also been totally wrong.

"Pete, I appreciate that you're worried about me. Really, I am. But the fact of the matter is I'm in love with Doyle. He's it for me. Right or wrong, I can't help the way I feel. I don't know if he'll ever want to love me back, but I have to give myself the chance to find out."

"I just don't want you to get hurt."

"There's a really good chance I will be," Thea replied, feeling a pinch in her chest at the painful truth of that statement. "But love is worth the risk."

"Okay," Pete sighed, "no more butting in. Unless you need me to," he added as they started walking back toward the table. "I'm still going to be your stand-in big brother."

"*Big* brother, huh?" She looked up at him with her head cocked. "You do remember that I'm older than you by like two months, right?"

"You are never going to let that go, are you?"

Thea grinned, having gotten the reaction she wanted. The humor of their usual banter quickly faded, however, when she saw that Seth was waiting at their table, staring out at the dance floor while talking to Lillian, who was sitting across from him typing on her phone, looking like she'd rather be absolutely anywhere else.

Thea could sympathize because she suddenly felt the exact same way.

Squaring her shoulders, she approached the table and took the empty seat next to Lillian, gratefully fishing out one of the last two bottles of water sloshing around in the bucket of half-melted ice and holding it to her face before opening it. "Wow, I'm totally beat. I think it's time to call it a night."

"I bought you a drink." Seth slid a large martini glass across the table toward her.

"I...oh." Thea stared at the familiar sugar-rimmed glass.

"A lemon drop martini," Seth prompted. "That's your drink, right?"

Since she hadn't developed a taste for them until her last year of college, she had no idea how he would know that, unless...She glanced at Lillian, who gave a small shake of her head. She hadn't mentioned it. That left only one other person. *Pete.* Thea gritted her teeth with renewed annoyance. Apology or not, he was so going to pay for being a blabbermouth.

"Thank you, but it's getting late and we really do need to be going."

Seth stared at her in mild confusion. "But...I bought you a drink." He nudged the glass a little closer toward her. "Go ahead, try it."

Not a chance. Even if she'd been in the mood to prolong the evening, Thea would have had to decline. One of the strictest, not to mention smartest, rules she'd ever been given, even before she'd reached the legal drinking age, was to never drink something that wasn't sealed or handed directly to her by the bartender. Even being an old acquaintance and a cop didn't give Seth a pass on that one. Date rape drugs had become a much too common occurrence to take stupid chances. Hence the bottled water on their table.

"And I appreciate the gesture, Seth, but I'm afraid we're leaving now." Thea looked at Lillian as she said it, daring her to argue, but Lillian was already starting to stand up. Clearly, she was totally onboard with leaving.

Seth clumsily got to his feet as Thea did, knocking the table in his haste and spilling the oversized drink. Thea barely scooted out of the way in time to avoid getting splashed. Seth didn't even seem to notice.

"I'll walk you to your car," he offered.

"That's okay. I have it covered." Doing something she rarely ever did, she sought out Daryl and gave him the signal that meant she wanted to be escorted out of the building rather than just discretely followed. From his new position on the wall, she realized that he must have followed her and Pete around the club when they'd left the dance floor so abruptly. What only earlier that night she'd considered overkill she now found oddly comforting, especially with the way Seth was looking at her.

For a minute, she really thought he might try to insist on walking her out despite Daryl's towering presence at her back. Thankfully, Pete broke the tension. He stepped between her and Seth to give her a peck on the cheek goodbye and then stayed there, effectively blocking Seth from trying to do the same. If he had, she was pretty sure Pete would have slugged him, and while she didn't usually condone violence, she was also pretty sure she would have been okay with that.

"It was great to see you again, Thea," Seth said.

Not wanting to lie, Thea didn't return the sentiment. Instead, she said, "Thanks for the dance and the drink. Goodbye, Seth." She didn't think he registered the finality in her choice of words.

Neither woman spoke until they'd settled into the back of the car Rick had brought around to the front of the club. It wasn't a limo, meaning there was no privacy glass to raise to keep Rick and Daryl from hearing their conversation, so Thea kept her comments to a minimum.

"Did you know he was bringing Seth with him?"

"God, no!" Lillian sounded honestly horrified. "I didn't even know he was planning on going out tonight. He must have overheard me talking to Mellie on the phone earlier about our plans." She shook her head. "I have no idea what he was thinking."

"According to him, he was thinking that maybe I'm too focused on, uh, one thing and not considering all of my options."

"This is what happens when men read *Cosmo*," Lillian said sadly. "One quiz and they start to think they understand the mysteries of the female mind."

"It was actually kind of sweet in a totally annoying, intrusive kind of way," Thea said. "You're lucky to have him as a brother."

"Yeah, tell me that again after he's followed you on a few of your dates."

Now *that* was a truly horrifying thought.

"Pete does have a point, though," Lillian continued, her eyes darting towards the front seat as she lowered her voice. "You have been totally focused on that one thing for a while."

"You're the one helping me with that *thing*," Thea whispered back, feeling confused and the teeniest bit betrayed. "You've never mentioned thinking I was making a mistake before."

"That's because I don't."

"Then what are you talking about?"

Lillian twisted the cord of her small purse between her fingers. "You met a lot of men tonight. And you had a good time. Right?"

"Right," Thea agreed slowly. "Your point?"

"How did they make you feel?"

Despite the urge to snap at her friend, Thea gave the question due consideration.

"They were all really nice," she said finally with a small shrug. "I had fun talking to them. After I finally relaxed and stopped trying so hard to not sound like an idiot," she added with a self-deprecating grin.

"That's good, but how did they make you *feel*?"

That's when she got it.

"Nothing like how *he* makes me feel," Thea said after glancing toward the men in the front seat, who were busy having their own low-voiced conversation. "Not even close."

"Some of them were better looking than him," Lillian pointed out.

"Prettier, maybe," Thea conceded, "but not better looking."

"And none of them did anything for you, huh? Not a single quiver of interest?"

"Not so much as a tingle."

Lillian stared at her for a second and then gave one slow nod before straightening in her seat and relaxing back into the cushion. "Okay. So now you know."

Thea tipped her head against the back of the seat and smiled faintly up at the roof. "I already did."

# CHAPTER 8

BRENNAN DOYLE WAS a morning person. A leftover habit from his Marine Corps days, he was up with the sun, showered, shaved, and at his office with a large mug of steaming coffee before most people had even cracked an eyelid and contemplated knocking their alarm clock across the room.

As always, there was the bottomless pot of coffee in the security cottage's kitchen/break area from which Doyle helped himself to a cup to tide him over while his own pot o' sludge was brewing in his office. Doyle got a terse report of "nothing going on" from Simon, who was still upset over his reassignment, checked the wall of video monitors out of habit, and then retired to his office to tackle the morning reports.

Nothing new had been found on the identity of Thea's mysterious letter-writing gift-giver. It was too much to hope that the freak would get tired of his game and crawl back under his rock. Doyle knew that all too often, people who had formed a fixation would cling tenaciously to their obsession, often for months, sometimes years, until finally something had to give. And with their letter writer, Doyle was inclined to believe that something was going to give soon. Not in months, but weeks, maybe only days. It made his gut clench into an icy ball when he thought about the danger Thea was in and how little he could do about it. Short of confining her to the estate until the creep was caught, all they could do was wait, watch, and worry.

*You could also tell Thea the truth,* a small voice said, but Doyle quickly squashed the whisper of conscience that continued to plague him. If he went against Frank Fordham's orders, then, yes, Thea would be aware of the problem, but he'd be out of a job. Not that that was what mattered to him. It was the fact that if he was fired, he wouldn't be around to ensure Thea's safety. That was what had him hamstrung. That was what made him follow orders he absolutely disagreed with. That was what was making him crazy.

He trusted Red and the rest of his people implicitly. They were good at their jobs. The best. They wouldn't be on the payroll otherwise. But when it came to Thea, *he* needed to be the one in charge of her safety. He couldn't be her actual bodyguard any longer, not since his promotion to chief of security, but he could manipulate and direct the safety net around her to his satisfaction to ensure nothing and no one ever touched her.

A net that was sadly thin at the moment, he admitted to himself grimly. With the senior Fordhams away, his staff had been neatly chopped in half. While the letters they'd used to deceive Thea and her mother were quite real, the actual threat was low-level to the point of being practically nonexistent. But the Fordhams were still rich and, if not famous, at least recognizable, and that made them potential targets. Especially overseas, where some groups considered kidnap and ransom a legitimate career path.

So eight of his most senior agents had gotten on a plane, and he had to use those who were left to run all of the estate's regular security as well as deal with the stalker threat he was forced to keep secret.

Damn Frank and his overprotective bullshit! This was exactly why Doyle was so keen to start up his own security business. He'd had enough of following questionable, and sometimes just plain bad, orders in the Marine Corps. He didn't want to have to keep dealing with that kind of crap in the civilian world as well. Becoming his own boss was the only sure way to avoid this kind of situation in the future.

He knew that he'd sort of let that plan coast for longer than he should have. In fact, he needed to dust off the half-finished application for the business loan he'd shoved in a desk drawer in his bungalow months ago and get it back to the bank. He might be needing a new job sooner than he'd expected.

But first, he needed to see Thea through the current danger. Once she was safe, he'd be able to leave with a clear conscience. In the meantime, he'd maintain the cover story and do his best to keep her safe, even if that meant curtailing a bit more of her freedom of movement.

Which there had been a lot more of in this past week than usual, Doyle remembered with a scowl. Not only had Thea and the rest of the Royal Court made several day-long trips to the shopping district in Boulder, but there had been two trips down to Denver, both to a nightclub named Platinum during the day when it wasn't open to the public, and both times the reports had made mention of Thea seeming a bit flustered and evasive about what the visits were for.

Finally, after Daryl had pinned them down for an answer, Lillian had grudgingly confessed that they'd volunteered to help their friend Des with Platinum's annual charity fashion show again but wanted to keep it quiet because Amelia's parents were likely to object and make her beg off since it might detract from the media's focus on the wedding.

Given Platinum's repertoire of cabaret singers, exotic dancers, and female impersonators, Doyle didn't think a conflict of schedules would be the reason the Westlakes yanked their daughter out of the project. She might have been allowed to participate in previous years, but that was before she was about to become Mrs. Future Senator.

*On the surface, the secrecy was logical, or as logical as anything those three did together ever was*, Doyle thought with a grin. Still, something about it bothered him. It wasn't like Thea to spend so much time away from home, and in the past week, she'd been gone more often than not. She hadn't even been by the security cottage to bug him about their runs or to bring him one of those never-ending plates of chocolate-chocolate chip cookies she was forever baking for him or to nag him for drinking too much coffee and not eating a healthy breakfast.

Now that he thought about it, there were a dozen little ways that he and Thea interacted on a normal basis, small intimacies that came from long acquaintance—friendly rivalries over their favorite sports teams, daily jokes in his email account, movie quotes tossed rapid-fire at each other whenever the opportunity arose, happy faces plastered all over his office and hidden in the most unexpected places for him to find when he had what Thea called one of his "grumpy days." Things he realized now he hadn't consciously thought about but were just always *there*.

And all of them had been absent this past week. Ever since he'd begged off their last run and sent her off to Fit with Kirsten.

Doyle frowned. Had he insulted her by doing that? He hadn't meant to. All he'd wanted to do was put some distance between them, push her back to a more comfortable distance so he wouldn't have to look at her in those sexy little outfits and feel like gouging his own eyes out for the things he was thinking when he saw her looking like that.

*Well, you got the distance you wanted, so what are you complaining about?* a voice taunted. His frown deepened. He'd wanted distance, yes, but he hadn't wanted to cut her out of his life completely. Not having her around at all was...

*Lonely.*

Doyle shook his head, growing impatient with himself. He missed his easy friendship with Thea the same way he'd miss Red or Daryl if they suddenly dropped out of his life. Because Thea was his *friend*. All there was between them was *friendship*.

*But there could be so much more.*

With an aggravated growl, Doyle shoved the traitorous thought away and exchanged the daytime report for Daryl's nightshift one, expecting the usual two or three lines outlining Thea's movement and any subsequent events that might be deemed related to her stalker, of which there had been few since she usually spent her nights at either Amelia's or Lillian's homes if she went out at all.

As he read, Doyle's jaw tightened in increments directly related to the information he was slow to comprehend. Thea had spent her Friday night... bar hopping. Not one. Not two. No, Thea and Lillian, sans Amelia, had danced their way through *three* different bars and clubs last night. Three!

And not her usual spots, either. No, the damn girl had avoided the places where she would be most likely be surrounded by friends and familiar faces—and therefore safest—and instead whiled away the night in places where the clientele was older, rougher, and usually out on the prowl for one thing and one thing only.

The little fool had been playing with fire and probably didn't even know it.

A tick started in his cheek when he reached the part of the report that disproved that notion. Evidently, Thea had known very well what the men in those bars were on the prowl for, and she'd had no qualms about them prowling around her like a pack of hungry dingoes. Two men had bought her and Lillian drinks at Farraday's, four had crowded their table at The Hole—what the hell had possessed those two little idiots to go *there* of all places!—and evidently Daryl had either lost count or given up trying when the girls had torched the dance floor at Blaze.

Damn, damn, damn! Didn't Thea realize how dangerous that was? Didn't she know she was like a wild flame, enticing men to gather around her, men she wouldn't have a clue how to handle if they got her alone, out of sight of her guard, for even a minute?

Did she think that because Daryl was there to watch over her, she had free reign to flirt and tease anything in pants, knowing she had a safety valve for whatever steam she built up in her poor, unsuspecting conquests? Did she enjoy being a cocktease?

Whoa!

Like a dash of cold water, that crude thought brought Doyle back down from the heights his temper had soared to. What the hell was he thinking? And, more accurately, what part of him had he been thinking with? Certainly, not his head. In his head, he knew that Thea might flirt and smile, but she was a good kid, and she'd never, *never*, cross the line into being a...God, he couldn't even think it again without cringing. Only the blistering heat of his temper had roused such a profane description.

*And just why had he gotten so angry so fast?* he wondered. Thea had gone clubbing before, and while the places she'd chosen last night weren't exactly of the most sterling reputation, neither were they dives. So why was this different from all the other times?

*All those other times she was with a group of her friends, and you knew she wasn't interested in any of them.*

Could that be it? Could he possibly be...jealous? No. Certainly not. Because in order to be jealous, he would have to care about Thea as more than a friend, more than a responsibility. It would mean that what lay between them was personal, no matter what he wanted to admit or deny, and that was unacceptable.

There was nothing else between them, so he wasn't jealous. Period.

What he was, was worried. Yes, that made much more sense than being jealous. Right now was the very worst time for Thea to begin developing new habits and doing things that took her out of the secure environments Doyle and his people were used to guarding her in.

Her actions last night had introduced new variables, unknown people who might or might not have something to do with the stalker, might very well *be* the stalker. At the very least, she had been in places where it would be difficult to keep a clear watch on her movements. Clubs, especially dance clubs, meant lots of people, lots of movement, and way too many opportunities for someone to get lost in the crowd in less time than it took to blink. *That's* what he was angry about.

He strangled the little voice before it could call him a liar.

So, what to do? Closing the folder with a thoughtful scowl, Doyle considered and discarded several options. Finally, he decided that he would put another person on Thea whenever she went out from now on. If she went out tonight, he'd call Daryl in from his night off so that he could keep a watch for any familiar faces from the night before. Not particularly a problem if Thea went back to any of the same clubs. But if she went somewhere else and one of those faces showed up, that would be a huge red flag.

Something like that would smell of coincidence, and if there was one thing Doyle was a firm disbeliever in, it was coincidence.

\* \* \*

"Nick, what a coincidence!"

After getting over the initial surprise of seeing one of her previous night's flirts in Pot and Kettle, Thea favored him with a genuine smile and gestured to one of the unoccupied chairs at the table she and Amelia sat at. Her friend cast a questioning look her way, and Thea gave a small nod, letting her know that yes, this was *that* Nick, the very one they had been discussing when he'd walked up and offered a tentative hello. They'd spent well over an hour chatting and laughing the night before, and she'd genuinely enjoyed his company. But the very last thing she'd expected was to see him again.

His honey-blond hair was lighter than it had appeared in the dim bar, and his light blue eyes a more vibrant shade than she remembered, almost like cornflowers. She cast an assessing eye from Nick to Amelia. Hmm. They looked good together. Similar coloring, similar calm natures...Then she sighed, remembering almost as an afterthought that Amelia was going to marry good old Chuck, while Nick was still nursing wounds from his wife's death. Not exactly an ideal situation when neither party was available, emotionally or otherwise.

Swallowing her regrets along with her matchmaking impulses, Thea made the introductions. "So, what brings you to Pot and Kettle? Don't tell me you dragged yourself all the way across town just for a cup of coffee," she teased, remembering that he'd mentioned he was staying at the Hyatt while he was in town for a business meeting that had been cancelled on Friday due to his missed flights and rescheduled for first thing Monday morning. The hotel was a good twenty minutes away, and there had to be a half-dozen other coffee shops between here and there, including, she was sure, one in the hotel lobby itself.

"Well, you did brag that this was the best coffee in Boulder," Nick replied, tapping his fingers against his steaming mug. He gave a sheepish grin. "Actually, no, it wasn't the coffee that brought me here. I heard you mention to Lillian last night that you were meeting your friend here for lunch, and well, I was hoping to bump into you."

"Oh." It was all Thea could think to say.

"I'm not hitting on you or anything," Nick rushed to say, correctly interpreting her sudden wariness. "I just didn't have anything to do today, and I really enjoyed talking with you last night, and I couldn't stand the thought of staring at the walls of my hotel room for the next forty-eight hours without going just a bit nuts, and..." He pushed a hand through his hair in agitation. "It sounded a lot less pathetic before I said it out loud," he admitted.

Pushing back his chair with a heavy sigh, he gave Thea an apologetic look. "I'm sorry. This was a really bad idea. I'm sorry I presumed to inflict myself on you like this, after only a few hours' acquaintance. I'm not usually so..."

"Lonely?" Thea said gently. She saw him wince.

"Creepy." But he didn't disagree with her assessment, either.

"You're not," Thea assured him. All the wariness that had welled in her fled. She might not be an expert on men, but she knew a wounded soul when she saw one. "Please, stay." She could see Nick turning it over in his mind, still on the verge of retreat, and was relieved when his tense muscles finally relaxed, signaling his decision to remain.

"Thanks." He gestured vaguely to the both of them. "Don't let me interrupt your conversation. I'm happy to just sit here and bask in the envy of every other man in the place that I'm sitting here with two beautiful women all to myself."

"Oh, no, that's okay," Thea sputtered, panic stealing her ability to speak. The last thing they needed to do was continue *that* conversation in front of Nick, considering he'd been one of the main topics of discussion. She shot a desperate look at Amelia.

Amelia blinked at her owlishly for a second before starting with an "Oh!" She recovered nicely, however, and smiled at their guest. "I mean, oh, no, we wouldn't want to bore you with all that, um, wedding talk. Flowers, invitations..." She made a queenly gesture that Thea recognized as being one Mrs. Westlake used quite often when she wanted to convey an etcetera without having to lower herself to saying it. It looked awkward coming from Amelia.

Evidently, she felt awkward using it, too, because she dropped her hand into her lap like it was a source of embarrassment and offered a weak smile.

"You know, those sorts of things. Not very interesting for you, certainly. Well, not just you, of course. I mean, they wouldn't be interesting to just about anybody who wasn't involved with the wedding, and, well, since you're not, you probably wouldn't be. Interested, I mean. In them." She looked at Thea, begging with her eyes for her to pick up the reins of the conversation before she totally strangled herself in them.

Choking back a laugh, Thea obliged. "So, was the trip all the way here worth it?"

Nick took a sip of his coffee and smiled at her over the rim. "Definitely."

She'd meant the coffee, of course, but suddenly she wasn't so sure that the same could be said for Nick.

# CHAPTER 9

**DOYLE HATED THE REPORTS** he read on Sunday morning even more than he'd hated the ones from Saturday. They confirmed that one of the "familiar faces" from Thea's Friday night excursions had, indeed, shown up again on Saturday night, this time at a different dance club than the one she'd gone to the night before. Worse, once he'd read Daryl's report, Doyle caught a feeling of familiarity in the description, and sure enough, there was the same description given in Sam's daytime report.

The guy had approached Thea and Amelia at the coffeehouse they frequented downtown, and Thea had greeted him as a known acquaintance, inviting him to join them, so Sam hadn't thought too much of it at the time. They were on the lookout for a stranger. Sam had no way of knowing that until about twelve hours before he'd witnessed that meeting, this guy *had* been a stranger and was, therefore, on the suspect list. Given that he'd now made contact with Thea three times in less than two days, that put him right at the top of it.

Reaching for the phone with the intention of calling both men into his office to give a more detailed, in-person report about the meetings they'd witnessed, Doyle growled in frustration when he realized that Daryl would be dead asleep after his second night shift in a row, and Sam was off today and had probably already gone off on the date he'd been talking about practically the whole week, taking a trip down to Denver for the day. Damn! That left only one person he could ask about this list-topping stranger that Thea had suddenly become so chummy with, and that was the lady herself.

Though he was loathe to do it, Doyle knew he had little choice. Besides, if there had been three meetings, he needed to know if there was going to be a fourth. If Thea had planned to see him again, Doyle would have advance notice so that he could put the best possible plan for protection and surveillance in place. And if she hadn't made any such plans, and this stranger-cum-suspect still managed to show up someplace where Thea was, then that would be almost as good as a neon sign pointing to him as their man.

Barely noticing the burnt ground taste as he drained the last remaining dregs of his coffee, Doyle went in search of Thea to begin the questioning. He found her at the pool.

Of course.

Gritting his teeth against the instant visceral reaction he had to the sight of that damned bikini, Doyle took a seat on the chaise next to her and did his best to only make eye contact, but it was hard, damn hard. Just like his—

"Good morning," Thea said over the top of her book.

"Good morning." *Eye contact, eye contact, eye contact...*

"So?" Thea lowered the book onto a raised knee, her upper body twisting slightly toward him as she looked over. The movement almost drew his eyes to forbidden territory, but he held onto his resolve. Barely. "To what do I owe the pleasure?"

Pleasure, pain, it was all the same right now, and all centered about three feet below his brain, which seemed to have taken an unscheduled break and left him unable to string two words together. "Uh..."

Looking slightly alarmed, she exclaimed, "Doyle, what? Is it my mother?"

"Who was that guy you were with last night?"

They both blinked in surprise, at the question as much as the rough voice that demanded it. Doyle cursed himself roundly. It was what he wanted to know but not how he'd planned to ask it. He'd meant to be calm. Thorough. Professional. Instead he'd come off sounding like a jealous jerk.

"Which guy?" Thea asked innocently, twisting her body just a tiny bit more toward him, the worry erased from her eyes. Maybe a little *too* innocently. But Doyle didn't have a lot of experience with a disingenuous Thea, so he couldn't be sure.

"Blond, about six foot, estimated age about thirty, drives a dark blue Toyota Camry rental. Sound familiar?"

Thea's mouth had opened in surprise as he spoke. Now she snapped it shut.

"My, my, my, your people sure do have a lot of time on their hands, don't they, to be able to provide you with such detailed reports," she murmured in amusement. "I'm surprised they didn't supply pictures as well."

Making a mental note to have whoever accompanied Thea from now on use their phones to snap pictures of everyone she interacted with, Doyle said, "Their job is to watch over you and protect you from potentially dangerous people and situations." Now, why did that suddenly sound trite, even to him?

"Since when is a date a dangerous situation?" Thea chuckled.

"Is that what it was? A date?" Somehow, that bit of information was like the jab of a needle between his eyes.

After considering it for a long moment, Thea finally pursed her lips.

"Wellll," she hedged, "I guess, no, it wasn't a date. Technically."

"So, this guy—what did you say his name was?"

"I didn't." Thea lasted almost ten seconds under Doyle's glare before she relented with a put-upon sigh. "Nick. Nicholas Hastings." She made a sour expression. "I'm surprised that wasn't already in the secret spy file you have on him."

It would have been, if he'd taken the time to run the rental car information before he'd come to speak to her, but Doyle didn't think she needed to know that. Instead, he asked, "What do you know about him?"

"He's single—a widower, actually—doesn't do drugs, and he's a great dancer." She shrugged nonchalantly. "What else do I need to know?"

*If he's the psychotic stalker who's been sending you sexually twisted letters.* But Doyle gritted his teeth and kept the words inside. "Why he's in town. Why he approached you in Farraday's. Why he showed up at Pot and Kettle yesterday and how he knew you'd be there."

"He's here on business. He didn't approach me; I approached him. And he overheard me mention that I was planning to meet Amelia for lunch and showed up because he enjoyed spending time with me, surprising as that may seem."

He wasn't sure why, but that last sounded almost like an accusation. He brushed a flicker of guilt away. "And last night?"

"Last night I asked him if he wanted to join us when we went out dancing since he doesn't really know anyone in town and he was bored out of his mind sitting all alone in his hotel room all weekend long waiting for his meeting on Monday. Is that a problem?"

*Yes.* "No, I guess not," he said and then couldn't help persisting, "But what do you really know about him?"

Thea stared at him a moment, her head cocked slightly as if she were trying to figure out a puzzle.

"Enough." A secretive smile curled her lips. "For now."

For now? *For now?* Why did that have the ring of the possibility for her to need to know more at some point in the future? That she might possibly *want* to know more in the future? And just why did that bother him so damned much?

"I don't want you seeing him again," Doyle said brusquely, assuring himself that it was as much for Thea's safety as for his peace of mind that he'd made the snap decision. It was the truth, even if it wasn't the whole of it, but he couldn't bring himself to admit it. There was something about Nick Hastings that he didn't like.

"You...what?"

The incredulous tone was Doyle's first hint that he might have been a bit hasty in issuing his decree.

"It's a matter of security," he explained carefully. "This Hastings is a stranger, and right now you're—"

"In a position to be a target, making me and everything I do a security risk, meaning I have to stay in sight of my bodyguards at all times, take no unnecessary risks, look both ways before I cross the street, don't take candy from strangers, yadda, yadda, yadda." Thea scowled. "I'm not a total idiot, you know. I wasn't planning to run off with the guy. But there's no reason I can't go out with him if I want to as long as one of your people tags along."

"I wouldn't be doing my job if I let you go into a potentially dangerous situation when I could have prevented it."

"A potentially dangerous situation?" She hooted with laughter. "Oh, my God, did you really just call a date a potentially dangerous situation?"

Okay, maybe that had been a bit over the top. But still.

"It is if we don't know anything about him except what he's told you," Doyle persisted. "You don't even know if any of it is true."

"So do a background check on him!" Thea exclaimed, throwing her hand up in frustration, dislodging her book and sending it tumbling to the ground. "I know at least two of your people are ex-spooks. It shouldn't be a problem for them to whip up a report that will tell you everything your little heart desires about him. But I can already tell you that you won't find anything more dangerous than a speeding ticket. Nick's a nice guy."

Something about the calm, firm assertion about a man she'd only met two days ago nettled Doyle.

"Ted Bundy's victims thought he was a nice guy, too, right up until he killed them," he growled as he snatched up the book, shoving it back into her hands before she had a chance to bend over and get it herself. He wasn't sure he could stand the sight without going insane.

"Nick isn't Ted Bundy, and I'm not planning on being anyone's victim."

Snatches of some of the twisted things the letters had contained about what the stalker wanted to do to Thea once he had her in his power brought a sudden grimness to Doyle's entire demeanor.

"No, you won't be. I can guarantee it. That's why you're not going to go anywhere with this guy again. Until," he added, holding up a hand to forestall the protest he could see forming on her lips, "I have a chance to check him out."

Thea's lips compressed as she obviously struggled with the high-handed decree.

"How long will that take?"

"A few days, maybe more." Probably less, but she didn't need to know that. The longer she was kept away from Hastings, the better. In a few days, she'd probably lose any interest in the guy, anyway. She always did. Aside from the one moron she'd hooked up with for a few months in college, in all the years that he'd known her he couldn't think of a single instance where Thea's interest hadn't waned by the second or third date. She just didn't seem to be able to focus her interest on any single person.

*Except you.*

The thought was as unwelcome as it was unbidden. There was a world of difference between a schoolgirl infatuation and adult interest, and Thea definitely fell into the former category. Definitely. Because she was still a kid and way too young for someone like him. Even if Hastings was only about four years his junior, and even if she did look like a centerfold in that damned thong bikini, and even if she did make every cell in his body stand at attention whenever she was around, especially his—

"What about tonight?"

The question dragged him from his wayward thoughts before they could do anymore damage to his already strained self-control.

"Tonight?" he croaked. He cleared his throat. "What about tonight?"

Thea nibbled her lower lip, drawing Doyle's attention like a hunting dog to where her white teeth tugged at the tender pink flesh. "Well, we sort of had plans for dinner."

"Break them."

With a huff, Thea said, "You don't just break reservations at Rudolfo's."

Which was the absolute truth. Not if you ever wanted to get a reservation there again before the next Ice Age. Rudolfo knew how to nurse a grudge.

"Then go alone."

That suggestion earned him a disbelieving snort. "Right."

"Take Lillian or Amelia, then." Anyone but Hastings.

"Lil already has a date, and Charles hit town today with his father and their campaign entourage, so Mellie's having dinner with them." Her nose wrinkled in annoyance. "There has to be someone who would be willing to bear my company for a few hours in exchange for a good meal."

It was then that Doyle saw the trap that had been laid. The one he had almost stepped right into, blinded by suntan oil and miles of skin. Damn, he had to come up with an excuse now, before she managed to ask him—

"What about Sam?"

"Sam?" Doyle blinked, feeling struck dumb by the name. *Sam?*

Thea nodded, smiling. "Yeah, Sam. He's off today, isn't he? Maybe he'd like to go with me."

Sam? She wanted to ask Sam to go to dinner with her, not him?

His pride pricked despite the fact that not seconds before he had been scrambling for an excuse not to go, Doyle said, "Sam's out on a date." He knew his tone was curt, but he didn't care. It bothered him that he hadn't been Thea's first choice. A lot more than it should have.

"Hmm. What about Rick?"

Grinding his teeth, Doyle replied, "He's on duty tonight." Was she going to ask every member of the security staff *except* him?

"Oh. Well." Thea's teeth tugged at her lip again as she thought.

Doyle felt a corresponding tug in his loins, and his temper flared at the unwanted arousal.

"You could always ask Simon," he said testily and then almost laughed at the look of horror that appeared on her face at the mere idea.

"And here I thought you were my friend," Thea said in mock moroseness, shaking her head. She sighed. "Guess I'll have to risk Rudolfo's wrath and cancel, after all."

It stung that the idea of asking *him* to dinner had apparently never entered her mind. "Do I suddenly have the plague or something?"

Thea looked surprised. "No, of course not. I just...I didn't think you'd want to go, that's all." *Since you've been going out of your way to avoid* me *like the plague for days.* The unsaid words were there as clearly as if they'd been spoken, and Doyle suddenly felt ashamed of his own childish actions.

"I'd love to go to dinner with you, Thea."

"Really?" She didn't look entirely convinced.

"Really."

After a long moment, a smile bloomed on Thea's face, wiping out the last traces of doubt. "Okay. The reservations are for seven."

"I'll pick you up at the main house at six-thirty, then."

As he walked away, Doyle grinned triumphantly at having successfully diverted Thea from her date with Hastings, blissfully unaware that he'd just been played like a pro.

*   *   *

She was going to dinner with Doyle!

Smiling serenely as she walked back to the house just as calm and nonchalant as you please, inside Thea was doing the Snoopy dance. It had worked!

It had actually worked! She had thought there had been signs of jealousy in Doyle when he'd switched Sam for Kirsten when she'd gone to the gym, but after the way he'd been going out of his way to avoid her this past week, she'd begun to have her doubts.

But Lillian had told her to go with her initial instincts and Des had agreed, saying that just the fact that Doyle was avoiding her was a promising sign that she was closer than she thought to breaching his reserve. And now they had a date!

She'd known that Sam was spending the day with Des's roommate, Sheila, just as she'd known that Rick was likewise unavailable. What she hadn't known was what Doyle's reaction would be when she suggested them as possible replacements for the temporarily off-limits Nick, with whom she'd never actually had dinner plans to begin with. She sent him a silent thank you for his unwitting part in her campaign and hoped he was enjoying the list of sightseeing ideas she had given him the day before.

She'd expected Doyle to be surprised by her choices, hoped he might be a tiny bit jealous, but had been shocked when he'd actually looked a little hurt. Doyle had been avoiding *her*. Why should he be hurt when she was simply returning the favor?

Sighing, she shook her head. She'd never understand the man. But for tonight, at least, he was hers, and for now, that was enough.

# CHAPTER 10

**DOYLE WAS HAVING** a good time.

The realization, made somewhere between the appetizer, a mouthwatering seafood platter which they'd shared, and the main course on which they'd gone in opposite directions, butter-soft filet mignon for him versus chicken tequila fettuccine for Thea, came as something of a surprise. A good one, but a surprise nonetheless.

Not too long after he'd finished congratulating himself over having routed Thea's budding interest in Nick Hastings, Doyle had slowly begun to understand the full implication of having shanghaied the empty seat at Thea's table.

He would be alone.

With Thea.

In public.

For hours.

And God knew what sexy little outfit she might decide to wear. Or how he was going to react to it, or, rather, how his *body* was going to react. Lately it seemed to have a very determined mind of its own where Thea was concerned.

He was in serious trouble.

Panic had very nearly sent him to the phone to call her and make some excuse for having to back out of their dinner arrangement—he wouldn't, couldn't call it a date—but uncertainty had prevailed long enough to let logic reassert itself. It wasn't as if this was the first time they'd gone out to dinner together.

He'd taken her someplace special for her eighteenth birthday. And her twenty-first. She'd even surprised him with dinner at Q's when he'd turned thirty because she said that he needed to celebrate the big three-oh, not sulk about it. He'd informed her in no uncertain terms that he did not sulk. Thea hadn't mentioned the S-word again for the rest of the evening, but her smirk had hinted that she had still been thinking it.

So, they'd eaten out before. Alone. In public. For hours. And nothing bad had ever come of it. So why was this any different?

Because those had been special occasions, and this was…what? Not a date. No, it was just two people who got along well together and liked spending time involved in their common interests going out for some good food, a few drinks, and maybe a little dancing if the band that sometimes played at Rudolfo's on the weekends was there.

Hell, it *was* a date!

No, definitely not. Doyle had thrust the word away and refused to acknowledge its existence for the rest of the afternoon. Instead, he'd immersed himself in his paperwork, setting into motion a detailed background check on one Nicholas Phillip Hastings of Chicago, while also reassigning one of his people to do surveillance on him as well. He might trust Thea to keep her word and stay away from Hastings, but that didn't mean he trusted Hastings to stay away from her.

He'd debated his choices, but with his people already spread thin, they'd been few. In the end, he decided to give Simon the assignment. It was the kind of "spook" work that he seemed to relish and would either give him a chance to prove himself or give Doyle the legitimate excuse he needed to give him his walking papers.

After that, he'd had nothing to do but wait. And think. And worry about what sexy little number Thea was going to be wearing when he picked her up at six-thirty. And how he was going to manage to drive all the way downtown in a state of semi-arousal, since that seemed to be his permanent condition lately whenever she was within ten feet of his unruly body.

Hell, who was he trying to kid? She didn't need to be anywhere in the vicinity. All he had to do was think about her wearing that itty-bitty, almost-not-there bikini and he was ready to go. It was like being fifteen all over again, except now he knew what he was getting all hot and bothered about.

And that only made it worse because there was no more chance of his fulfilling that particular fantasy with Thea than he had with any of the *Sports Illustrated* swimsuit models that had hung over his bed as a teen.

His brain knew that, but somehow his body managed to ignore the facts and followed the fantasy. He'd had to take a second shower just before it was time to pick Thea up at the main house. An ice-cold one.

But the effort had been futile once he'd seen her descending the front steps.

The dress she'd chosen wasn't sexy in the explicit sense of the word. The neckline wasn't overly daring, her shoulders were covered, and the back didn't plunge to her derriere. Technically speaking, it was a moderately conservative evening dress. But the way the soft plum-colored fabric hugged her body, clinging to her in all the places a man's hand would want to cling: at the breast, at the luscious curves of her hips, at the ripe mounds of her derriere…God, it was enough to drive him insane, seeing her like that and knowing she was forbidden fruit.

*Only because you decided she was,* his inner devil had taunted. *Nobody else considers her off-limits.*

*This was Thea,* he'd reminded himself firmly as he'd helped her into his car. Thea who'd cried in his arms like her thirteen-year-old heart was breaking when her dog, Pebbles, ran away and was hit by a car.

Thea who cheated at Scrabble by making up important-sounding words and then was insulted rather than embarrassed when a trip to the dictionary proved her perfidy.

Thea who had sweet-talked his staff into buying two hundred boxes of Girl Scout cookies one year, just so she could show up Tara Winchell, her rival and archnemesis throughout most of middle school. Sucker that he was, forty of those boxes had been his. He hadn't been able to look at a cookie of any variety without getting nauseous for almost a year afterward.

And yet…

Was he really being fair by continuing to see her as that gamine girl he'd befriended when he'd first come to work on the estate? Was he ignoring the fact that she was now all grown up so he could also ignore the burgeoning desire he felt whenever she was near? Was he really that much of a coward?

The questions had slowly wormed their way through his thoughts during the drive to the restaurant. They were only reinforced by the looks of male appreciation Thea garnered on the way to their table. He wanted to snarl at every man who sent her one of those assessing looks, to tell them to keep their roving eyes and their lecherous thoughts off of her silk-wrapped body.

God knew that made him a hypocrite—he'd certainly given his share of appreciative stares to anonymous women over the years—but this was different. This was Thea these men were mentally undressing. She deserved better.

The lady in question seemed totally unaware of the looks being sent her way. Or, if she did notice, she dismissed them without the usual preening that he was used to seeing from Margo. When men admired Margo, she always shot him a little smirk, just to make sure he'd noticed her being noticed.

Funny, he'd never really thought about that before, but now that he had, he found it annoyed him. Especially when compared with the smile Thea gave him as they were seated. Not one that said "Look at all the other men here who want me. Aren't you lucky you're the one I'm with?" but said instead "I'm really glad to be here with you."

It was that smile that had lightened his mood and allowed him to fall into the easy, familiar banter the two of them had always enjoyed. The meal passed in a comfortable blur of topics from baseball to movies. But when Doyle brought the subject of Amelia's upcoming wedding up over dessert, Thea's expression lost some of its joyful exuberance and turned wistful.

"Trouble in paradise?" Doyle probed gently.

Thea chewed her lip for a second before shaking her head. "No. I don't think so, anyway. It's just…" She sighed. "I just worry about Mellie. She's such an easygoing person and so willing to do whatever it takes to make everybody else happy, sometimes to the point of making *herself* insane. I just can't help but worry that between her fiancé's political aspirations, her mother's Olympic-class social climbing, and her future mother-in-law's determination to make everything ten times harder than it needs to be, that Mellie's going to be so busy doing what everyone else wants that she's going to forget she's supposed to care about what *she* wants." Thea cocked her head slightly. "Did that make any sense at all?"

"Strangely enough, yes, but only because I'm used to you." Thea smiled at his teasing, her whole face brightening. Doyle felt a shaft of something more than desire zing through him. Something more emotional than physical. Something he really didn't want to examine too closely, so he shoved it away.

It took a long second before he could gather his scattered thoughts and pick up his side of the conversation again. "She, uh, wouldn't marry him if she didn't think she could handle the lifestyle that goes along with his career."

Thankfully unaware of his sudden inner turmoil, Thea lifted one shoulder in a half-shrug. "I know. But I can't help it. She's one of my best friends. I want her to be happy, and I'm not so sure that Charles knows how to manage that. Or even if he cares. He spends so much time stomping around the country with his father trying to establish himself in the party that he'd probably never think to come and see her if his personal assistant didn't put it on his itinerary. And even then, she sees more of Oliver—his assistant—than him."

Thea scowled, stabbing her fork into her cheesecake as though it were a stand-in for the man in question. "Sometimes I think Charles is marrying Senator Westlake's connections instead of his daughter, and Mellie just comes along with the deal as the fully trained political hostess. Kind of like the toy surprise you get with your burger and fries."

"You do realize that you've just equated your friend's marriage to a Happy Meal?"

"You know, I'll be satisfied if 'happy' figures into things in any way it can."

Although he knew Thea's concern for her friend wasn't entirely unwarranted, having had the misfortune of meeting the future in-laws in question,

Doyle selfishly didn't want it to put a damper on the evening, not when he was enjoying himself in Thea's company for the first time in weeks.

Deliberately, he picked up his fork and helped himself to a large bite of Thea's cheesecake. It was difficult to swallow without choking on laughter at the look of affronted chagrin that crossed her face at the sneak attack.

"Nope." He made a show of smacking his lips. "Definitely as good as ever."

"And why would you think it wasn't?" Thea watched him lick the fork clean with obvious resentment.

"Well," Doyle drawled slowly, eyeing her plate again, "I figured since you were mutilating it rather than inhaling it like you usually do," he paused a second while she sucked in an indignant breath, willfully ignoring the way her breasts heaved upward against the silk, "that there must have been something wrong with it."

"Well, you thought wrong, mister." Wary of the covetous looks Doyle was still throwing at it, Thea moved her plate to where he'd have to lean over her to get at it. "Dessert stealing is a very serious offense, you know."

Doyle twirled his fork between his fingers, fighting a grin. "Is it, really?"

"Yes."

"I hadn't realized that."

"Ignorance of the dessert laws is not an excuse."

"Are you going to read me my rights before you haul me in?"

Thea's lips twitched. "I think maybe we can avoid any hauling, since this is your first offense—this *is* your first offense, isn't it?"

With as innocent a look as he could manage, Doyle replied, "Of course."

"Of course," Thea echoed, sounding less than believing. A sudden, speculative light lit her eyes. "You will, of course, be expected to make restitution."

"Resti—" Doyle followed her gaze to his own plate, heaped with one of the most decadent slabs of Black Forest cake this side of the Atlantic. "Oh no. You're not getting my cake. Sorry. Uh-uh. Go ahead and call the sweets police, babe, because I'll go down fighting before I surrender any of this." With good reason. The pastry chef was originally from Germany, and made an authentic *Schwarzwalder Kirschtorte* worth every overpriced penny Rudolfo paid him.

"Just a bite," Thea cajoled.

"No way."

"Come on," she pouted, "just one itty-bitty bite."

"Forget it."

She dipped her head and gave him her best pretty-please smile.

"Just one teensy, little—"

"Oh, God, all right!" He had stolen a pretty large piece of hers, after all. He supposed it was only fair. "One *tiny* bite, and then we're even, right?"

Mimicking his earlier almost-innocent expression, Thea replied, "Of course."
Doyle couldn't hold back a snort of laughter. "Yeah, right."

Only years of trained reflexes allowed him to intercept Thea's hand as her fork pounced on the prize. He wasn't surprised to see that the tines had already made indents staking out a piece that was considerably more than tiny.

What did surprise him was the frisson of heat that enveloped him as his skin touched hers, a heat that seemed to follow some internal beacon straight to his groin. He should have let her hand go. He should have. But he didn't.

Instead, he picked it up and replaced the fork much closer to the edge of the cake, allowing her a piece of his precious dessert that was more than itsy but still smaller than bitsy. It was all he could do to force himself to release her. He kept his eyes on the cake, not daring to let her see the confused, heated expression he was certain was in his eyes.

After a moment's hesitation, Thea pushed her fork through the thick layers of chocolate cake, cherries, and whipped cream. Like it was a lodestone, Doyle's eyes followed the cake as it made the short trip to her mouth, realizing only too late how big a mistake that was.

Her lips closed around the fork, and his unruly body jerked as though she's closed them over something else. He struggled to talk down his stirring dick, but it was impossible, not with Thea making those soft pleasure noises as she chewed her plunder.

"Oh. My. God." Thea opened her eyes wide and stared at him. "That was... amazing." The satisfied look on her face was one he was used to seeing in the bedroom after a night of mind-blowing sex. It unnerved him to see it on Thea, but it also sent a shiver of desire through him as well.

God, if she could find that much pleasure in a simple piece of chocolate cake—well, okay, a *fantastic* piece of chocolate cake—how much more would she find in long hours tangled with him in the sheets, straining and sweating and...

*Jesus.* Doyle swallowed, fighting to get his suddenly ragged breathing under control. These were not thoughts he should be having about Thea. But once there, the images refused to be erased, and Doyle knew that some of what he was feeling must have showed in his eyes because he could see the same flash of awareness and heat reflected back at him from hers. Neither of them spoke.

Silently, Doyle reached over and rubbed a small dab of whipped cream from Thea's lip with his thumb. He could hear her breath catch. He caressed her lip again, even though the cream was already gone, and felt her warm breath against his skin as it left her in a rush. He shouldn't be doing this. There were a thousand reasons why. This was Thea. They were in public. This wasn't a date. This was *Thea.*

But none of his reasons mattered when he felt the small flick of her tongue as it darted out and connected for the briefest second with his thumb. This time it was his breath that caught. Reason fled, and all he could think about was how he was going to get Thea out of the restaurant and someplace private while disguising the fact that he had the erection of the century from the rest of the diners they'd have to walk past on the way out.

It was an indication of how far gone he was that he didn't notice the woman standing at his shoulder until she spoke. "Brennan, darling!"

*Son of a bitch.*

Just like that, the sensual spell that had been weaving around him was broken, and reality slammed back into place with painful clarity.

"Hello, Margo."

# CHAPTER 11

DOYLE SMILED UP at the lushly figured redhead standing beside him, although it felt more like a grimace as he struggled to tame his still-raging blood. Normally, he would have stood, as any gentleman should, but at the moment it was out of the question, although it was amazing how quickly his arousal was fading at the sight of her when usually his body had the exact opposite reaction. In any case, he wasn't going to question his rapid deflating; he would simply be thankful for it.

"I thought that was your car out in the parking lot," Margo purred, slipping a hand onto his shoulder and leaning down to kiss him, giving him an unobstructed view down her plunging neckline. Strangely, the sight of her bountiful breasts had no effect on him whatsoever.

Without forethought, he turned his head at the last second to give Margo his cheek, rather than his mouth, which had been her target. Her hand tightened for a telling second on his shoulder, announcing her displeasure at the avoidance. Damn, what did she expect, a full-on lip-lock in the middle of the restaurant? With Thea sitting right across the table?

*Oh, hell.* Doyle glanced over at Thea. She had a serene, mildly inquisitive look on her face that to anyone else would have passed as polite interest and nothing more. But knowing Thea as he did, he could read the tense set of her shoulders, the artificial smile that curved her lips, and knew that she was anything *but* serene.

There was no avoiding it, so he did the introductions. "Margo, I don't think you've ever met Thea before. Thea Fordham." He wasn't entirely sure why he needed to stress that this was his employer's daughter, but there was something in Margo's eyes that he didn't like. "Thea, this is Margo Klein, a…friend."

Margo laughed, although it sounded slightly sharp to his ears.

"Oh, Brennan, don't be silly." Her hand caressed his shoulder in a familiar manner that could almost be called proprietary. "We're *so* much more than friends." She turned her gaze to Thea. "So, you're little Cynthia," she said, her tone mildly amused as she gave Thea a thorough perusal that even Doyle knew was meant to be insulting. "Brennan talks about you all the time. Cynthia this, Cynthia that." She smiled. "It's really quite entertaining."

Thea offered a sharp smile and returned the insulting perusal, the tiniest hint of a sneer teasing her lips in a way Doyle recognized as being a trademark of the haughty Mrs. Westlake.

"Really?" She raised her glass of wine in a dismissive manner, also *a la* Westlake. "Funny, he's never mentioned you at all."

*Ouch.* Doyle was aware that Thea had scored a direct hit even before he felt Margo stiffen. He couldn't fault Thea's retaliation since Margo had launched the first salvo, but the trick now was going to be keeping the skirmish from escalating into an all-out war. He'd excelled at tactics in the Corps, but even he had cause to doubt his abilities when faced with two women clearly skilled in the art of the cutting comment.

"Are you waiting for your table?" he asked, drawing the conversation back into neutral territory. Or so he thought.

"Oh, no. I've already eaten. Except for dessert," Margo added in a huskier tone.

"Why don't you bring your date over to say hello," Thea said. "I'd love to meet him. I'm sure Doyle would, too."

"So sorry to disappoint you, Cynthia dear, but my dear friend and dinner companion," here she was sure to place an emphasis on the fact she didn't consider it a date, "Doctor Nathaniel Cummings, was paged to the hospital just as we finished our meal. He was needed for some emergency, an accident or something." She waved a negligent hand. "It happens all the time, what with Nate being in such demand for his skills as a surgeon." This last sounded more petulant than proud.

"How terrible for you," Thea murmured.

Margo gave her a hard glare and then turned to Doyle, her expression once again turning coy. "So, you see, since time was of the essence for Nate, I insisted he go directly to the hospital and not waste the time it would take to drive me home first. I was going to call a cab, but then I remembered seeing your car in the lot when we came in and I thought maybe I could impose on you to give me a ride."

Doyle thought he heard Thea mutter "how convenient" under her breath, but when he glanced sharply over at her, she was still smiling that serene, unnatural smile. He'd never realized before how much he hated that smile.

He also hated being put in this position, but what could he do? There was no polite way of refusing, something he was sure Margo was well aware of. Damn her!

"We'd be happy to give you a lift."

"We?" Margo's smile faltered for the briefest second before it returned at full wattage. "Oh, but, Brennan, you know how little room there is in the back seat of that car of yours," she purred, giving his shoulder another meaningful stroke. It was hard to resist the urge to shake her hand off, especially when he saw the brittle edge Thea's smile took on at the implied intimacy in said back seat. What the hell game was Margo playing?

"You're right, of course," Doyle said tightly. "No need for you to squeeze into the Charger when Rick can drop you off in comfort with the Expedition." His words had two opposite effects on the women. Thea's smile turned genuine, while Margo's hardened into what could only be called a snarl before she recovered and gave him a wounded pout.

"Rick?"

"One of my men. He's on duty out in the lounge. He'll see you home safely." Although at that moment he couldn't vouch for the bodyguard's safety, considering the fire that was shooting from Margo's baby blues.

"On duty?" Margo's lips pinched together. "I thought *you* were here to babysit her." The implication was clear. If Doyle wasn't there in the capacity of bodyguard, then he was there as something else. Something less official. More personal. And clearly, Margo didn't care for that, not one little bit. Doyle didn't know where this sudden possessiveness of Margo's came from, but he did know that he didn't like it. Especially when Margo had admitted being here with her own "dinner companion."

"*Her* hasn't needed a babysitter since she was twelve," Thea interjected. Her pose was still relaxed, but Doyle figured she was going to have the cut-crystal design from her glass imbedded in the soft flesh of her palm by the time they left if she didn't ease her grip. "*Her* is in the middle of dinner with a friend." A not-so-subtle hint that Margo was intruding on their meal, delivered in a calm, sophisticated manner that only underscored Margo's rudeness.

Doyle started to fold his napkin. "Come on, I'll introduce you to Rick."

"No!" Margo laughed nervously and adjusted her tone to a more cajoling level. "I mean, no, I couldn't even think of taking away little Cynthia's bodyguard. He does have his job to do, after all. What if something were to happen to her on the way home?"

"Oh, don't worry," Thea said. She swirled her wine and gave Doyle a slow smile. "I'll be in excellent hands."

Just like that, the heat that had subsided came roaring back to life between them, hotter and more urgent than before. All Doyle could think of were hands, his hands, on Thea, covering her, caressing her, teasing, testing, exploring...

Blood pounded in his ears as he watched Thea's smile falter and then bloom again into a more seductive curving of wine-moistened lips, her eyes darkening with desire. Desire. For him. Thea wanted him. And, God help him, he wanted her as well, wanted with a desperate need that made him break out in a cold sweat. With Rick chauffeuring Margo home, he'd be completely alone with Thea. No watchful shadow, no reports being filed.

No safety net to keep him on his best behavior.

Because, if he was honest with himself, that was the reason he'd had Rick tag along tonight. Not so he could relax his vigilance and enjoy himself, not because it would have been cruel to deny Rick a meal he'd been, by his own admission, looking forward to all day, but so that he'd have a legitimate reason to keep himself in line, stay within the boundaries already established for his relationship with Thea. The *proper* boundaries.

In short, he'd known his resolve was weakening, so he'd brought along a chaperone. A lowering thought, but there it was.

With Rick out of the picture, he'd be back to depending on his own willpower, of which he was well aware he was currently in short supply. But was that necessarily the bad thing he'd once thought it to be? Maybe it wouldn't hurt to explore these new feelings, this new awareness of Thea as a desirable woman rather than the hero-worshipping teenager he'd labeled her for so long.

But not tonight.

Oh no. Being alone in the car with her tonight would be a Very Bad Idea in big freaking capital letters. Without Rick as a safety net, it would be way too easy to let things get out of hand, because while the back seat of the Charger might be a tight squeeze—*okay, bad choice of words,* he cursed himself as a thin sheen of sweat broke out on his upper lip—the front seats were more than comfortable. And they reclined. A lot.

The idea of allowing himself to be attracted to Thea was still too new, too strange, too...tempting. And though he was pretty certain that she was right there with him on this attraction thing—hell, she'd *licked his thumb,* for Christ's sake!—they were still light years apart in experience, with him as the one who had to know best and make sure things didn't progress too fast or out of control. For either of them.

What he needed was a little time and space—especially space—to think it all through, to make a rational decision that didn't originate between his legs. His head—the one on his shoulders—knew that, but his mouth was refusing to say what needed to be said, clearly having thrown in its lot with the other, smaller head that was currently clamoring for attention again beneath his napkin.

Manicured nails digging into his shoulder brought him back to himself. "Brennan, *darling*, you wouldn't send me home with a complete stranger, now, would you?"

There it was. The excuse he could use to extricate himself from the situation he wasn't yet ready to face. He grabbed onto it like a drowning man.

"No, of course not. I'll take you, and Rick can bring Thea home. If that's okay?" he asked belatedly of Thea, finally gathering his nerve to look at her again, afraid of getting caught again in the heat that had ensnared him just moments before.

He needn't have worried. There was no heat. The only thing that he saw was shock. And hurt. And then nothing at all as the bland mask fell firmly back into place.

*Fuck.*

"Of course," Thea replied. With barely a flick of her hand, she drew their waiter to her side and asked for the check.

Already feeling guilty at his knee-jerk decision to abandon Thea in favor of the woman he knew he *could* keep his hands off of, Doyle reached for his wallet. "I'll—"

"Don't be ridiculous." Thea's voice was calm, serene, all that was gracious, but the look she shot him was like a punch in the gut. He was used to adoration, mischievous humor, and lately sometimes even speculative female interest gleaming in her gaze. Never before had he seen…nothing.

Her eyes were flat with no emotion whatsoever, as if she were looking at someone she didn't know. No, worse. As if she were looking at someone she didn't *want* to know.

"This was my idea. It's only right that I pay for it."

Well, ouch to the nasty double entendre. Doyle ground his teeth as she signed the check, wondering how things had gone so wrong in the space of just a few short minutes. Then the pressure on his shoulder reminded him how. Margo.

"Was there anything wrong with your desserts, miss?" The waiter was looking askance at the practically untouched slices of cake.

"No, they were lovely," Thea assured him with a smile. "Franz needn't worry. His desserts are still decadent enough to die for." The smile faltered slightly, and Doyle knew she was remembering the moment that had passed between them over that decadent cake because he was as well. He didn't think he could erase that memory from his mind with sandpaper. "It was the appetites that were lacking, not his skill." The waiter looked appeased and whisked himself away.

"Shall we ask them to box yours up to take with us for later, darling?" Margo asked in a seductive, husky voice, stroking her fingers over the nape of his neck just in case anyone within ten feet had missed her staking her claim. "You know how you like to get creative with whipped cream."

Doyle gritted his teeth. Getting through the drive to Margo's was going to be a true test of restraint and not for the reasons she seemed to be thinking. Damn, she'd never been like this before, never so blatantly possessive and crude. Why now?

"No, I don't think so," he ground out. He stood abruptly, satisfied when the movement forced her hand from his neck, but she was quick to capture his arm in its place. Her hands, strong from the years of massage therapy she did at Fit, were like steel bands, trapping him to her side even when Thea rose, forcing her to scoot her chair back on her own. Doyle chafed at being held back, but, short of a scene, he knew there was no way to detach himself from Margo to do the polite thing and assist Thea.

"Well, it was *so* nice to meet you, Cindy. Do have a good night." Margo flashed her a victorious smile. "I know we will."

"Always a pleasure to meet one of Doyle's friends, Margie," Thea answered coolly.

"Margo," came the snapped correction. Thea simply gave her a bland look.

"Oh, of course. My mistake." Rather than apologetic, her tone said she really didn't care one way or the other, that the name of one of "Doyle's friends" was inconsequential. To reinforce that sentiment, Thea glanced past them and smiled. "Do excuse me, but I must pay my respects to the deputy governor and his wife before I go." With a dismissive nod one might give a servant, she sailed past them.

Doyle had to resist the urge to applaud her poise in slapping down Margo's pretensions. Then, realizing that he had a seething tantrum waiting to happen attached to his side like a limpet, he made a beeline for the front door. After depositing a fuming Margo with the valet to wait for his car, Doyle ducked back inside and located Rick Channing to tell him about the change in plans. He ignored the disapproval in his subordinate's eyes and beat another hasty retreat, once more cursing the fact that the evening had deteriorated to the point where he was cast in the part of the villain in practically everyone's eyes.

He'd been placed in a no-win situation by fate and the red-haired virago waiting impatiently for him outside, and he was none too happy about it. Margo was pleasant company most of the time, in an uncommitted, unattached sort of way. What they had was fun. Nonexclusive. Not even remotely serious. But this sense of clingy possessiveness she'd shown tonight made him wonder if, possibly, she had seen their relationship in a very different way. If that was the case, then maybe it was time to either set her straight or set her loose.

*   *   *

*Damn him!*

Thea fumed in thundering silence during the interminable ride home. At first she tried to make normal conversation with Rick, refusing to be seen as sulking over Doyle's blatant defection, but her bodyguard-cum-chauffer seemed as stilted and uncomfortable as she did with the effort, so they'd finally both given up. Rick's awkwardness only served to make her own even worse.

Not only had Doyle humiliated her, he'd done it in front of a witness. No, *witnesses*, plural. No way did his exit with that red-haired bitch go unnoticed. Thea had seen too many familiar faces in the restaurant to even hope that her aborted dinner date would go unmentioned. Mrs. Westlake wasn't the only old tabby that enjoyed the hell out of dissecting every one of her social gaffes as a way of reminding themselves how absolutely superior they were to the uncultured New Money in their midst.

After thanking Rick for driving her home, she breezed in past Graham, her father's butler/major domo, with a cheery smile that she actually managed to hang onto until her bedroom door was locked behind her and she could vent the red-hot fury that had been simmering since the moment Margo had first appeared.

"Damn, damn, damn!" She only just resisted the urge to fling her purse across the room. "Of all the rotten, unthinking, *horrible* things he could have done!" Finally, the sob that had been choking her broke free. She dropped into the oversized chair by the window as she fought back a second one, refusing to let herself be reduced to such a pitiful state.

"I am not going to cry over you, Brennan Doyle," she swore viciously even as she swiped at the tears that were leaking through her lashes against her will. "You're an unbelievable bastard, and I don't even know what I ever saw in you."

At least she was honest enough to know she was lying to herself. She knew exactly what she saw in him. He was smart, and funny, and while he'd never admit it, he had a soft streak in him a mile wide, especially when it came to women, children, and animals. He was everything she'd ever wanted in a man. Brains, personality, looks, all wrapped up in one irresistible package. He was far from perfect, but he was perfect enough for her.

Why couldn't he want her the way that she wanted him? It had seemed like he did there for a minute; she could swear it. The look in his eyes had made her feel hot and cold and slightly dizzy, and she'd been so lost in the unfamiliar sensation that she would probably have done anything he wanted. A small shiver ran through her as she remembered the feeling. No, she would have *definitely* done anything he wanted.

Unfortunately, what he'd wanted was to send her home like some unwanted package.

That thought restoked her anger and forced her once again to her feet, sending her pacing in increasing agitation around the room, hands clenching and unclenching impotently at her sides. She stopped when she caught sight of herself in the full length mirror near the dressing table and forced herself to do a critical analysis of her appearance.

Aside from the too-bright eyes shining out of her flushed face, she thought she looked just as attractive as Margo "more-than-a-friend" Klein. Thea wasn't as stacked as the older woman, but she had nice curves, and the silk of the dress she'd spent hours choosing showed them to elegant perfection. Or so the saleswoman and Lillian had both agreed when she'd bought it.

"Perfection," Thea said mockingly to her reflection, spreading her arms wide. "Then why are you here alone in your room talking to yourself while he's over at Margo's doing…" Preferring not to dwell on just what Doyle was most likely doing with or to Margo, she dropped her arms and sighed. "All dressed up and no place to go. And no one who'd want to go with you even if you did."

*Nick would.*

The errant thought brought a smile to her face. Yes, Nick probably would take her out someplace if she asked, even if he did have his meeting to go to in the morning. He didn't seem to mind spending time with her. He wouldn't dump her for somebody else if they came along and rubbed their breasts on his arm, unlike some other jerks she knew.

Thea glanced at her watch. It was still early. Twenty minutes to drive there, a half hour in the lounge for drinks, an hour tops, and Nick could still be tucked in bed before eleven. Plenty early for the good night's sleep he'd said he needed.

She was already pulling up the Hyatt's website on her phone for the hotel's phone number when her promise to Doyle inconveniently sprang to mind. Damn! She'd sworn she'd steer clear of Nick until Doyle gave the all-clear on his background check. It was a stupid, stupid promise. She'd only made it in the first place to keep Doyle happy. And why should she care about making Doyle happy now, when he'd just managed to make her feel the crappiest she'd ever felt in her entire life?

She knew Nick would never hurt her. He was just a nice guy who'd found a friendly face in a city full of strangers. They got along well. Better than well. Nick made it easy to talk to him, almost as though they'd known each other for years instead of days. He made her feel good. Attractive. Interesting. And right now her ego could use all the balm she could manage to scrape together.

After copying down the phone number, Thea's conscience began to nag at her. No matter what Doyle had done to her tonight, he was still her father's security chief, in charge of looking out for her well-being, and she *had* made a promise.

She sighed and put down her phone. As tempting as it was to thumb her nose at Doyle in a blatant act of rebellion, it wasn't fair to use Nick that way. It was poor repayment for his company and friendship.

*It just isn't fair!* she railed silently. *After all this time, things were just starting to go right. He was just starting to notice me, and then* she *had to come along and ruin what had been shaping up to be my deepest fantasy coming true.*

Margo.

Thea bared her teeth. A bottle-dyed redhead with a gravity-defying bosom that couldn't possibly be attributed to nature and clearly a threat to all of Thea's well-laid plans. She wasn't stupid; she knew Doyle had had women in his life over the years, some for longer than others, although none had seemed to be able to pass the six-month mark, something Thea had secretly taken great comfort in.

But knowing those women existed and actually coming face-to-face with one of them were two different things. Seeing Margo had made her more real. Seeing her hanging all over Doyle had been agony, especially when he hadn't done anything to peel her off of himself. Seeing him leave with her had just about ripped out her already shredded heart.

Why? Why did he do that? He could have stuffed old Margo in the back of the Charger (and Thea was so not going to think about the hints that had been dropped about that backseat, although she doubted she'd ever be able to sit in it again) if she really didn't want to catch a ride with "total stranger" Rick, which any way you cut it was a pretty lame excuse since he was one of Doyle's own men and therefore totally trustworthy. Yes, as annoying as it would have been to have to share Doyle for as long as it would have taken to drop Margo off at her apartment, Thea could have coped. But being ditched entirely for the obnoxious redhead was unacceptable.

Painful.

Humiliating.

And all too typical of the way her ongoing pursuit of Doyle always seemed to turn out.

That sad truth hit home with enough force to make her sit on the bed with a deflated slump. Was she really that pathetic? Had she totally misread everything about the evening? She hadn't asked Doyle to take her out, after all. All right, yes, she'd manipulated him a teensy bit by suggesting other alternatives while leaving his name conspicuously off her list of potential dinner dates, but *he'd* been the one to act insulted by the omission. *He'd* been the one to suggest himself as escort. It wasn't like he'd had to do it to save her from social ruin or anything. He'd done it because he wanted to.

Hadn't he?

Dear God, had she made him feel so sorry for her dateless state that he'd felt he *had* to take her to dinner? Had what she'd thought the best evening of her life been nothing more to him than a…a pity date?

Thea groaned and threw herself backward onto the mattress. Now she felt humiliated for a whole different reason. But it made sense. Doyle had been his usual nice self, and she'd misinterpreted "nice" for "interested," and he'd known it. She'd licked his *thumb,* for God's sake!

Faced with the ride home together, knowing that she was thinking all the wrong things, it was no wonder Doyle had grabbed the opportunity Margo had presented. He'd not only gotten out of what was sure to have been an extremely uncomfortable ride, but he'd also gotten his point across to Thea about how things actually stood between them without having to utter a single word.

With that lowering realization firmly in mind, Thea stripped herself out of the dress she had so hopefully put on just hours before and ignored the tempting array of silks and satins now populating her lingerie drawer, instead drawing on her oldest pair of cotton pajamas for comfort before crawling under the covers. It was too early for bed, but all she wanted to do was lose herself in the oblivion of sleep so she could hide from the sickening certainty clawing her gut that she'd finally, and irrevocably, humiliated herself beyond all repair.

# CHAPTER 12

**THEA WAS AVOIDING HIM.**

Drumming his fingers on the folders strewn over his desktop, Doyle felt a certain sense of dread weighing heavily on his chest. It had been three days since that disastrous night at the restaurant, and for each and every one of those days Thea had managed to be up and off the estate early enough to avoid him and come home late enough to accomplish the same.

At this rate, the only way he was going to get a chance to talk to her was to have the person on escort duty call him when they were heading back to the estate so he could stake out the garage and pounce on her when she got out of her car.

Doyle shifted uncomfortably in his chair. The mere thought of pouncing on Thea's lush, nubile body was still enough to stir him, which proved he was totally out of his mind. Four days ago, he would never have entertained ideas of Thea and sex together in the same mix. Well, okay, there had been that time when she was wearing that thong bikini, but hell, he was only human!

But now…

Now, he couldn't seem to think a coherent thought without erotic images intruding into it. But damn it, he just couldn't forget that look that had been on her face, in her eyes, when he'd shared that bite of cake with her. When he'd wiped that stray dab of cream from her lip. When she'd touched her tongue to his bare skin. She'd been aroused. Deeply aroused. And she'd wanted *him*.

Now he couldn't even get close enough to say one word to her.

Damn it to hell!

Well, at least he knew where she was, and it wasn't with her new "friend" Nick. And a damned good thing, too, considering what his guys had been able to dig up on him already with more to come. It was too soon to be sure, but everything was beginning to point to Hastings as their stalker. The most damning evidence so far was his frequent cross-country travels for work. Once they matched his itinerary to the postmarks on the letters, they'd be able to take it to the local D.A. and get the bastard off the streets, and, more importantly, away from Thea, once and for all.

But while his cyber experts tackled that endeavor, Doyle was stuck with little more to do than ponder how he was going to handle Thea's silent treatment, if he could call it a silent treatment when he was never within a hundred yards of the person in question. It was more like an escape and evade maneuver.

Doyle gave a grim smile. E&E had been his forte in the Corps, but damned if Thea wasn't giving him a run for his money.

She'd spent the last two days holed up at Amelia's house, supposedly helping out with the last minute arrangements for the engagement party being held a week from Saturday, according to what she'd told her daily escorts. Knowing Amelia's mother, however, Doyle thought it much more likely she was simply helping her friend keep her sanity in the midst of dictatorial chaos.

Being able to avoid him was merely a bonus.

He blew out a breath as he shoved his chair back and spun around so he could grab the coffee pot on the credenza. His nerves were already jangled from too little sleep, but he needed the caffeine kick to make it through the morning. Maybe he'd take a power nap at lunchtime to make up for the restless nights that had been plagued by an uncomfortable mix of guilt and sexually frustrated dreams. Or maybe he'd go to the gym and work off some of the nervous energy that was making his skin feel jumpy, like an electrical current was running just below the surface.

But, no, if he did that, he might very well run into Margo, and that was the last thing he wanted to do. He'd been as neatly sidestepping her these past few days as Thea had been him, and, judging by the increasing number of hang-ups on his voice mail, Margo was none too pleased about it. He probably should have made a clean break with her the other night, but she'd already been more than a little annoyed when he didn't take her up on her offer to come up for coffee and "dessert." He hadn't wanted to make it worse by ending things while sitting in the car in front of her apartment building in full view of her neighbors. She usually kept it well-hidden, but Margo's temper was like cordite. It burned hot and fast and usually ended with a bang.

Not that he understood why she'd gotten so upset with him in the first place. They hadn't been on a date. There should have been no expectations of "dessert" or anything else. Carefully, he reviewed the conversation just prior to his hasty exit—he refused to call it a retreat—from the restaurant. Margo had needed a ride, and he had needed an excuse not to be alone with Thea.

Nope, he hadn't said anything to lead Margo to any wrong conclusions about his motives or expectations. Granted, she'd been acting disagreeably possessive at the time, and he hadn't done much to dissuade her—yet another mistake on his part, not protesting the way she'd acted toward Thea, but he'd thought calling her on her unacceptable behavior might have just made the situation worse.

Still, he'd offered nothing more than a ride. Anything else had been a total product of Margo's imagination.

*Then why is Thea avoiding you?*

Try as he might, Doyle couldn't forget the instant of pain that had crossed Thea's face when he'd agreed to pawn her off on Rick, and no matter how he tried to sugarcoat it with excuses, that was exactly what he'd done.

No two ways about it, he was a dick.

He'd handled the situation badly, but he hadn't exactly been in a position to explain himself and his reasoning at the time, which, in hindsight, had been more than a little faulty. He needed to make those explanations now and try to make amends for his brutally stupid mistake.

Which he couldn't do unless he could pin Thea down in one place.

Well, when Thea came home—eventually—he'd be waiting. She might try, but she couldn't hide from him forever.

* * *

"You can't hide from him forever, you know."

Doing her best to ignore the comment that had been unceremoniously lobbed into the conversation, and not for the first time, either, Thea kept her head bent to the seating chart that had long ago bored her to tears, partly because she didn't know most of the people on it, but mostly because it was a futile endeavor.

Any of the changes Amelia wanted to make to it would undoubtedly be ignored by her mother, just like every other suggestion her friend had made regarding her engagement party. And, judging by the names on the seating chart, it was looking less and less like an gathering of friends and family so much as a who's-who of the Washington political scene.

She squinted at the chart and pointed. "Is that the vice president?"

"Yes." Amelia made a frustrated gesture with her hands. "Thea, it's been three days. Don't you think you should talk to him?"

"I'll bet your mother was steamed that she only snagged the vice president and not the big guy himself," Thea said, steadfastly ignoring the question. "Quite a let-down in her social expectations, huh?"

"He'll be at the wedding. What are you going to do about Doyle?"

Thea blinked in surprise. "Really? I thought your mother was kidding about that."

"Yes, he'll be there. He's one of my father's cronies. Who cares about him? What about *Doyle*?"

"That's so cool. Think he'll mind me getting my picture taken with him?"

As Amelia made a strangling noise deep in her throat, Lillian reached over and plucked the seating chart from Thea's hands and flicked it down the polished dining room table. The heavy vellum spun crazily before coming to rest halfway down the twenty foot length of mahogany, well out of reach.

"Hey, I was looking at that," Thea said indignantly.

Lillian snorted. "No, you were hiding behind it."

Thea drew herself straight and stared her friend in the eye.

"I was not hiding." She held Lillian's steady gaze for a long time—all of five seconds—before she slumped back and mumbled, "Okay, maybe I was hiding a little."

"A lot."

Thea glared. "Don't push it."

"Someone has to."

"I'm humiliated. I think that deserves a little compassion, don't you?"

"We gave you two whole days to sulk. That's all you get."

"I was not..." Thea thunked her head back against the heavy wooden chair and glared at the mural-covered ceiling, since she had about as much chance of getting sympathy from the archangels painted up there as from her friends at the moment.

Especially since she knew she *had* been sulking. Big time.

"Fine. Whatever. Can we talk about something else now? Please?"

"We haven't talked about *this* yet."

"Mellie, how's your dress coming?"

"Thea..." Lillian's tone was pure exasperation.

"I already told you what happened. There's nothing else to talk about," Thea insisted, knowing even as she did that it was a futile fight. Once Lillian grabbed hold of a subject, she wouldn't be happy until she'd wrung it dry.

"You gave us the 'See Spot Run' version of what happened with absolutely no details and then refused to talk about it again."

"More like the 'See Doyle Run' version," Thea muttered under her breath, remembering with fresh pain the humiliation of watching Doyle stroll out the door with that she-barracuda dangling from his arm.

"See, that's the part I don't get," Amelia chimed in. "You said everything seemed to be going so well up until he, well..." She gestured vaguely.

"Bolted? Ran for the door? Dropped me like a hot potato?"

Amelia squirmed. "Well, yeah, that."

Thea shrugged. "I *thought* everything was going great. Obviously, I was wrong."

"Maybe not," Lillian said.

Thea shot her an incredulous look.

"Hello, abandoned before the end of the date for another woman," she said. "I may not be a dating expert, great guru o' love, but I'd say that qualifies as not great."

"What were you doing right before Mountains showed up?" Lillian persisted.

Even through her depression, Thea couldn't hold back an amused snort at the nickname Lillian had adopted for Margo. She'd said that she had overheard her brothers calling the overly endowed redhead that once, adding that after so many men had scaled those silicone peaks, they wouldn't have been surprised if there was a Sherpa guide or two lost somewhere in the massive depths of her cleavage.

Unfortunately, her amusement waned as she recalled the last few minutes of that painful night.

"We were having dessert," she sighed. "I was teasing him about sharing his chocolate cake since he'd stolen a bite of my cheesecake, and, oh God, it was soooo good." She closed her eyes and wallowed in the memory of the deep chocolate cake melting on her tongue and then gave herself a mental shake. Like then, she opened her eyes, and remembered what she'd seen.

"Doyle was…" She gave a shaky laugh. "Well, he looked like he wanted to dive into my mouth after the cake, to tell you the truth. And then he reached over and wiped a little bit of whipped cream off my mouth, and…" *And I couldn't resist tasting him.*

But she didn't say that. She couldn't. She wasn't even comfortable remembering that she'd been that bold, that impulsive. The flare of heat she'd thought she'd seen in his eyes had made it worth it, an acknowledgement that she was a desirable woman to his desiring man.

Too bad she'd thought wrong.

"And?" Amelia prompted.

"And then Margo showed up." It was like a dash of frigid water, ruining everything that had come before.

"And then?"

"And then he left with her," Thea said, her voice flat.

"Just like that?" Lillian prodded. "She showed up, and he just jumped out of his seat and ran off?"

"No, first she insulted me with a few catty remarks—which he didn't do anything about, I might add—before rubbing herself all over him and getting him to agree to take her home." The memory of Margo touching Doyle with the self-assurance of someone who knows they have that right burned painfully deep in her chest.

"So, it wasn't his idea?" Lillian asked thoughtfully.

"No, it was hers. She said her dinner date was a doctor who got called to the hospital, so she was stranded, and she just *happened* to see Doyle's car in the lot, so would he mind giving her a lift home." She rolled her eyes to express how unlikely she found it that Margo had just "happened" to do anything where Doyle was concerned.

"And he agreed?"

"Well…" Thea's brow wrinkled as she thought. "No, not right away. He offered to send her with Rick." She brightened at the memory and then slumped again just as quickly. "But as soon as she hinted she'd rather go home with him, he agreed, and it was 'so long, Thea, you don't mind, do you?' And off they went."

"Wait, he asked you if you minded?" Lillian asked sharply.

"Well, yeah, but—"

"And you didn't say something?" Her friend's voice was growing louder and more shrill by the second.

"Um, well, no. I mean, he'd already offered the ride. Asking me was just an afterthought. What could I say?"

"You could have said 'hell, yes, I mind!' and told him to let her either go with Rick or call a cab, but that no way in hell was he going to dump you in the middle of your date." Shaking her head, Lillian gave her a disgusted look. "T, I am seriously disappointed in you."

"He'd already made his decision," Thea said, feeling defensive and just a little hurt at this sudden and unexpected lack of support. "I wasn't about to get into a tug-of-war over him in the middle of a restaurant."

"She's right about that," Amelia said. "It's not likely Mount…er, Margo would have given in gracefully. Or quietly."

Thea nodded. "She was on him like a barnacle, and I don't think she was going to let herself get scraped off easily. Not that he tried very hard," she added bitterly. She looked at Lillian with a mutinous glare. "Besides, I shouldn't have to beg my date to stay with me. He should want to stay all on his own. And Doyle didn't." She felt her composure slip a little as that painful reality settled on her chest like a boulder all over again.

"Maybe he had a reason," Amelia offered, her face soft with sympathy.

"Sure he did." Thea blinked back tears that she refused to let flow. She'd done enough crying over her one-sided love for Doyle over the years. It was time to finally admit she'd been wasting her time. "He wanted to go off and play King of the Mountains," she said with a sardonic twist of her lips.

"Or maybe it was more like hide-and-seek," Lillian mused, tapping a finger against her chin thoughtfully. Thea blinked.

"Well, that's just an ick thought I didn't need. Thanks *so* much."

It was Lillian's turn to blink. Then she scowled. "I didn't mean it like *that*. Get your mind out of the gutter."

"Then what did you mean?" Thea demanded, embarrassed that her thoughts had evidently strayed to Nastyville alone. But really, what else was she supposed to think, when that redheaded silicone factory had made it clear as Waterford what she was really inviting Doyle home for?

"I meant that maybe Doyle was feeling the need to retreat and regroup, and Margo provided a convenient excuse." When both Thea and Amelia continued to stare at her, she sighed and explained. "You said you were having a good time."

Thea nodded. "Up till the end, yeah."

"You were even trading desserts, which even though you won't elaborate, I'll assume was more than just a matter of simple taste testing to compare notes."

Thea blushed.

"Hmph." Lillian tapped her finger on her chin again. "You said he looked like he wanted to dive into your mouth." Thea nodded. "And maybe more than that?" Another nod, another blush. "Like he couldn't wait to get you into the car and tear your clothes off?"

Stifling a groan at the very thought of Doyle's warm hands slipping the clothes from her body, a sensation it seemed more and more unlikely that she was ever going to experience anywhere except in her dreams, Thea said, "That's what I thought, but obviously I'm not the greatest judge of what a man is thinking. Maybe he was just thinking about whether or not to order a second piece of cake to take home with him since I'd made him share the first one."

"Or maybe you are. Don't forget, the man in question had a nasty habit of running scared where you're concerned."

Like he had the first time he'd seen her in that embarrassing thong bikini. Like he had from their daily runs. *Hmm.* Thea turned the possibility around in her mind. Was it possible that she *hadn't* misread the heat in Doyle's eyes? Had he wanted her so badly that he'd forced himself to take a giant step backward? It was an interesting idea, which went a long way toward soothing her oh-so bruised feelings, but it was still just a theory.

"Think about it," Lillian persisted. "If he hadn't wanted it to be a date, he could have just told Rick to stay home and gone with you by himself, which would have made him your de facto bodyguard and on duty. He didn't, so that means he wanted to be with you. *You*, not her."

"True," Thea allowed, not wanting to read too much into it, since she seemed to be doing a lot of that lately. "But if that's the case then he should have said something instead of just letting me think he was being an insensitive jackass."

"Oh, sure," Amelia snorted, "he could have said 'Thea, I have to take Margo home now because if I don't, I'm afraid I'll lose control and have my wicked way with you in the car.'"

"Wicked way?" Thea repeated with an amused grin.

"She's been reading those regency romance novels again," Lillian said, rolling her eyes.

Amelia blushed but defended herself by saying, "It's better than saying 'I'm afraid I'll strip you naked and do the nasty with you in the backseat,' isn't it?"

Covering a surprised laugh with a cough, Lillian said, "You're right. Wicked way it is."

Thea was too busy reliving the horrible images of Doyle's backseat that Margo had planted in her mind that night to be amused. She shook her head, trying to shed the disturbing images like a dog shedding water. Nasty gutter water.

"Whatever he might have said, he didn't, and all of this is just supposition, anyway. He might have wanted to go, and he might very well have spent the night at her place after he brought her home."

"The only way you're going to know for sure is to ask him," Lillian said.

That earned a disbelieving laugh. "Oh, right, that would be a conversation I'm going to run right out and have. 'Excuse me, Doyle, can you tell me if you boffed dear old Margo after you walked out on our date last Sunday?' Like that'll ever happen!"

"Not that part." Lillian slashed her hand through the air in annoyance. "The other part. About why he took Margo home and not you." She shook her head. "You're being dense on purpose."

She was right. The very last thing in the world Thea wanted to do was ask Doyle that question. It was kind of like offering yourself up to the guy with the gun and just begging him to put that final bullet right through your heart. If she didn't ask, she could hang on to that last slender thread of hope, deep down inside, where she could almost convince herself that Doyle had left her there for noble reasons, that he did care despite the evidence to the contrary, that she hadn't entrusted her heart and soul to a man who could so carelessly trample and discard both without so much as a backward glance.

She was a coward, and she knew it. She didn't like it, but she knew it.

Evidently her friends knew it, too, because they weren't about to let the subject drop.

"Did you ever think that Doyle might have gone looking for you first thing Monday to explain and maybe even apologize?" Lillian asked.

"Yes," Thea mumbled. But she'd also thought that maybe he wouldn't. Which was why it was so much easier to hide out at Amelia's and lick her wounds, rather than sitting at home listening to her heart shred a little more every minute.

"Or yesterday?" Lillian persisted.

"Yes," Thea said again, this time with a bit more bite. "And before you say it, today, too. I get it, okay? I'm in major avoidance mode."

"Well, that's about to change."

"How?" Thea asked warily. She inwardly cringed at the sight of both her friends getting to their feet in unison, as if to underscore that it was two against one.

"First, we're getting out of here."

"But...but..." Thea grasped at desperate straws. "But what about the engagement party?" she stammered.

"You mean the one that's already been planned down to the last crudités?" There was dry humor in Amelia's voice, but there was also an undertone of resigned hurt that instantly made Thea feel like a jerk for wailing and whining about her Doyle issues when Amelia was going through worse problems of her own.

"Mellie, I'm sorry," she started. Amelia waved the apology away.

"I'm used to it. Besides," she added with a wry grin, "this is the first time I've been allowed to even look at the seating arrangement since it was finalized. How did you manage to smuggle it out of the War Room?"

As always, Amelia's name for the small home office that had been taken over by the two dragons for their wedding planning brought a snort of laughter. Between the phones, scanner, and seriously high-tech computer that Mrs. Westlake had had installed expressly for plotting...er, planning her only daughter's wedding, the room had definitely taken on the air of belonging to a general marshalling for a major invasion.

Or, in this case, a Major Society Event. The only difference between the two was that the weapons of choice would be sharp tongues rather than swords, although they could draw blood just as easily, and, in the case of Society, be just as deadly.

"Oliver slipped it to me," Thea said.

"Oliver?" Amelia looked first surprised and then affronted. "The last time I asked to see it, he told me I'd have to apply to either Mrs. Davenport or my mother for permission. Can you believe it? *Apply for permission?* To see my own damn seating chart for my own damn party?" She seemed ignorant of the two jaws that had dropped at her double-damning and instead continued in an aggrieved tone, "But you, he lets see it, just because you asked. Well, that's just...shitty!" With an annoyed huff, she drooped back into her seat, arms crossed over her chest as she stared at the wall in petulant silence.

Stunned that something as seemingly innocent as wheedling the seating chart from Charles's personal assistant to justify her lingering presence at the Westlake estate could have produced such an offended outburst, Thea exchanged a worried look with Lillian. She, too, seemed surprised, but she simply shrugged. Amelia was clearly more upset about having her engagement party shanghaied by the dragons than she had let on, but what could they really do about it now?

It was far too late to try and wrest control back, and Thea wasn't sure that Amelia would have wanted to even if she could. She might have endured her parents' never-ending political parties, but she had never enjoyed them. Thea worried that Amelia's wedding had turned into simply another event that she had to struggle through and endure, rather than the start to the happily-ever-after she wanted and deserved.

Knowing that pity was the last thing Amelia wanted, Thea offered the only thing she could to take some of the sting out of the situation. "Well, ah, he didn't exactly *just* let me see it," she said. "I had to bribe him for it."

That got Amelia's attention, although her body remained rigid with anger. "A bribe?"

"Yeah, a bribe. Didn't you try that when he first said no?"

"Of course not!" Amelia huffed, indignant. Lillian snorted.

"And your father's a politician?" Lillian blew an air kiss at Amelia in response to the glare she got.

"What did you use?" Amelia asked, half-curious, half-aggrieved.

Thea shrugged. "The usual." A grin kicked up her lips. "A dozen of Rosa's homemade honey oatmeal raisin cookies."

Lillian bit her lower lip, possibly to keep from drooling. "The ones that are big enough to use as Frisbees?" she asked longingly.

Amelia was less enthused. "The ones that my mother banned from the house?"

"That was only because your chef got miffed that everyone liked them better than his prissy little petit fours," Thea pointed out. It had been an ugly scene. Lots of yelling in French, followed by the threat of resigning if such déclassé foods were ever allowed into "his domain" again.

Choosing her status-symbol chef over common sense—it was only cookies, for pity's sake—Mrs. Westlake had issued her ultimatum. Nothing from Rosa's kitchen was ever to pass her hallowed doors again. Ever. Thea had rolled her eyes but agreed for Amelia's sake. Her friend had enough troubles without getting involved in a war of the kitchens.

"Whatever the reason, she's going to blow a blood vessel if she finds out about them."

She couldn't be sure, but Thea thought she detected a hint of glee in Amelia's statement. "Don't worry," Thea said with a wink, "Oliver knows he's carrying contraband. He'll keep them out of sight."

He'd grinned like a kid who'd just been given a much-longed-for present when she'd shown up at the office door with her baked offering, and he'd been as eager as she to keep their transaction a secret. Technically, he worked for Charles, but he'd been appropriated by the dragons for party planning and obviously wasn't any more enamored of his temporary bosses than Thea was.

Not that he'd ever said as much, but it had been clear in his quick capitulation and the conspiratorial, heads-together whispers as he'd covertly slipped her the chart. She found it hard to believe that he'd been such a hard-ass to Amelia.

Then again, Amelia hadn't brought him cookies you could land a small aircraft on.

Wanting to get her friend's mind away from her wedding woes, Thea said, "So, where are we headed?" It was only after the words were out that she remembered that her friends had been about to drag her out of the protection of the Westlake estate and into the real world, where Doyle held the tattered remains of her heart and her pride in his large, strong hands.

She looked around the room, desperately wondering if she could manage to contract some hideously contagious disease in the next two minutes so that she'd have to be confined to one of the guest rooms for a week or three. Then she groaned silently when she heard the one thing she'd known she was going to hear, the one thing she'd dreaded and hoped for most.

"Where else? Swimming!"

# CHAPTER 13

**THIS WAS SUCH A BAD, BAD IDEA.**

The thought rolled through Thea's head for the hundredth time, as though if she told herself that obvious fact enough times, she might somehow gain the strength of will to jump up off her lounger and make a life-saving run for the house. Well, okay, maybe *life-saving* was overstating it a bit. But definitely pride-saving. Dignity-saving.

Heart-saving.

With a barely suppressed groan, she shifted restlessly and tried to have faith in Lillian's assurances that dragging herself out of hiding and into a confrontation—er, conversation—with Doyle was the best move. Easy enough for her to say. It wasn't Lillian's feelings being forked over for another skewering.

Still, Thea knew she couldn't keep hiding out at Amelia's. If nothing else, the constant proximity to one or both of the dragons, depending on whether the Davenports were in town or on another leg of their cross-country fact-finding tour for the senator's economic committee, was almost as unpleasant as dwelling on why she wanted to avoid Doyle in the first place.

Lillian and Amelia had both seemed of a like mind in why Doyle had ditched her: self-preservation. Thea just wished she could be as sure as they seemed with their conclusion. She really, really wanted it to be something as simple as that, just a more intense form of his usual shying away when the emotions between them started to shift toward anything remotely sexual. The alternative was just too damned painful to bear.

So, here she was, stretched out by the pool like a sacrificial offering—for some reason the staked goat in *Jurassic Park* kept leaping to mind—waiting to see if Doyle would come willingly to her or if she was going to have to go beard him in his den. She wasn't entirely sure which would be worse.

No, that wasn't true. Going to him would be a thousand times worse.

At least if he came to her first, she wouldn't feel...what? Like she was sixteen years old again, following him around with what she'd thought at the time was great nonchalance, making farfetched excuses to pop into his office, or following him on his rounds, or just "coincidently" showing up at the various places around town he liked to frequent during his off hours?

This time she did groan. God, she'd been such a dork. The question was, had anything changed? Was she still chasing after someone that just didn't want to be caught?

"Stud alert at nine o'clock," Lillian murmured from beside her. Thea fought to keep from jerking her head around to see. Easy. She needed to stay calm. Cool. Unaffected.

She needed to throw up.

"Come on, Mellie." With catlike grace Lillian sprang up from her lounger and dragged on her wrap. "Let's see if we can get Rosa to scare us up some of those cookies that your mother's kitchen Nazi hates so much." Then, as if sensing Thea's muscle's twitch in anticipation of getting up to go with them, she jabbed a finger in her direction and said firmly, "Stay."

"Woof," Thea muttered as her friends performed their strategic retreat. She knew she had a better chance of Doyle speaking freely without an audience, but she still felt a shiver of nerves dance up her spine. She'd avoided this confrontation—no, *conversation,* she reminded herself again—for days. It was time to clear the air. But oh, how the craven part of her wanted to run and hide in the kitchen with milk and cookies instead.

"I hope I didn't chase them off."

Thea had to swallow before answering to loosen her tongue from the roof of her suddenly spitless mouth.

"Ah, no, they're on a junk food mission. Mellie's mother has laid down the law at her house about what can and can't be eaten. No starch, no sugar, no chocolate," she ticked on her fingers. "With the engagement party coming up, she can't chance getting a zit that would be seen by all the Washington movers and shakers that are going to be there. Lord knows something as horrible as a pimple might ruin poor Chuckie's entire political career."

Doyle made a noise that might have been a suppressed snort. "So she abides by her mother's rules at home to keep the peace and comes here to get her Twinkie fix."

"Something like that."

"Very diplomatic."

"That's our Mellie. Always eager to please." It was impossible to keep the hint of dismay she felt for her friend from coloring her words. She hadn't missed the way Amelia was still pressing her stomach all the time when she thought no one was looking or how she was now popping antacids like they were breath mints. The wedding plans and the tag-teaming of the dragons were taking their toll on her, and something was eventually going to have to give. Thea was just afraid that something was going to be Amelia.

"Speaking of food," Doyle finally said into the growing silence, "I, ah, had a good time the other night. At dinner."

Thea wasn't entirely sure how to take that. "The food was good," she answered noncommittally.

"It always is." Doyle shifted. "I meant, I enjoyed being with you for dinner."

Again, not exactly clear, but she started to get a little hopeful. "It was too bad you couldn't stay to enjoy the rest of dessert," she said, watching him carefully from behind her dark-tinted Bvlgaris. Unfortunately, his eyes were as protected by his shades as hers were.

"Yeah, I, ah, well..." He blew out a frustrated breath. "I'm sorry Margo was so..."

Catty? Bitchy? "Rude?"

"She's normally a very pleasant person," Doyle said, ignoring Thea's suggestion. "I don't know why she acted that way."

Ah, but Thea did. Margo had found out that "little Cynthia" wasn't so very little after all, and if she'd caught any of the cake-sharing byplay—which Thea definitely thought she had, given the venom she'd been spitting from word one—she'd probably guessed that Thea's interest in Doyle might very well be reciprocated. Hopefully, she amended, mentally crossing her fingers. Hopefully.

Taking a deep breath, Thea threw her pride to the wind and said boldly, "She probably just didn't like seeing you on a date with another woman."

She might not have been able to see his eyes, but she could very much see the way his body went suddenly still and wary. Her heart began to pound painfully in her chest as she waited for the words that would either save her or flay her.

"Well, it ah..." Doyle cleared his throat. "It wasn't, ah..."

*Don't say it,* she wailed pitifully inside her head. *Please don't say it.*

"It wasn't really a *date,*" Doyle went on, stumbling through his words totally unaware at what havoc they were wreaking on Thea's heart. "I mean, it was a date, but it wasn't really a *date* date. It was a...a friends date."

"A friends date," Thea repeated numbly.

"Yes." Doyle nodded jerkily. "Like the time you took me to Q's for my birthday."

She hadn't tried to suck his finger into her mouth at Q's, but she couldn't bring herself to point that out. Nor had he looked at her like he wanted to devour her on the spot. But obviously he hadn't this time, either. She must have imagined it. Or maybe he had, but only because she'd made a sexual advance with her tongue and he was a guy and he couldn't help but respond. For a second, anyway. Clearly, that was as long as she was able to hold his interest as anything other than a—God, she wanted to choke on the word—*friend.*

"You do consider me your friend, don't you?" Doyle sounded hesitant, almost as though he was waiting for her to pitch some kind of fit.

Somewhere deep inside, she was weeping, but she wouldn't let it show. Not for a second would she ever let Doyle know how much his words were killing her, a piece at a time. Later. Later she'd bleed. But for now, she pulled the tattered remnants of her pride around her, inadequate protection though it might be, and smiled up at him. "Of course, I do."

Relief blossomed across his face. "Good. That's good. Because that's really important to me. Your friendship. I...I really value that. A lot."

"Sure. That's great." Trying hard to collect her thoughts from their downward spiral, she drew on the only thing she could think of to salvage what little pride she had left. "Oh, did I tell you? I heard back from one of the firms I sent my résumé to. They're very interested."

"That's great!" He sounded genuinely pleased. *And why not,* she thought morosely. *Isn't that what a* friend *would feel?* "Which firm is it?"

"Matrix Design." Her heart double-thumped as she waited for his reaction.

Doyle's brow wrinkled for a second before recognition hit. "Isn't that the firm you interned with last year?"

"Yes." The one in California. A thousand miles away. One of the dozens of résumés she'd sent out almost two weeks ago after the fiasco with Janice Timberlake and had regretted ever since. "They sent an email yesterday saying they'd love to have me back. Full-time." And she'd been feeling so miserable that she'd almost sent back an immediate acceptance. Only a last-minute bout of panic had kept her from hitting send.

"Wow." Doyle rocked back on his heels for a second before smiling. "That's great, Thea. Congratulations."

"Thanks." Did his smile look uncertain or relieved? She just couldn't tell.

"Are you going to take it?"

"I...I haven't decided yet. I have to think about it. Consider my options and...everything else."

She didn't really know what she'd expected. Maybe that he would say he didn't want her taking the job, didn't want her moving so far away. But Doyle simply nodded and didn't say anything at all.

Thea got to her feet, suddenly feeling much too naked and far too vulnerable and unable to bear hearing him spout another word about friendship.

WHAT THE LADY WANTS

She grabbed up her wrap and clutched it in a tight ball in front of her, partly to cover herself and partly to keep her hands from shaking.

"I think I'll see what Lil and Mellie were able to beg out of Rosa. I'll..." She swallowed and cut a quick glance at Doyle and then had to look away, afraid he'd see the torment in her eyes despite the dark lenses. "I'll see you around, Doyle."

Then she walked as fast as she could without running toward the house and the comfort of junk food and her friends.

*   *   *

"You told her *what?*"

Doyle winced at his brother's shout as he jerked the phone from his ear. Rubbing the offended organ, he sighed and said again, "I told her I valued her friendship. A lot. Well, I do," he said defensively when Austin groaned. It was a sound of disgust he had heard quite often from his oldest brother, although it had been years since he'd experienced it. Funny how neither years nor a few thousand miles of wireless connection made it any less humiliating.

"Well, what was I supposed to say?" he demanded, annoyed that Austin could still make him feel ten years old again to his brother's worldly sixteen. "I love your bikini and want to rip it off your body with my teeth?" Now *he* wanted to groan. That damned bitty bikini had stripped him of his ability to form a coherent sentence. Again. Hell, it had almost put him into full caveman mode. He was lucky he hadn't drooled all over her dainty little feet.

"Yes!" Austin shouted, eliciting another wince. Then, in a more conspiratorial tone he asked, "Was she really that hot?"

*God yes.* "That's not the point." He'd be damned if he'd discuss Thea's body with him. He needed to burn that bikini. Or build an altar to it.

"Uh, yeah, I think it is." Austin had adopted his wiser older brother tone. "You obviously want this girl, and from what you've told me, it's pretty obvious she wants you, too. What isn't obvious is why you two can't seem to get your acts together and do something about it."

"It's not that easy," Doyle started.

"Yeah, yeah, boss's daughter, trust, duty, blah, blah," Austin cut in. "She's legal, isn't she?"

Doyle scowled. "She's twenty-two."

"So I don't see what your problem is."

"I never said her age was an issue." Austin's silence called him on that lie. "Okay, so maybe she is a little young. For me, anyway."

His brother snorted. "Yeah, I forgot, you're the old man of the sea."

"Twelve years—"

"Is nothing." There was a faint sound of crinkling paper, and Doyle knew his brother had opened one of his ever-present rolls of Life Savers. He smiled at the familiar habit, one begun when his brother had first started dating his wife, Rebecca, ten years earlier and she'd broken him of his smoking habit, something even their mother, with all of her well-honed Irish-Catholic guilt, had never been able to do. When Austin had traded his Luckys for Pep-O-Mints, that was when they'd all known it was true love.

That was what he wanted, Doyle realized suddenly. He wanted that clarity, that light bulb that proclaimed "this is the one." He hated all this fumbling and guessing and knots in both his gut and his chest every time he thought about either having Thea in his life or *not* having her there.

"How did you know?" he asked quietly.

As always, his brother seemed to follow his train of thought effortlessly. "First time I saw Becca, I felt like I'd stepped on a live wire in the middle of the street," Austin reminisced fondly. He chuckled. "Damn near got myself run down by a bus when I stepped off the curb to cross the street to get to her before she disappeared in the crowd. Once I caught up to her, of course, it took more than a little convincing to get her to even give me her name and some downright pleading to get her phone number. She didn't feel the same immediate *zing* that I did, but I got her to come around in the end."

Doyle had felt a zing all right, but he didn't think that was what his brother was talking about. "So, what you're saying is that you knew right away she was the one, but she didn't?" Well, hell, that didn't help at all.

"What I'm saying, little brother, is that you'll never know if she's the one unless you give yourself—and her—the chance to do more than dance around each other like you have been. Date her. Kiss her. Hell, take her to bed. She's a big girl," he said firmly, cutting off Doyle's automatic protest before he could get it out, "and if she doesn't have a problem seeing you as a hot guy she'd like to bump uglies with rather than just her father's ancient and decrepit head of security, then there's no reason you should, either."

That image nearly blurred Doyle's vision and sent his pulse up a notch. "And what if it doesn't work out?" he asked. "What if I..." He gestured futilely.

"Screw her silly," Austin provided helpfully, clearly amused at his brother's reticence.

"*Make love* to her," Doyle forced out between clenched teeth, "and things don't work out? What happens then?"

"What, do you think she'd go all rich bitch on you and have daddy dearest fire your ass?"

He didn't even have to think about it. "No. She's not like that."

"So what's the problem?"

"The problem is, what do I do if things *do* work out?"

There was a long pause on his brother's end. "Uh, *what?*"

"What if things do work out between us? What if we fall in love, get married, the whole nine yards. What then?"

"Then you pop out a few kids and live happily ever after?" Austin sounded as though he was feeling his way through a minefield with his answer. Doyle knew exactly how he felt. He'd been negotiating that same minefield for the past few days himself.

"And where exactly do we live this fairy tale life? Do I move her into my bungalow here on the estate? Expect her to cook and clean and do the laundry like a good little middle-class housewife?"

"Okay, you know Becca would rip you a new one if she ever heard you say that, right?"

Doyle ignored him, although he knew it was the truth. "What I'm saying is how can I expect the princess to move out of the castle and give up the life she's accustomed to and live at the level I can afford to provide, which doesn't even come close?"

"So she's a prima donna, is she?"

"Well, no."

"Cares about status, bank accounts, flashy cars, how much bling you can cover her with?"

"Of course not."

"Needs to have servants to do everything for her? Couldn't find her way around a kitchen or a laundry room with a seeing-eye dog? Wouldn't dare chip a nail opening the car door for herself?"

"That's not what I'm saying," Doyle growled. Thea was none of those things.

"Then, brother-mine, I think the one with the problem here isn't Thea. It's you."

Doyle wanted to protest, tell his brother he was dead wrong, that he didn't give a flying fuck about Thea's money or his lack thereof, but he knew it would be a lie. As always, Austin had called it true.

He *did* care.

It bothered him more than he wanted to admit that should he take the chance and pursue this...this whatever it was with Thea, the end result would be either him grudgingly using Thea's fortune to let them live in the manner she was used to or Thea grudgingly living on his salary and learning to deal with his more modest lifestyle. Either way, someone wasn't going to be happy, and he'd already seen firsthand how arguments over money could destroy a marriage before it even got started.

Once again, Austin seemed to read his mind.

"Don't go comparing you and Thea to what happened with Donny and the bitch-whose-name-won't-be-spoken," Austin warned. No one mentioned their ex-sister-in-law's name, even out of their brother's hearing. She'd caused so much grief and pain in the seven years they'd been together that Donny still refused to trust another woman in his life even thirteen years after she'd finally walked out, taking their daughter with her. Every member of the Doyle clan would rather chew glass and drink vinegar before uttering her name.

"She was a money-grubbing lazy bitch who thought she caught a free ride when she got pregnant, who spent every cent Donny made a week before he made it and then complained that there wasn't more," Austin continued. "I don't see a single similarity, and if you say that there is, I just might have to get on a plane and come out there to knock some of the stupid out of you."

Doyle didn't doubt that his brother meant his threat. "No, I'm not saying that. It's just…" He sighed, rubbing the back of his neck wearily. "What if we get together and I can't make her happy?"

"And what if you get together and you do?" Austin countered. He made an exasperated sound. "Look, didn't you tell me that she was looking for a job? Decorating houses or something, wasn't it?"

"Interior design," he acknowledged, even as the hard knot in his chest tightened at the reminder of Thea's earlier announcement about the job offer. The fact that the firm she'd interned with wanted her back wasn't a surprise; he'd seen the pictures of the jobs she'd done for them. What *had* surprised him was the fact that she was actually considering the offer. And the casual way she'd dropped that bombshell on him just now…it had nearly rocked him off his size twelve feet. It had also unnerved him enough that he'd finally broken down and called his brother for advice.

"She any good at it?"

"Very." And that wasn't just loyalty talking. Thea had not only done over most of the rooms in the main house over the past few years, she'd also put her hand to his own bungalow as well. He ran a hand over the soft, brown corduroy of the sofa, remembering the reluctance with which he'd dragged his feet when she'd first suggested the makeover, and the bullheaded stubbornness with which Thea had countered until she'd finally gotten her way. Doyle didn't know much about decorating, but he did know that she'd managed to turn a temporary living space into a real, comfortable home.

"Sounds to me then that she plans to earn her own paycheck rather than live on daddy's money for the rest of her life."

Doyle frowned, thinking that over. "Yeah, I guess so," he finally conceded. Now that he thought about it, Thea had also mentioned finding an apartment once she'd finally gotten that elusive job. Still, that didn't mean she wouldn't use some of her trust fund money to supplement her salary to get a nicer place, something more upscale than a single bedroom shoebox with a view of the alleyway. Surely she couldn't expect to live entirely on her paycheck, especially at first. Could she?

"And what about you?" Austin plowed on.

"What about me what?"

"When are you going to get off your ass and get your business up and running?" his brother demanded.

Doyle winced when he considered the loan papers still gathering dust in his desk drawer. "I'm still nailing down a few details," he hedged.

"You've been 'nailing down a few details' for the past year."

"I'll get to it," Doyle snapped. "Right now, I've got more important things to do." Like keep Thea safe.

Austin was immediately contrite. "Sorry, man, I know there's a lot of shit going on right now that you need to worry about." He knew about the problem with the stalker in only the vaguest of details, but he knew his brother well enough to understand that any threat to someone under his care would be taken deadly seriously and assume primary importance.

He wasn't, however, willing to give up his point.

"But you had everything figured out and ready to rock and roll a year ago," he continued, ignoring Doyle's disgusted groan. "This other stuff is only a few months old. So, you have to ask yourself, what kept you from following through back then?"

The very question he'd asked himself any number of times when he'd gotten a call from the business officer at the bank who'd preapproved him all those months ago based on his business plan, asking if he was going to be filing his loan package soon, or when the real estate agent he'd asked to keep an eye out for decent properties in the price range he figured he could handle called with a new listing.

He gave his brother the only answer he'd had to give either of them, as well as himself. "The time just wasn't right."

Austin snorted. "You're either blind or so deep in denial you're going to start shitting pyramids. What wasn't right was the fact that Thea was away at college, and if you left to start your own company while she was, you wouldn't get to see her when she finally came back for good."

Denial rose to Doyle's lips, but he paused, considering his brother's words. Had he subconsciously been subverting his business plans in order to have access to Thea? No. Impossible. He hadn't thought about her in terms of anything other than his employer's young daughter until just recently.

Or had he? Memories of a dark night and a very naked Thea flashed through his head. He hadn't been able to see anything under the midnight water, but he'd imagined it and it had been enough to torment him for weeks afterward. They'd both acted as though the skinny-dipping incident never happened the next time they'd seen each other. But had his own subconscious hung onto that image, that instant of desire, and filed it away under unfinished business?

He just didn't know.

Austin wasn't done hammering away at his point just yet. "Have you considered that if you were running your own security firm, you wouldn't have to worry about whose money you were living on because you'd both be earning paychecks that didn't have the name Fordham anywhere on it?"

No, he hadn't. The idea held some appeal. A lot, in fact. Granted, he wouldn't be drawing much money from a newly formed business at first, but security paid extremely well and he'd nurtured a great many contacts over the past few years that would let him assemble a client list that consisted of some very heavy hitters. He wouldn't be rich, but he wouldn't exactly be making minimum wage, either.

And then he remembered Thea's bombshell.

"She got a job offer." His voice was flat and monotone, betraying none of the turmoil the words caused. "In California."

"Did she take it?"

"Not yet. But she's thinking about it." And somehow, that felt like a betrayal, even though he couldn't logically explain why that might be.

"So...?"

"So?" He really hated when his brother got that 'take the slow child by the hand so he doesn't get lost' tone.

"So make her think about why she should say no."

"It's a good job," Doyle forced himself to admit. "Maybe she should say yes."

"Then maybe you need to think about whether you're willing to drag your ass to California with her to start up your business out there. You know that would really chafe Mom's butt," he couldn't help but add in that cheerful way only siblings could when someone else was the focus of their mother's ire. "She already hates that you moved more than halfway across the country."

"Thanks for the reminder," Doyle replied, but his brain was spinning around the idea his brother had lobbed out there like a hand grenade. He *could* open his business pretty much anywhere. California had more than its fair share of rich and famous that required constant security. But that would mean committing to something he wasn't sure he could—or even wanted to— commit to. Everything was still too crazy and surreal when it came to Thea.

"Look," Austin said finally into the silence, clearly picking up on his brother's reluctance, "stop getting ahead of yourself. Just start at the beginning and let the end take care of itself. Ask the girl out. She wants you to. *You* want to. So just do it. See where it leads. Maybe you get together. Maybe you don't. What's the worst that could happen?" The unmistakable wail of a child echoed over the line, causing Austin to heave a martyred sigh that didn't fool Doyle for one second. His brother loved his kid to pieces.

"Looks like my peace and quiet is over for the afternoon." The wailing got louder, indicating Austin was walking toward his daughter's room. "I swear, one day this kid is going to break the sound barrier." He sounded more proud than aggrieved at that pronouncement.

"I'll let you go." He knew Austin would need both hands for diaper duty. His niece was thirty pounds of unrepentant trouble, who'd managed on more than one occasion to elude both her parents while in the middle of a diaper change, but most often her father, who tended to underestimate the mischievous spawn of his loins.

The last time she'd made it all the way to the living room before being corralled, but not before mooning old lady Tevstock and her visiting sister the Sister across the street through the full-view glass door his sister-in-law had been so proud to have installed just the week before. Sister Mary Alice had told his brother that she'd pray for them.

The way the little demon seed was going, Doyle was pretty sure they'd need it. "Give Chelsea and Becca kisses for me."

After pocketing his cell, Doyle wandered aimlessly through his small but comfortable bungalow. He tried to picture Thea living there, sharing his space, sharing his bed…God! He dragged a hand down his face. He had to stop thinking about the sex part of this equation.

The worst part was he *could* see it, all of it. And he liked it. A lot.

Was he so wrong to worry about the disparity in their social standings? Austin had made a good point, one Doyle had avoided admitting to on his own. Thea wasn't a snob or a diva or a Paris Hilton clone who lived for the next party or fashion show or tabloid headline. She hadn't been born to money, so she had a healthy respect of "real" life at her core. So why did he expect her to balk at his desire not to live on any more of her father's money than what came in his paycheck?

Pride.

Small word. Nasty aftertaste. And, if he was completely honest with himself, the root of his current dilemma. He'd worked hard all his life, first in the Corps and then at his security job, working up from newbie staff member to head of the entire detail, all on his own merit. He'd known when he'd come to work for the Fordhams that it was temporary, that he was still trying to decide what he wanted to do with his life after having his plans for a career in the Marines literally blown out from under him by a roadside bomb.

The wound had been minor, but his mother had nearly lost her mind to the fear that the next one wouldn't be and had dragged a promise from him to not re-up when his contract expired. Red Fields had contacted him shortly after getting out about giving security work a try, and Doyle had decided it would do as an interim job while he considered his options, although he would have been lying if he said that the fact it was a few thousand miles away from his mother's smothering love and care hadn't been the biggest attraction at the time.

After a year, he'd known he'd found something he enjoyed enough to make a career of. Always driven and just a little anal about control, he'd started making plans to one day open up his own business. The promotion to head of security had sped up his timetable considerably. He could have gone ahead any time in the past year after he'd been preapproved for a more than adequate business loan to cover start-ups and scoped out enough talent to put together a more than decent team.

As Austin had pointed out, though, for some reason—and he wasn't willing to admit that reason had anything to do with Thea—he'd never found quite the right time to actually get the ball rolling.

Once he did, though, money would be tight, regardless of the wealth of his clients. All new businesses operated in the red for at least the first year, if not longer. He'd have to find a place to live, too. His draw from the business would probably end up being less than he currently was making once he factored in living expenses that were now part of his more than generous salary package, so that would mean a one-bedroom or even a studio. Even if Thea found a job with a decent salary, he couldn't expect her to carry the brunt of the household expenses. He'd have to...

Whoa! He took a huge mental leap backward. Austin was right again. He was getting *way* ahead of himself here. He hadn't even kissed Thea. Why was he worrying about marriage?

Because deep in his mind lurked the specter of his brother Donny's miserable face whenever he talked about all he'd given up to marry his high school sweetie when she'd suddenly turned up pregnant the week before graduation despite swearing up and down she had been on the Pill.

Gone was the football scholarship. Gone was the opportunity to move on to the pros, which had been Donny's lifelong dream, one he'd worked damn hard for until Holly-the-Bitch had slapped a ball and chain around his leg and anchored him to Boston. Gone was the happy, carefree brother who'd always been the upbeat optimist in the family.

Slowly, day by day, month by month, Doyle had watched the smile fade to a bitter scowl, the jokes turn to vicious barbs, and his brother disappear inside a cold, angry shell that not even his family could penetrate.

Pride had been his brother's downfall as well. He hadn't told anybody his reasons for the sudden marriage when he should have been planning to head off to LSU. Hadn't asked for help when the bills became an overwhelming burden and he was forced to drop out of community college and take a second job. Hadn't leaned on any of his brothers—or his sisters, for that matter—when his marriage had started to implode, taking his already shaky relationship with his daughter, Meagan, into the shitter as well thanks to Holly's venomous influence. His pride had made him stand alone for all those years. And he was still standing alone.

*Pride was a damned fool thing,* Doyle realized with painful clarity. And he'd be a damned fool as well if he let his get in the way of finding out if there was something to this attraction between Thea and himself.

He was heading for the door to corner the object of his sudden revelation and apologize for being such an idiot when his cell phone rang.

"Doyle," he answered impatiently and then listened to Red Fields speak the only words that could have deterred him from his chosen course.

"We got another letter."

# CHAPTER 14

"**THAT DRESS REALLY** is perfect for you."

"Mm-hmm." Thea stared absently into the fitting room mirror, not seeing anything of the elegant sapphire blue sheath she was wearing. All she could concentrate on was the shattered shell of her hopes and dreams. It was all she had thought about, all she *could* think about for the past three days.

"Céline was right when she said the color would make your eyes look like 'fathomless pools a man could drown in,'" Lillian drawled in a fair imitation of the boutique owner's over-affected Parisian accent.

"Mm-hmm." Thea had taken a chance on Doyle and she'd lost. Big time. *Really* big time. So big that there felt like a huge crater had been dug into her chest and hollowed everything out that used to belong there. A dinosaur-extinction sized crater. Which was actually pretty fitting, since life as she knew it had ceased to exist.

"But the outfit won't really come together until we glue the big horn onto the middle of your forehead and hang you from the ceiling of the reception hall like a piñata."

"Mm-hmm." She needed to stop putting off sending her reply to accept the job offer from Madison Helmsworth at Matrix. Moving to California would be hard, but it might be the first step to starting the healing process. Maybe when she got home she should...

Lillian's words finally penetrated the fog that had surrounded her brain for the past seventy-two or so hours.

"What?" Thea looked into the mirror at her friend, who was standing a few feet behind her with a half-pitying, half-exasperated look on her face. It was the pity that hurt the most.

"Sweetie, I'm sorry things didn't work out the way—"

Thea threw a hand up to forestall the rest. "I knew it was a risk. I'm a big girl. I can handle it." The look Lillian gave her in the mirror said they both knew she lied. Thea tried again. "It hurts to know I gave it my best and still didn't walk away with the prize, but I'll live." Alone. Without Doyle. Without the beautiful little babies with black hair and long-lashed hazel eyes she'd started to dream about holding. Another spasm of grief tightened her chest as she realized her loss anew.

An arm slipped around her shoulders, and Thea leaned her head against her friend's with a sigh, accepting the hug but fighting the tears. She wasn't a pretty crier. If she let loose now, she'd be facing Céline and her assistants with red, puffy eyes and blotchy skin. Not her best look.

Thea had spent half the previous day with a cold washcloth on her face trying to undo the damage of the crying jag she'd indulged in after getting off the phone with her mother. As much as she'd wanted to unburden herself to the one person in the world she knew would be on her side and give her unquestioning support no matter what, Thea had bitten back the words that had trembled at the tip of her tongue, begging for escape.

Instead, she'd listened with honest awe to her mother's descriptions of the Great Wall and the Forbidden City, the highlights of the third leg of their four-destination world tour. Their final stop was a restful week in Fiji, with them making it back home with just two days to spare before Amelia's engagement party.

Her mother had sounded so happy, so re-energized, so *healthy*. After everything she'd been through, both medically and emotionally, there was just no way Thea could spoil that sense of contentment for her. The problem with Doyle was hers, and she'd find a way to deal with it.

Eventually.

Just as she had then, Thea pushed her hurt away to its own private corner to be picked at later. She bumped her head against Lillian's again in a thank-you-but-I'm-okay-now gesture and blinked the silly moisture—they were *not* tears—from her eyes. Straightening, she looked purposefully into the mirror.

"So, think we'll blow the socks off those stuffy politicians or what?" She grinned and then did a double-take as she noticed for the first time the image bouncing into the mirror from the ones behind them. Lillian's classically cut Versace might be as demure as her own in front, but there was a whole lot less of the back than Thea remembered.

In fact, there *was* no back, at least none to speak of. The opening in the deep fuchsia silk that had once been screened by lace now dipped in a wide, open V that ventured far enough down so as to hint at the beginnings of the separation at the upper curves of Lillian's butt cheeks.

Thea couldn't help it. She gaped.

Noticing her reaction, Lillian grinned. "Like it? I had Céline do a few last-minute alterations."

Thea choked on a laugh. "Holy hell, Lil, Mrs. Westlake is going to shit flying monkeys!"

The grin turned evil. "Good. Serves the old witch right for badgering Mellie into picking bridesmaids dresses that make me look like Stumpy the No-Legged Pumpkin."

Wincing in sympathy, because the poofy cut of the melon-colored dresses really had been the worst choice possible for Lillian's petite stature, not to mention that the color turned Thea's own healthy bronzed complexion a rather sickly sallow color (both facts she was pretty sure had been a deciding factor in the final choice), Thea said, "Somehow I don't think that anybody who sees you in this will even care what you look like in the other one."

Not that it really mattered to Lillian. Thea knew she was merely using the outrageous dress as a way to focus the dragon's spite onto herself rather than let it rain all over poor Mellie, as usual. They wanted to give her a chance to enjoy her engagement party, despite her mother's best efforts, conscious or not, to ensure otherwise.

With that in mind, Thea mirrored Lillian's evil grin and did a slow turn for her friend's benefit. The soft sapphire silk of her gown flowed over her body like a caressing hand. Except where it parted company from her body altogether along the deep side slits that rode her long legs almost all the way to their tops. The alteration was unnoticeable while she was standing still. But when she moved, there was a whole lot of leg action going on. Thea was rewarded for her like-minded thinking by a whoop of surprised delight.

Throwing a conspiratorial arm around Thea's waist, Lillian gave a decisive nod at their reflection. "Definitely flying monkeys." And for the first time that day, Thea felt the pain threatening to strangle her loosen just a little bit.

\* \* \*

"He's not our man."

Frozen in the act of pouring his fourth—or maybe tenth—cup of coffee, Doyle took a long second to digest the words he had not wanted to hear. Slowly, he turned his chair back to face his desk. Red Fields stood in his open doorway, file in hand, and looking none too pleased with his own pronouncement.

"Hastings fits the profile," Doyle protested, even though he knew Red was as familiar with that fact as he was. "His lack of personal relationships, his solitary work, a higher than average intelligence, his extensive travel…"

"The travel is actually the part that gets him off." Red stepped forward and dropped the folder on Doyle's desk. "Rick verified Hastings's work itinerary against credit card records and hotel, airline, and rental car reservations. Not one of the cities Hastings was in matches up to where the letters were postmarked from, not on the dates they were mailed or within a month prior."

"He could have made a side trip to mail them, a layover or a car ride or something."

Red was already shaking his head. "Rick tracked all the layovers, and none matched. As for taking a drive to a postmark city, the cities Hastings was in on and around those dates were far enough away to make it practically impossible for him to have made it there and back in less than a day, and the records reflected no unexplained absences from his scheduled meetings."

"Damn it!" Doyle slammed his mug down, causing the hot coffee to slosh over the brim, scalding his hand. With an aggravated hiss of pain, he shoved the injured web between thumb and forefinger into his mouth to soothe the burn. Red wordlessly vanished and reappeared with a stack of paper towels, which Doyle took with an ungracious nod of thanks.

He spent the next few moments cleaning up his mess, all the while spinning this new information around in his mind. It had to be Hastings. It had to be! He had shown up in Boulder right around the time the gifts had started to accompany the letters. He had "bumped into" Thea at not one but two different locations and been invited along to a third because of it. Thea had made plans to go to dinner with the man—an actual date, damn it!—before Doyle had intervened. He was working his way closer to her, ingratiating himself, plotting for the ultimate moment when he'd have the chance he wanted to get her alone and—

He pushed the rest of that thought far away. The last thing he wanted whirling around in his head was a picture of what that sick bastard had described in his last letter as "their coming ultimate union." In detail. Details so graphic and depraved that even a hardened ex-SEAL like Red had paled when he'd read it.

"The letter mentioned talking to her. Touching her, damn it!" Doyle threw the wadded up paper towels into the trash with enough force to rock the can sideways before it finally settled back on its base. That was what had really sent him over the edge when he'd read it. *When you smiled so invitingly at me, and your soft hand touched mine in that secret caress, I knew the pleasures you were offering, the pleasures I will take. And I can't help but wonder as I think of you every night as I lay in bed, is your skin that amazingly soft all over? I'll know the answer soon, my love. Soon.*

"It was an admission that there had been actual contact," Doyle ground out, struggling to suppress the rage those words provoked. "It came within days of her meeting Hastings for the first time. That's too much of a coincidence for me to swallow."

"Just because the writer claimed contact doesn't mean it actually happened anyplace but in his own mind," Red pointed out. "You know the psych profile for intimacy-seeking stalkers says they can imagine an entire relationship out of nothing more than passing someone on the street. Or even if they did actually encounter each other, it could have been as simple as Thea paying and getting change from a cashier at the coffeehouse, or the ticket taker at the movies, or her keys from a valet, or…"

"I get the point." Doyle dropped his large frame into his chair on a frustrated sigh. "It could be anyone, anywhere that she's had casual contact with or someone she hasn't even been within a hundred yards of. Which leaves us exactly nowhere."

"The postmark was local, so we at least know he's here in Boulder."

Somewhere Hastings wasn't any longer. "That does nothing to make me feel any better."

Red leaned his hip against the side of the desk and crossed his arms. "Look, I know you don't want to hear this…"

Doyle barely resisted the urge to say "then don't say it," even though he had a pretty good idea what his second-in-command was going to say. And no, he didn't want to hear it. But maybe, just maybe, it was time to start following his gut instead of his orders.

"*If* this guy has somehow gotten close and *if* he's in a position to get close again, the best way to protect Thea is to let her know exactly what it is she needs to be protected from. Otherwise, she might miss something important, something that might warn her that she's in danger." Red shifted roughly in the hard wooden chair, clearly agitated by the restraints imposed by their employer. "Despite what her father thinks, she's a big girl. She can handle the truth without freaking out."

Breath hissed from between Doyle's lips. "I know she can. But Mr. Fordham refused to reconsider his orders when I talked to him." After the last letter had arrived and left his entire staff in want of a shower after reading its graphic rape fantasies, Doyle had been certain he'd be able to convince Frank to change his mind, given the new urgency of the local postmark.

No such luck. The term "control freak" had been invented for people like Francis T. Fordham. He'd insisted nothing be done until he was back home himself to take care of it.

"But he did give you permission before he left to confine her to the estate if it came down to a matter of her safety," Red reminded him.

Yeah, he had. And wouldn't that just go over wonderfully with Thea when he couldn't even explain to her exactly *why* he was essentially putting her under house arrest for the next five days. Not that it would stop him from doing it if he felt her safety was no longer guaranteed by her security detail, but that was a nightmare best saved for a last resort.

Once he played that card, he'd never get an ounce of cooperation out of Thea again. The stalker was too close, Thea was in danger, and they had jack shit to go on. All in all, he wasn't feeling very good about their chances of avoiding a total clusterfuck before the whole thing was over.

"It's an option if we need it," was all he said. What went unsaid, but both men understood, was that even if they locked Thea up snug and tight, their problem didn't go away. The stalker wouldn't just pack up his pen and paper and go home. Well, he might, but he'd be back. He was fixated. Unless he found someone or something else to hang his psychotic attachment onto—not that Doyle wished that particular joy on anyone—he would continue to see Thea as the object of his lust and the only one with whom he could, in his own rambling words, "find his future permanent happiness."

No, the problem wasn't going to go away. Which meant they had to catch the sick prick, because until they did, Thea was a target just by breathing, no matter where she was, safely inside the estate walls or not.

"Have we heard anything back from the Feebs?" Doyle asked.

They'd finally brought the FBI into the mix after the presents had started arriving. The multistate postmarks together with the personal delivery of the candy had allowed them to put forth the probability that the stalker had crossed state lines in his pursuit of his obsession. That had made it a federal crime, and that had allowed Frank Fordham to tug a few strings and get the Feds involved.

As much as Doyle had disliked losing control of the situation, he was smart enough to know that it had reached a point where his security staff, as competent and diversely talented as they were, would be more effective in dealing with the threat if they had some official help. They were set up to protect, not investigate.

That didn't mean that he wasn't going to keep his fingers in the mix, however.

"Still no match on that partial print from the box of chocolates from AFIS." They both knew the odds were against there being one. As extensive as the FBI's Automated Fingerprint Identification System was, it could only match against the prints it had on file. If they were lucky, their freak had a record.

Doyle hadn't been feeling very lucky lately.

"What about the chocolates themselves?"

"Not tampered with." There was the same hint of relief in Red's voice as Doyle felt when he heard them. At least Thea's stalker wasn't trying to poison or drug her. Yet. Still, it relieved a small knot of tension about the consequences if one of the "gifts" managed to get through to her before they could intercept it.

*Another good reason to tell Thea about what was going on,* the reasonable part of him urged.

And yet…he couldn't do it. Frank hadn't said the words, but it had been very clear after their last conversation that if Doyle went against his orders, he'd be out of a job the same day the Fordhams returned from their trip. Doyle couldn't let that happen. The only way he could ensure Thea's safety was if he was there for her.

To be there for her, he had to keep his job.

To keep his job, he had to continue lying to her.

Therefore, he would continue to lie to her, no matter how much he hated it.

He might have totally screwed up in every other way with her, most recently with his infamous "I value your friendship" speech—which, he admitted reluctantly, he had dragged his feet about following up on and apologizing for, *again*—but in keeping Thea safe, he wouldn't fail.

He couldn't.

Which still left him with one huge problem. If their letter writer wasn't Nick Hastings, then who the hell was it?

\* \* \*

"Mmmm." Like a cat with its cream, Lillian closed her eyes in pleasure as she licked the thick whipped topping from the rim of her hazelnut mocha latte. "If it could bring home a paycheck and pick up its own socks, I'd marry it."

Thea, used to her friend's communion ritual with her twin vices of chocolate and caffeine, simply smiled and took a mechanical sip of her own triple-shot cappuccino, willing the caffeine to kick in. She was starting to drag, and it was barely two o'clock. A week of little to no sleep would do that. The worst of the dark circles had been dealt with thanks to a little help from some judiciously applied concealer, but her body was beginning to show her in other ways that it was starting to run on empty.

Doyle didn't want her. Fine. She'd always known that, somewhere deep down where all her insecurities squirmed and hid, even when she'd been swimming deep in denial and hoping for her fairy-tale ending: the prince sweeps the princess into his strong arms, declares his never-ending love, and they ride off into the sunset, together forever.

She snorted to herself and took another sip. Some princess she was. Any princess worth her salt could get her prince to go to one knee and declare his eternal devotion. What did she get? An avowal of undying friendship.

Friends.

Right.

Perfect.

Sometimes life really sucked.

Her phone vibrated on the table, indicating a new text message. She checked the sender, and then deleted it without reading it. Seth again. Somehow he'd gotten her phone number, and for the past two days he'd been sending messages that she had absolutely no interest in returning. Hopefully, he'd eventually take the hint and go away. If not, she might just have to change her phone number. Again.

"I still think we should just cancel for tonight," Thea said, taking another pull on her cappuccino, willing the caffeine to kick in.

"No," Lillian protested. "Just because Mellie can't make it doesn't mean we can't still have a fun night out."

They had made plans to take Amelia out to Club Platinum as a sort of pre-engagement-party party, but she had called and begged off just a little while ago. Charles, along with his father and the rest of their entourage, had unexpectedly made another fly-by visit to Boulder and he had evidently asked her to go out to dinner with him. Just the two of them. Amelia had sounded so enthused by the prospect of actually being alone in the same room with her fiancé without at least two parents and a campaign manager in attendance that Thea hadn't even given her a good teasing over bailing on her own party. Amelia so rarely sounded enthused about anything to do with her wedding these days; Thea hadn't had the heart.

"I'm not sure I'm really in the mood," Thea said.

"Oh, come on, it'll be good for you." Putting down her drink, Lillian tapped her phone with one finger. "I can call up Carlos and Miguel and see if they're free."

The dark-haired twins from Blaze. Thea knew that Lillian had started seeing one of them, not that she could remember which one. She was almost tempted to say yes, simply because she was getting sick of her own company, and another Saturday night spend moping around her bedroom sounded like even less fun than going out with people she barely knew and pretending to have a good time.

Before she could answer, though, Lillian said, "Hey, isn't that Nick over there at the counter?"

Surprised, Thea looked up and connected with Nick Hastings's emerald gaze as he swung away from the condiment bar with his doctored coffee in one hand and a gigantic cinnamon bun in the other. He looked a bit off balance at finding both of them staring right at him, but a pleased smile quickly overtook his face and he started walking their way.

A smile tugged at Thea's lips in response. Yeah, sometimes life sucked. But sometimes, if you were really lucky, it took pity on you anyway.

# CHAPTER 15

**CLUB PLATINUM WAS PACKED.**

Currently the premiere hotspot on the Denver clubbing circuit, the eclectic mix of tasteful elegance and flamboyant trash had become not just a huge tourist draw, but the destination of many locals as well. The door charge was higher on weekends, but the show inside was worth the price.

And only part of it was on the stage.

As Thea and Lillian led a somewhat wide-eyed Nick through the crowd, Thea couldn't seem to keep from second-guessing the decision to have him come along with them tonight. Called back to town for more meetings and left at loose ends until Monday again, Nick had been totally onboard with the last-minute invitation, even offering to pay for the evening out of appreciation for their company, an offer which Thea had quickly but politely declined. Letting him pay would have made it feel too much like a date.

There had been one tricky moment when she had remembered her promise to Doyle concerning Nick and had to excuse herself to make a quick cell phone call from the ladies' room, but where she'd expected and planned for Doyle's earlier resistance, what she'd gotten instead was a quick agreement.

Granted, Doyle had seemed a bit distracted and harried, like he was impatient to get back to something she'd interrupted, but still! He'd sounded more than happy enough to okay the outing. He'd even told her to have fun.

With. Another. Man.

If she'd needed a final nail in the coffin on her doubts about how Doyle felt about her—or, rather, *didn't* feel about her—there it was. And it hurt. A lot.

She'd gone back to the table where Nick and Lillian had been involved in a surprisingly heated discussion about the practicality of hybrid cars, of all things, and managed to smile and even participate in the conversation for almost ten minutes before suddenly "remembering" a promise to Rosa to stop at a specialty store while she was in town and pick up a few things for her Sunday baking. Since Lillian was in love with just about anything that came out of Rosa's kitchen, she'd practically shoved Thea out the door, but not before making plans to pick up both her and Nick for their club outing.

So here she was.

On a date.

With Nick.

Okay, it wasn't really a date, considering Lillian made them a threesome. And that Lillian had been the one to ask Nick along in the first place. And it was Lillian who was driving. But it was Thea's hand that Nick had a hold of as they plowed through the crowded club, and it felt...nice. Comfortable. Safe. Almost...brotherly.

Thea groaned to herself. That was exactly how it felt. Like she was holding hands with one of Lillian's brothers. Platonic. Uninspiring. Sexless.

Damn it.

She was pulled from that depressing line of thought when Nick eased closer to her and whispered—or rather, practically shouted so as to be heard over the noise—in her ear, "What kind of show did you say we were going to see here?"

Despite her inner turmoil, Thea couldn't help but smile. They'd kept Nick in the dark about just what the entertainment for the evening at Platinum was going to be. It was always fun to see how long it took for the uninitiated to catch on. Although she did feel a twinge of apprehension since they really didn't know Nick well enough to be sure how he'd react, Thea just grinned and whisper-shouted back, "It's really hard to explain. But you'll love it. The performers here are all amazingly talented." And they were. It was that dedication to quality that kept Platinum at the top of everyone's "must" list.

Lillian, who had been forging their way through the tightly packed sea of bodies like a miniature ice-breaker cutting through the North Atlantic, suddenly came to a stop and gave someone a hug. When she pulled back, Thea saw that it was Desmond. Only he was in full Desdemona Darling regalia, which meant that they'd gotten lucky and he, or rather, *she* was going to be performing that night. Since buying into ownership of the club, Des's onstage time had been seriously scaled back in favor of more managerial duties.

Careful of the artfully applied stage makeup, Thea hugged their friend as soon as Lillian had moved out of the way. Des returned the embrace with equal care and then smiled down at Thea from atop three-inch heels that had her topping out over six feet and asked, "Who's your new friend, and whatever happened to the delish Doyle?"

Choosing to stick with the first half of the question, Thea took a step back and made room for Nick to move up to her side. "This is Nick Hastings. Nick, this is Des." And left the introductions at that. Des could decide what to let Nick know or guess. It was impossible to see anything left of Desmond. In costume and makeup, there was only Desdemona, and as strange as it sometimes was for Thea to admit it, Des was gorgeous.

Des's dark, Mediterranean eyes were shadowed and sultry, those Val Kilmer lips becoming more Angelina Jolie under their glossy coating. A wig covered Des's short-cropped hair, so natural looking even a touch wouldn't give it away. And as for the breasts...Well, there were some things about Des's transformation Thea didn't care to think about too closely because at the moment Des had more cleavage than she did.

Extending a perfectly manicured hand, Des beamed a wide—and if Thea wasn't mistaken, interested—smile at Nick. "How nice to meet you, Nick. Very, very nice."

Somewhat tentatively, Nick accepted the extended hand. Evidently he'd noticed the gleam in Des's eyes as well. "Nice to meet you as well." He smiled, retrieved his hand, and dropped his arm quickly around Thea's waist. He couldn't have been any clearer if he'd hung a "not available" sign around his neck.

Des, being Des, ignored the gesture and gave him a slow, face-to-foot perusal, lingering in a few places long enough to make Nick squirm.

"Not on your team, Des," Lillian murmured, although she looked more amused at Nick's discomfort than sympathetic.

"You never heard of switch-hitters?" Gaze finally back on neutral territory, Des sighed and ran a fingertip over the corners of her mouth, ostensibly to wipe any lipstick smudge, but in reality a gesture that meant she found Nick drool-worthy. Thea fought back a grin. She really needed more gay friends so Des could stop striking out with her straight ones.

"The place is really packed tonight," Thea said, hoping to divert the current conversation into safer waters. "I hope we can find a table."

Des arched a perfectly plucked brow that said without words that *of course* it was packed, and, *of course,* there were no tables to be had. This was Platinum, after all. Then she surprised Thea by saying, "You have a table reserved stage side. Follow me." With a swish of skirts, she turned on her stilettos and started shooing people out of her path with a mere flick of her hands. Miraculously, they parted like water around a very determined rock, making the rest of the trip much easier than their struggle from the front door had been.

Once they made it to their table, Thea saw that Des hadn't lied. They were tucked right up against the runway that jutted out from the stage onto what was a dance floor on other nights. Plucking the reserved sign from the red and gold tablecloth, Des pulled out the seat that gave the very best view of the stage and smiled invitingly at Nick, who hesitated briefly before taking it. Whether it was because a woman had held a chair for him or because he'd been seated before Thea and Lillian or if it was because of the avaricious gleam in Des's eyes, Thea wasn't sure, but when she saw Des's hands slide from the chair back to Nick's shoulders, she decided the game had gone on long enough.

"Stop teasing, Des," she scolded. Des gave her a pouty smirk but backed off.

"First drink's on the house. Enjoy the show, kiddies." With a wink for Nick and a questioning glance for Thea, Des retreated back the way they'd come, the crowd once again parting like magic before her. Once she was out of sight, Nick visibly relaxed.

"Sorry about that," Thea said, feeling bad that Des had gotten such a kick out of making Nick squirm. "Des can be..." she trailed off, at a loss. Des could be so many things.

"A pushy bitch," Lillian supplied and then grinned impishly when Thea shot her a sour look. "Tell me I'm wrong."

"It's okay, really," Nick reassured them. Although Thea noticed he did glance over his shoulder as if to reassure himself that Des hadn't doubled back. "I guess I've been a little out of touch. I don't seem to remember women being quite so...ah...," he cleared his throat uncomfortably, "...up front about what they want. I wasn't ready for it."

"Nobody's ever quite ready for Des," Lillian quipped.

"Ain't that the truth." But Thea worried exactly how Nick was going to react when he realized that the woman who'd been so up front about her appraisal of his...up front was really a man. Would he be amazed at the seamless illusion Des managed? Offended? Another horrible possibility dawned on Thea. Would he think they'd set him up? That they were laughing at him, at his discomfort, watching Des drool over him like a hungry wolf?

She cringed at the thought. Nick might not inspire anything more than a mild like in her heart, but she'd already come to think of him as a friend in the making and she definitely didn't want him to think their evening out was some nasty joke at his expense.

More than ever she wished she'd just stayed home and sulked in her bedroom like she'd originally planned.

As a waitress materialized and took their drink orders, Thea took a quick look around. Her shadows had found a space along the wall. Thea gave a small smile in answer to Daryl's nod of acknowledgement. Francine would be somewhere at his side, although her less than statuesque build kept her hidden by the crowd. That had been Doyle's one condition to her outing. Two guards, one female, so she'd have both an inside and outside guard when she made a trip to the ladies' room.

That had rankled. Perhaps, under normal circumstances, she would have even argued, in part because it was fun to spar with Doyle and see how far she could push him, even knowing she'd lose in the end. But now...now, she'd just accepted the bodyguards without a whimper because she simply didn't care anymore. Let the whole damn security detail follow her into the toilet. What did it matter? What did anything matter anymore?

With a determined smile, Thea turned her attention back to Lillian and Nick and away from her maudlin pity party. It was Saturday night, she was out with her friends, and she was going to have a good time, even if it killed her. So what if Doyle didn't want her? So what if he'd crushed all her girlish fantasies and womanly dreams? She'd survive.

It might take a few dozen boxes of hand-crafted chocolates from Recchiuti's and a couple hundred gallons of Häagen-Dazs Rocky Road to do it, but she'd get over him and move on. Eventually. Even the almighty Doyle wasn't worth wallowing over for the rest of her life. In the end, she'd get over him.

But oh, the pain until she got there was excruciating.

When the lights finally dimmed for the first act of the night, Thea had already inhaled one piña colada, and her second was quickly going the way of the first. Nick was still nursing his beer, and Lillian had a pitcher of iced tea to serve herself from, her usual drink of choice when she was driving. Having no such constraints, Thea took another healthy swallow, drawing so hard on the straw that it clogged with the half-frozen liquid.

"You're going to give yourself brain freeze," Nick said, leaning in close to whisper, this time not because of the noise, but because of the quiet that had started to settle over the room.

Even as he said the words, she felt the intense agony slice through her forehead.

"Too late," she groaned, massaging the spot between her eyes that had borne the brunt of the cold-induced pain, eyes squeezed tight as she rode out the wave. A few long seconds later the pain began to ease, and she cautiously opened her eyes in a squint, thankful for the dim lighting that hid the mortified rush of embarrassment heating her cheeks.

The blush only increased when she noticed that her drink had mysteriously vanished and been replaced by a glass of Lillian's iced tea. Knowing she'd been silently chastised, and rightfully so, she accepted the new drink without complaint.

As they all turned their attention to watch the performer that had sashayed out onto the stage and started to sing, Thea cursed herself roundly. Getting drunk wouldn't change anything. Come morning, the only difference would be that instead of being alone with her misery, she'd have the company of a wicked hangover to deal with. She knew that much from sad experience. Too much beer at her pity party after the Dave Disaster in college had been an excellent teacher. She'd done a lot of thinking after she'd finished praying to the porcelain god and crawled to bed, and she'd decided that no man would ever be worth going through that again.

So why had she been sucking down the coladas like they were chocolate milk?

Simple. This wasn't about just any man. This was about Doyle.

*Simple?* No, nothing about this mess with Doyle was simple. In fact, it was as complicated and confusing as hell.

Her budding buzz evaporated, leaving her with a suffocating sense of hopelessness. Mortified to feel the press of tears at the back of her eyes, she hastily excused herself and wended her way to the ladies' room at the back of the club.

As rude as it was to leave in the middle of the show, it meant the bathroom was empty. Knowing she would have only a minute, maybe less, before losing any chance at privacy, Thea wet a paper towel and pressed it first to her eyes and then her cheeks, which were flushed with a combination of alcohol and jagged emotion. Then finally she lifted her hair and draped the cool towel across the back of her neck.

The door pushed open. "Everything okay?"

Thea sighed and nodded, removing the towel and scrunching it into a tight ball before shooting it at the waste can. "Yeah, Francine, everything's fine. I just...need a minute, okay?"

With a look rife with sympathy, the bodyguard gave a quick look around, verifying the room was empty. Thankfully, Francine refrained from pointing out that Thea should have waited for her to have that done first before coming in alone. With a quick nod, she retreated silently into the hall. As the door shut behind her, Thea had the awful feeling that Francine knew *exactly* what was wrong, and she stifled a groan.

"I'm pathetic." She rummaged in her bag, repaired her makeup as best she could, and gave herself a stern stare in the mirror. "You *will* go back out there, you *will* have a good time, and you *will* get Doyle out of your mind once and for all."

But even as she pulled the door open and let the sounds of Lady Gaga into the tiled room, she knew that while she could handle the first two orders, the third was going to be practically impossible.

# CHAPTER 16

**THEA WAITED UNTIL** the applause signaled the end of the first act before she exited her refuge and started twisting her way through the miniscule space between tables. She was so intent on getting back to her seat before the next performer took the stage that she never saw the person coming in the other direction until it was too late. With no room to sidestep, the collision was inevitable. The only saving grace was that neither one of them was carrying a drink.

"Oh, I'm sorry. I wasn't looking…"

"Wow, sorry. The lights are so low that…"

Even as she tried to step back from the unexpected contact, Thea felt the hands that had come up to steady her tighten on her upper arms, as though unwilling to let go. A quick frisson of unease blasted through her. For a second, she had the terrible thought that Seth had somehow tracked her down. Then the fingers holding her flexed and disappeared, and the man they belonged to chuckled.

"Okay, when I'd hoped I'd run into you here, I wasn't thinking quite so literally."

The familiar voice brought her head up and she managed to make out the smiling face in the dim light. A small laugh of relief puffed through her lips.

"Oliver. Hi." She started to ask what he meant about hoping to run into her, but the rise in music warned that the next act was about to begin and they were standing in the way of people's view of the stage. "Do you have a table?"

It was Oliver's turn to laugh. "Are you kidding? I was lucky to get a seat at the bar. Which," he added ruefully, "is most likely gone by now."

"Come on, then. We have a table over here." She squeezed past him and led the way, wondering as she did why she'd extended the impulsive invitation. She liked Oliver well enough, and he'd proven a surprisingly helpful ally when it came to smuggling wedding plans out of the War Room, but she'd never associated with him in a social setting aside from several of Mrs. Westlake's interminable dinner parties. He was always either dogging Charles's steps with an electronic tablet taking notes or rattling off information, or on the phone making one of the seemingly hundreds of calls and contacts that were necessary when an up-and-coming senator-in-the-making was in town to do the rounds.

Somehow, she'd never pictured Charles's personal assistant as someone who'd enjoy the type of entertainment that Platinum provided. He was just as buttoned-up and starchy as his boss. At least he'd always seemed that way. Maybe there was a wilder side to Oliver Pratt that he just didn't show the world.

Thea considered that for all of a second. Nah.

They made it to the table just as the music signaled the next act.

"Look who I found," Thea said, sliding into her seat. It was the small hesitation in Oliver's movement before he took the open chair next to Lillian and nodded a stiff hello to Nick that had her remembering too late that Lil had mentioned once that she didn't think Oliver liked her very much. Thea thought it was more a case of diametrically opposed personalities head-butting each other rather than actual dislike, but, still, it made for an awkward seating arrangement.

Short of being obvious and swapping seats with her friend, there wasn't anything she could do about it now, so instead she focused her attention on the stage, where one of Des's best friends was launching into a spot-on rendition of Madonna's "Like a Virgin." If Thea hadn't seen the transformation herself once, she'd be hard-pressed to believe that "Madonna" was really a tax accountant named Harold who was going slightly bald on top and tended to stutter when he was nervous.

Being on-stage in his other persona, he was confident, charismatic, and entirely sure of himself and the hold he had on his audience. Seeing the utter joy on his face, Thea could understand why Des had fought so hard for part ownership of the club. In doing so, he'd ensured that no matter what other acts were brought in, the drag burlesque would always remain. This wasn't just work for these performers. This was a vindication of life.

During the applause at the end of Harold's act—which had included a sassy encore of "Material Girl"—Thea leaned in and made the introductions between Nick and Oliver. The two shook hands, but there was almost no time for further conversation before the next singer took the stage. Finally, there was a short intermission, and the house lights rose slightly, allowing the waitresses to swarm the tables and fill drink orders before the second half of the show began.

"So, Oliver," Lillian said, shifting in her seat to look at him with a raised brow, "fancy meeting you here." Thea winced inwardly at the tone and was relieved when Oliver didn't rise to the obvious bait.

"What, I can't just be here to have a good time?" Oliver asked, raising a neatly manscaped brow.

Lillian gave it all of a half second's thought. "Yeah, no. Not a chance."

Oliver's lips pinched a bit. "When Charles decided to take Amelia out to dinner instead of going over some changes to his speech for the engagement party, I was left at something of a loose end. Since Amelia mentioned your plans to bring her here tonight for a little girls' night out, I thought I'd come and check the place out for myself."

And suddenly Oliver's presence made sense. Thea opened her mouth but heard her own question coming out of Lillian's mouth as a sharp accusation instead.

"Charles told you to check the place out, didn't he?"

"Of course not." But Thea could tell by the way he stiffened his spine he was lying. Or, at least, not telling the entire truth.

"But he might have mentioned that he was a little concerned about what kind of club Platinum was," Thea said softly, trying not to let her anger at Charles's heavy-handed tactics come through. "And maybe he hinted that you could come and take a look, since you were suddenly free for the night?"

Free because Charles had launched a preemptive strike and asked his fiancée out to dinner. Not because he had finally wanted to spend some time alone with her, as Amelia had rather giddily assumed, but simply to prevent her from going someplace that the arrogant son of a bitch hadn't yet had vetted as being suitable for the future Mrs. Senator to be seen at.

"It might have come up in conversation." Oliver shot Lillian a dark glare when she muttered something under her breath that was too low for Thea to hear, but evidently he did. "Charles has every right to be concerned with what his fiancée does," he snapped. "Her actions reflect directly on him. One misstep, one indiscretion, and his entire campaign can implode before he even sets foot in D.C."

"As if Mellie would ever do anything to hurt him," Lillian said, her chin coming up in preparation for battle on their friend's behalf.

"Oliver," Thea said, hoping to steer away from outright warfare, "Amelia's grown up with the dos and don'ts of living under the political microscope. She would never do anything to hurt Charles's campaign."

"Not intentionally, no," Oliver conceded, "but the senator was concerned about her adamant refusal to withdraw from the exhibition going on here next month. She's been very stubborn about it."

"First off, buster, that 'exhibition' is a fashion show, put on every year to raise money for charity, and no one said boo when Mellie signed up to do the catwalk, which her dad—you know, the *other* senator—would have been the first to pull the plug on if he'd thought it was even the teensiest bit questionable."

"Hey, Lil," Thea said, seeing the tidal wave that was about to roll over the unsuspecting man, "maybe you should, you know, pull it back a notch?" Plus, it wasn't exactly true that Senator Westlake had approved of his daughter's participation in this year's fashion show. He just hadn't been informed of it at the time.

"Second of all," Lillian charged on, "maybe, just *maybe*, if Charles would deign to spend a little more time with the woman he's supposed to marry in, oh," she looked at her watch, "nine months, instead of following daddy dearest all over the country glad-handing the money people, he and his father wouldn't have to worry quite so much about where she was spending all of that free time and with whom!"

"Um, Lil, really, you gotta bring it back to Earth," Thea tried again, starting to get the feeling that the evening was about to implode in a spectacular fashion.

"And thirdly," Lillian said, turning far enough in her seat that she was almost nose-to-nose with Oliver.

"Oh, damn," Thea sighed in defeat.

"If your boss thinks he's going to manage Amelia like some stuffed poodle that doesn't have a brain for herself, he'd better think again, pal, because Mellie might have a soft heart and a sweet-as-sugar disposition, but she's *nobody's* fool, and there's no way she's going to put up with it. She deserves to be treated with love and respect, not like a chess piece to be moved where she might do him the most good and pushed to the side when she isn't needed."

"As if you have any idea what it takes to make a successful career in politics," Oliver replied, his voice heavy with derision. "Charles Davenport is going places, and he's going to do important things. He needs someone at his side that's going to be useful to him, not a hindrance. Amelia understands her place, even if you don't."

"Her place?" Lillian repeated disbelievingly. "Her *place?*"

Thea saw red. All thoughts of being the voice of reason were lost under the wave of rage on her friend's behalf.

"Her place is in a loving relationship," she said, leaning forward on her forearms as she caught Oliver's attention away from Lillian. "Half of a team, not just a minor player."

Oliver looked at her as though shocked that she was siding with Lillian on this. "How can you not understand?" he asked. "There can only be one person leading the way. The other has to follow. Someone has to sacrifice their own wants and needs for the greater good. It's the only way it can work."

"And that someone has to be Amelia?"

"She knew exactly what she was getting into when she agreed to the marriage."

"I wonder about that," Lillian muttered.

"You said it yourself. Her father was a senator," Oliver pointed out.

There wasn't anything either of them could say to that. It was the truth. Amelia knew all too well what a political marriage entailed as far as sacrifice. Thea just couldn't stomach hearing her friend's future described in such brutally callous terms.

Her distress must have been evident, because Nick, whom she'd almost forgotten about, put his hand over hers on the table and leaned in toward Oliver. "I think maybe this isn't the place for this particular discussion."

Whether it was the thread of steel that underlay Nick's quiet voice or the reminder that they were discussing a very private issue in a very public venue, Oliver closed his mouth with a surprised snap.

"You're right, of course," he finally said, his gaze bouncing from Thea to Nick, looking slightly distressed at the thought of what he'd been saying in front of a stranger.

He ignored Lillian, which Thea thought was probably for the best.

Oliver's gaze focused on Thea again, his expression earnest if still ill at ease.

"I just wanted you to understand..." He grimaced when the house lights flashed, warning that the second half of the show was about to begin. Standing, he said in a rush, "You'll see that I'm right. No matter what happens, you have to believe it's all for the best."

Watching Oliver disappear into the crowd as the lights came down, Thea shook her head and offered Nick a weak grin. "Sorry about that. There was no excuse for him to be that—"

"Obnoxious?" Lillian snorted into her glass.

"No. Yes," Thea corrected, changing her mind. Oliver had been a bit of a shithead. But if she was going to continue to be effective at smuggling wedding plans out of the War Room, she had to stay on his good side.

Nick gave her hand a quick squeeze and a pat before releasing it. "I won't lie and say I have any idea what that was all about, but it didn't seem like it was anything you or your friend would want being overheard. It sounded pretty private."

As appreciative as Thea was to Nick for defusing the situation, she didn't feel comfortable discussing the whole Amelia/Charles problem with him. He was, after all, a virtual stranger for all that she liked him. Instead, she nodded and said only, "It's complicated and definitely private. So, thank you."

"Yeah, and thanks for getting him to leave," Lillian added, saluting Nick with her glass. "He would have ruined the rest of the evening if he'd stuck around." She shook her head at Thea. "What were you thinking bringing him over here?"

"I was just being polite," Thea replied defensively but hadn't she wondered the same thing herself when she'd first extended the invitation? It was those damned manners again. They got her into trouble every time.

Then again, if she hadn't asked him over, they wouldn't have found out about Charles's ulterior motives. Not that there was much they could do with that information. If they told Mellie, she'd be heartbroken. Worse, she'd probably just make some excuse for Charles that cast his actions in a better light, just like she usually did. But if they didn't tell her, she wouldn't know what Charles had been up to, and he'd be free to pull the same high-handed crap on her again.

It really was a no-win situation.

As if sensing her inner turmoil, Nick leaned his head next to hers and whispered, "Do you want to go?"

She shook her head and dredged up a smile that was only partially false. "No, I'm fine. Besides, if we leave now, we'll miss the best part. Des usually closes the show."

"Riiiight. Your friend Des." He sounded so bemused as he finally put it all together that Thea couldn't help but laugh, feeling the last of the tension from the unpleasant scene with Oliver fade away. She patted Nick's arm and grinned.

"Trust me. You're going to love it."

# Chapter 17

**"SON OF A BITCH."**

Tossing Daryl Raintree's report down on his desk, Doyle leaned back and scrubbed his hands roughly over his face, fighting down the urge to growl like the damn dog in the manger he clearly was. Nick Hastings. The son of a bitch had turned up again. Twice in one day. Although, to be fair, he'd accompanied Thea to the club only after she'd called and asked for Doyle's approval. Which he'd given. Reluctantly. But what the hell else could he have done?

It had been the first time she'd spoken to him since the infamous "friendship" incident, and what had she called to talk about? If he had finally finished the background check on Hastings because she wanted to go out with him if he had.

He'd been so off balance by the out-of-the-blue question that he'd given her the go-ahead before he could come up with a good reason not to. It was only after he'd hung up that the questions had started crowding his mind.

Like, why the hell was Hastings back in Boulder? Hadn't Thea said he'd finished his business and gone home to Chicago? Why had he sought Thea out again after she'd cancelled their dinner arrangements the last time he was here? And how had he found her? He hadn't contacted her at the house, of that he was positive. That meant he'd either called her cell to arrange a meeting at Pot and Kettle or else he'd just happened to run into her there.

Doyle's gut was burning. He didn't like coincidences. The fact that the last letter had shown up after Hastings had left town and now he was mysteriously back, he liked even less.

Red said his travel itinerary didn't match their postmarks. Fine. He didn't doubt Red's thoroughness. But he just couldn't let the possibility go that maybe, just maybe, this bastard had worked out a system to get his letters mailed by someone else, someone they hadn't connected to him yet, to throw them off the trail. Someone who didn't have a clue that they were aiding and abetting a budding psychopath.

Hell, who was he kidding? Deep down he wanted Hastings to be their perp not because it would be the easiest answer, but because he didn't like the fact that Thea was suddenly interested in spending time in his company. And enjoying it.

He snorted and let out a weary groan, shoving his chair back and reaching for his jacket. He was a sad, sorry bastard. God forbid Thea should have some fun. She rarely dated, and other than that jackass kid back in college she hadn't formed a lasting attachment to any man.

Except him.

Up until now, he'd been too blind—no, too damned chickenshit—to do anything about that important fact. He'd kept Thea very firmly in the little box marked "off-limits." But now...now the box was open and, just like Pandora, he couldn't possibly put everything back inside and close the lid again, even if he wanted to.

And if he was finally very honest with himself, he found he really didn't want to.

He was still scared as hell that things wouldn't work out the way he wanted, the way he needed them to. The memory of Donny's miserable face at Christmas when everyone else's kids except his were gathered at their parents' house because Holly-the-bitch had dragged their daughter down to Florida to spend the holidays with her parents loomed in his mind like a specter of Christmas Future. Mothers almost always got custody. Add to that the war chest of money and lawyers that would be at Thea's disposal, and he'd be royally fucked.

Damn it all to hell. Austin was right. Doyle really did keep playing the worst-case-scenario card. They hadn't even gone on a real, official date yet— he refused to think of their dinner at Rudolfo's as their first date, not with the way it had ended, which he'd done such a poor job of explaining to her when he'd tried—and his sorry brain had them divorced and fighting over nonexistent kids.

Suddenly that image was replaced by a different one, one of Thea big and round and glowing with love for the child growing inside her. Just the thought was enough to make his gut clench in longing. She'd make a great mother. He knew that without question. She had a natural instinct for people. It was what made her so good at her design work. She knew how to listen, and how to get people to talk, and how to make them feel she was really getting what they were telling her.

It seemed she even knew how to get through to a big dumbass jarhead who didn't know a good thing until it came up and shook a micro-bikini in his slack-jawed face. Because now that he'd decided he wanted her, he wasn't going to give up. If she was still pissed at him—and by the way she'd been avoiding him lately he had to think she was—he'd just have to convince her to give him another chance.

The timing sucked, though. Her father's edict meant he had to keep lying to her, and Thea had a deep, abiding hatred of liars. Once she knew the truth, she'd be pissed at him for a whole different reason than the one she was avoiding him for now. That meant two heavy strikes against him before he even got well and truly in the game. That was okay, though. Now that he'd decided to play, he meant to play to win.

The other problem he was having trouble dealing with was Margo. Things had been on a downward slide with her for a while now, long before his whole Thea revelation. She'd been company, a warm body in his bed when the mood struck, and they'd had a good time while it lasted, but she'd started to get a little too clingy for his tastes recently.

It had become clear to him that it was long past time to put a definitive end to their relationship after the stunt she'd pulled at the restaurant. They'd never been an exclusive item, much as she might like to hint otherwise, and to act the way she had made it clear that they were past done, even if he hadn't decided it was time to take his head out of his ass in regards to Thea.

He'd tried to get ahold of Margo several times in the past few days so he could do just that, but she'd been ignoring his calls as neatly as he'd previously ignored hers. He had a feeling she knew what was coming and was trying to avoid the inevitable.

Pulling out his phone, he gave it another try. As with all of his previous calls, it rang five times and then rolled over to voice mail. He almost hung up and then hesitated. Normally, he would consider leaving a breakup message on someone's voice mail regardless of the circumstances a pretty shitty thing to do, but with Margo continuing to duck him this way, he really didn't have much choice. He refused to play her game any longer.

"Margo, I wanted to do this face-to-face, but you're making that impossible, so here it is. What we had was nice, but it's time for us both to move on. We both knew it was only casual between us, so I don't think you should be too surprised by what I'm saying, but I also don't want you to have any hard feelings, so please call me back after you listen to this so we can talk about it." He thumbed the phone off and tossed it on the desk with a sigh. He waited a few minutes, certain that Margo would have listened to the message as soon as he'd hung up, but the requested return call didn't come.

Margo was still avoiding him, so he couldn't resolve that situation.

Thea was still avoiding him, so he couldn't do anything about that situation, either.

That left the puzzle of the stalker to deal with.

Calling Red and Kirsten into his office, Doyle pulled out the copy of the latest letter that had arrived four days ago and forced himself to read it again. Twisted obsession, sick words of love mixed with frightening promises of pain and punishment if he was disappointed. It was just as disturbing now as it had been the first time he'd read it.

"Where are we on analysis?" he asked when Red took his chair.

"We just got the preliminary report from the Feds."

"Let me guess," Doyle said, scowling. "Nothing."

"No fingerprints, no watermarks, no obvious DNA on either the letter or the envelope," Red confirmed. He sighed. "Damn, I miss the days when people actually had to lick the damn flap and stamp."

"There was one anomaly, though," Kirsten said.

Doyle straightened in his seat, his senses going on alert. Up until now, there hadn't been a single thing out of the ordinary about the letters that could help them narrow down their search for the sender. If there was something, anything, that broke the established pattern, it could mean that their perp had made his first mistake. A mistake meant he was one step closer to being caught.

Referring back to her tablet, Kirsten continued, "There was a tiny smear of some foreign substance on the bottom edge of the paper. We're still waiting to hear back on the analysis, though."

Feeling his bubble of excitement start to deflate again, Doyle said, "That's it?"

Kirsten scowled, tapping her stylus against her leg in an annoyed staccato. "So far. The Feebies aren't exactly thrilled about having to deal with us. When I pushed, I was reminded rather pointedly that they're sharing information, not the investigation, and they'll do so at the agent-in-charge's discretion."

"Wonderful." Doyle pinched the bridge of his nose tiredly. Damn. The last thing they needed was some rod-up-his-ass Feeb withholding something important just to prove a point. Frank Fordham's connections might have gotten the FBI involved, but even he couldn't force them to play nice now that they were.

"Do the best you can," he told Kirsten. He grinned slightly. "Dazzle them with your charm."

She curled her lip in distaste. "I'd rather shoot them with my gun."

"Whatever works." Doyle looked to Red. "Have we heard back from the head of Davenport's security detail? What was his name? Rogers?"

They'd dealt well with Paul Kent, the head of William Westlake's security, over the years due to—or perhaps in spite of—the close friendship of the daughters of the two households. The fact that it was Frederick Davenport's security team that had taken charge of the upcoming engagement party rather than Kent and his people was an annoyance he'd gladly pawned off on his second-in-command.

"Don Rogers. Real horse's ass." The look Red shot Doyle promised retribution for being made liaison with said ass. "He's still giving us grief about how many of our people we can have inside the venue and whether or not they can be armed."

"What the hell does he want us to do if there's an incident?" Kirsten asked indignantly. "Throw shrimp at the bad guys?"

"Evidently Rogers is getting his own grief from the Secret Service about how many armed people are going to be on the premises," Red told them.

"And he's passing it along," Doyle guessed.

"Ayup."

"Guess that means Mrs. Westlake actually got the vice president to attend." Kirsten sounded less than awed. In fact, she sounded downright grumpy. High-end politicians usually meant a lot more grief for their security details all around. They were already dealing with several senators and congressmen, both sitting and retired. Adding one of the White House crowd to the mix was just going to make everyone's life that much more miserable.

"He did make one good point, though," Red said. "The venue is huge, but it still only holds so many people comfortably. Even if everyone who attends only brings one asset for security inside with them, that already doubles the attendance. More than that, and…" He spread his hands.

"And it gets ridiculous." Doyle could see the logic in it. Two hundred guests outnumbered by four hundred security people…Yeah, that had clusterfuck written all over it.

"And probably unnecessary," Red continued. "With the VP and all the other high mucketies attending, there won't be anyone who steps foot inside that building that hasn't been searched, background checked, and vetted back to his forefathers. There won't be a single busboy or janitor who hasn't had Secret Service crawling up his ass to take a peek. Outside of the panic room at the main house, that catering hall could very well be the safest place on the planet for our Thea to be."

No, the safest place for her to be was somewhere far away from Boulder, but since Doyle knew there was no chance in hell of that happening, he had to accept that the security measures put in place for the party would be enough. But he was damn well going to be that one asset they had on the inside.

"Fine," he snapped finally. "Tell Rogers we'll stick to his inside plan for now, but the rest of our people will be staged outside and everyone *will* be armed." There was no compromise on that as far as Doyle was concerned. "I'm sure Paul told him the same thing."

"I wonder if he wet himself before or after he tried to tell Hans he couldn't bring his guns to the party," Kirsten mused with a malicious glint in her eyes. Doyle let out a bark of laughter, which was echoed by Red.

Hans Gruber was the head of Rupert Beaumont's security. At six-five and two-hundred-sixty pounds, the man was not only built like a tank, he had the personality of one as well. The fact that he shared the name of the terrorist from the first *Die Hard* movie did not amuse him at all, and grown men had been known to flee from his wrath if they made the mistake of uttering anything that even sounded remotely like "yippee-ki-yay."

Thea swore that she had once seen him crack what might have been a smile, but Doyle wasn't sure it was even possible. As far as he knew, the man had only two expressions: don't-piss-me-off and you've-pissed-me-off-and-now-you-must-die.

Yeah, he could bet that Rogers had wet himself, just a little.

"You know the Washington elite aren't going to be settling for just one asset," Kirsten pointed out.

"When it's their show, they don't have to," Red replied and then asked Doyle, "Want me to explain to Rogers what's going on? It might help change his mind if he knows why we wanted more assets on site for such low-risk—his words—clients?"

"I'd prefer not to if it can be helped." They'd managed to keep the existence of the letters from all but a select few. Only the chief of police, his deputy chief, and the detectives directly involved in the case knew their content. The city was far too small and gossip far too rampant to do otherwise.

Especially with Peter Beaumont on the force. If he caught one whiff of the actual story, he wouldn't last ten minutes before his sister ferreted it out of him.

"But," Doyle allowed after a moment's thought, "if things escalate between now and the party, give him what you think he needs to know to get him to change his mind."

Even with background checks and insane amounts of security in place all around the catering hall, Doyle still wasn't convinced it was enough. Because if anything happened to Thea on his watch, he wasn't certain he would ever survive the guilt of having failed her when it counted most.

# CHAPTER 18

TELL AMELIA OR NOT TELL HER.

That was the question that chased around Thea's mind like a spastic hamster as she circled the track at Fit. The headache she'd awakened with that morning had more to do with the moral dilemma poking at her conscience and disturbing her sleep than from any residual hangover effects, thanks to Lil's timely intervention.

After popping a few aspirin and taking a long, restorative shower, she'd decided to do what she usually did when she was faced with a problem she couldn't seem to solve. Go for a run. The soothing repetitive motion usually freed her mind to ponder other things. In the past, she'd worked through a room design that wasn't coming together or how she could convince a client that the really horrid choices they were making weren't *wrong* so much as not exactly *right*. More recently she'd used the time to plot out her next move in the ongoing campaign to get Doyle to notice her.

Much good that had done her.

But today…today she was trying to figure out whether or not she would be helping Amelia by telling her what they'd learned from Oliver the previous evening or hurting her. Was it really her place to explain to Amelia that her fiancé was a manipulative, self-serving bastard?

But was it her place to keep her from knowing the truth? She already knew what Lillian would say when she called her later and asked her what she thought they should do. Painful or not, she'd want to sit Amelia down and give her the facts. And maybe that *was* the best choice.

But maybe it wasn't.

With a frustrated sigh, Thea started her cool-down several laps early, drawing a surprised glance from Sam, who started to slow his own pace to match Thea's. Thea shook her head and motioned with her hand for him to continue. There was no need for him to cut his own run short just because she was feeling edgy and unsettled.

He hesitated and then nodded and picked his pace back up to his usual long-legged lope when she indicated she wasn't planning to leave the gym, just move over to the weight equipment where Kirsten was making use of the free weights. It was the one benefit to using the club's track rather than the more peaceful and private trails on the estate that she usually preferred. Well, that and the fact that it was miles away from Doyle. She was determined to finally let that ship sail without diving off the dock after it like a love-sick idiot.

It was hard. Really, really hard. But she was trying. All she had to do was get through one day at a time. One hour. One minute without thinking about Doyle, without craving his affection, his smile, his kiss.

And didn't she just sound like a freaking addict working her way through withdrawal?

Settling on her back on the padded bench, Thea hefted the five-pound free weights and started a series of butterfly curls. If she was going to end up being photographed and seen by half the country at Mellie's wedding, she was going to be darn sure there wasn't an ounce of arm flab visible in that horrid bridesmaid gown.

Thea grimaced. God, she hated that dress. But she and Lillian hadn't put up a fight, hoping that by letting Mrs. Westlake have her way on that, she might be more inclined to give Mellie more input on her own gown. So far, that hadn't worked out so well, but there was still time for a miracle.

"Well, well, if it isn't little Cynthia."

*Crap.*

It was difficult, but Thea managed to hold back the groan that wanted so badly to escape at the syrupy voice. She ignored Margo's snide greeting, keeping her eyes focused on the ceiling as her arms curled in smooth, unhurried arcs, hoping, praying, the woman would just walk away.

She *so* wasn't in the mood to deal with her bitchiness this morning.

"Decided to come slumming with the regular folks again today, huh? Let everyone see that you're just like us?"

Thea could almost hear the air quotes around those last words. Really, the woman was poking at the wrong place if she was looking to get a rise out of her. She'd spent the first half of her life as one of the regular folks. She'd grown up in a two-bedroom ranch with a postage-stamp-sized yard and a roof that leaked when the wind blew from the west.

"I'm surprised you don't have a private gym up in that mansion of yours. It's not like you couldn't afford it."

There would have been if her father hadn't decided to turn the space into a solarium for her mother instead. Since her father's idea of a good workout consisted of taking the stairs down one floor from his office to the conference room rather than using the elevator, the space had definitely been put to the best use. Still, right now she wished he hadn't been quite so altruistic.

"It doesn't matter how often you come out of your castle and play at being normal. He's never going to want you, you know."

Ahh, now they were getting to the crux of the matter. The words stung, but Thea didn't let it show. She just kept curling the weights, breathing, breathing, breathing. It didn't matter that she knew the older woman was right. It didn't. And if she told herself that enough times, she might even come to believe it in say, oh, twenty years or so.

"God, you're such a child," Margo taunted with a soft laugh. "Look at you, pretending not to hear what you don't want to admit to. Brennan always said you were nothing more than a little girl playing at being a grownup. Looks like he was right about—Hey!" She jumped back with a yelp as one of the dumbbells dropped to the ground inches from her toes.

"Sorry," Thea said, not in the least. "It slipped." She sat up on the bench and gave a quick shake of her head to Kirsten as she put the other weight down and grabbed up her towel to dab at the perspiration on her face. No intervention needed.

"Slipped my ass," Margo hissed. "You did that on purpose."

"Maybe you shouldn't have been standing so close." *Or been such a bitch,* she added silently. Thea picked up the weight she had dropped and replaced both on the rack in their proper cradles. When she turned back, she sighed, seeing that Margo was still standing there, her posture tight and aggressive, fists clenched at her sides.

Great, just great. Thea really didn't need this right now. All she wanted was a hot shower and to go home where she could try to figure out what she was going to do about Amelia and Charles. A public brawl was *not* on the agenda, as much as she might like to knock Little Miss Attitude on her ass.

But Margo, it seemed, had no qualms about making a spectacle of them both. She got in Thea's way as she tried to walk past her toward the locker room, refusing to let her pass. "How dare you?"

Thea tried to step around again but was blocked once more. She sighed. "You don't want to do this, Margo," she said quietly. "Just walk away." She shot another look at Kirsten, who was quickly approaching with a determined look on her face. Thea made an abortive gesture with her hand to call her off. The only danger Margo posed was to Thea's already shredded feelings.

"Such a little princess," Margo sneered. "Thinking you can buy anyone and anything with daddy's money. Well, you can't buy Brennan. He knows what he wants, and it isn't you!"

Accepting the slice to her heart with barely a wince, Thea shook her head. "I've never tried to buy anyone, least of all Doyle. He decides who and what he wants all on his own."

"He wants *me*!"

The hint of desperation in those words made Thea take a long, objective look at the woman uttering them. At first glance, she could understand why Doyle would be interested, even if she didn't like it. Margo was tall, attractive, and had curves enough for two women. She dressed to accentuate her assets and wasn't shy about letting more than a hint of her impressive cleavage show.

But up close like this, Thea could see the faint fan of lines starting to edge her overly made-up eyes, indicating she was probably closer to forty than to thirty, as Thea had first guessed. It was a good job, but her wavy auburn hair owed more to a high-end salon than it did to nature, and the blue eyes that were glaring at her with such anger and determination had the bland uniformity of color that usually came from colored contacts.

Together with the enhanced bustline that Peter Beaumont and half of Boulder drooled over, Margo had certainly put together a package meant to grab a man's attention. What she hadn't yet figured out, it seemed, was that there needed to be something worthwhile inside all that pretty outer wrapping in order to keep it.

Suddenly feeling unaccountably sorry for the woman, Thea shook her head again and said, "That's between you and Doyle." It was as gracious as she could be under the circumstances, since she'd so obviously lost what Margo had won.

She made one more attempt to step around the other woman, only to be brought up short when Margo grabbed her by the arm. As she stared at the offending hand, every drop of sympathy she'd been feeling dried up in a heartbeat.

"Let. Go." Thea was actually proud that she managed to sound so calm when what she really wanted to do was haul back and deck the woman.

"Leave him alone. Do you hear me?" Margo not only didn't let go, she actually tightened her grip. Fingers strengthened by years of doing massage therapy sank into the tender flesh of Thea's upper arm with enough force to cause real pain. "He's mine, and I won't let some stupid little girl like you steal him away!"

All of the lessons with Doyle and his team kicked in without thought. Just as Kirsten was reaching to grab hold of Margo, Thea's free hand went for

Margo's elbow, her thumb digging into the front crevice as her fingers curled into the back where the radial nerve lay. Instantly, Margo's grip loosened as she gasped in pain.

Training and inclination had Thea itching to follow-through and put her attacker to the floor, but sanity and the awareness that they had an audience prevailed. She drew in a shaky breath, refusing to rub her sore arm—damn, she just *knew* there were going to be bruises there—and glared at the other woman. "Don't you ever put your hands on me again."

Cradling her arm to her body, Margo spat out, "Bitch!" There were watery tears in her voice, but even more so there was rage.

"When the need arises," Thea agreed with a sharp smile. "Now get the hell out of my way, and stay out of it."

"Or what? You'll sic your bodyguards on me?" Margo sneered the question, but she looked worried when she darted glances at both Kirsten and Sam, who had sprinted over and now flanked Thea on her other side.

Thea spread her arms out. "Did I need to have them help me just now?" She lowered her arms and picked up the towel she'd dropped. "Leave me alone, Margo. If you see me in the future, walk the other way, and I'll do the same. Don't talk to me, don't approach me, and don't you ever, *ever,* put a hand on me again, or so help me God I'll make sure you regret it."

Spinning on her heel, Thea stalked toward the locker room, Kirsten on her like glue. It was hard, but Thea willfully ignored the avid attention of the few other gym patrons who had caught wind of the budding argument in the weight area and had been not-so subtly waiting to see if it was going to explode into an all-out catfight.

Great, she thought in disgust. Just wait till wind of this juicy little tidbit made its way back to Mrs. Westlake. She'd be lucky if she was even allowed to *attend* Amelia's wedding, much less participate in it.

# CHAPTER 19

**USUALLY WHEN SHE** was going somewhere to meet with her friends, Thea would drive her own car and her guard *du jour* would follow in one of the unobtrusively bland sedans from the security carpool. When she was going someplace alone like the gym, however, she usually chose to ride with her shadow and enjoy the company.

Today, though, she wished she'd chosen differently. The last thing she wanted right now was company, and she knew if she opened her mouth to try and hold a normal conversation, she'd end up ranting like a lunatic. Thankfully, aside from inquiring if she needed any medical attention for her arm and asking if she wanted to file a police report—both of which she'd declined as both unnecessary and incredibly humiliating—Sam and Kirsten were both wise enough to remain silent on the ride home.

If it had been only Kirsten in the car, Thea might have given in to the overwhelming urge to vent her fury and frustration, but Sam's presence held her back. Which was a good thing, because what might have made her feel better in the short-term would definitely have opened up a whole other set of issues about just why Fit's massage therapist had gone all Fatal Attraction on her. Kirsten had been close enough to hear most of the conversation. She could draw her own conclusions without Thea connecting the dots. So Thea sucked it all up, kept her mouth shut, and hoped she wouldn't explode before she got home.

She made it but only just. As soon as the door to her room shut behind her, she let out the shuddering breath that was the dam break for the tears that had been making her eyeballs ache for the past ten minutes. It was stupid to cry, but it was either that or scream.

How dare she? How *dare* she?

Bad enough she'd gotten Doyle to abandon her at the restaurant. Bad enough that she'd taken him home and done who knew what with him until the wee hours. Bad enough that she'd won and Thea had lost. Bad enough that she'd chosen to rub Thea's face in it.

In public no less.

But the worst, the absolute worst of it all, was what she had said. *"Brennan always said you were nothing more than a little girl playing at being a grownup."* Doyle had said that? About her? To that silicone-breasted bitch?

That was the strike to the very center of her heart that Thea was certain she'd never recover from. She'd already accepted—if not yet found a way to deal with—the fact that Doyle didn't love her. Wouldn't love her. Ever. But she'd at least thought she still had his respect, his friendship. Hadn't he given her the "I value your friendship" speech just last week? But no friend would ever ridicule another in such a way. Ever. It was mean, and spiteful, and…and…

And not at all like something Doyle would have said about her, not to Margo or anyone else for that matter. Ever.

The tears had evidently flushed the adrenaline-induced veil of stupid from her brain, because now that she thought about them, rather than simply reacted to them, the words that had made her want to throw up simply made no sense. Not coming from Doyle.

But coming from Margo? Oh, yeah, they made perfect sense.

The bitch was good. She'd known just where the chink in Thea's emotional armor lay and attacked it with the deft hand of a master.

Point to her.

Feeling marginally better and knowing that her time was limited, if not already almost up, Thea headed for the shower that she'd forgone at Fit in favor of a fast getaway. She doubted Sam or Kirsten would wait until the end of the shift to file their reports about the incident, and she knew that no matter what else lay between them Doyle wouldn't shirk his duties as the head of Fordham security to come see her for the details. She preferred to be clean and dressed when that happened.

She was still toweling her damp hair when the sharp knock came. Staring at her own tight expression in the mirror, she sighed, rolled her shoulders to try and loosen the tension knot that had settled there, and walked to the door. There was a second knock before she got there, this one quicker and harder, betraying Doyle's impatience.

"I'm fine," she said as she opened the door, trying to head things off. Judging by the harsh lines on Doyle's face that betrayed his inner fury, it wasn't going to help. Above and beyond his job, Doyle was a protector by nature. Someone he considered under his protection had been threatened, and despite the fact that there had been more insult than injury, he'd still feel responsible.

"I'm fine," she repeated, trying for a more reassuring tone when he continued to stand in the doorway, staring at her. "Really. It was nothing. Almost nothing," she amended.

"What happened?" His voice was low, even, and nowhere near calm. There was a guttural edge to it that Thea had never heard before. It sent a small frisson of fear through her. Or was it excitement?

Unnerved by her conflicting reaction to Doyle's alpha male dominance display, she spun and stalked back into her suite, heading toward the sitting room side as she blotted the ends of her hair with the towel.

"Since you've obviously already gotten an incident report, you already know. Why should I go over it again?"

"Because I want to hear it from you." She practically jumped when he spoke from right behind her. She hadn't heard him follow her. Damn sneaky Marine training.

Trying to cover her reaction, she gave a snarky laugh and dropped into one of the cushy velour chairs that flanked the fireplace.

"So who don't you trust? Me, Sam, or Kirsten?" When Doyle just continued to stare, his arms crossed over his broad chest, she picked at the edge of the towel in her lap and sighed. "Okay, that was a dumb thing to say. I just don't see...Fine." It was clear he wasn't going to let it go, so better to just get it over with as fast and painlessly as possible. "I was at the gym, and your friend Margo came over and started being bitchy, so I left. End of story."

"Try again."

Thea sighed. "Okay, I was at the gym, and your friend Margo came over and started being bitchy, so I tried to leave. She grabbed my arm. I threatened to smack her in her big fat mouth, and I left." She was intrigued by the way his mouth tightened into a grimace every time she used the phrase "your friend Margo."

"Better, but I'd still like the full version."

"Why?"

"Humor me."

"Maybe I don't want to." It was just too damn embarrassing.

"Do it anyway."

Thea didn't care for the tone of his voice or the way he was towering over her, arms crossed, looking down at her like she was a recalcitrant child. In fact, at that moment, she didn't care for very much of anything, much less being interrogated by the man who was the reason she was having such a shitty day in the first place. She jumped to her feet, tossing her head defiantly.

"I'll file a report."

She moved to stalk past him, head held high, only to bump into his chest as he stepped in her way, effectively body-blocking her escape. Refusing to step back, she tilted her head up and glared at him, fighting not to melt under that wicked hazel gaze. "Move, Doyle."

"Not until you tell me what the hell happened today."

"*Move.*"

"Thea," he growled, narrowing his eyes. It was enough to finally pop the bubble of her control.

"Fine! You want to know what happened? Here it is. I was at the gym, minding my own business, when *your friend Margo,*" she punctuated each word with a finger into his chest, "came over and started making nasty comments. I tried to ignore her, but she kept pushing and bitching. Finally I had enough and tried to leave. But was she smart enough to just let me go? Oh, no, not *your friend Margo.*" She poked again.

"Stop calling her that," Doyle muttered, rubbing the spot she was abusing.

"Why? She is, isn't she? You know, your 'friend'?" She air-quoted it and got the satisfaction of seeing Doyle look uncomfortable. Good. The bastard deserved it.

"So I tried to leave because getting into a public brawl was not how I planned to spend my Sunday morning, but evidently too much silicone induces severe brain damage because your...Margo," she settled for sneering the name since Doyle looked ready to snatch her hand up if she tried to poke him again, "grabbed my arm."

Doyle took half a step back, but it was only to catch her right arm in his hands and give it a quick inspection. The feel of his hands on her skin, sensitized by the recent hot shower, sent a zing of jangled nerves to places far removed from her arm. As he smoothed his palm up over her elbow to the tender flesh of her upper arm, she barely controlled a shiver. This was bad. Very bad.

"The other one," she mumbled and then cursed herself for the admission. Sure enough, Doyle immediately sent his hands questing along her left arm, starting at the wrist and flowing upward, until they reached the line of faint bruises that had already started to blossom on the inner flesh of her upper arm. She flinched when he touched them and then nearly flinched again when the touch turned to a caress.

Oh man, she was in so much trouble.

"That bitch." The words hissed out through clenched teeth, barely audible but for the fact that they were standing so close. So close, in fact, that Thea could see the flush that colored Doyle's tanned cheeks. Anger? Or...arousal, maybe? His fingers were still stroking softly over her bruised arm, as though his touch alone could make it better. His breathing was a little ragged, almost matching hers. And his lips were close. So very close. Close enough that if she just went up on her tippy toes, she could...

God, what was she thinking! She was doing it again. Doyle was checking up on her, making sure she was okay. That was *all*. Just like before, she was reading something into it that just wasn't there.

Pathetic, pathetic, Thea.

Suppressing a groan, Thea eased herself from his grasp and took the step back that she should have taken when she first bumped into him.

"So, thanks to all the self-defense lessons you insisted I take, I broke her hold without having to break anything else and told her to stay the hell away from me in the future." She shrugged uncomfortably. "That's it."

"That's it?"

Thea swallowed. She nodded. "Yeah. That's it."

"And where was your security detail while all of this was going on?"

"Oh, no. Don't even try to make it about them," Thea said hotly. "I waved Kirsten off. There was no reason for either her or Sam to get involved until things got physical, and by then I'd already taken care of the matter, so there was nothing left for them to do."

"Hmm." Doyle stared at her, studying her with such intensity that it was all she could do not to squirm. The man would have made an excellent cop. All he'd have to do was use that silent stare down on a suspect and they'd willingly confess to everything they'd ever done wrong. And probably a few things they hadn't.

Right now, the only thing saving her from babbling like a fool was the fear of total humiliation. Self-preservation evidently trumped Doyle's super-stare.

"Why was Margo hassling you?"

"Why do you think?" She barely refrained from rolling her eyes. Could he *be* any denser?

"Because of me."

"Ding-ding-ding." She shrugged again, trying for nonchalance, but the small smile she forced felt freakish rather than self-assured. "She was warning me off. I told her I got it."

"Got what?"

He sounded so wary that Thea wanted to cry, but instead she pulled up her big-girl panties and sought to reassure him. "That you and she are...you know. Together."

"No."

"No?" She cocked her head questioningly. "No, what?"

"No, we are not together. Margo and me. We're..." Doyle scrubbed at his face and shook his head, looking adorably frustrated and put upon. "We were never a real couple to begin with," he said, starting over.

"Could have fooled me," Thea muttered and then bit her lip when she realized she'd said it out loud. She glanced apologetically at Doyle, who was scowling, and silently promised not to interrupt again.

"We were never an exclusive couple," he amended, "and the last time I was even out with her was almost a month ago."

"A week." Thea wanted to slap a hand over her wayward mouth. So much for her promise. But, really, couldn't the man tell time?

"No, a month," he said firmly. Then his expression faltered. His eyes closed for a second as though on a painful memory. "Rudolfo's." He refocused his gaze on her before she could mask the intense shaft of pain that single word and its accompanying humiliation brought her, and his expression hardened. "I really screwed up that night, Thea, I won't lie. I should never have taken the coward's way out by leaving with Margo like that. But I did, and I hurt you when I never meant to do that. I was just trying to keep things from getting out of hand between us. I am so sorry."

Humiliation upon humiliation. She'd been right. She'd put him in an awkward position, and he'd grabbed at the opportunity Margo had presented to extricate himself from her misguided attempt at seduction. Tears she'd thought long since spent pressed hotly behind her eyes, seeking escape, so she did the same.

Ducking her head, she pushed past him, aiming for the privacy of her bathroom. "I'm sorry, I have to…"

"Damn it!" Steely arms closed over her from behind, effectively pinning her arms to her sides.

"Let me go, Doyle. Please!" There was no way he'd miss the tears thickening her voice, or the desperation, but rather than let her go, he tightened his hold instead.

"God, I'm screwing this all to hell and back," he muttered into her hair. "I'm sorry, sweetheart. I was a jackass. Leaving with Margo…it was self-preservation."

Thea stilled. Sweetheart? Had he just called her sweetheart?

Doyle was still talking, his mouth pressed close to her ear. "I wanted to take you home that night. You have no idea how much. But I knew, I just knew that if I did, I wouldn't settle for a kiss goodnight. You had me so freaking crazy, I was afraid…" He laughed, the sound derisive and bitter. "I was afraid. That pretty much sums it up."

"Of me?" Thea asked tentatively. She was still reeling from the sudden confession.

"No. Of me." He sighed, rubbing his cheek against her like a cat scent-marking a beloved possession. "You opened my eyes, sweetheart, made me see that I'd been missing a very important fact all this time. You grew up. But then, I guess that was the whole point of these past few weeks, wasn't it? Getting me to wake the hell up?"

Heat bloomed along Thea's cheeks as she remembered the lengths to which she'd gone to achieve just that. "Yeah, kinda."

"Mmmhmm." He chuckled softly, and she relaxed. "Well, it finally worked. That night at dinner, I realized that I'd just been holding off the inevitable. The blinders were off, and there was no going back. I wanted you."

"Wanted?" Past tense?

"Want. Badly."

His words thrilled her, but she was still afraid of making the wrong assumptions. If things went wrong this time, she knew there would never be another chance for them.

She leaned into him a bit more, asking with her body was she was too chicken to ask with mere words. "How badly?"

Muttering a curse under his breath, Doyle closed that last increment of space between their lower bodies, and Thea felt the hard ridge of his erection press into her backside. "This badly."

"Oh," she breathed, shocked and delighted at the evidence of his arousal.

"Yeah, oh. God, you're killing me," he groaned when she pressed back against him and shimmied her butt just a little. "This is the shape I was in after you practically made love to that piece of chocolate cake that night. The only thing that was keeping me in check was the fact that Rick was there. Didn't you wonder why I didn't give him the night off?"

"Yeah, a little," she admitted, although at the time she'd been beyond thrilled that by keeping her security detail in place, it was an indication that Doyle considered their evening out to be personal, rather than business.

"I couldn't very well kiss you, or touch you, or do any of the other things you had me wanting to do that night with him following us home."

"That would have made for an interesting report at the morning briefing," Thea agreed, giggling when he tightened his arms around her in mock punishment for her cheek.

"You have no idea how interesting," he whispered in her ear, sending shivers down her spine at the dark promise in his tone.

"You could show me."

"Oh, I intend to." The press of his erection emphasized the words. "But first I have to finish explaining."

"You don't have to." Thea tried to turn in his arms to face him. He resisted at first and then finally gave in, letting her spin but not relinquishing his hold, as though he were afraid she'd run away if he let her go.

As if.

"You wanted me," she said, bringing her hands up to his chest, relishing the hard play of muscles beneath the soft cotton. What she really wanted to do was throw her arms around his neck, but she didn't quite have the nerve just yet. This was all still too new and unexpected. She was terrified of screwing something up. "It freaked you out. I get that. And then Margo showed up."

"And then Margo showed up," Doyle repeated, only when he said it, it sounded like a curse. "She took me by surprise, and then when she asked for a ride home…I should have sent her home with Rick."

"Yeah, you should have."

"If I had, I would have had you half-stripped with my mouth all over your body before we made it halfway home."

The image sent a wave of damp heat through her, and her breasts tightened painfully. "I wouldn't have minded in the least."

"I would have," Doyle growled. "What I feel for you is worth more than a quick grope in the back seat of a sports car. Which," he added emphatically, "Margo has never been in for *any* reason."

Thea grinned. Evidently she wasn't the only one who remembered Margo's veiled references to her "intimate" knowledge of the contours of that back seat. Then the grin faded.

"But you're still together, right? I mean, exclusive or not, you're still involved with her." Because Thea didn't poach. And she didn't share.

"I suppose technically, yes. But not for lack of trying to change that fact," he added quickly as she started to pull back from him. "I decided last week it was past time to end things with her, but she's been ducking my calls. So I finally left her a message this morning, telling her we were over. I just don't know if she listened to it yet or not."

"Oh, I'm pretty sure she did," Thea said, remembering the hint of desperation in the other woman's eyes as she declared Doyle "hers." Again she felt the unwelcome twinge of sympathy.

"That doesn't give her the right to accost you." Anger flared in his eyes. "I'll be having a talk with her about that fact later today, as well as setting her straight about how things stand between her and me. Believe me, this won't happen again."

"Even so, I think I'll just stick to running on the grounds for a while, just to keep the peace," Thea said, only half joking. Because once Doyle actually broke things off with her in a permanent, never-going-to-change-his-mind way, Margo seemed the type to take her spite to a nasty level.

"You don't have to. Margo won't be at Fit anymore."

Dismay bloomed. "Oh, Doyle, you didn't."

"I didn't have to. The manager heard about what happened from several of the people there this morning. There's no way they'd keep her on after she went after a member like that. He called here to assure me that there wouldn't be any further incidents. Hey." He slid a finger under her chin, tipping her face up to his. "Margo losing her job isn't your fault. It's hers. Don't feel bad about it."

She did, though. The woman was a royal bitch and had caused her no small amount of grief over the past week, but she still hated for anyone to lose their livelihood.

"You're still doing it," Doyle chided.

"I can't help it." She sighed. "Maybe if I call them —" She stopped when Doyle brought his finger up over her lips, silencing her.

"Not. Your. Fault."

She couldn't help it. Staring into his eyes, Thea's inner imp made her flick her tongue out and lave his finger, just as she'd done at the restaurant that night. This time, however, there weren't a few dozen people sitting in the room or a jealous sort-of girlfriend storming the scene.

This time there were just the two of them, and Thea watched, fascinated, as Doyle's pupils dilated and his nostrils flared. The flush she'd noticed earlier on his cheekbones darkened, making them look sharper and sexier. As if Doyle needed any more hotness. He already had her sizzling, and he hadn't even kissed her yet.

An oversight he didn't waste any time correcting, replacing his finger with his lips and giving her a whole new use for her tongue.

# Chapter 20

**THEA'S LIPS OPENED** under his with little coaxing. Doyle could feel the softness of her lips, the eager warmth of her tongue as it met his, and a part of him was amazed that this was actually happening. This was Thea. *Thea.* For all the doubts he'd had, for all the agonies he'd suffered trying to decide the rights and wrongs of it all, he knew now that this was exactly what he had wanted to happen.

Right here. Right now. This was his woman, and he was going to stake his claim before another bout of stupid made him resist the idea again.

*Woman.* God, yes, Thea was all that and more. He could feel the firm globes of her breasts pressing against his chest as she wrapped her arms around him. One of her hands sifted through his hair as the other clutched his shoulder as though to hold him in place. He almost laughed. Like he was going to go anyplace but where he was right at that moment.

Finally given the freedom to explore, he felt like a kid let loose in a candy store, not knowing what treat to start with first. Deciding to start at the top, he rubbed both hands along her back, feeling the play of her shoulder blades, the soft curve of her back as it dipped toward her waist and then flared out again in a sexy curve at her hips.

Once there, his hands took opposite directions. One curved around to cup her ass, lightly kneading it to the accompaniment of Thea's tiny moans, which sent even more heat to Doyle's already rock-hard dick. He'd promised himself that he'd go slow, that he'd ease her into lovemaking, but his body was going to give him trouble keeping that promise. All he wanted to do at that moment was strip her naked and climb inside of her for the next week or so.

The other hand, which had been sliding up her ribs, finally found its destination and curled around her left breast. It was a lovely handful, and all he kept picturing was the way the luscious mounds had glistened under her fingers as she'd smoothed sunscreen all over them. He'd tried not to look then, but now all he wanted to do was look, and taste, and touch.

Settling for touch, he caressed the soft mound gently, rubbing his thumb over and over the crested peak he could clearly feel beneath the barrier of her clothing, a barrier he wanted gone. Now. But he forced himself to go slowly, to savor each step as they took it. Everything was a first for them, and he wanted each and every memory of this first time to be perfect. For both of them.

Thea gasped slightly into his mouth as he lightly pinched the erect nipple and then shuddered and moaned when he did it a second time, easing the slight sting with more caresses each time. She broke her lips from his to take a deep, hitching breath and then sent a rain of almost frantic kisses along his jawline as her hands slid down and caught the edge of his polo shirt and started dragging it upward.

"Slow down," Doyle said, even as his body cooperated and pulled back from her just enough to let the material slide free.

"Slow down my ass," Thea muttered, still tugging at his shirt. "I want you naked. Now."

Hiding a grin at her bossy impatience, Doyle took over and finished drawing the shirt over his head. He let it drop to the carpet and waited as Thea stared at his chest. Standing there while she looked her fill made him feel like a damned idiot, but the greedy look in Thea's eyes as they roved over his bare upper body made it worth it.

Almost hesitantly, she placed both palms against his pecs, her fingertips curling slightly inward like a cat flexing its claws before she leaned in and placed a gentle kiss at the very center of his sternum.

Next to his heart.

Unfamiliar emotion clogged his lungs at the simple gesture. Too much. Too soon. His instinct was to put things back on a more physical level, so he hooked a finger under the bottom of her T-shirt and tugged playfully. "My turn."

He thought she might say something about his reaction—or, rather, lack of one—but instead she simply smiled that Thea smile, the one that said she knew exactly what he was thinking, and took a step back, both figuratively and literally.

Where Margo would have used the opportunity to put on an act, all coy hesitations and sexy poses, Thea simply skinned the top up and off, dropping it onto the floor next to his. She seemed to falter for just a second, enough to let him know that she wasn't quite as blasé about the whole thing as she was trying to play it, before gathering her resolve and letting her lacy bra follow.

Beautiful. Absofuckinglutely beautiful.

She stood there, her head held proudly up like a glorious Boadicea, but he could see the flicker of anxiety just beneath the surface. He of all people knew just how little experience she had with intimacy. The fact that she trusted him enough to bare herself like this for him was humbling as well as arousing.

Reaching out a hand, Doyle stroked the soft flesh of her upper chest first and then circled down slowly until the back of his fingers brushed over one rigid rose-colored crest, tightening it even further and drawing a tiny whimper from her.

"Beautiful," he murmured, covering it this time with his palm, bringing his other hand up to cover her other breast at the same time.

He stroked both globes, bringing his thumbs over the peaks, loving the small gasps she made every time he did. Some women didn't enjoy having their breasts touched and teased, but clearly Thea did, a fact for which he would be eternally grateful.

Using that knowledge, Doyle leaned down and took one nipple into his mouth, laving it with his tongue and drawing his teeth gently across it just to see what reaction it would bring. The small yip he got had him looking up, worried that he'd stepped wrong, but the almost frantic look on Thea's face reassured him that it had been a good sound, not one of distress.

Wanting freer access to Thea's luscious body than standing would provide, he maneuvered her backward three steps until her legs bumped the edge of the chair she'd recently vacated. Pressing her into it, he pulled her legs apart and went to his knees between them, immediately reclaiming the nipple he'd left damp and wanting. Thea's hands went to his head, first petting his hair as he worshipped her breasts and then clutching it as her moans became more frantic and breathy.

She started squirming in the seat, and he realized that she had started tugging at his hair, trying to get him to lift his head. Worried that he'd hurt her with his enthusiastic attentions, he pulled back, only to have his mouth claimed hungrily by hers as she pushed at his shoulders. He resisted, unsure of what she wanted, until she ripped her mouth from his and panted, "I want to touch you, too!"

The image of Thea's hot, little hands running free over his body was enough to send the remainder of his blood supply south in a painful rush. The next time she pushed, he went over backward, taking her with him, cushioning her against his chest as they went to the thick, soft carpet. She laughed, obviously knowing that she'd only moved him because he'd allowed it, and then hummed in pleasure as she studied the options laid out before her.

The anticipation was killing him by slow inches, but he swore he'd allow her to take things at her own pace for as long as he could stand it. Which, judging by the way his dick was throbbing inside his too-tight jeans, wouldn't be very much longer at all.

Propping herself on her elbow beside him, Thea ran her free hand across his chest, stopping to run a fingertip around each of his nipples on the way by before leaning in and touching her tongue to the one closest to her. He felt rather then heard her hum again as the disc tightened under her attention.

He'd never thought his nipples were sensitive enough to be a source of arousal for him, but Thea was proving that belief wrong as she licked, sucked and lightly nipped, sending wave after wave of electric sensation straight to his groin, a spot that didn't need any additional stimulation at the moment. He already felt like he was going to burst long before they got to the main event.

His concentration was focused so tightly on what Thea was doing with her mouth that he entirely missed the fact that her hand had gone questing all on its own. The little minx had managed to undo the button on his jeans, giving her just enough room to slip her soft hand inside. He jerked when her fingers brushed the sensitized tip of his penis and then let out a harsh groan as they curled around him in a gentle squeeze.

Fighting the urge to either throw her to the ground and fuck her brains out or jerk off in the soft cocoon of her hand, Doyle struggled to remain still and allowed her to explore. A small breath puffed out of him as Thea's thumb found the drop of liquid on his tip and smoothed it around and around with infinite slowness. God, the witch was trying to drive him crazy! She caressed, stroked, and explored until his entire body was twitching with anticipation and need.

"You're killing me," he finally groaned, his head thudding back against the floor as her nail scraped ever so lightly against the sensitive underside of the crest.

"Then I finally got something right." The smug satisfaction in her voice had him smiling.

"Sweetheart, there's not a damn thing you could do wrong right now." The assurance was barely out of his mouth before he caught her wrist as her fingers gave a firm stroke to his shaft, sending another pulse of liquid from the tip and a warning tingle that said he was close. Too close. "Except sending me over before we get to the best part."

The pout that came to her lips made him want to kiss it off, so he did just that. Sliding her hand free of his shaft brought a groan of disappointment from her and a groan of almost-too-much from him as she gave a last little flick to the tip with her thumb. He rolled her onto her back and straddled her hips with his knees, giving her a mock chiding glare.

"Naughty, Thea."

She gave him a smile so steamy he could practically feel himself break into a sweat. "Only as naughty as you want me to be."

With a groan, he pressed his forehead to hers. "Lord, woman, you're going to make me insane." He caught the hand that was trying to sneak its way back into his pants and pressed both of her arms to the sides of her head, pinning her in place with gentle care as he stared down at her, taking extra care with the arm that Margo had bruised. She tested his hold and then sighed and gave him a disgruntled glare, which morphed to uncertainty when he gave her what his sisters had dubbed his "pirate smile."

"My turn again."

He dropped an exquisitely gentle kiss on her lips, building it slowly, nibbling at the lushness of her bottom lip before thrusting inside with slow, languid strokes. Thea fell into the kiss willingly, never noticing when he released his hold on her arms and sent one of his hands down to her waist.

His fingers teased at her belly button, dipping inside in mimicry of things to come, before sliding past the elastic band of her yoga pants to the edge of her panties. Lace and silk, and no doubt a match to the luscious little scrap of a bra she'd been wearing. He had a moment to wonder if she'd always worn such sexy underwear under her very proper clothes and then decided it was better he hadn't known if she had. That kind of knowledge would have driven him insane.

*Would* drive him insane, every time he saw her from now on.

Pushing past the lace, his fingers found only smooth skin before dipping into folds that were already drenched with her arousal. They groaned in unison, Thea rolling her hips up to meet his touch.

"You're so hot and wet for me," Doyle groaned, pushing his fingers further, making her lower body buck again. "So ready."

"I've been ready for weeks," Thea panted and then tossed her head back on a moan when he found the tight bundle of nerves he knew could throw her over the edge. He circled it, toyed with it, relishing the combination of whimpers and moans that he drew from her with every touch. He dipped back down to her opening and brushed it slowly with just the tip of his finger, back and forth, pushing just barely inside before pulling back and teasing again.

After his third foray, Thea growled and slapped a hand against the floor in frustration. "God, you're making me crazy. Stop— ah!" Her words cut off with a gasp and then a groan as he finally pushed his finger all the way inside. "God, yes!"

The combination of Thea's breathy cry and the sensation of her tight passage clinging to his finger was nearly Doyle's undoing. His dick throbbed once, twice, and it took every ounce of concentration he had to hold back the orgasm that was just another throb away. He pressed his face to Thea's breasts and panted with the strain.

No way in hell was he going to come in his pants like some kid on his first date. When he finally went, it was going to be inside her, riding the waves of Thea's own orgasm, knowing he'd taken them both to paradise together.

Thea's hand petted the top of his head tentatively. "Brennan?"

The sound of his name in that breathy voice, his *first* name, the name she'd never used before in all the years they'd known each other, almost ruined his control.

"I just...need a second here," he gritted out, struggling with the fierce emotion that one simple word had caused. To distract her, he moved his thumb up to her clit while his finger remained buried deep inside. The first brush made her gasp, the second whimper, and the third drew out a groan so sensually charged that all of his efforts at holding back were very nearly shot to hell. Just the sounds of Thea's arousal and pleasure were evidently enough to destroy every bit of self-control that he had.

With speed born of desperation, Doyle jerked his hand free, ignoring the sense of loss, and scooped Thea up in his arms. She gave a startled squeal but threw her arms around his neck willingly enough as he stalked toward her bed. He needed to get her there, *now,* before he took her on the floor like some rutting bastard.

Finally, *finally,* they were there, and he tossed her onto the silky red comforter with a growl of satisfaction before following her down.

# CHAPTER 21

**THE SENSATION OF FLYING** through the air was fleeting, ending with a soft impact on the feather-top mattress that forced a surprised gasp from Thea's lips. She barely had time to recover before Doyle's mouth closed over hers again, the kiss both tender and a bit frantic, and everything she'd ever dreamed of on those long, lonely nights in this very bed.

So many fantasies, and not a single one of them lived up to the actual event in any way, shape, or form.

Not surprising, when her entire previous sexual experience had been limited to Dave, the schmuck who had given her less pleasure during the entire five months he'd spent in her bed than Doyle already had with just his mouth and hands in less than half an hour.

Who knew that there was so much more to be had when the man in your bed was actually a man and not some college kid whose entire knowledge of how to make love came from the Forum section of *Penthouse*.

Doyle's mouth slipped from hers and worked down to her ear, nipping at the tender flesh just below it, then soothing the sting with his tongue. A shiver rolled through her at the sensation. God, it was amazing, these things he was making her feel. Hot and cold, shivery and frantic...every one of his touches set off a new sensation, and every one of them zinged straight to her core. She already felt hot and swollen there. By the time they finally got to make love, she was afraid she might just implode at the first stroke.

Slowly, methodically, Doyle kissed his way down her neck, to her shoulder and then to her breast. She caught her lip in her teeth as he suckled first one hard nipple and then the other, finally unable to hold back the groan that had been building inside.

That seemed to be what he'd been waiting for because he dropped a final kiss on each peak before moving further down her body, his lips questing over her belly to the small indent of her navel. He laved the rim in a lazy circle before dipping his tongue inside, just as his finger had earlier.

It shouldn't have been erotic—it was just a belly button, for God's sake—but the small penetration sent a shaft of empathetic heat to her already superheated vagina.

God, he was killing her with pleasure!

Fisting her hands in the comforter, Thea fought not to squirm as Doyle's hot breath touched the sensitive skin just above the edge of the stretchy yoga pants that he had pulled low on her hips. She wanted, *needed* him to get where he was going, but he seemed intent on taking the scenic route, pausing to admire her hip bones and draw little circles on them with the tip of his tongue, driving her crazy and stringing her nerves so tight she was certain she was going to shoot right off the bed at any moment.

"Brennan," she groaned, finally giving in to the need to squirm, hoping he'd take the hint.

"Patience is a virtue," he admonished, but there was laughter in his voice.

"Not right now, it isn't," she replied on a growl, wondering how she could possibly have enough brain cells still firing to come up with the correct movie quote. Maybe because it was true. Now wasn't the time to be patient. Now was the time to be demanding.

Only she didn't know how.

Luckily, Doyle was through teasing. He pushed back from her and grasped the band of her yoga pants, yanking them down her legs and tossing them aside. Then he froze. Thea's breath caught at the look of sheer masculine admiration on his face, and she made a quick mental note to thank Lillian for her insistence on the new undies. She couldn't imagine feeling quite so sexy in her usual plain white bikini briefs.

Recovering from his momentary brain-freeze, Doyle slipped two fingers under the black lace and slowly drew her panties down and off. Once again, he stood and stared. It was difficult, but Thea fought off the urge to reach for the edge of the comforter to shield herself, although she could feel her cheeks heating and her insides twitching anxiously. Aside from Dave, nobody except her doctor and the nice lady who'd done her recent waxing—so embarrassing!—had ever seen this much of her.

The panties slipped from Doyle's fingers unnoticed. "Jesus wept," was all he said, but it was enough.

Emboldened, Thea smiled and lifted her chin toward his unbuttoned but still zipped jeans. "You, too."

The speed with which his shoes, jeans, and boxer briefs were off and on the floor was startling, leaving her only a second to admire the perfection of Doyle's nude body before he grasped her ankles and tugged. She gave a startled yip as she felt herself slide easily on the smooth silk toward the end of the bed, even though she knew Doyle would never let her fall off the edge.

He pulled until her butt was near the bottom of the mattress, her legs dangling but not reaching the floor. She looked up at him quizzically and got another of those smiles that belonged on a Scottish Highlander or a Viking marauder.

"Still my turn."

Before she could protest that, or even consider if she wanted to, he went to his knees and put a hand on each of her inner thighs. She drew in a breath that came out as a shaky moan when she felt his warm tongue slide slowly up the crease of her folds, bottom to top and then back. Then he did it again. And again. The fourth time, he found her clit and circled it with the tip of his tongue in a teasing swirl.

Her hips grew a mind of their own, lifting toward the sensation, shamelessly begging for more. Doyle obliged, closing his lips over the tiny bud and suckling ever so gently.

It was like someone had put an electric charge to her body. Her back bowed, and her hands, too far away to touch him, flexed then fisted instead on the comforter as her head thrashed from side to side under the onslaught. Every pull sent a new wash of sensation through her, until she was panting out an intelligible garble of oh Gods and ahhs and "Yes. Yes. YES!". There was a familiar tightening in her womb, building and intensifying, and she wasn't certain if she wanted to embrace it or hold it off just a little longer.

As if reading her mind, Doyle took the decision from her, inserting one strong finger into her as he continued to lick and suckle, and then a second. He stroked in and out slowly, and the added stimulation took her over the edge between one heartbeat and the next. Her body convulsed, the pleasure whipping along her nerve endings and dimming her vision to a starburst of white and black, a hoarse cry of primal pleasure ripping from her throat as she rode the waves of pulsing completion.

She'd only ever climaxed on her own before; Dave had never managed to pull off even that small achievement, always too focused on his own orgasm to pay attention to whether or not she was with him at the end. The difference between what she'd felt before and what she felt now was like the difference between a sparkler and a Roman candle. She felt consumed. Burned. Reborn. And yet...

It wasn't enough.

As she slowly came back to her senses, she looked down her body to see Doyle still kneeling at the foot of the bed. Waiting. When she met his expectant gaze, he smiled slowly, pressed a single kiss to the inside of each thigh, and stood.

*Oh. My. God.*

She'd had only a quick glance of him before. Now, she drank in the sight: tanned skin, hard muscles, lightly haired chest glistening with a faint patina of sweat, and rampantly, urgently erect. His penis stood out from his body, curving slightly back toward his belly, the tip so engorged it was very nearly purple. Thick veins ran its length, and as she stared she swore she could see them pulse as they sent even more blood to the already swollen head.

Doyle swore under his breath in what she thought might be Gaelic and reached for her hands. She allowed him to slide her the rest of the way off the bed and onto her feet, although her legs wobbled slightly under her for just a second. Doyle grabbed the comforter and yanked, stripping it ruthlessly from the bed and tossing it aside, pulling the blanket and top sheet down as well in one swift motion before urging her back onto the bed.

She scooted up toward the middle, never breaking eye contact as he climbed onto the bed and crawled toward her like a beast stalking his prey.

"Why?" she asked, meaning the comforter. She'd enjoyed the cool smoothness of the silk against her bare skin.

Still moving on all fours, he growled, "No traction." She barely had time to form her lips into an "oh" of understanding when he was on her.

This time, the kiss was anything but gentle. It consumed, ravished, devoured, and she sank quickly under the heady sensation of Doyle's loss of control, the one thing she knew he valued above all else. That she could bring him to this state told her that this wasn't just physical, wasn't just lust run rampant. This was more. And it was mutual.

Doyle tore his mouth from hers and swore again. Definitely Gaelic.

"I didn't bring..." He made a sound deep in his chest of frustration and annoyance that she felt through their touching bodies, sending a shaft of something electric to her core.

"In the drawer," she panted, flinging a hand out in the general direction of her nightstand. She fought the urge to giggle when Doyle practically dove for it, coming out with the sealed box of condoms she'd found wrapped up with a bow in one of the bags of new lingerie, with a sticky note attached with the words "Stage 4" written in Lillian's distinctive handwriting.

She watched as he ripped the box open and grabbed one of the foil squares, swiftly sheathing himself in the ultrathin latex with hands she was gratified to see were shaking just a little bit. Good. She was feeling kind of shaky herself. It was nice to have company.

Then he was over her, his knees gently pushing hers apart, his hazel eyes a vivid green with his arousal as they stared down reverently at her face. Waiting.

"Yes," she replied to the unspoken question. Yes, she wanted this. Wanted him. Now. Here. Like this, in the bed where she'd spent so many restless nights fantasizing about this very thing, and, she realized now, never even coming close to the reality of it. This went beyond fantasies. This was her fairytale. Her greatest, bestest wish coming true

With infinite care, Doyle placed the head of his erection at her opening, teasing in just a bit and then retreating, again and again, sliding a fraction deeper each time, until she could feel the thickness of him forcing the walls of her channel apart. The sensation of him filling her was almost overwhelming, nerve endings sending pulses of pleasure out with each stroke, making her writhe and squirm and arch, instinctively trying to take more of him, all of him, inside her, and not just the small increments he was allowing.

Her hands ran along his ribs and found his ass, squeezing the hard muscles and trying to urge him deeper, faster. Doyle simply chuckled—rather evilly, she thought—and kept to his set pace, one that was most definitely meant to drive her insane before he was through.

"Brennan, please." She hated that it sounded like begging, but she was beyond caring. She needed more of him. All of him.

Now, damn it.

Two more strokes, three. On the fourth—hallelujah!—he finally, finally sank all the way home.

And stopped.

Feeling the need to wail, Thea looked up at him, about to protest, but was stopped by the look on his face. He looked...enraptured. Like he'd finally found something he hadn't known he'd been looking for. They stared at each other for several long seconds, and Thea felt a well of emotion in her chest that echoed the look on his face.

"*Mo chroi,*" he whispered. Then he began to move, slowly at first, keeping each stroke measured and even, but soon his tempo began to change, speeding up just a little but still not enough to satisfy the need clawing inside her. Realizing she was in no way going to be able to influence his choice of speed, Thea released her hold on his buttocks and instead drew her hands up his back, letting her nails graze the damp skin in a long, lazy path along his spine.

She felt it then, the small stutter in his previously rock-steady tempo. She stroked him again, pressing her nails just a bit harder, and felt it again.

Definitely a stutter. She grinned, knowing that she'd just found the chink in Doyle's armor.

With infinite deliberateness, she scored a wavy path up his lean back, along the spine on the way up, further out toward the ribs on the way back down, sussing out the spots that affected him the most and using them shamelessly. Within minutes, all smoothness was gone from Doyle's movements, and finally, with a harsh curse, he planted his hands at the sides of her head and gave her exactly what she'd wanted, pistoning his hips with a speed that she knew would have had them bumping the headboard had they'd stayed on top of the silk comforter as she'd wanted.

Pleasure built inside her with every strong stroke, filling her as surely as Doyle did, until finally, finally, she couldn't hold it inside any longer and it burst, dragging a cry from her lips and making her dig her nails deeper into Doyle's back as she pulled him even closer and deeper, wanting him with her in the climax.

And then he was, his back bowing as he came with a growl of pure pleasure that had him incapable of actual words as he stroked through his release. He thrust once more, deeper than any before, and held himself there, head back, eyes closed, as though absorbing every last sensation before he finally relaxed, his body curving back down over hers.

He met her eyes and smiled. Not the Viking smile, but the one that said all the tender things that men seemed genetically incapable of uttering aloud except in instances of extreme duress. Her mother had warned her once that getting a man to say "I love you" was akin to landing a man on the moon: it seemed impossible at first, but with a lot of patience, invested time, and dedication to the cause, it could be done, though rarely duplicated.

*"Mo chroi, m'anam."* With those whispered words she didn't understand, Doyle leaned toward her. Lifting her face for the expected kiss, Thea was shocked when his lips fell short of the expected target. Instead, he placed a single, gentle kiss on her chest, between her breasts.

Right next to her heart.

Who needed words, anyway?

# CHAPTER 22

"**WILL YOU GO TO** Mellie's engagement party with me?"

Doyle was on his back in the middle of Thea's queen-size bed, Thea tucked up against his right side. Still caught in the lazy afterglow of what had to be the most amazing sex he'd ever had, he was momentarily confused by the question. His brain wasn't exactly back up to fully functioning speed, which was the only excuse he had for the inane answer he gave.

"I'm already going."

He could feel Thea smile against his shoulder as she continued to trace small circles through the short, dark hair on his chest. "No, I meant will you go with me, as in *with* me."

"Ah." Another brilliant response. God, if an hour in bed with Thea could destroy this many brain cells, he'd be a drooling idiot by the end of the week. Of course, getting to that state would be a hell of a lot of fun.

Just the thought of a week in bed with Thea was enough to warm his blood again. He would have sworn he was too spent to recover so quickly, but the proof against that was already stirring between his legs. Good thing they'd drawn the sheet up partway before collapsing into an exhausted pile after he'd taken care of the condom. If Thea thought to go another round, she just might kill him.

"Doyle!" The accompanying tug on his chest hair drew a pained grunt from him but served its purpose of dragging his attention back to the question at hand. "It's a simple question. Yes or no?"

It should have been a simple question. But it wasn't. There were things at play that Thea wasn't aware of. Dangerous things. Things he had to protect her from. Because if he lost her, if anything at all were to happen to her, he'd be gutted. Devastated. Destroyed.

Then again, what better way to protect her than from right by her side the entire night? Not to mention the fact if he was counted as a guest, he'd be able to get a second man inside the venue without Rogers being able to bitch about it.

"Yes," he said finally.

"You don't have to sound so enthusiastic," Thea huffed, tweaking his chest hair again to emphasize her displeasure. Doyle laughed. He twined the fingers of his free hand with hers, saving himself from any further retribution.

"Yes, Thea, I would love to be your date to Amelia's party." He punctuated his acceptance by dragging her hand to his mouth and kissing her palm and then turned the gesture slightly carnal by catching the web of her fingers with his teeth and nipping just a bit before laving the sting away with his tongue.

Thea made a sound low in her throat in response. His dick stirred again, and he had to fight the urge to just roll her underneath him and risk more brain cells dissolving by slipping into the warm welcome of her body for a second go.

"I want you again, too," she murmured in his ear, indicating that she hadn't missed the tent he was making in the sheets. "But you have work, and I have to get dressed and decide whether or not to ruin my best friend's day or not."

"What? Why?"

Thea sighed, her warm breath tickling across his chest. "If you knew something, something that could make someone really upset, something bad, would you tell them or would you keep it to yourself?"

For a split second Doyle had the panicked thought that Thea had somehow found out about the letters, but he quickly dismissed the idea when he connected the question to her first comment about ruining her friend's day.

"I guess it would depend," he answered slowly, "on whether or not the something was dangerous or not." His conscience tweaked, hard, but he ignored it.

"Dangerous, no. Potentially devastating, probably."

"Emotionally, financially, socially…?"

"Definitely emotionally." She groaned and snuggled deeper into his side, her hand still entwined with his on his chest. "I know I should tell her. I just don't want to. Mellie is under so much pressure already, what with the party this week, and the wedding, and dealing with the dragons. I'd really hate to dump something else on her head right now, but…"

"But she might hate it more if you kept it from her?"

"Yeah." Thea used the hand trapped between them to pinch his side. "Why do men have to be such jerks?" she demanded.

"Ouch." Giving her ass a retaliatory swat, he scowled. "Why do I get punished for something her idiot fiancé did?"

"Sorry." She kissed his shoulder and peered up at him apologetically. "Charles is a sneaky bastard and a shit."

"Well, he *is* a budding politician." Doyle endured another pinch, this one deserved, and asked, "What did he do?"

He listened while Thea sketched out what she'd learned from Charles's personal assistant about the reason for the last-minute dinner that had kept Amelia from attending the club as planned. A part of him understood why Charles—or, more likely, his father—had wanted the club vetted. Platinum was popular, but it wasn't exactly mainstream, and politicians were always conscious of things that might come back and bite them in the ass later on in their careers, especially in this day and age of camera phones and instant media streaming. Once something was out there, it was out there forever.

But the other part of him, the part that knew the three friends and how they watched each other's backs in the tricky and sometimes nasty social world they lived in, knew that both Thea and Lillian would see the tactic as a gross betrayal of trust on Charles's part. Doyle also understood Thea's hesitance in clueing their friend in to the facts.

Amelia Westlake was the one the other two looked out for the most, their weakest link if he had to put a term to it, although Thea would probably punch him if she ever heard him say it out loud. No one wanted to bear bad news to the ones they loved and protected.

He should know.

When she was done talking, Thea lay quietly in his embrace, absently running her thumb over and over his, until finally she said, "I don't know what to do, Doyle."

"Then ask yourself, if the situation was reversed, would you want Amelia or Lillian to tell you?"

"Yes. Absolutely." There wasn't any hesitation in her answer. "It might hurt to hear, but I'd rather know the facts than flounder around in the dark believing in something that everyone else knew wasn't the truth." Turning her head slightly, she pressed a kiss to his chest. "Thanks."

This time, his conscience didn't just tweak, it kicked him straight in the gut. "I didn't say anything you wouldn't have figured out on your own anyway."

"Still, it was nice to have you to talk it over with. I like this." She raised herself up on her elbow slightly so she could look down at his face. "I really like this. All of this. You, me, the talking…"

"The sex," he couldn't help adding, giving her a teasing leer.

"Oh, yeah, the sex absolutely rocked," she agreed with a grin, but it faded to something just a bit uncertain that made his heart hurt. "You're not going to change your mind, are you? I mean, I'm almost afraid that once we leave this room, you're going to start having doubts and regrets and then things will get all kinds of weird between us again and—" Her words were muffled under the two fingers he placed over her mouth.

"Not going to change my mind." He stated it as firmly as he could without sounding pissed, because he was a little. Did she really think he'd take her to bed and then just decide he didn't want her anymore? "Not going to have doubts. And the only weirdness is going to be when your parents come home in three days and I have to tell your father that we're seeing each other."

He watched her eyes widen almost comically and answered her unspoken denial. "Yeah, I do. He's your dad and my boss. He needs to know how things stand between us." Definitely *not* a conversation he was going to enjoy, but there was no way around it.

"But...," she spluttered under his fingers.

"Like he wouldn't figure it out on his own if we spent more than five minutes together in a room with him?" The man hadn't made his millions by being unobservant. And Thea was his only child. His little girl. His baby.

Oh, yeah, he was *really* going to hate having that conversation. The only thing worse would be having to defend his inadequacies to the man in front of Thea.

Thea sighed and sank back down at his side. "I guess you're right. But shouldn't I be the one to tell him? I mean, he is my father."

"No, I'll talk to him. Call me old-fashioned, but that's what men are supposed to do. You," he added with a smirk, "get to tell your mother."

"That won't be a problem. She's always liked you. It's Lillian I don't want to tell. She's just going to gloat that her plan worked."

A few things clicked into place. "Ah, so I have her to thank for the new jogging clothes and that teeny, tiny bikini you were almost wearing?"

She preened just a bit. "Liked it, did you?"

"Liked? I damn near swallowed my tongue, woman!" He smiled when she giggled and then added, "You're going to have to burn it, though, because if anyone else ever saw you wearing it, I'd have to kill them." And he meant it. Just the thought of anyone else on his security team wandering by the pool and seeing Thea wearing that scrap of material she laughingly called a bathing suit made him want to do murder. Yesterday, he would have called it protectiveness. Today, he knew it for what it really was.

Possessiveness.

Funny how the thought didn't freak him out the way he'd thought it would. Thea was his, to have and protect and keep all other male eyes the hell off of. Period.

"What if I promise to only wear it for you?" Thea glanced up at him, batting her eyes in exaggerated coyness. His temperature rose several degrees at the thought.

"That would be acceptable."

She laughed and then groaned. Patting his chest, she said, "As much as I'd rather spend the rest of the day just like this, we really do have to get up now. I have some bad news to give, and, if I don't go do it now, I just may chicken out again."

There it was. His crossroads. His gut clenched, and Doyle reached a decision, one he still wasn't one hundred percent sure was the right one, but given the conversation of the last half hour, he knew it was the only one he could live with.

Curling his arm around her, he pulled Thea back to his side as she started to rise and held her there, ignoring her surprised look and focusing on the ceiling as he spoke.

"Before you go, there's something I need to talk to you about."

# CHAPTER 23

**SOMEONE WAS STALKING HER.**

The thought rolled around and around in Thea's brain as she drove on autopilot through the familiar roads to the Westlake estate. Someone was watching her, maybe following her, definitely fantasizing about her...

Her gaze jerked to the rearview mirror. The dark blue sedan was still faithfully glued to her bumper, but somehow it didn't give her the measure of comfort she'd thought it would. Maybe she should have asked Daryl to ride with her. Or she could have ridden with him. Or she could have just stayed at home, safely locked behind the estate's walls and watched over by the elaborate surveillance system she'd always hated knowing was there in the past. Never before had she been so grateful for those cameras' intrusive presence.

Common sense told her to stay where it was safe. Sheer stubbornness had made her leave. No one, not even some psychotic freak with a torture fetish, was going to force her to cower under the covers for the rest of her life.

Of course, being brave had been easy while she'd still been inside the gates. Now, out in the big, wide world, she found that she wasn't quite as sanguine about facing her fears head on. At least now she understood why she'd been saddled with the extra security details for the past month.

A flash of anger helped burn the fear away for a few seconds. Damn her father for insisting on keeping such a huge secret from her!

Not that she didn't understand his motivation. Her father's love for her and her mother bordered on the obsessive sometimes. Hadn't she had to move over a thousand miles away to attend college just to get a breath of free air? So she really shouldn't be surprised that he would insist on keeping her in the dark and wrapped up in cotton for her own good.

But to lie to her? And to make Doyle lie as well? Damn it, she had a right to know that she wasn't just in some vague danger from a few overpaid executives with a grudge against her father's business practices, but rather the direct target of a deranged, and evidently very smart, very determined, lunatic.

She felt a twinge of regret over the way she'd blown up at Doyle when he'd told her the truth about what was going on. Lying was her one real hot button. After all of the crap she'd gone through with Dave's lying and cheating, she had zero tolerance, and Doyle knew it, which was what had pissed her off more than anything.

To his credit, he hadn't offered up any excuses. He'd laid out the facts and then let her have her say. Which she had. Loudly.

In her own defense, though, she'd realized pretty quickly that she was venting her anger on the wrong person and wrangled her temper under control before she'd really gotten on a roll. No matter what she and Doyle were to each other, at the end of the day, he still worked for her father and was bound by his orders, as annoying and wrong as they might be.

No, Doyle didn't deserve her wrath. That prize belonged to her father. And oh, was she going to have it out with him when he got home. How could he think he was protecting her by leaving her in the dark about someone wanting to hurt her?

Anger was replaced by the hollow ache that had started in the pit of her stomach when she'd first understood the full implication of the situation. Someone actually wanted to hurt her. Who? Someone she knew? A total stranger? Someone she talked to every day, or someone she'd never spoken a single word to except in their twisted mind? The danger could come from anywhere, anytime. No one, no place was really safe.

All of Doyle's paranoia about Nick suddenly made perfect sense. Thea shuddered, but she knew in her heart that it wasn't him. Seth, on the other hand, definitely hit all of the points on the creepy stalker checklist, including the fact that he'd somehow gotten her private phone number despite both Peter and Lillian swearing up and down that they hadn't given it to him. Judging by the fire in Doyle's eyes when she'd told him about Seth, he'd agreed.

Thinking she might be able to help figure out who was doing this to her, she'd insisted on seeing the letters for herself. That had been a mistake.

The first few letters Doyle had showed her were like the one she'd gotten in the mail and given to him weeks ago and then totally forgotten about—creepy, but almost innocent. Saw you, liked you, want to be with you. Middle school stuff.

By the third, though, things had gotten a little less innocent and a lot more personal. Scary personal. Intimately so. By the fifth, she hadn't been able to get through the whole thing before she'd dropped the photocopy to the table and walked out of the room, wanting nothing more than to go take another shower. A hot one. Unfortunately, there wasn't any brain bleach for her to use to cleanse the horrific images from her mind.

Doyle had refused to show her the rest of the letters. Not that she'd wanted to see them after that. She just couldn't imagine how they could possibly be any worse than the ones she'd already seen, but if the look on Doyle's face was any indication, they must have been.

Although what could be more horrific than having some maniac's initials branded into the flesh of her inner thighs as proof of her acceptance of his total possession and ownership, she didn't *want* to know.

She tried to push the memories away and concentrated instead on negotiating the turn into the ornate wrought iron gates that opened ponderously before her. If she didn't stop thinking about it, she just might have to pull over before she reached the house, and she was pretty sure Mrs. Westlake wouldn't appreciate her puking in her rose garden.

She parked on the side of the garage behind Amelia's Mercedes hybrid but didn't move to get out even after shutting the engine off. She leaned her head on the steering wheel and tried to corral her emotions.

God, what a day.

First the very public confrontation with Margo, and then the amazing hour of passion with Doyle, and then finding out she'd been fixated on by some sicko with a perverted sense of courtship. Now she had to go tell her friend that the intimate dinner she'd been so excited about had been just one more manipulation by the politically ambitious idiot she was engaged to.

At this rate, she was going to have to start borrowing some of Mellie's antacids.

Determinedly, she pushed thoughts of the letters into a cramped little corner of her brain and hoped they would stay there. One crisis at a time was all she could deal with and right now was the time for Amelia's.

Royce, the Westlakes' very proper butler, informed her that Amelia was in the family dining room having a light luncheon, giving her a conspirator's wink as she passed him a large plastic baggie of Rosa's homemade contraband from her tote. Oliver hadn't been the only member of the household to resent *Monsieur La Chef's* hissy fit and Mrs. Westlake's resultant goody ban.

Royce and the twice-widowed housekeeper, Mrs. Massey, were particularly fond of Rosa's baking, and, if Thea wasn't mistaken, of each other as well. Since both of them had run interference between Amelia and her mother on more than one occasion, she was more than happy to return a favor.

She also knew the value of a peace offering, hence the second baggie of gooey oatmeal-chocolate chip yumminess in her tote for Oliver. She had a feeling that after their tiff the night before, he wasn't going to be as accommodating as he'd been in the past when she asked for a favor. But she'd gotten Doyle to agree to be her date, and she wasn't wasting a second getting the seating arrangements squared away to secure his place at her side.

Even though it was what her bodyguards always did when she went to visit one of her friends, Thea still felt a rush of panic when Daryl gave her a nod and turned down the short hallway that led to the security office situated at the front of the house. She fought it down, inch by inch, reminding herself that she was just as safe inside the Westlake's home as she was in her own. Probably safer.

Too bad logic didn't mix well with panic.

Knowing the longer she stood there, the more of an idiot she looked like, Thea put her feet into motion and forced herself to move. As she approached the dining room, she heard voices. Amelia and her mother.

Thea groaned silently. She really didn't want to deal with the woman at the moment, and she definitely couldn't tell Amelia what she needed to tell her while she was there. She wondered briefly if it was too late to escape back out the front door and then had another, less cowardly thought. If the dragon was occupied here, it might be the perfect opportunity to catch Oliver alone.

Backtracking, she hurried down the corridor to the small office the mothers had usurped as their own. Damn. It was empty. But the door stood ajar and the light was on, indicating that whoever had been inside had only just left and expected to return soon. Thea hesitated on the threshold. No Oliver, so there was no reason for her to go inside. Still…it was forbidden territory. Sacrosanct. Totally off-limits to everyone but the dragons and their minion.

The lure was just too great.

Giving a swift look both ways down the hall first, she slipped inside. The room was larger than she'd expected, easily twice as big as the room she'd set up as her own temporary office at home. Of course, there were three people using this one, so it made sense they'd need more space.

The faint aroma of Coco Noir lingered in the air, letting her know that Mrs. Westlake had recently been there and might very well come back at any moment. Thea's heart picked up a few beats at the implied risk, but strangely, after finding out she had a deranged admirer out there stalking her, the threat of the dragon's wrath really didn't measure up.

Two desks flanked the right and left walls, one with a computer that had a swirly screen saver slowly rotating through the colors of the rainbow in random, abstract patterns. Next to the computer was an open can of Red Bull energy drink, the recycle bin beside the desk already half-full of the slender blue-and-silver cans. Good. That meant Oliver was around somewhere.

The third wall had a table that was stacked with various envelopes, notepads, and books of invitation and place-card samples that she was pretty certain Mellie had never laid eyes on. She was tempted to peek, but a whiteboard on an easel in the corner drew her attention. It appeared to be a checklist for the upcoming engagement party.

Except it didn't contain the usual items like caterer or flowers or limos. No, it contained the names of every major news outlet in the country, followed by a ranking of the top anchors and reporters attached to each of them. Stars denoted some kind of ranking system, and checkmarks seemed to indicate which would be attending.

There were a lot of checks.

Thea ground her teeth in frustration. Damn the Davenports, and damn the Westlakes, too. That many news people in attendance could only mean one thing. They were going to turn what should have been a celebration of their children's future happiness together into a media feeding frenzy by announcing Charles's nomination to the upcoming primary race.

How could they? How *could* they? Charles would have to have been in on it. But what about Amelia? Had any of them even thought about what this would do to her? Had they even *told* her? Or was she going to be blindsided the night of the party when all attention shifted from the happy couple to focusing instead on the newest Democratic *wunderkind* throwing his hat into the political ring?

Her hands tightening on the strap of her tote in impotent fury, Thea swore violently under her breath. She couldn't let them do this to Mellie. It would kill her. Truly rip her heart out. And yet…there wasn't a damn thing Thea could do to stop it. Judging from the names checked off on that list, half of the most important men and women from both the print and broadcast media were coming. To disinvite them would be political suicide. There was absolutely no way to stop the Davenport juggernaut.

Thea swore again, this time using a few of the words she'd learned from Red when he didn't know she was around to hear them, only to have her words break off into a muffled scream as a hand came around to cover her mouth from behind.

# CHAPTER 24

"SHH! MRS. WESTLAKE is right down the hall."

It took several seconds for the familiar voice to penetrate the thick fog of panic that had gripped her at the same time as the hand. Still, relief didn't come immediately. The dark, violent words from the letters she'd read were still too fresh in her mind. It could have been anyone who'd snuck up on her. Surprised her. Done...whatever to her.

Thea shuddered. She'd never considered herself a coward before, but right then, it was all she could do not to run back to the security office and tell Daryl he wasn't allowed to ever, ever leave her side again.

*Ever.*

The hand over her mouth reeked of a strong combination of floral soap and hand sanitizer. Wrinkling her nose in distaste, she shoved at the arm, dislodging the hand and swatting at Oliver as she turned, taking a step back as she did to put a little space between them.

"What the hell did you do that for?" she demanded, wiping her mouth to try and get rid of the lingering aroma of Purell. She saw Oliver's mouth tighten a little but wasn't about to apologize for her language.

"You screamed," he said, as though stating the obvious.

"I screamed *after* you grabbed me." Hah! Point to her.

His brow furrowed slightly before smoothing back out again, an expression she'd often seen on Charles when he was working hard at not looking like he had to think about the answer to a question. "You were cursing."

"Quietly." Mostly, anyway.

"You know how Mrs. Westlake feels about that kind of language."

Strongly enough to ban both Thea and Lillian from the house for several months back when they were seniors in high school and she'd caught them trash-talking the cheerleaders who'd been giving Lil a hard time because she'd gone on a date with one of the football players one of the girls had wanted for herself.

Still…"She's all the way down in the breakfast room."

Oliver looked like he was going to argue and then asked instead, "What were you doing in here?"

"Looking for you, actually."

"Oh?"

She supposed the wary look in his eyes was warranted after the previous night. "How difficult would it be to make a minor tweak to the guest list?"

"For the wedding? Well, since it hadn't been finalized yet—"

"No, for the party."

"The party?" He stared at her. "You mean the engagement party? The one that's in six days? *That* party?"

She thought she could see the vein in his temple beginning to pulse. Quickly, before it could burst, she said, "I'm not really adding another body. Technically." She winced. "I mean, I just wanted to let you know that I'm going to be using my plus-one after all."

Amelia had encouraged both her and Lillian to bring dates to the engagement party, wanting them to have a good time instead of just holding her hand. Lillian hadn't been hanging onto a man long enough to get one through the required background check to make the guest list, and Thea hadn't wanted to bring anyone if it couldn't be Doyle, so they'd both declined the offer.

Despite that, Amelia had insisted that a seat be left available at their table for each of them, just in case they changed their minds; one of the few fights she'd actually won. Of course, the only other people at their table were Thea's and Lillian's parents, and Amelia's great-aunt Josephine, who would spend the evening talking about her half-dozen dogs and almost as many ex-husbands and would most likely be asleep in her seat long before dessert with the aid of a few too many cocktails.

Unfortunately, the vein in Oliver's temple didn't stop throbbing as she'd hoped. "You've decided to bring a date?"

"Well, yes. Is that a problem?" She wouldn't put it past one of the dragons to have commandeered those two extra seats without telling Amelia. An invitation to this party was the Washington equivalent of winning the golden ticket. Any seat left unoccupied was wasted real estate.

"There isn't enough time left to do any of the necessary background checks," Oliver gritted out.

"Oh!" Feeling stupid, Thea gave a small laugh. "Sorry. You don't have to worry about that," she said, patting his arm in apology for giving him unnecessary agita. "He already has the necessary clearance or whatever you call it."

"He does?"

Thea nodded. "He was going to be working, well, I guess he'll *still* be work-ing, but I'm hoping he'll be able to spare at least a little time to enjoy himself."

It felt incredibly silly to keep dancing around just saying Doyle's name, but once Oliver knew, Mrs. Westlake would know and then *everybody* would know. Thea didn't want her parents finding out about her and Doyle that way. Not that she thought either one of them would have a problem with their rela-tionship, but it just seemed rude for everyone else to know before they did.

Oliver blinked, appearing slightly confused. "This is rather...sudden, isn't it?"

"No, it's actually long overdue. Some people are a little slow on the uptake." But once they got going...*Whoo boy!* Memories of exactly how effec-tive Doyle could be in going slow flooded her, making her body tighten in anticipation of doing it all over again that night after she made him dinner in his bungalow. Maybe she should stop and get a dessert from Rudolfo's. Something decadent and sinful that they could share in bed after they...

Mortified by where her thoughts had strayed, Thea could feel twin flags of embarrassment burning her cheeks as she struggled to focus back on the conversation.

"I'm sorry. What did you say?"

The small smile he gave her only served to deepen her embarrassment, as though he knew *exactly* what she'd been thinking.

"Just that sometimes people miss what's right in front of them."

"Yeah, sometimes, but I think we're both finally on the same page now, so, um, are we good here? With the seating thing, I mean?" Where was a convenient hole when you needed one to crawl into?

"Don't worry." Oliver smiled and patted her arm. "I'll take care of everything."

"Great. Thanks." She made it as far as the door before remembering her bribe. Digging into her tote, she dragged out the plastic baggie of cookies and practically threw it at him. "Here. These are for you. Bye!"

It was a less than graceful retreat, but at that moment all Thea wanted was to get away. Dignity was a distant memory. She fast-walked down the hallway, ducking into the powder room that Oliver must have used and locked the door, leaning back against it with a groan. Holy, holy crap!

Putting her hands to her cheeks, she could still feel the heat burning there. Sure enough, looking in the mirror, she cringed at the flushed, wide-eyed person blinking back at her. Never before had she had such a visceral reac-tion to just thinking about sex. Then again, the only sex she'd had to think about before had been mediocre at best. Sex with Doyle had been...more. Much, much more.

It hit her then, standing in the Westlake's blue and beige powder room with the tiny Tiffany sconces and gold-flecked marble countertop. It was more because it hadn't been just sex. She could still feel his touch on her skin, feel his breath on her throat, taste his mouth on her lips, because they'd connected at a much deeper level than just the physical.

They'd made love. Passionate, desperate love.

She'd be fooling herself if she thought that meant that Doyle loved her. Yet. It was too soon for that, especially for a man like Doyle, who always considered his every move very carefully beforehand, sometimes with painful thoroughness. But it did give her hope that he would find his way to that state sooner rather than later.

Remembering the look in his eyes as he laid that kiss next to her heart, the words he'd whispered against her skin—she didn't know what they meant, but they had to mean *something* special, didn't they?—she thought he might already be partway there.

After splashing some cool water on her cheeks to try and put out the fire there, she squared her shoulders and went in search of Amelia. She found her still in the dining room, poking at the remains of a poached chicken breast with steamed broccoli and rice. It was one of Mellie's favorite dishes, and one that Thea knew the chef prepared exceptionally well, so the fact that more than half the meal remained uneaten was a very bad sign.

Feeling a little guilty to be relieved that Mrs. Westlake had departed sometime during her foray behind enemy lines, Thea plopped down into the chair next to her friend and snagged a piece of fresh bread, the aroma of which reminded her that she hadn't taken the time to stop for lunch herself before coming over. Then she remembered why her appetite had been lacking and put the bread back down uneaten.

"Is it too late to go into the Witness Protection Program, do you think?" Amelia asked, spearing her fork into a broccoli floret and staring at it morosely.

"I think you have to witness a crime to qualify for that particular perk from the federal government," Thea replied. Her heart hurt to see her friend so miserable.

Amelia let out a cynical laugh. "I think this whole dog-and-pony show qualifies as criminal, don't you?"

For Amelia to say something like that, something had to have happened. Something bad. Unfortunately, Thea thought she might have an inkling or two about what that something might be.

"What's wrong?" She touched her friend's arm, trying to get her to look at her. Amelia refused, continuing to stare at the floret as though it fascinated her. "Mellie?"

"I sort of almost slept with Charles last night."

Thea did a slow blink. That certainly wasn't what she'd expected to hear. "Um…okay?"

Amelia laughed again, an unhappy sound to go with her expression. "No, not okay. Definitely not okay. It was…" She let her fork drop, the sharp ringing of metal on fine china making Thea wince. "A disaster."

All sorts of unpleasant possibilities flashed through Thea's mind. She hesitantly asked, "He didn't make it good for you? Or…?"

"We never got far enough to make it good."

"Okay, what? I'm confused."

"That makes two of us."

"Mellie, use your words. What happened?"

"Oh, God." Amelia slumped back in her seat—the second of her mother's rigid rules to be broken in as many minutes—and covered her face with her hands. "We went to dinner. I thought we were going to the restaurant at his hotel, but he brought me up to his suite instead. He had a table set up there with a waiter standing by to serve us and everything."

"That sounds romantic," Thea hedged, but knowing what she did about Charles's motives made her sound more questioning than encouraging.

"I thought so, too. At first."

"And then?"

"I tried to get him to talk about the future. Our future," she clarified. "What we were going to do after the wedding, where we would live. Children." The word sounded so wistful that Thea wished Charles would walk into the room so she could punch the insensitive bastard right in the nose.

"Do you know what my future sounded like? His future. *His* career, *his* job, *his* need to have the right wife, the right family connections, the right everything! Oh, and he's sure that having kids would make the constituents very happy, so he was all for that, just not right away. Maybe after he'd had a year or two in office. A pregnant wife would do wonderful things for him at re-election time."

No, she wouldn't punch his nose. She'd kick him in the balls.

"The worst part is, I kind of expected all that," Amelia went on, finally lowering her hands to look over at Thea. Her eyes were red and glassy with unshed tears that she furiously blinked back. "I know what a politician's wife is expected to do, to give up. I've watched my mother all these years, planning her life around my father's, and then planning my life around that."

"And you didn't want that for yourself," Thea reminded her gently.

Amelia shrugged. "I hadn't planned on falling in love with a politician, no, but Charles just kind of blindsided me."

*Steamrolled her was more likely*, Thea thought, remembering the whirlwind courtship he'd staged over the course of a few short months before popping the question. "So, if that wasn't what upset you, then what happened?"

Amelia closed her eyes and then opened them again, pushing back from the table. She caught Thea's hand in hers and silently tugged her out of the room and up to her bedroom. Once inside, she closed and locked the door, then threw her arms around Thea's neck and burst into tears.

# CHAPTER 25

**ALARMED, THEA HUGGED** her friend hard, letting her cry out the anger and frustration that had evidently been festering inside. She'd known Amelia had been sublimating her true feelings with smiles and antacids, but this breakdown said that things were far worse than either she or Lillian had ever guessed.

"I'm...sorry," Amelia hitched through her sobs several minutes later, obviously trying to stop but clearly unable.

"Don't you dare be sorry." Thea hugged her even harder, determined to let her cry out every last tear she had to cry. "What are friends for if not to leak tears and snot onto each other when they need to?" As she'd hoped, Amelia let out a wet bubble of laughter and the sobs eased, slowly turning into hiccups that signaled the end of the storm.

But not the end of the problem.

Murmuring a faint "excuse me," Amelia disappeared into the en suite bathroom. Water ran. While her friend washed her face and gathered her composure, Thea curled up on one of the two large upholstered chairs that sat in the bay window overlooking the side gardens. They'd been straight-backed Chippendale chairs up until two years ago when Amelia had begged Thea to redesign her room from the antiques showpiece she'd lived with most of her life into something she could actually be comfortable in.

Thea had understood exactly what her friend had been asking her to create: a sanctuary. So, during one frantic midwinter break, she'd done just that. Gone were the heavy walnut and marble, replaced by lighter woods, brighter colors, and an overall softer feel.

The only antique to remain was a mahogany dressing table with a mirror that was so old that the reflection was slightly warped. Amelia said she loved it because it had been a sixteenth birthday present from her great-aunt Josie. Personally, Thea thought she liked it because it had bugged her mother that it was somewhat less than perfect.

Amelia had loved the final result of the makeover. Mrs. Westlake...not so much. Thea was pretty sure she only let it stay in its new, livable state because it wasn't a room that would ever be in the public eye.

Amelia came back dry-eyed, looking as though something vital had been drained out of her along with the tears. She dropped into the matching chair at the bay window, kicking off her shoes and curling her feet up underneath her in what even Thea could tell was a self-protective gesture. She was dying to know what happened, but forced herself to wait until Amelia told it at her own pace.

"Men suck," Amelia said finally with a sigh. She rolled her head on the chair's high back to peer out the window. "Do you know that Charles has never once tried to do more than kiss me?" Since it was clearly a rhetorical question, Thea remained silent. "He's kissed me hello, kissed me good night, even kissed me once or twice just to kiss me. But he's never once tried to do more."

"Maybe he was being a gentleman?" Thea suggested, though she doubted that. More like he hadn't scheduled time for anything more in his day planner.

"Pretty to think so, right?" The unfamiliar cynical tone was back in Amelia's voice. "Truthfully, I was starting to get a little worried he was gay."

Thea let out a surprised huff of air, not quite a laugh because it wasn't funny, but not quite a word because she honestly couldn't think of the right one to say. Of all the things she'd imagined, that certainly hadn't been on the list.

"Last night, I decided it was the perfect time to find out if the problem was him or me. I mean, how often are we ever alone together, right? And there we were, in his hotel suite, no parents, no Oliver, no agenda. Just him, and me, and a bed. So," she finished with a shrug, "I seduced him."

Again, nowhere near what she'd expected. Amelia was the model of propriety her mother had molded her to be. She didn't stick a pinky out of place—except when Thea and Lillian were there to coax her into it, of course, which was why Mrs. Westlake had discouraged their friendship with her daughter from the start. They encouraged her to bend the box a little, like going to Club Platinum or Blaze.

Amelia had evidently done them one better and totally blown a big old hole in the box, and she'd done it all by herself with no input from them.

And it didn't appear as though it had gone well.

"How did he, uh...?"

"Respond?" Amelia bit her lip and then gave Thea a sheepish grin. "Well, he's not gay, anyway." The grin slipped away. "I think I'd almost rather he was."

"What happened?" Thea asked gently.

"We were on the bed, and things were going the way I'd hoped. It was…nice."

Nice? Thea couldn't imagine describing sex with the man you loved as simply "nice." Not after experiencing what she had just that morning with Doyle. It was hot, frantic, mind-blowing, toe-curling, even earth-shattering. Nice? Nuh-uh.

"He'd turned the lights down low, which was good because, truthfully, I was pretty nervous about getting naked in front of him. But I did it," she stated proudly and then gave a cheeky grin. "I wore some of the lingerie that Lil picked out when we went shopping for you. I'll have to tell her she has good taste. Charles liked it. A lot." She managed a giggle. "I think I shocked him, actually."

"Good." Thea tried to picture the look on the usually unflappable politician's face when his quiet little fiancée stripped down to a set of racy, lacy undies. She couldn't do it.

"Things kind of went fast after that." Pink tinged her cheeks. "Maybe a little too fast, to tell you the truth. I was still pretty nervous and he was pretty eager, and…it was just starting to feel really good when…"

"When?"

"He stopped." The words were barely a whisper.

"He stopped?" Thea repeated. "Like, he realized he was going too fast and slowed things down?"

"No, I mean he stopped." The pink had turned a bright red, and Amelia wouldn't meet Thea's eyes as she rushed on. "He got up and sat on the edge of the bed. At first I thought he was opening the nightstand to get, you know, protection."

"But he wasn't," Thea guessed, dreading where this was going.

Amelia shook her head. "He was answering his phone."

"He…" Thea shook her head, certain she must have heard wrong.

"Answered. His. Phone." Amelia spat each word as though it were a curse and then angrily wiped at the tear that ran silently down her cheek. "I hadn't even realized he'd put it there, and I didn't hear it ring. He must have had it on vibrate."

"You…he…" Thea closed her mouth with a snap, unable to string out a coherent response. She'd known Charles was an ambitious bastard, but this! It went beyond being merely insensitive. It was heartless and cruel, and she was absolutely going to make the bastard pay for every tear he'd made Amelia shed over him.

"I thought, okay, maybe it was something important, and he *had* to answer it," Amelia went on.

"*Nothing* is that important," Thea countered harshly. "Not even if it was the president himself." She stopped and slid a sideways look at her friend. "It wasn't...?"

"No," Amelia replied with a short laugh and then sobered. "I think it was Oliver."

Which reminded Thea of why she'd come over to speak to Amelia in the first place. But somehow, Charles's perfidy in derailing Mellie's night out with the girls paled to insignificance compared to what the rest of the evening had brought about. Still...

"Remind me we have to come back to him," Thea said, not wanting to interrupt her friend before she was finished. "What happened after Charles answered the phone?"

Amelia looked intrigued enough by Thea's comment to want to ask more and then sighed and said, "He talked. I left. That's it."

"So not it." Thea rolled her hand. "He started talking and you...?"

"Waited, damn it." Amelia grimaced at the admission. "At first I couldn't believe he'd done it. Then I thought, he'll tell Oliver he'll call him back and put the phone down in just a second. But he kept talking, and talking, and then he got up and went into the other part of the suite where they have their little portable office set up. He never even said a word to me." She sounded so bewildered and hurt that Thea clenched her fists in impotent rage. "It was like he forgot I was even there."

Every word that came to mind would have gotten her banished for life by Mrs. Westlake, so Thea settled for asking, "Do you want to kill him yourself or do you want me to help?"

"Believe me, the urge was there to do worse than that," Amelia told her, surprising Thea with the ring of truth behind the words. Amelia was the least likely person she knew to do any kind of violence. She'd sucked at every self-defense class she'd ever taken, much to the despair of Paul Kent and the rest of the Westlakes' security staff.

"Then what?"

"When I finally realized he wasn't coming back, I got dressed and went out to the living room to get my bag. He never even turned around to look at me when I came in. So, I went down to the desk, had them call me a car, and came home."

Thea couldn't miss the way Amelia's hands crept around to grasp her stomach as she finished her recitation, telling the missing ending to her tale. She's most likely gone straight to her bathroom and thrown up her fancy dinner when she'd gotten home and then sucked down half a bottle of Maalox to stop the acid the unpleasant evening had churned up from eating straight out her belly button.

"Did the bastard call you when he realized you'd left?" Preferably to beg her forgiveness for being such an insensitive prick.

"He called," Amelia replied and then added grimly, "this morning."

Way too late for it to count as anything other than another insult to poor Amelia's pride. "What did he have to say for himself?"

"I have no idea. I wouldn't answer my cell."

"Good for you!"

"Then he called the house."

"And?"

"I still wouldn't talk to him."

"Yes! Make him squirm."

"Oh, he's going to have to do a lot more than squirm," Amelia said, her eyes narrowing angrily. "He's going to have to crawl."

*For all of about five seconds before he was forgiven given Amelia's track record,* Thea thought morosely, but it was still good to see her friend making an effort to stand up for herself. She'd need to do a lot more of that if she was going to survive life with the overambitious jerk she was marrying and his demanding mother.

"Of course, Mother doesn't understand why I'm so upset about the evening being ruined, and it's not like I can exactly explain that it wasn't *dinner* that got interrupted—"

"God, no!" Thea exclaimed, picturing the disaster that conversation would provoke. Mrs. Westlake wasn't exactly a forward thinker when it came to sex. The fact that Amelia was still a virgin at the age of twenty-two was a testament to the stranglehold she kept on both her daughter's morals and her privacy. It wouldn't matter that Amelia and Charles were engaged. She'd view the events of the previous evening as yet another failure Amelia would have to do penance for.

"—soooo, now she's mad at me for acting 'childish,'" she air-quoted with a grimace, "and I have a bad feeling she's going to get Charles's mother involved if I don't pick up the next time he calls."

Tag-teamed by the dragons. Thea shuddered. "Maybe you should just answer and tell him he needs to come apologize face-to-face."

"Yeah. I should." She worried at her lower lip with her teeth for a second and then said quietly, "But what if he doesn't think he has to apologize? What if he doesn't think he did anything wrong?"

"Then you set him straight."

"But if it was an important call—"

"Don't." Thea jabbed a finger at her friend. "Don't start rationalizing, and don't start excusing him. He treated you like crap, and there's no reason important enough in the world for that." She could sense Amelia starting to waffle in her resolution and decided the time was right to throw another log on the fire under Charles's sorry butt. "Remember our plans to go to Platinum last night?"

"I'm really sorry I had to cancel on you that. I was really looking forward to it. But when Charles asked me to…" It only took a second for Amelia to put it together. "He asked me to dinner to keep me from going out with you and Lillian, didn't he?"

Thea nodded. "Yeah, he did. And he sent Oliver to the club to check it out."

"To vet it." She shook her head in disgust. "So the whole evening was a sham. He never wanted to spend time with me. No wonder it was so easy for him to just…" She made a strangled sound in her throat and clenched her hands into fists as though she were picturing someone's neck there for the wringing. "I am so *sick* of being manipulated," she raged in a strangled voice. "All he had to do was ask me not to go. He didn't have to make up a lie."

As much as she didn't want to defend the jerk, Thea felt obligated to point out, "He did clear the evening to spend time with you. Maybe it started out as an excuse to keep you away from the club, but you did get to spend some quality time alone together. Before, you know…," she trailed off, knowing there was no good way to describe the debacle of bedroom interruptus.

Amelia remained silent, but she seemed to be considering what Thea had said. Finally, she nodded. "I guess I'll just have to see what he has to say for himself and take it from there." She offered a tired smile. "Thanks. If I hadn't gotten that all out, I think I probably would have had a nervous breakdown. Either that or run off and joined the circus."

It was an old joke from their first years of friendship. When life at the Westlake house had gotten too intense for Amelia, as it often had in the years before the senator's bad heart had forced him to retire, Thea and Lillian had offered to join her in running away to a fun and carefree new life in the circus.

They'd made elaborate and outrageously detailed plans for their new careers—Thea on the high wire, Lillian as a trick rider on horseback, and Amelia as a lion tamer. Lillian had even sketched out costumes for each of them to wear, complete with tons of sequins and lots of colorful, ridiculously large feathers. Since then, it had been their private code for wanting—or needing—to escape the pressures of their all-too-real lives.

"Why do that when you've got a circus of your very own right here to star in?" Thea teased, relieved that Amelia had recovered enough to find her sense of humor again.

"Yeah, but the clowns are running the show, so what chance do I have of ever getting center ring?" It was said jokingly, but there was all too much truth in those words. Amelia might have ceded control of her wedding plans to the dragons, but as much as she'd insisted otherwise, she wasn't happy about it. The big question was, would she have the strength to try to wrestle ownership of that center ring back?

And what did it say if she didn't even want to try?

There didn't seem to be much else for them to talk about after that. As much as Thea wanted to share her news about the about-face her relationship with Doyle had taken that morning, she knew it would be cruel to bring it up after Mellie's own disastrous evening. The same went for news about her apparent stalker. Throwing that out there now would be akin to tossing gasoline on her friend's already smoldering nerves.

Doyle had wanted her to tell both Lillian and Amelia as soon as possible with the reasoning that they were the people who were usually closest to her when she was off the estate grounds and, therefore, would be in the best position to spot anything, or anyone, suspicious or unusual. Now, Thea debated the wisdom of telling Mellie at all. She already had more than enough to worry over. She didn't need Thea's problems heaped onto her own. Not now.

Maybe she would tell her next week, after the party, when things had calmed down a bit. Because she knew there *would* be a party, no matter the outcome of Amelia's talk with Charles. No way would any of the parents, Westlake or Davenport, let anything spoil their plans to launch Charles's career with all possible fanfare and media coverage.

Not even an unhappy bride.

# CHAPTER 26

"I WANT TO GO TO the airport with you to pick up my parents."

Doyle didn't even pause to consider it. "No."

Frowning, Thea dropped the basket of muffins she'd used as an excuse to visit his office on his desk with a thump. "Why not?"

"Because I said no." Was the woman being purposely slow, or did she really not understand what a disaster that would be?

"Is this about the stalker?" She thrust her chin up defiantly, making Doyle want to kiss her on it. Which was the problem. Why couldn't she see that? He stepped closer until he was crowding her against the desk.

"No, it has nothing to do with that, and everything to do with this." He leaned in close, leaving just a whisper of breath between their bodies. Thea instinctively arched into him, tipping her head up for the kiss she expected. He didn't think she even realized she was doing it. Doyle kept his lips just above hers and whispered, "You want me. Your body gives you away. There's no way your mother wouldn't notice."

Thea frowned up at him, obviously displeased. "You want me, too." Not a statement, but more of a demand.

"Damn right I do, which is something your *father* wouldn't miss, which is why you're not coming to the airport." He palmed the back of her head and held her as he kissed her, long and deep, before finding the willpower to let her go.

God, she made him crazy! He'd never experienced this kind of desire before. After four nights of having her in his bed, his body should have been sated enough that he could be around her without acting like a horny sixteen-year-old who'd just figured out how his dick worked.

Before he could step back, Thea grabbed both sides of his face and pressed her mouth back to his in a kiss even more carnal than the one before. Her arms slid around his neck, anchoring him in place and pressing the front of her body tightly to every aching bit of his. It took every ounce of willpower he possessed to not grind himself into her to relieve some of the pressure building in his groin.

Just as they were reaching the point where Doyle wasn't certain he could keep from lifting her onto his desk and seeing what she was wearing under that long, wispy skirt she had on, Thea broke the kiss with a gasp for air. She pulled back just enough to be able to look at him without either of them going cross-eyed.

"We're telling them about us when they get home." Again, not a statement, but a demand. Doyle smiled gently, sensing her underlying anxiety.

"Yes, we're telling them about us when they get home."

She searched his eyes and then gave a brisk nod. "Okay, then."

Doyle stepped back and let her slip around him. Turning, he watched her check her clothes and hair quickly before opening the door. Doyle bit back a grin at her wasted efforts. The rosy, swollen lips and the flushed cheeks were more of a giveaway than a slightly rumpled blouse.

His staff were trained observers. Just because they hadn't come right out and said anything didn't mean some things had gone unnoticed, like, for instance, the fact that Thea had spent every evening so far that week at his bungalow, not leaving until well after dawn each morning. Something, he realized with a sigh, that wasn't going to be happening again anytime soon. Not with the senior Fordhams back in residence.

The thought of not having Thea in his arms while he slept at night brought a curious ache to his chest. It had only been four nights, but already it felt so comfortable and natural to have her there that he wasn't entirely sure he'd be able to sleep easily with her gone. Which was ridiculous, but there it was.

*A problem for later,* he decided. After he gauged Frank Fordham's reaction to the news of his security chief's involvement with his daughter. Adult or not, Thea was still the man's little girl. There was always the chance things could get ugly before they got resolved to everyone's satisfaction.

And that wasn't even taking into account the fact that he might very well be fired for telling Thea the truth against orders. *That* was the real reason he didn't want Thea going with him to the airport. He planned to set Frank Fordham straight about everything that was going on as soon as humanly possible, which was why he was going with the limo himself to make the pickup. The fact that Evelyn Fordham would be right there next to her husband listening to the same hard truths was something that Frank would just have to deal with. Doyle was done with lies and misdirection. From here until the end, everything was going to be aboveboard.

The possible consequences were just too serious to do otherwise.

A quick look at the clock told him he still had about half an hour before he and Simon needed to leave for the airport. He smiled faintly to himself, thinking he could have avoided the entire argument with Thea simply by telling her who the assigned driver was for the trip. She would have found half a dozen excuses not to go all on her own.

Poor Simon. The man had begged more than once to have a chance to redeem himself by being put back into the rotation of Thea's detail. So far Doyle had resisted, not wanting a mutiny on his hands from Thea. But Simon had been persistent to the point of becoming a pain in the ass about it, so Doyle he had finally relented and made him a part of the party detail for Saturday. He'd be outside, out of Thea's sight, so there wasn't anything she could really bitch about. With luck, she'd never even know he was there.

Just as he was reaching for the muffins Thea had left behind, a brisk knock barely preceded the door being shoved open and Red slipping into his office. Doyle tensed. Sensing the unspoken question, Red shook his head. "No. Nothing in today's mail."

"Damn." Doyle relaxed, but only slightly. "It's been over a week. I expected there to be another one by now." Judging by the perp's previous escalation, there *should* have been another letter by now, or possibly even another attempt at a gift of some sort. Especially after the way the last letter had bragged about how they were soon finally going to be together "as they were meant to be." His appetite gone, he dropped the muffin back in the basket untouched.

"Maybe he got spooked," Red suggested, taking one of the chairs opposite the desk. He peered into the basket and plucked out a blueberry muffin.

"By what, though? It's not like we're any closer to figuring out who he is," Doyle added in disgust.

"Maybe he's gone. He'd taken things as close to reality as he could without actually following through. Maybe it was time for the fantasy to end before it could be ruined for him by realizing it was never going to happen anyplace but in his twisted little head." Breaking the muffin in half, Red took a large bite.

"Much as I'd like that to be the case, we can't count on it." Not when Thea's safety hinged on their response to the threat the stalker posed. They couldn't assume anything other than that he was still out there, still focused on her, still intent on somehow getting to her. Anything less was leaving her open to danger, and that was unacceptable.

Whether they ever received another letter or not, they couldn't lessen their guard. Not until the perp was identified and neutralized.

"Did we get anything more on the analysis of the foreign substance on the last letter?"

"Yeah, actually. It turns out it was honey."

"Honey?" Really? "So, what, our guy's a beekeeper?"

"Or a baker, or a little old lady who likes honey in her tea, or…"

"Yeah, yeah, I get it. It doesn't help us at all." Doyle pinched the bridge of his nose. "Damn it! We're getting nowhere with this."

"There's always one thing we can do."

Doyle knew exactly what he was going to suggest. "No."

"It might be the only way to draw him out."

"I said no, damn it! We are *not* using Thea as bait!" The very thought had his guts twisting in agonizing knots.

"You wouldn't be, not exactly."

"Not any way."

"Hear me out," Red insisted. He didn't want to, but Doyle gave him a terse nod. "Go out. Let the two of you be seen together. If he's watching her, he'll blow a gasket thinking she's being unfaithful to him." He grinned at his boss's expression. "What, did you really think it was a secret for more than five minutes? We had a pool going on how long it would take her to finally wear you down. Besides which, you can't keep that stupid moony look off your face whenever she's within ten feet of you."

"Fuck you," Doyle muttered, feeling his cheeks warm. "I damn well don't moon."

"Like a goddamn schoolboy." Still grinning, Red popped the last bite of muffin into his mouth.

"Ah, hell." Doyle stopped arguing. He probably did moon. God knew he'd caught himself staring off into space more than once when something triggered a memory of how Thea's skin had felt gliding along his, or how her hair had smelled as he pressed his face into it as he thrust inside her, or how…

He jerked his attention back to Red, who was all but laughing at him now. Which was as close as the older man would come to giving his stamp of approval.

Clearing his throat uncomfortably, Doyle said, "I don't like the idea of baiting him. It could be dangerous. He's already nuts. Make him mad, and he could act out violently and unpredictably."

"And if we're expecting it, we can mitigate the danger."

"But not eliminate it."

"No," Red conceded. "We can't eliminate it. But is she any safer while we just wait for him to make his next move on his own?"

No, she wasn't. That didn't mean that Doyle was comfortable actively putting her at potentially greater risk.

"I'll consider it," was all he would commit to. He'd have to think it through, weigh the pros and cons. And, probably most difficult of all, he'd have to try to take his personal feelings out of the equation. Because try as he might right now, he couldn't think objectively. And that wasn't just bad. That was dangerous.

"Everything's in place for Saturday," Red informed him, acknowledging that the discussion had been tabled for the moment. "We finally got every-one vetted by Secret Service, so we shouldn't get any more grief from Rogers about anything."

Doyle restrained a grin. Interaction between his second and the head of Davenport's security had been less than friendly from the start and grown even less so as the day of the party drew closer. Watching the gruff former SEAL deal with the snob from D.C. had become a source of great amusement to the entire security staff. Bets had been laid on how long Red would hold out before he finally gave up on being diplomatic and resorted to intimidat-ing the jackass instead of negotiating with him.

"Why the hell did it take so long?" Doyle asked. "It should have been routine."

Red shrugged. "Evidently something blipped on one of the background checks, so they went back and reran them all for everybody on staff, even the ones not on the party detail. Just to make sure they didn't miss anything." His tone said it was more likely because they were just being assholes.

"What?" Doyle sat up straighter. "On who?"

"Poole."

Doyle's Spidey-sense gave a small tingle. "Impossible. His background check when he got hired came back clean."

"Evidently the Secret Service has better tech people than we do, because they found a juvenile record from when Poole was sixteen that got expunged after he completed court-ordered counseling."

"If it was expunged, then it shouldn't have popped." Just like it hadn't popped for them. Expunged records basically erased the fact that a crime or arrest had ever happened. It was meant to give people a second chance, so prospective employers didn't let their impression get influenced by some-thing done while the person in question had been young and stupid.

Just like Doyle's was being influenced now. Suddenly, all of those requests to be put back on Thea's personal detail took on a much more ominous tone.

"I want him off the party detail."

Red didn't look surprised, but he did look determined. "If you do that, you might as well just fire him, because no one's going to want to work with someone you show that kind of blatant distrust for."

"I don't have any reason to fire him."

"Secret Service cleared him, so you don't have any real reason to pull him from the detail, either," Red countered, crossing his arms.

Doyle wanted to argue, but he couldn't. He knew he was thinking with his emotions and not his head. "Fuck."

"You could always just ask him about it yourself."

He could. But if he approached the problem like the head of security and kept his personal feelings for Thea out of the equation, he knew he probably shouldn't. People given a second chance didn't deserve to have the rug ripped out from underneath them.

The problem was, his feelings for Thea weren't so easy to discount. He wanted her safe, even if it meant trampling other people with unfairness in order to achieve it.

The alarm on his watch beeped. Glancing at it, Doyle stood, swiping a muffin for himself as he did. It was a safe bet there wouldn't be any left when he got back. His people were notorious scavengers when it came to any treats out of Rosa's kitchen. "Time to head for the airport."

Red stood as well, his hand making a quick trip to the basket for another muffin as he did. He saluted Doyle with his booty and followed him out. "Isn't Thea going with you to pick up her folks?"

"No."

Red looked at him for a long second before bursting into laughter as he figured out the reason.

"I don't moon, damn it," Doyle growled, pushing past his friend with a none-too-gentle shove of his elbow. Red's laughter followed him all the way outside. *Hell*, he thought, a smile tugging at his lips, he not only mooned, he also grinned like a fool, and maybe even drooled, just a little, whenever Thea was around. He might not have had his light bulb moment just yet, but he knew when he was well and truly hooked.

Still on edge over the news of Simon's somewhat questionable past, Doyle chose to slide into the rear of the limo rather than ride up front with him. He needed to think things through before he made any decisions there. The Secret Service might have cleared Simon to work the party, but they didn't know about the stalker. A call to Don Rogers just might be in order.

Aside from not wanting to deal with those issues, he needed the time the ride the airport took to prepare himself for the coming conversation with Thea's parents. He might like and respect them, but in the end it didn't really matter what the Fordhams said when they found out about his relationship with their daughter. It didn't even matter if they fired him. Thea was his now, just like he was hers, and no matter what happened, he wasn't letting her go.

*   *   *

Thea could tell just from the way Doyle emerged from the back of the limo that things hadn't gone well with her father. He had his impassive game face on, the one that kept all his thoughts and feelings bottled up and buttoned down, but his usually fluid movements were stiff and jerky, making him appear like a marionette whose strings were being yanked too hard.

As she watched her father emerge next, it wasn't too difficult to see just who had been doing the yanking. Frank Fordham looked more like he'd just come from fighting off a hostile takeover than a month jetting around to some of the most exotic places in the world. Lines of tension bracketed his mouth, which was missing its usual boyish smile, and his shoulders as he reached back to help her mother out were as stiff and tight as Doyle's were.

Not good.

Hoping to snap some of that tension, Thea hurried over to the limo, her smile turning genuine the moment she saw the glow of health that exuded from her mother's face despite the pensive look that shadowed her eyes. A worry Thea hadn't even realized she was carrying slid off her shoulders. Whatever else had happened in the past month, at least her parents' vacation had done its job.

"Mom!" She flung herself into her mother's open arms, absorbing the love and safety that embrace had always offered unconditionally. They hugged for a long minute, both of them just a little teary when they finally broke apart, which made them both laugh. Her mother gave her a kiss on the cheek.

"I missed you, sweetheart." Evelyn Fordham used her thumb to wipe off the smudge of coral lipstick that had transferred to Thea's face.

"Missed you, too, Mom. You had a good time?"

"It was incredible. The experience of a lifetime. I can't wait to show you the pictures."

Thea grinned. If she knew her mother, there were probably thousands of them. Literally. Her mother had never met a picture she didn't like, refusing to delete even the worst out of focus ones, insisting there was still a memory attached to them even if it was a little blurry.

"What's someone got to do to get a hug around here?"

With a huge smile, her father grabbed her up into a bone-crushing embrace. Thea thought there was a hint of desperation in his grip, which was bordering on painful before he finally eased up and stepped back, although he kept hold of her arms as he looked her up and down as though to make sure she was in one piece.

"I'm fine, Daddy," she assured him, hoping to head off the overprotective look that was gleaming from eyes that were several shades lighter than her own deep blue.

"Of course, you're fine. Why wouldn't you be?"

Thea sighed. Great. They were going to play the pretend-it-didn't-happen-and-it-will-go-away game.

"Maybe because I have some psycho writing me love letters that would make the Marquis de Sade blush?" she replied, deciding it was time to take the bull by the horns.

"We are not discussing this." He released his hold on her arms, as though distancing himself from the matter.

"We *are* going to discuss it because you obviously don't understand just how wrong it was to keep this from me."

"From us," her mother added, stepping up next to Thea, arms folded firmly across her chest as she bent a look of severe displeasure on her husband.

Thea almost felt bad for him. Her father never won when the two women in his life joined forces on something and he knew it, but he clearly wasn't going to cave on this matter without putting up a valiant effort.

"How is it wrong to want to protect the people I love most in this world?" he said finally.

"How is keeping the threat a secret protecting me?" Thea demanded. "Not knowing there was a stalker watching me put me in more danger, not less."

"You were never in danger, not for a second," her father said, his voice very certain. "There were guards with you every time you stepped foot from the property. I made sure of that."

"And because I didn't understand exactly what it was they were trying to protect me from, I made their job ten times harder than it needed to be!"

"I pay to have the very best," her father replied harshly, "and I expect them to be able to do what they were hired for. If they can't, then they don't work for me anymore. End of story."

That sounded ominous.

"Fine. Putting aside the issue of my *needing* to know about what was going on," Thea said, switching gears, "what about my *right* to know?"

A wary look flashed in his eyes. "What do you mean?"

"The threat, the letters, they're aimed at *me*. Doesn't that simple fact mean I had the right to know about them?"

"Sweetheart, I just didn't want you being bothered by this."

"Bothered?" she repeated, not sure she'd heard right. *"Bothered?"*

"Why should you have to worry your little head over something that was already being handled?" *By the grownups* hung unspoken at the end.

In that moment, Thea realized that Doyle wasn't the only man in her life that had been having trouble seeing her as a capable, reasoning adult since she'd come home. Her father clearly still saw her as a silly little girl who needed to be coddled and cosseted, allowed to play at life but not to be trusted to make her own decisions about the really important things.

That knowledge made her heart ache a little bit.

"Why not?" she asked, the sour taste of disappointment coating each word. "Because I'm rich and privileged or because I'm just a child?"

"Because you're my daughter," her father snapped back, "and I love you enough to want to protect you from the parts of life that aren't always pleasant. Is that such a terrible thing for a father to want?"

Before she could answer, Thea felt two strong hands slide onto her shoulders and the steadying warmth of Doyle's sturdy presence at her back. She only barely resisted the urge to lean back into all of that strength he offered and take comfort in it.

"Sir, I would respectfully suggest that you not raise your voice when you're speaking to Thea," Doyle said, his tone low and calm and dead serious.

"Why are you still here?" her father demanded, his gaze flicking quickly to where Doyle's hands were, the implication making his eyes narrow. "You don't work for me anymore, remember?"

Thea's gasp was lost under Doyle's reply.

"Yes, sir, I remember. But I'd still suggest you not yell at your daughter."

Reaching up with one hand to cover one of Doyle's, Thea glared at her father. "You *fired* him? How could you?"

"How could I?" Her father sounded incredulous that she would even ask. "He ignored my direct orders. Worse than that, he not only told you about those God awful letters, he let you read them! How could I *not* fire him?"

"I insisted he show them to me," Thea said, wanting to make her part in things very clear. "I didn't give him a choice."

"He had a choice. He just made the wrong one." Her father's gaze turned frosty as he shifted it back to Doyle. "Letting her read those letters was unconscionable. I would have let you go for that alone, even if you hadn't disobeyed orders."

The way Frank's lips curved into an angry scowl emphasized the small scar just to the left side of his upper lip. Ever since she was a child, Thea had used that mark as a gauge of her father's temper. The more pronounced the scar, the angrier her father was. Right now, it was about as bad as she'd ever seen it.

"I happen to agree with you, sir," Doyle said, his hands tightening on Thea's shoulders briefly. "The last thing I wanted was for Thea to be exposed to what was in those letters."

"But you let her read them anyway."

Doyle nodded. "Because I trusted her to know her own mind. Thea has a good head on her shoulders, and I think we all tend to overlook that fact once in a while in our eagerness to protect her. She wanted to know exactly what she was facing, so I let her. Within reason," he added.

Meaning they would have started selling snow blowers in hell before she ever got to see those last few letters. Which Thea was absolutely okay with. She'd had enough nightmares from the ones she had read. She didn't need more fuel for the psychotic bonfire.

"For what it's worth, Frank, I think he did the only thing he could do under the circumstances," Evelyn said to her husband. "From what Brennan told us in the car, things have gotten worse since we left, and without any real leads, it was just getting too dangerous to keep Thea in the dark any longer." To Thea she added, "The first I heard of any of this was in the car just now. If I'd known anything about those letters, I would have been on the first plane home." The fine lines beside her mouth were a sure sign of how tightly she was holding onto the fear and fury Doyle's revelations had stirred. Thea appreciated her mother's forced calm. One of them needed to be the voice of reason, and Thea was pretty sure it wasn't going to be her.

"Which is precisely why I didn't tell you," her father said, taking her mother's hand in his. "There was nothing you could have done by being here, and the worry was exactly what the doctors said you needed to avoid."

The tenderness in the way he looked at her mother softened Thea's anger slightly. She understood how he felt. Hadn't she been willing to go along with the whole bodyguard routine when she'd thought her mother might back out of her trip if she balked?

But lying and reasons aside, there was one big issue that needed to be dealt with. Immediately.

"Daddy, you can't fire Doyle."

"I already did."

"Then un-fire him." She felt a surge of panic at her father's unrelenting scowl. She had to get him to change his mind. She had to. "You know he did the right thing. You can't fire him for that."

"I can," her father disagreed. "But somehow I don't think that's the only reason you want me to keep him on staff." His too-shrewd gaze took in the comfortable way she stood under Doyle's touch. "What the hell else has been going on here while we've been gone?" he demanded.

"Why don't we continue this discussion inside?" Thea's mother looped her arm through her husband's. "I get the feeling that we might want a little more privacy for this."

Her mother had a point, but Thea wasn't budging until she got an answer. If her father didn't change his mind about Doyle, any other explanations were moot. "Dad?"

"I can't just let people disregard my orders because they think they know best," Frank growled, running a hand through his hair in frustration. "It's bad business practice. If I ran my company that way, it would have imploded years ago."

"I understand that." She really did. Her father had taught her more about successfully running a business in one summer than all her years at college combined. "But this isn't the office, and I'm not an acquisition or a spreadsheet. Can't you make an exception for me? Please?"

"Frank, you've always prided yourself on hiring people intelligent enough to have sound enough judgment to make hard decisions when their backs are up against the proverbial wall," Evelyn said. "Brennan was here and you weren't, and he made a decision. A good boss would back his employee up, even if that decision wasn't exactly the one he would have made for himself."

Her father didn't look convinced, but he did look like he was thinking.

"Besides," her mother continued, shooting Thea a knowing smirk, "unless I miss my guess, Brennan is going to be spending a lot more time with the family in the future in a non-employee capacity, and I think it might get a little awkward sitting down to Thanksgiving dinner across the table from the son-in-law that you once fired."

Thea nearly swallowed her tongue. "Mom!"

Her father looked nearly as shell-shocked as she felt. "Son of a—" He shook his head. "Fine. You win. He's rehired, or unfired, or whatever you want to call it." Glaring at Doyle, he added, "We'll be talking about this."

"Yes, sir," Doyle replied.

Thea stepped back so she was standing next to Doyle instead of in front of him and took his hand in hers, squeezing it tightly. "*We'll* be talking about this," she said, just so both men realized she intended to be a part of whatever conversation they planned to have.

Her father looked like he was going to argue. Instead, he chuckled ruefully and asked Doyle, "Are you sure you know what you're getting yourself into?"

Doyle gave Thea's hand a gentle squeeze and replied without hesitation, "Yes, sir. I do."

Thea might have felt insulted if she hadn't caught the sad, almost resigned look that flashed across her father's face before he turned toward the house, taking her mother with him. Why would he look sad?

As if reading her mind, Doyle slipped his arm around her and said quietly as they slowly followed in her parents' wake, "Try to go easy on him. He just realized that his little girl isn't his little girl anymore."

"It's about time everybody noticed that," she grumbled, but she felt a small pang of loss herself at that realization. Things were changing. Nothing was ever going to be the same. But as long as she had Doyle by her side, she knew she could face anything.

# CHAPTER 27

"I THINK I'M GOING to throw up."

Casting a worried glance at Lillian, Thea rushed to Amelia's side and put a comforting arm around her tense shoulders.

"Just take a deep breath, sweetie. Everything's going to be fine." She gently urged her pale and shaking friend onto a small sofa, glad that they had followed her when they'd noticed her slip into the small room the banquet hall had set aside for the hosting families' use.

Lillian followed, sliding one of the dainty wastebaskets a little closer before she took the chair to the side of the sofa. Just in case.

"What's wrong?"

"Nothing. Nothing's wrong. I just…"

"Got a little overwhelmed?" Thea supplied gently, although "panicked" might have been a more accurate description.

Tilting her head back, Amelia took a deep breath in through her nose and then let it out slowly. "Sorry." She offered them a weak smile. "I'm okay now. I just needed a second."

It was a total lie, but Thea wasn't about to call her out on it. From the second she'd appeared on Charles's arm at the party, Thea had been watching her as had Lillian, both doing their best to make sure no one, especially the dragons, gave their friend any grief tonight.

At first, it had appeared that Charles was finally stepping up to the plate, giving Amelia the attention she deserved as his fiancée. He'd kept her anchored to his side the entire time they'd been circulating through the large ballroom, greeting everyone briefly, stopping only to talk to a select few. It was easy to see who those select few were: the movers and shakers of Washington politics. Family and longtime friends barely got a moment's attention.

Less easy to see had been the fact that although Charles kept Amelia at his side, he had, for the most part, ignored her. It had taken Thea almost a full hour to come to that realization, partly because Amelia was so good at keeping a serene smile on her face regardless of her actual feelings, and partly because she was enjoying her own time spent with Doyle. For that, especially, she felt incredibly guilty.

It was only when she'd compared the two men that she'd realized something was wrong. Doyle was constantly touching her—a hold on her elbow as they walked, tucking her hand through his arm as they stood talking to people, a light brush of his fingers at her waist when she leaned in to say something to him privately.

And always, always, he made her a part of the conversation. Whether they were speaking with one person or five, regardless the topic, he always made certain she was included. If he noticed her eyes glazing over as they discussed the hottest new tech stock, he deftly turned the conversation to something else. If she had an opinion to voice, he listened, even debated if he disagreed, but she was always allowed her say.

Not so with Charles.

Once she started to really pay attention, Thea realized that although Amelia was smiling, she wasn't talking. She'd greet everyone they approached—most likely by name, if Thea had to guess, since her friend had a memory like a steel trap when it came to details like that—and then she'd stand quietly by her idiot fiancé's side as he chatted away, only speaking again to bid her good-byes when they finally moved on.

Never once did Charles try to include her in the conversation. Never once did he touch her except to lead her from one spot to another, like a well-trained puppy, where she then stood patiently yet again until he was ready to move on. Never once did he show through any kind of body language that she was anything less than superfluous.

Rather than being half of a couple, Amelia had been reduced to a mere accessory.

Doyle had noticed Thea's growing agitation and after a few moments of observation, he'd easily picked up on the source. Thankfully, rather than warning her against interfering, he'd simply kissed her temple and said quietly, "Try not to draw any blood. Too many cameras in the room" and sent her on her way to rescue her friend.

But Amelia had somehow managed to rescue herself, and like a rabbit seeking the safety of its burrow, ducked into the small withdrawing room, her two friends hot on her heels.

Noting Amelia's still pale complexion, Thea asked, "Have you eaten anything yet tonight?"

"Um, no. We've been too busy greeting our guests."

Grinding her teeth against the angry words that wanted to come out at that, Thea asked instead, "When did you eat last?" Because knowing Mellie, her nervous stomach had kept her appetite at bay for longer than was healthy.

"Um…" From the pinched look on Amelia's face, Thea knew she was trying to remember. And couldn't.

"Lil."

"I'm on it." With a worried frown, Lillian slipped out of the room in search of food.

"I'm okay," Amelia insisted again.

"You'll be even better after you eat something."

"Dinner is going to be served in a little while. I can wait until then." She cast a furtive glance at the door. "I should be getting back."

"You can take ten minutes for yourself."

Amelia shook her head. "Someone will be looking for me."

It was nothing less than the truth, so Thea walked to the door and turned the lock with a decisive snap, although whether she was ensuring no one could come in or that Amelia wouldn't leave she wasn't certain. Probably a little of both. "They'll just have to wait."

"You don't understand," Amelia began.

Thea went to sit next to her. "I do, sweetie. Really, I do." She saw the instant that Amelia comprehended that she really *did* understand what had been going on because tears filled her friend's moss-green eyes, making them look like shiny emeralds.

"Oh, T, it's awful," she whispered. Her face crumpled, and Thea gathered her into her shoulder as she began to sob quietly. Thea would have preferred great, heaving sobs and big, ugly tears. Crying was supposed to be a release. Holding back and letting only the tiniest of pressure out when it finally got too bad wasn't healthy. Like so many other things Amelia did.

Had been trained to do.

Mrs. Westlake deserved a good punch in her expensive rhinoplasty.

"I thought you and Charles had smoothed things out about last weekend," Thea said when Amelia finally sniffled and pulled back. She reached over to the table next to the sofa and grabbed the box of tissues discreetly disguised in a cloisonné box.

"I thought so, too." Dabbing at her eyes and then her nose, Amelia looked confused. Lost. Thea thought she should have been looking angry. But knowing her friend as well as she did, she knew that Mellie would be looking for some way to blame herself for Charles's neglectful attitude.

So she was pleasantly surprised when Amelia said, "I don't know what's wrong with him tonight. He's gone out of his way to be so nice to me all week. He's come by almost every day for lunch, and he's called on the days he didn't. He's even been sending me more of those little handwritten notes every morning. They were really sweet. Romantic, even."

"So why is he being such a—" Thea bit off the word that leapt to mind.

"Butthead?" Amelia filled in for her. They both burst into laughter. Amelia's amusement faded, though, leaving behind the lost look again. "I don't know. No. That's not true. I do know, and I'm not going to pretend anymore. He's more interested in his career than in marrying me."

Her chin wobbled for a second before she firmed it, resolve shining in her eyes. "I refuse to become my mother, damn it. I'm not going to live my life in his shadow, waiting for some crumb of affection."

A soft knock interrupted her, and by the time Thea came back from letting in Lillian and her haphazardly piled plate of appetizers, Amelia's resolve seemed to have fled. She dutifully picked at the offerings, but she seemed sunk in her own thoughts. Unhappy ones, judging by the pinched look around her eyes.

"So," Lillian said to Thea as they watched Amelia shred her second roll, "you and Doyle looked all cozy and couple-like out there. Looks like my plan worked out just the way I said it would." Her smug expression froze, and she darted a quick look at Amelia. "Oh, honey, I didn't mean to…"

Amelia waved her apology off and even managed a small smile. "It's fine. I'd rather talk about someone else's relationship, anyway. And they did look good together."

"Well, duh," Lillian replied, rolling her eyes.

"What did your parents have to say about you two being involved?"

"Not too much, really, although I'm pretty sure my dad gave Doyle the 'if you hurt my little girl, you're a dead man' speech when I wasn't around, not that either one of them will ever admit it to me."

"What about your mom?" Amelia asked.

Thea grinned ruefully. "She told my dad he couldn't fire his future son-in-law without making the holidays weird."

Amelia looked shocked. Lillian sputtered into laughter.

"How did Doyle react?" she asked.

*Surprisingly well,* Thea thought. In fact, he'd seemed quite at ease with the implication that they weren't just dating but heading for something more permanent. Marriage. Kids. The whole domestic package. It was what she'd dreamed of, hoped for, for more years than she cared to admit. Now that she practically had it in the palm of her hand, she found she was just a little wary of believing in it. It would hurt too much of it turned out not to be true.

"Well, he didn't run away screaming or start to twitch, but we didn't really get to—" She was cut off by the strident knock on the door. All three friends turned to stare at the door as the knob jiggled furiously before the knocking came again.

"Amelia Ann, open this door. At once!"

The sound of her mother's voice drained all of the amusement from Amelia's face.

"Guess my reprieve is over," she sighed, watching with resignation as Lillian went to unlock the door. Mrs. Westlake sailed in the second the lock was snapped open, almost clipping Lillian with the edge of the door. She never noticed, her eyes pinned like lasers on her daughter.

"What do you think you're doing hiding in here while you have a roomful of guests waiting?" she demanded. "People have been asking for you."

"I doubt that." Thea barely heard the words muttered under Amelia's breath, but evidently her mother had bat ears. She heard her just fine.

"Don't talk back to me, young lady. I expect you to behave properly, despite the example of the company you insist on keeping." She glared meaningfully at Thea, who had taken the opportunity to shift on the sofa and let a little more thigh show through the high slit of her dress.

Mrs. Westlake's thin nose quivered, but she refused to be sidetracked from her harangue. "Poor Charles has had to continue greeting your guests all by himself."

"Poor Charles," Amelia repeated sourly. "To tell you the truth, Mother, he was doing just fine for the both of us even when I was standing right beside him, so I don't see how my absence can make any difference at all."

Thea couldn't tell who was more surprised, Amelia or her mother.

Narrowing her eyes—the Botox must have been wearing off—Mrs. Westlake said sharply, "Don't you dare take that tone with me, young lady. This is your engagement party. People expect to speak to the bride as well as the groom. It's your responsibility to make all of your guests welcome."

Sensing that things could only degenerate from bad to disaster, Thea jumped into the fray. "Mellie was feeling a little lightheaded because she missed lunch, so she came in here to eat something and rest until she felt better before going back out to face the crowd."

"Yeah, it would be terrible if she fainted in front of all those inquisitive reporters," Lillian said, picking up the distraction and running with it. She gave a theatrical shudder. "Who knows what they might start thinking about why she did." Her hand touched her own stomach lightly in suggestion.

Mrs. Westlake looked properly horrified by the possibility.

"Rumors like that could ruin Charles's reputation." She glared at her daughter. "Make sure you're not feeling lightheaded anymore when you come out. I'll have to say something about you being gone, though." She tapped a brightly lacquered nail to her chin. "Your dress. Yes, that will work. Something was spilled on your dress and you had to have it taken care of." She nodded decisively. "If anyone asks you, that's what happened. Understood?"

"Perfectly," Amelia replied, sounding weary. She stared after her mother as the door snicked shut behind her. "It would ruin Charles's reputation," she repeated, shaking her head. "What about me, Mother? Wouldn't being pregnant ruin my reputation as well?"

She pressed her fingers into her temples, making Thea curse to herself. One ailment had been eased only to make way for another. Pouring a glass of water from the Baccarat carafe, Thea handed it to Amelia, who had already dug one of the migraine pills she'd only recently started needing out of her handbag. She swallowed it with a faint grimace. "Thanks."

"I could always get us something stronger," Lillian offered, only half joking. "One of the bars is right around the corner."

"Totally tempting," Amelia said, "but getting snookered would probably ruin Charles's reputation, too, so I guess I'd better not." She took a compact from her bag and checked her makeup, freshened her lipstick, and gave herself a practice smile in the mirror before rolling her eyes and sticking her tongue out at her image.

Rising, she smoothed her dress down. It was a beautiful silk and lace creation in a pale, almost icy blue, and suited Amelia's coloring perfectly, if not her personality. It was obvious she hated it. *But then*, Thea mused, *when had anything about the evening ever been about what Amelia wanted?*

"Okay," Amelia announced, throwing her shoulders back and tilting her chin up defiantly, "I'm ready. Let's go face the hordes."

As it turned out, it wasn't the hordes she needed to worry about facing. It was the dragons. Both of them swooped down to intercept the trio almost the second they emerged, neatly extracting Amelia from the protection of her friends.

"There are people you need to speak to immediately before they feel slighted," Mrs. Davenport said, one long-taloned hand taking firm hold of Amelia's arm as she steered her future daughter-in-law toward the far end of the room.

"And after that, you need to speak to the Dowlings," Mrs. Westlake chimed in, striding closely at her other side. "They were *very* disappointed you didn't come and see them first thing."

Amelia threw a pleading look over her shoulder, looking very much like a condemned prisoner being led off to the gallows. Thea started to follow, but Lillian shook her head.

"No, no, I've got this shift. You go and dance with your man and have a little fun." She waggled her eyebrows meaningfully before spinning on her four-inch heels and sashaying after the threesome forging determinedly through the crowded ballroom, her daring backless gown drawing more than a few looks of appreciation from men as she passed.

Thea briefly considered tagging along to offer her own support but then shook her head with a smile. Lillian was more than capable of running any necessary interference. And she really did want to dance with Doyle at least once tonight. Then she'd track down Mellie and see if she needed help with a strategic escape to the powder room.

Turning, she almost walked straight into Oliver, who grabbed her arm to keep them from colliding, just as he had at Platinum, while managing to hang onto the full champagne flute he carried in the other without spilling it.

"Oh!" She let out a rueful laugh as she steadied herself. "We have to stop meeting like this," she quipped, trying to ignore the sweatiness of his palm against her bare skin.

"Do you have a minute?" he asked, not responding to the jest with a smile of his own.

"Um, sure, I guess. What's up?"

"Charles needs to speak with you. It's important," he added when she hesitated.

The seriousness of his face and tone made Thea bite back her knee-jerk refusal. She was pretty sure Charles knew she didn't like him all that much, not that it would matter to him one way or the other. But if he was seeking her out—well, sending his minion to seek her out—then what he had to say probably had something to do with Amelia, and was, therefore, something she'd make the time to listen to.

"Sure," she said, stepping back to disengage from Oliver's hold, which had stopped being helpful and was now simply uncomfortable. "I guess I can tear myself away from the festivities for a few minutes." She thought she saw a flash of temper spark in his eyes right before he offered her his arm. It was the gentlemanly thing to do, especially since they'd be moving through a lot of people and were likely to get separated otherwise. Still, she couldn't explain the great reluctance with which she tucked her hand into the crook of his arm.

"For you." He offered her the glass of champagne he held. "You look like you could use it."

Accepting the drink out of politeness, she gave Oliver a bright smile. "Thank you." Knowing Francine would be following wherever they went as her official shadow for the evening since Doyle was technically her date, she said with a flourish of her glass, "Lead on, Macduff. Let's go see what good old Chuckie wants."

# CHAPTER 28

"LOST YOUR LADY ALREADY, young man?"

Doyle broke from his casual—or so he'd thought—perusal of the room and looked down at the diminutive woman standing beside him. He'd been introduced to Josephine Pierce earlier in the evening and had liked her immediately. Brash and opinionated as only the elderly could be and get away with, she'd put a much needed infusion of humor into the evening, giving a spot-on and often sharp-tongued rundown of the milling guests and glitterati.

Still, he was a little surprised that Amelia's great-aunt had approached him to chat. They had little in common, although he supposed they were kindred spirits in a way: invited yet unwanted guests. From what Thea had told him, Meredith Westlake considered her aunt a bit of an embarrassment and had only extended the invitation because it was proper etiquette to do so, fully expecting her to do the polite thing and decline.

Unfortunately for her, Josephine hadn't obliged.

"Ma'am," he acknowledged, dipping his head respectfully while politely ignoring her question. "Can I get you something to drink?" When she nodded regally, he turned to the bartender. "Bourbon, neat."

He'd already seen her knock back at least two of them like they were water. Not that they seemed to have affected her at all. The woman might be well past the three-quarter century mark, but she apparently had a cast-iron stomach and the constitution of an army mule.

The old woman cackled gleefully, tapping her heavy wooden cane against the floor to punctuate her laughter. Doyle got his toes out of the way just in time.

"Finally, someone who understands what a real drink is. Thought you'd try to pawn some of that prissy champagne off on me like everyone else has been doing, or, worse, one of those silly old-lady drinks. I like a man who appreciates a good whiskey."

"I'm more of a beer man, myself."

"But not tonight," she said shrewdly, glancing at the half-full glass of ginger ale he held.

"No," he acknowledged. "Not tonight."

"Too bad," she sniffed. "The way the night's shaping up, you might be wishing you'd had a good stiff shot or two."

Doyle had a feeling she was right.

"Can't go wrong with a good, cold beer, though," Josephine mused as she accepted her drink from Doyle, "unless it's one of those damned fruity micro-brew monstrosities. Man would get himself laughed straight out of Texas for drinking something like that in public."

Refraining from comment, Doyle simply smiled and sipped his soda. He knew if he gave her the slightest encouragement, she'd be off and running with a topic she obviously had very strong opinions about. He recognized the type. His brother-in-law, Sean, was the same way. Give him a topic, any topic, and he could debate you on its merits until your ears bled and you were begging to agree with him.

Then he'd change sides, just to be contrary.

Sensing she wasn't going to get the rise out of him she'd been hoping for, Josephine harrumphed and turned her attention where Doyle's had already gone, to the seething mass that clogged the enormous ballroom. The vaulted ceilings and numerous skylights kept the room from feeling closed in, but there was no way that several hundred people could occupy the space and not be considered a crowd.

Somewhere in that mess was Thea, most likely sticking to her friend's side like a preemptive Band-Aid. Doyle felt a huge pinch of sympathy for Amelia's situation, but the newly emerging possessive part of him wanted Thea back at his own side. He tried to tell himself it was because it was the only place he could be absolutely certain Thea was safe, despite the fact Francine was watching over her, but he knew he was lying. He wanted her there because she felt *right* there.

"I thought it might be that way," Josephine mused eventually, sipping her drink with obvious relish.

Doyle tore his attention away from his search with great difficulty. "What way, ma'am?"

She clucked her tongue. "Stop 'ma'aming' me, young man. Makes me feel old."

"Only if you stop 'young manning' me. Ma'am," he added deliberately and broke into a smile when she did as well.

"Fair enough, fair enough." She sipped her drink, her gaze roving over the crowd, before answering him. "Took you for just young Cynthia's escort when we were introduced before. I can call *her* young, can't I?" she challenged, although Doyle could see the spark of humor in her dark eyes.

"She's not here to object, so I don't see why not," he replied amiably. Even as he said it, his gaze reflexively went back to the crowd. She and Lillian had followed Amelia into the private withdrawing room a pretty long time ago. Surely she had to be almost done doing whatever it was those three did together by now.

"And that's what has you all tied up in knots, isn't it?"

She rapped her cane again, drawing his attention back to her and her knowing smile. "Ma'am? Ah, sorry. Mrs. Pierce."

"Never mind, never mind." With a flip of her wrist, she finished the last of her drink and handed the empty glass to Doyle. "Would you see me back to my seat? Dinner will be served shortly, and I don't trust this lot not to knock me on my keister when the feed bell sounds. Free food comes in second only to free booze with the Washington freeloader crowd."

Doyle subdued a laugh. No wonder Meredith Westlake considered her aunt persona non grata. Her opinions were as free-flowing as the two hundred-dollar-a-bottle champagne and went down much less palatably.

Taking her free hand and tucking it into his elbow, he helped the elderly woman to where their table had been set into a corner, so far from the dais where Amelia, Charles, and their parents were to be seated that it was practically in a different room. Thea had been quietly pissed when she'd seen the placement, saying simply it wasn't where their table had been on the chart she'd looked at the previous week. Evidently there had been some last minute reconfiguring in guest ranking, and they'd been shuffled to the back to make way for someone that had been deemed more important.

Settling his elderly charge into one of the comfortable red velvet chairs, Doyle once again scanned the surrounding crowd. Still no Thea. Worry was beginning to nibble at the edges of his instincts. He tried to ignore it, but he'd relied on those instincts for far too many years to not heed them now.

"No sense going to look for her now," Josephine said, evidently noting his agitation. "She'll be back when dinner's announced. You'd probably just pass each other in the chaos. Although you may want to have a waiter get you a bud vase for that," she added. "A nice touch, but it'll be dead by the end of the evening without water."

"What?" Doyle forced his attention to her words, frowning because they made no sense. "I'm sorry. What do you mean?"

"The flower." She nodded her head across the table to where Thea's place card sat. A single red rose lay across her plate. "Very nice. Mysterious *and* romantic."

Doyle stared at the rose that hadn't been there when they'd first arrived. Confusion quickly morphed into something close to panic. Uttering a curse under his breath, he stalked around the table and snatched up the piece of paper that was neatly folded under the flower, knowing he was improperly handling possible evidence and not giving a damn.

His fingers shook slightly as he opened the single piece of paper. The familiar spidery script jumped out at him even as everything in him screamed in denial. One line only this time: *Tonight you're finally mine.*

No. Not here. Not with all of the layers of security in place. How the hell could the bastard have gotten in? How had he gotten this close with none of them knowing?

Where the hell was Thea?

Cursing himself for ignoring the instincts that had been nagging at him ever since she'd gotten out of his sight, Doyle pulled the earpiece that had been tucked inside his tuxedo collar into place, activating it and the mic clipped to his sleeve. "Francine, sitrep, please." He waited for her to report, but got only dead air. "Francine, what is your location?" Still nothing.

*This isn't happening.*

His instincts now screaming at him, Doyle practically knocked a waiter off his feet as he bolted toward the withdrawing room, ignoring Josephine's worried call and the irritated glares from the people he jostled along the way. None of them mattered. Thea. Only Thea mattered. He had to find her, had to make sure she was safe.

*Please, God, let her be safe.*

Not bothering to knock, he slammed into the private room, his heart pounding.

Empty.

Doyle activated the mic again. "Red, we have a breach. Our perp is in the building." His expression was grim as he turned and headed back into the seething mass of guests. "I've lost visual on the Lady, and Francine isn't responding. Have everyone move to their secondary locations and hold until I say otherwise."

They had contingency plans ready for all of the ways things could have possibly gone wrong that evening. Moving his people to their secondary locations put them in position to block exits and start a search pattern if the absolute worst happened and he didn't find Thea somewhere safely circulating with her friends and Francine's equipment simply on the fritz.

By the time he finally found Amelia ensconced in a small alcove with both mothers and an older couple who had the pinched, inbred look of someone who'd smelled something unpleasant, his temper was almost as raw as his nerves. He was sure there was at least one tray of shattered glasses somewhere in his wake, and most likely a Secret Service agent or two who were cutting through the crowd toward his location. That was just fine with him. He wanted everyone he could get at hand if it turned out his worst fears were warranted.

And it appeared that they were. Panic scorched his tongue like acid when he saw that Thea wasn't with her two friends.

"Doyle, what the hell?" Lillian asked in surprise. From the way she and Amelia were staring at him, he could only assume he looked as wild as he felt.

"Where's Thea?" he rasped. *Please say she was just here. Please tell me she just went to the ladies' room a second ago. Please tell me that I didn't let her fall into the hands of that sick bastard because I thought she was safe here.*

"She went to find you," Lillian replied. A little of his panic seemed to be rubbing off on her, her eyes widening when she added, "Like, ten minutes ago, at least. Maybe more."

"Shit!" He ran a hand through his hair in frustration. It was possible they'd just missed each other in the crowd, but he thought, no, he *knew* that wasn't the case. Not with the note, and not with Francine not responding.

Mrs. Westlake drew herself up like a puff adder getting ready to spit.

"Mr. Doyle! You will watch your language or I'll be forced to ask you to remove yourself from these premises."

"Honestly, Meredith," Mrs. Davenport chided, "can't you exert a little more control over your staff? I mean, really!" She turned to coo apologetic words to the horrified couple standing beside her, having made it clear that the offense was entirely her co-hostess's fault and responsibility.

"It's him, isn't it?" Lillian's voice quivered slightly.

"What is going on?" Amelia demanded, looking first at Lillian's stricken expression and then Doyle's anguished one. "What's wrong with Thea?" She stamped her foot and gave Doyle a hard shove in his shoulder. "Tell me, damn it!"

Faintly registering Mrs. Westlake's outraged gasp of shock, Doyle remembered that Thea had chosen not to tell Amelia about the stalker until after the party. Deciding it would take too long to explain, he focused on Lillian, who at least appeared up to speed on the situation.

"He's here," he said in a low, dangerous voice. "He left this on the table for her." He waved the paper that was half crumpled in his fist.

Looking frustrated at being ignored, Amelia grabbed at the paper, her brow furrowing as she read it. "Why would Charles leave a note like that for Thea?"

Everything inside Doyle stilled, frozen by words he heard but couldn't quite comprehend. He stared down at Amelia. "What did you say?"

The menace in his voice made her cringe, but then she straightened her back and shook the paper. "This is Charles's handwriting, but there has to be some mistake. He must have meant to leave the note for me." She looked from Doyle to Lillian and back, as though expecting them to understand. "'Tonight you're mine'? Hello? Engagement party. Right?" When they didn't immediately agree with her, she looked to Lillian. "What's going on that I don't know about?" she demanded. "Tell me!"

Doyle ignored the demand and jabbed a finger at the paper she held. "Are you certain that handwriting belongs to Charles Davenport?"

"Yes," she insisted, while at the same time Constance Davenport said from behind her shoulder, "Of course, it isn't."

Something close to a growl came out of Doyle's throat. He nipped the paper from Amelia's fingers and shoved it in Mrs. Davenport's face. "Is this or is this not your son's handwriting?"

"I just told you that it isn't," she replied, bringing a hand up toward her throat in a subconsciously defensive gesture of a prey animal faced with a slavering predator. "Charles has absolutely lovely handwriting. I wouldn't have it any other way. That scrawl belongs to his assistant, Oliver Pratt."

"No," Amelia insisted. "The letters. Charles wrote me letters. They were… personal." Her cheeks reddened. "He wouldn't have had Oliver…," she trailed off as the truth sunk in. "He dictated love letters for Oliver to write," she said in a flat tone.

"Charles is much too busy to handle something as trivial as personal correspondence himself," was Mrs. Davenport's condescending response. "That's what he has a personal assistant for."

Doyle didn't give a damn about any letters. "You're absolutely positive about the handwriting?"

"Why would I lie about something as ridiculous as that?" she sniffed. "Now, what is this all about?"

The idea that she was lying to protect her son slid briefly through his mind, but Doyle quickly discarded it. No way even someone as smug and arrogant as Charles would think he could get away with grabbing Thea from his own engagement party. It had to be the assistant.

Pieces clicked into place in a way they had refused to before. The postmarks from around the country. The hints of intimate knowledge. The inferences of personal contact. Everything lined up with Pratt's movements as part of the Davenports' entourage as they stomped around the country drumming up party support for Charles's upcoming primary bid and their stops in Boulder to visit his fiancée and her family.

All the time and effort put into protecting her from the bastard who was stalking her, and she'd been totally accessible to him every time she'd gone over to visit her friend.

There were dozens of security personnel in place both inside and out of the banquet hall. He had to believe there was no way Pratt had been able to find a way to escape without notice, not with Thea in tow. He'd taught her well enough not to go with an abductor without putting up a fight.

He refused to consider that she might not be in any condition to resist.

"Heads up, team," he said, stalking away toward the nearest exit. "We have a Level One situation. The Lady is most likely with Oliver Pratt, Davenport's assistant. Five ten or eleven, blond hair, glasses. He's our letter writer. Find them. Whatever it takes, he doesn't leave the grounds with her." Having given unspoken permission to shoot to kill if it was deemed necessary, Doyle hoped none of his men had to act on the command.

He wanted the pleasure of killing the bastard himself.

# CHAPTER 29

"SO WHERE DOES CHARLES plan to have this talk, in a broom closet?"

The snarky question was muttered half under her breath as Thea turned down yet another hallway in the nonpublic area of the banquet hall. She'd allowed for the fact that he might want a little privacy, depending on the topic he had in mind, but this backroom cloak-and-dagger act was just a little silly.

Surely they could have found a quiet alcove somewhere in that monstrous ballroom where no one could overhear them. Then again, with a room full of top-notch reporters salivating for a story and the age of cell phone cameras catching everything that went on everywhere and instantly flinging it around the world at three times the speed of sound via social media, she could understand his paranoia.

Understand it, just not appreciate it. She really wanted to dance with Doyle before the night got too crazy and she missed her chance. And she had a feeling that the moment the toasts and speeches began, crazy was the least things were going to get.

Plus she wanted a drink. One that *wasn't* the overpriced, far-too-dry champagne Mrs. Westlake had insisted be the only brand the catering hall offered to guests. Thea was thirsty enough that she almost regretted depositing the glass Oliver had given her onto a passing waiter's tray untouched. Almost.

Enough was enough. Just before they turned a corner, she stopped and turned to look behind her. She didn't like that Francine wasn't anywhere in sight. "Oliver, I need to wait for my—"

The burst of pain as she was slammed into the wall knocked the unfinished words from her head with a startled cry of pain. A burst of light and then darkness filtered her vision on impact.

"What...?" The question was reflexive, her brain unable to grab hold of what was happening enough to make sense of it.

"Bitch!" The harsh curse was accompanied by hard hands grabbing her shoulders and slamming her back into the wall a second time. This time her head connected solidly enough to bring her vision down to a single pinpoint of light for a few seconds. A pained whimper escaped her lips.

"You stupid, teasing *bitch!*" Hands pounded the wall beside her head. Thea cringed, waiting for another blow as her spinning head scrambled to level itself and start functioning again. What had happened? Why was someone shouting at her, hitting her?

*Stalker.*

The word jumped up through the rest of her jumbled thoughts with stunning clarity amid the chaos. Somehow, her stalker had gotten in and had found her. Had he jumped Oliver to get to her? Was he hurt? Dead?

Even as she thought it, her brain was slowly starting to shuffle the rest of the pieces back into order and she knew. Even before her vision cleared and she found herself staring into the hot, angry, pale glacial-blue eyes of her attacker, she knew.

"Oliver." She blinked tears of pain back, trying to focus on him despite the fact that her head was throbbing as though it were going to explode. "Stop. Please. You're hurting me."

"Hurting you? *Hurting you?*" She cringed again as he shouted the words, sending the throbbing pain up a notch to near excruciating. "What the hell do you think you've been doing to *me?*"

"I've never done anything to hurt you." Calm. Reasonable. And totally the wrong thing to say, judging by the explosion that followed.

"Oh no? What do you call stringing me along all these months, huh? Coming to see me every chance you got, bringing me little presents, all smiles and flirty niceness, like you were a sweet girl. A nice girl. A girl who *knew her place.*" The last three words were accompanied by more pounding on the wall, the last one close enough that his fist grazed the side of her head.

She tried to turn away, but he grabbed her jaw roughly and forced her to focus on him. "But it was all an act, wasn't it?" he hissed, his breath hot on her face. "You aren't any of those things."

"Oliver, I'm sorry if you misunderstood." It was difficult to talk with the bruising grip he had on her face, but she had to try, had to reason with him before things got worse. Her mind shied away from the hints the letters had given as to just how much worse.

"I was helping Amelia with the wedding plans. That's why I came to see you so mu—" She gasped as his grip tightened, bringing tears of pain to her eyes.

"You came to see *me*." His pale blue eyes flashed with savage intensity behind the round lenses of his glasses. "The rest was just an excuse, so Mrs. Westlake wouldn't guess."

"Oliver—"

"No!" He shoved her head back against the wall. Only being an inch away this time meant the impact wasn't as great; it was little more than a bump, really, but the previous two blasts had left her head tender enough that she still felt as though someone had taken a baseball bat to her skull. "You came to see me."

She realized fuzzily that it wasn't just anger in his eyes. There was a whole lot of crazy in there as well. And you just didn't reason with a crazy person. You couldn't. The best she could do was humor him, get him to stop hurting her, and stall until her security detail got there.

*Come on, Francine, where are you?*

"Okay," she whispered. "You're right. I-I came to see you." She stared at his ear as she said it, knowing she was a crappy liar, but hoping that terror might lend a little credulity to her performance. She saw a smile curve his lips and breathed a small sigh of relief.

"I knew it. I knew it." His hand loosened on her jaw and skimmed up her cheek in a caress. It was difficult, but she managed not to shudder. "We were meant to be together."

Seconds passed, and she could sense the anger building in him again, but she honestly had no idea why or what she could do to diffuse it.

"We were meant to be together," he repeated, but this time there was no tenderness in the tone. It was hard and mean and scared the hell out of her. She jumped when he shouted in her face, "Say it!"

"We were meant to be t-together." Her mouth was so dry, the words were barely audible, and she had to stuff down the sob that wanted to follow before it could escape. God, how had this happened? How had she misjudged someone so completely?

She'd actually *liked* Oliver. They'd been coconspirators. She'd brought him cookies and he'd passed her wedding information. They hadn't exactly been friends but had been friendly. Where in all that interaction had she missed the basic fact that he had a few screws loose?

"You're mine."

"I'm yours," she repeated dutifully, hoping to avoid another painful prompt.

"That's right. You're mine. You're mine." He murmured the words over and over as he stroked her cheek. It wasn't so much a gesture of affection as one of possession. She endured it, fighting to gather her thoughts, fighting to conquer the panic and remember what she needed to do to get away since it seemed help wasn't coming anytime soon. She'd been taught this. Why couldn't she remember what she should do? Damn her fuzzy head! *Think, damn it!*

"Oliver," she said cautiously, "we should get back to the party. We're going to be missed. It won't look right if we're gone too long." If she could remind him that there were people who might be looking for them, maybe some semblance of rational thought would resurface. Oliver had always been about making sure things looked right.

"Who's going to miss us, Thea?" The caress turned harsh. "Your *date*? Is that who's going to miss you?"

Crap. Crap! She'd forgotten about the crazy.

"He's not my date," she started, but Oliver grabbed a handful of her hair, gripping it painfully as he brought his face close to hers. It hurt, but at least he hadn't beaten her head against the wall again.

Yet.

"I was so thrilled when you came to see me the other day about the seating arrangements, telling me you wanted to make sure I was going to be sitting by your side." His voice was deceptively gentle again.

"I never said..." Swallowing, Thea bit off the rest of her protest. Oliver had evidently put his own warped interpretation on her somewhat veiled request. Pointing out he'd been wrong wasn't going to help her now.

"I was so certain you'd decided to end the little game we were playing, keeping our love a secret," he continued as though she hadn't spoken. "I thought you were finally ready to acknowledge what was between us openly. And what better place than at the party, where all your friends and family would be? It would have been almost like it was *our* engagement party. That's how I started thinking of it. As our party."

"Oliver..."

"Imagine my surprise when you showed up with *him* at your side." Disgust practically dripped from the words. "That's when I knew. You're aren't really a nice girl at all, are you, Thea? You're a tease. Just a slutty little tease."

She couldn't hold back the yip of pain that the tightening grip on her hair elicited. "Doyle's my bodyguard. Just my bodyguard." She struggled to keep her voice calm. "My father worries about me, and he insisted—"

"Bullshit!" Oliver spun away, his hand tearing free of her hair, taking more than a few strands with it.

The pain was worth the freedom it brought, though, and Thea drew a deep breath, her mind finally starting to clear enough for her to remember all the things Doyle and Red had taught her about getting away from an attacker. The hallway was narrow, which limited her options and her avenues of escape. Since she had no idea what lay in the direction they had been heading, her only safe choice was to head back the way they had come. Back to the ballroom.

Back to Doyle.

She just needed to pick her moment.

"He's not just your bodyguard, Thea," Oliver said, sneering her name disdainfully. "Do you think I'm stupid?"

*No, I think you're scary crazy.* "He's head of my father's security."

"You've fucked him, haven't you?"

The question shocked her, which was kind of ridiculous, considering the situation she currently found herself in. Unfortunately, her surprise must have registered as guilt because Oliver's expression darkened to the violent rage it had held when he'd first slammed her into the wall.

"Unfaithful bitch!"

She saw the hand coming toward her too late. Although she tried to turn to avoid it, his open palm still struck her face with enough force to rock her off her feet, the sound of flesh hitting flesh obscenely loud in the narrow space. Pain exploded again through her head. She fell to her knees, her hands just barely keeping her face from slamming to the carpet.

Gagging on the bile welling up in her throat, she gasped for breath through the hair he'd torn from its fancy arrangement that now hung down in her face. The idea of puking on him had appeal, but then the nausea receded, and she was left with only the pain.

"You'll learn."

"Learn what?" The words sounded thick and strange.

"Your lessons. Get up." A hand grasped her arm and yanked her to her feet.

Thea tolerated his touch because she knew she needed to be off the floor before she could make a move. But even as she found her balance and turned toward him with the intent of going for his eyes with her recently manicured nails, she was brought up short by what he held.

A very small, very deadly looking gun.

He chuckled at her shocked expression. "Don't worry. I know how to use it."

She wasn't sure if that was meant to reassure her or threaten her. It didn't really matter. Either way, it meant she was seriously screwed.

# CHAPTER 30

**SHE WAS GOING TO DIE.**

The very real possibility hit home about the same time as the door they'd passed through at the end of the hallway clicked shut behind them, locking them out of the building. There was no escaping back inside now. No hope of running back to the safety of Doyle and Francine. No hope of waking up and finding that all of this had been some horrible, horrible dream. She was stuck in the dark alone with a crazy man with a gun.

Things were probably not going to end well.

No, damn it! She stomped on the defeatist thoughts that were threatening to choke her into submission. There might not be anybody around right this second, but if Oliver planned to take her away someplace, he'd have to get his car and that meant dealing with the valets.

And security.

Silently, she gave thanks for the pompously arrogant Davenports and their insistence on inviting the vice president and his gaggle of Secret Service agents. According to Doyle, their mere presence had upped the game for all the other security details in attendance. No one would admit to liking the Federal agents, but everyone wanted to look good in front of them.

For the first time since Oliver had revealed himself to be her stalker, Thea felt the universe come into balance. Things weren't going to be pretty or easy, not when Oliver had a gun shoved in her ribs, but neither were they hopeless. She just needed to be ready to take advantage of any opportunity that presented itself.

The door they'd come out of was on the opposite end of the building from the ballroom, just about as far from the parking lot as you could get. There was a narrow, concrete walkway that curved around back, and she stumbled more than once as Oliver started pushing her along it. Her delicate stiletto heels might have been a dream to glide over a polished dance floor in, but on an uneven surface in the dark, they were an accident waiting to happen.

Oliver must have thought the same because he pulled her to a jolting halt after her next stumble. "Kick them off," he ordered.

Thea found herself strongly adverse to even that small act of disrobing for him. "The dress is too long to walk in without them," she said, realizing it was true. "I'll trip."

"How could you wear that?" Oliver demanded, pushing her into motion again after a moment's thought. Evidently, her argument made sense to him. Which was good, because the idea starting to form in her head would need the shoes to succeed.

"Wear what?"

"That slutty dress." It sounded like he was gritting his teeth. "It's just like you, isn't it? It looks all sweet and nice, but the truth is right there, just waiting to be revealed."

His fingers flexed around her upper arm, making her wince. The bruises Margo has inflicted there were just starting to fade, the area still slightly tender. She had a feeling the new batch of bruises was going to be much more spectacular. "You'll learn, though. Oh, yes, you'll learn."

Obviously, the high slits in her gown that Doyle had found so intriguing when she'd slid into the Charger were a big red flag for Oliver's temper, so Thea thought it wise to steer the conversation someplace else. "You said that before. What am I going to learn?"

"Your lessons."

"What lessons?"

"How to behave yourself. How not to tease a man, lead him on, make him think you want him, and then just ignore him the next time you see him like he's no better than a piece of trash at the side of the road."

There was a vehemence to his words and an underlying anger that frightened her as much as the words themselves.

"I never ignored you, Oliver," she said tentatively. "I never treated you like that."

"You did!" he insisted. "I sent you things, presents, and you never once thanked me for them. I thanked you every time you brought me something. Every time!"

*The cookies*, she realized dimly. She'd brought him cookies.

"But you never even acknowledged my gifts," Oliver ranted on. "You just took and took, like it was your due, and I wasn't even worth a simple thank you for the effort."

"What…" The question remained unspoken as the memory of her conversation with Doyle about the stalker flashed through her mind. There hadn't just been letters. Recently, there had been presents. Flowers. Chocolates. The gifts of a man courting a woman.

Of Oliver courting her.

"I didn't get them," she told him, opting for the truth.

"Liar."

"No, really, they were stopped by security when they were delivered, and I never…" Too late, she realized her mistake.

"Stopped by the man you're fucking, you mean."

Deciding it wouldn't help her cause to say that she hadn't been sleeping with Doyle back when the "gifts" had been intercepted, Thea said instead, "I would have thanked you if I'd gotten them, Oliver. Really." She tried to sound grateful. "The chocolates were my favorite kind. It was sweet of you to go to the trouble to find that out." Creepy, actually.

"I overheard you and Amelia talking about it," he boasted, making her skin crawl. How many other private conversations had he eavesdropped on while at the Westlake house?

"What about the flowers?" he asked, sounding eager for more compliments.

"Um…" She hadn't seen the flowers. Had he forgotten that fact? Maybe he had. "They were very pretty."

"Pretty." He sounded disappointed. "It's never enough for you, is it?"

"What?"

"I give and give and give, but you're just too spoiled to appreciate the value of the act instead of the value of the gift. Everything has to be bigger and shinier and more expensive. But you'll learn," he promised. "I'll teach you to appreciate everything I do for you. Every single thing."

There was such dark promise in those words that Thea stumbled again, and this time it had nothing to do with her shoes and everything to do with the pictures her mind drew from the words in those god-awful letters. *You'll scream and cry and beg at first, but in the end, you'll come to understand. The lessons will be hard won, but they'll make you a better woman, the perfect woman for me. Only when you've been cleansed of your past through the blood of true penance will you be ready to serve me as you were meant to.*

Oh, *hell* no! No way was this sick bastard teaching her any lesson, much less ones that promised screaming and blood. She tensed her shoulders, wondering how much longer it was going to be before they got to the parking lot. The building was huge, but they surely must have walked almost all the way around…

They weren't heading for the parking lot.

Fear chased through her like a ghostly wind at the realization. She'd been so damned smug in her certainty that he was going to walk right into the arms of the people who would thwart his nasty plans and save her. What she'd forgotten was that as twisted and crazy as he was, one thing Oliver didn't seem to be was stupid.

He'd managed to elude detection for months, even while living right in their midst. What had made her think he'd just blindly walk out into a parking lot full of people wearing guns and allow himself to be caught?

Stupid, stupid, Thea.

"Where are we going?" she asked as she started to slow her steps against the insistent pressure of the gun in her back.

"To your new home."

"But you live in Connecticut." Or so she thought. She'd never given much thought to where Oliver actually lived. Truthfully, she'd never really given much thought to him at all.

"I rented a place here shortly after I decided you were the one. I thought it would be good for you to stay close to home while you were getting settled into your new role as my wife."

Coming from a normal man, that might have sounded thoughtful. From Oliver, it proved that he'd been planning this ending right from the very start. Nothing she could have done, nothing Doyle could have done, would have changed anything.

"I'm not going to be your wife, Oliver," she said, deciding that this was as far as she was going to go with him. If they made it as far as the car he most likely had hidden somewhere, she'd be lost. If she was going to make a stand, it was going to be here and now. And if he shot her…well, she'd actually prefer that to what he had in mind for her.

"You will." He pushed her, but she dug her heels in and pushed back. "Stop fighting me! You'll be sorry later for defying me like this," he threatened.

She let herself stumble again, which removed the gun from her back for the split second she needed to make her move. With every ounce of strength she could muster, she stabbed one four-inch heel down into his instep above his shoe while at the same time thrusting her elbow back into his sternum and slamming her head back into his face, which hurt her already sore head a lot worse than she'd expected. Any of those three attacks on its own might not have been enough to free her, but coming all at the same time, they served up just enough pain and surprise to do the trick.

Oliver's grip slackened as he let out a pain-filled grunt, his hands automatically going to his face. Thea immediately stepped forward with a tiny wobble, turned, and put her shoes to their second-best use after dancing.

The kick she delivered to his crotch landed with satisfying force, driving a metal-tipped stiletto deep into soft flesh. It wasn't a grunt Oliver gave this time, but a high-pitched scream.

She let out a yell fueled by rage and fear as her second kick, this time with the pointy toe, connected with his arm and knocked the gun from his already slack fingers as he dropped to his knees, curling protectively over his wounded groin. The gun disappeared into the darkness. Thea briefly considered looking for it and then decided against it. She'd do better to run for the front of the building and find help while Oliver was still slightly incapacitated.

Help actually found her first.

Ironically, it came in the form of her least favorite bodyguard. At that particular moment, all past offenses were forgotten, and she nearly knocked Simon off his feet as she ran into him. The primitive part of her brain could only think *safety*.

"Oliver," she gasped, trying to talk past her heart which had somehow crawled up into her throat. "It was Oliver."

"Where is he?" Simon was methodically trying to peel her off of him as he asked, his eyes constantly tracking over the darkness around them.

"B-back there." She finally allowed herself to be partially disentangled but still hung onto his arm, wanting, needing, the contact to keep from shattering into hysterical pieces. "He has a gun."

Almost before the words were out of her mouth, Simon was shoving her away, down behind him. There were two gunshots, almost on top of each other, and she watched in horror as Simon's body jerked with the impact and fell beside her on the ground, unmoving.

# CHAPTER 31

"IT'S HERS."

Doyle closed a fist around the diamond-tipped hairclip Daryl had handed him, fighting back the primitive urge to roar out his anger and frustration. Precious minutes had already been wasted convincing that fuckhead Don Rogers to allow Doyle's team into the building to search. Too many minutes. Only the intervention of the Westlake's security chief, Paul Kent, had kept Doyle from shooting the bastard.

Francine had already been located, alive but incapacitated, in one of the empty offices beside the withdrawing room Thea had last been seen in. Kirsten and Rick had headed toward the kitchen, Doyle and Daryl the back hallways, while Paul ordered up a medical evac for Francine and put his own team on high alert. The rest of Doyle's team remained stationed outside in case Pratt managed to make it out of the building with Thea.

Now, Daryl had finally turned up their first clue. Doyle recognized the hairclip as being one of a pair nestled in Thea's thick hair earlier that evening. He should. He'd spent enough time fantasizing about pulling them out and letting that glorious mound loose as she rode him to completion in his bed.

Now, it was a symbol of his failure to protect what was his responsibility—no, his *right*—to protect. And it was eating him alive.

Tightening his grasp until the tip bit painfully into his palm, Doyle tried very hard to keep his mind from picking at the possible reasons it had come to be laying in the hall. None of them were good, and he needed to concentrate on what he needed to do to get Thea back safely rather than what he'd failed to protect her from.

Later, when she was safe, then he'd have plenty of time to dissect his failures and wallow in self-loathing over them.

Slipping the clip into his pocket, he signaled for Daryl to continue down the hallway. They cleared each room they passed with quiet efficiency. All empty. Finally, there was no place else to go except through the steel door with the glowing exit sign above it.

It was pitch dark outside. A glance up showed the bulb missing from the fixture above the door. Doyle's heart thumped wildly. That simple act of preparation meant that this wasn't a spur of the moment act. Pratt had planned to take Thea tonight. That meant he'd also have planned for his escape. He of all people would know how much security would be on the premises that evening.

And exactly where it would be.

Damn it to hell! That meant he'd have stashed a car or more likely a van of some kind nearby to make his escape. Doyle gave a terse update into the mic, ordering Sam to have all exits from the parking lot blocked immediately. It was doubtful Pratt would have been stupid enough to leave his vehicle there, but Doyle wasn't taking any chances.

The dark walkway curved around the back of the building. The location of both it and the door meant it was a service entrance, and one not much used, judging by the state of the cracked concrete. That meant none of the impressive illumination the walkways through the cocktail garden and around the pond and waterfall boasted, but for that Doyle was actually grateful. They knew who they were chasing, but Pratt didn't know anyone was following. For the moment, the advantage was theirs. With luck, the darkness would keep it that way.

Suddenly, the sound of raised voices echoed from further down the path. Using hand signals, he directed Daryl to his left as they broke into a run.

There was a strange high-pitched squeal followed by a primal, gut-wrenching scream that had him putting an extra burst of speed on. If that bastard had hurt her...

The sight that greeted him wasn't what he expected. A dozen yards in front of him was a man on his knees, curled over on himself, whimpering in pain. Several yards further away was Thea, trying to climb Simon like a monkey. Simon was doing his best to peel her off, but Doyle knew she was a lot stronger than she looked.

Doyle slowed to a cautious walk. For a second, just a second, he forgot everything else and simply savored the sight of her, whole and unharmed. He had no idea what she'd done to Pratt—that had to be who the asshole on the ground was—but he knew he'd take great pleasure in hearing the details of it. Later.

The hairs on the back of his neck lifted, his instincts screaming that something bad was about to happen. Even as he thought it, he started to raise his gun, but not before Pratt had lunged awkwardly off to the side to grab for something on the ground.

It was one of those moments he'd experienced in the Corps, one of those life and death moments where time slowed to a crazy, frame-by-frame speed and everything happened so slowly you thought surely you had plenty of time to see what was happening, adjust, and react, but in reality everything had really sped up to the point where you didn't even know you'd reacted until after the whole thing was already over with.

Doyle fired at almost the same instant Pratt did. He knew his bullet found its mark. Knew that Pratt was dead before his face even hit the ground. Compared to some of the shots he'd had to make in combat, this one had barely rated any effort at all. But the price might have been the highest he'd ever had to pay in his life because he couldn't tell which of the two people lying on the ground past Pratt's limp body had been shot.

Trusting Daryl to take care of Pratt, Doyle ran for Thea, who—thank you, God!—was back up off the ground where Simon had evidently shoved her and was kneeling at his side. Even in the moonlight he could see the blood glistening on the front of Simon's dark suit and on Thea's hands as she pressed against the wound, trying to stop the flow. He yelled into the mic at his wrist for help and an ambulance and then dropped to his knees on Simon's other side so he could assess the damage. Thea looked up at him, eyes wide with shock.

"He got shot for me," she said, her voice incredulous at the thought. "He pushed me aside and took the bullet." A tear overran her welling eyes and slid down her face. "The idiot."

There was a smear of blood on her chin that he wasn't certain had come from Simon. Rage welled in him, but he fought it back. He'd check her inch by inch for injuries later. Now, he needed to concentrate on the critically wounded man on the ground in front of him.

"He did his job." It was a lot more than that, and Doyle made a mental note to see that the kid knew it. Hell, he'd throw him a fucking parade. How did you repay the man who'd saved the life of the woman you loved?

*Loved?*

*Well, shit. It's a hell of a time for that damn light bulb to finally go off,* he thought viciously as he stripped off first his specially tailored tuxedo jacket and then the low-profile holster that went beneath. Popping the studs, he pulled his shirt off and quickly folded it into a thick pad.

"Move your hands, sweetheart."

She did as he ordered, making a small keening sound of distress as he gently examined the wound. Judging by the size of the hole, Pratt's weapon had been a small caliber, and it had struck high on Simon's left shoulder.

With luck, it had missed both bone and vital arteries and he would recover without any lasting physical impairment.

Simon roused with a moan as Doyle pressed the makeshift bandage onto the wound, putting more pressure on it than Thea had. Simon blinked up first at Doyle and then at Thea and managed to look satisfied. "Din't screw up," he slurred. "Safe."

"You did good," Doyle acknowledged.

"Got shot."

Doyle grinned at the disgust in the words. "Yeah, you're gonna have to work on that part."

"Thank you, Simon," Thea said, squeezing his hand as she blinked back tears. "I'm sorry you got shot because of me."

"Th'job."

"No, it was my fault," she insisted. "The first thing out of my mouth should have been that he had a gun. I'd knocked it out of his hand, so I didn't think…" She broke off on a shuddery sob. "I'm so sorry."

Doyle took a second to digest her words. "You knocked the gun out of his hand?"

She nodded, sniffling. "After I kicked him in the balls."

"After you…" After a few seconds of doing a fish imitation, Doyle let out a rueful laugh. "You're an amazing woman, Cynthia Fordham."

She smiled up at him a bit mistily. "It's about time you noticed."

Other words crowded his tongue, trying to force themselves out before another chance of losing her arose, but he bit them back. Not the time. Not the place. First there was Simon to get to the hospital and then the mess with Pratt's death and the shitstorm of fallout that was bound to follow. There was a ballroom full of reporters that were going to make a meal of the night's events, and two senators that weren't going to be happy about it.

It was going to be a long night.

*　*　*

Chaos reigned outside the reception hall.

The lights from all of the police cars and ambulances bathed the night blue and red. People were shouting, talking, asking questions, but it was all just background noise, making no sense to Thea's ears. Sitting on the back bumper of one of the ambulances, she watched it all with numb detachment, wishing Doyle was still at her side.

Logically, she knew she was perfectly safe. Daryl and Sam were there to make sure of it. But that didn't mean that she *felt* safe. In truth, she felt exposed.

Betrayed.

Violated.

The very solicitous EMT who had just finished checking her over must have noticed her shiver because he draped a thin blanket around her shoulders. She wanted to thank him, but she couldn't seem to muster up the energy. She couldn't seem to do much of anything.

"Oh, my dear Lord, Cynthia!"

Suddenly her parents were there, her mother hugging her and sobbing, her father looking alternately furious and teary. The warmth of her mother's embrace helped to thaw some of the freezing cold of shock that was holding her captive.

"Are you all right?" Her mother smoothed Thea's wild hair back, making a pained sound when she saw the reddened swelling on the side of her face from when Oliver had hit her.

"I'm fine," Thea assured her, even though her cheek was throbbing in time with the pounding in her head. "Really, I am. I'm just a little bruised and a lot scared."

"I'll believe it when a doctor tells me," her father said. His tone left absolutely no room for argument. Which she wasn't about to do, since the hospital was exactly where she wanted to go. She needed to find out what was happening with Simon and Francine, both of whom had already been taken away by ambulance. No one knew what had happened to Francine or if they did they weren't telling her. She needed to find out. She needed to be there, making sure they were getting the best possible care. If either of them died...

She shoved the thought away. No one was going to die for her tonight. No one.

Except for Oliver.

"Thea!"

The shout barely gave her time to brace for the impact as Lillian practically threw herself at Thea, hugging her tightly before reluctantly pulling back to make way for Amelia, who also hugged her. It wasn't until Amelia pulled back and Thea saw the smear of red across her friend's ice-blue gown that she remembered she was covered in blood. Simon's blood.

She shivered again.

"I ruined your beautiful dress." A tear leaked down Thea's face as she stared at the stain, unable to look away. There had been so much blood.

"Forget my dress," Amelia replied. "Are you okay? What happened?"

"You don't know?"

"We heard bits and pieces, but none of it made any sense. Someone said one of the guards was shot!"

"Simon," Thea replied, her voice cracking. "Simon got shot. Protecting me."

"From Oliver." Lillian sounded incredulous. "I can't believe it was him."

"Why didn't you tell me what was going on?" Amelia demanded. "I'm your friend, damn it. You should have told me."

"I didn't want to give you something else to worry about before the party. I wanted tonight to be perfect for you." Thea gave a short, horrified laugh. "I guess that was a great big fail, huh?"

"Like any of this was your fault," Lillian scoffed. She leaned in to hug her friend again, whispering quietly, "I'm glad Doyle killed him."

Clearly, Lillian knew more than she was letting on.

"Me, too," Thea whispered back.

"Where is she?" The strident voice cut through the surrounding din, making Thea cringe. She didn't think she was the only one, either. The last person she wanted to deal with right at that moment was Mrs. Westlake. The craven part of her thought just for a second about escaping into the back of the ambulance and shutting the doors, but she toughed it out and waited for Amelia's mother to appear.

When Mrs. Westlake rounded the back of the ambulance, she zeroed in on Thea immediately. "Cynthia Fordham. How *could* you?"

Thea blinked. "Excuse me?"

"I knew it was a mistake, allowing my daughter to associate with you, but this…this is beyond inexcusable! Do you have any idea how much damage you've done?"

"Mother!" Amelia gasped. "Thea is the *victim* here."

"And you," Mrs. Westlake continued, turning on her daughter, "you should be inside helping Charles deal with the press, not out here with…" She trailed off with a horrified gasp. "Your dress! What have you done to your dress?"

"It has blood on it, Mother," Amelia said, her voice flat and angry. "Blood from the man who was shot protecting my best friend from the crazy man who tried to *kidnap her.*"

"Oh, no, no, no, this won't do. You can't go back inside looking like that. If someone were to get a picture of you like that…no, absolutely not." Mrs. Westlake spun to glare at Thea again. "You have ruined *everything!* Do you have any idea how much work it took to arrange for this kind of press coverage? How much exposure this was going to get for Charles's primary bid? And now the only thing the morning headlines are going to be talking about is how one of your security people shot and killed someone during the party. If they make any mention of Charles at all, it will be as a footnote."

"Mother," Amelia said grimly, "shut up."

Mrs. Westlake stiffened. "I beg your pardon, young lady?"

"You heard your daughter, Meredith." Thea's mother took a step toward the other woman, putting herself almost between her and Thea. "Shut. Up."

There was an almost comical moment when Mrs. Westlake gaped at her in surprise. Evidently, she hadn't noticed the rest of her audience. Then her mouth snapped shut and she drew her arrogance around her like a cloak. "Evelyn. I didn't see you there."

"Obviously. You were too busy chastising my daughter for something that wasn't her fault instead of begging her forgiveness."

"Now, see here—"

"No, you've had your say. Now you're going to listen to me. My daughter has been terrorized, kidnapped, assaulted, and very nearly...," her voice wobbled slightly, "...very nearly killed tonight and you have the *nerve* to complain that you and your future son-in-law aren't going to be getting enough of the headlines? Are you insane?"

"Well, of course, I didn't mean to imply—"

"Has it occurred to you that it's *your* fault that all of this happened?" Evelyn persisted, taking another step closer. "The man stalking my daughter was in your employ all this time, after all. If you want someone to blame for tonight's disaster, you might try yourself."

Panic flashed over Mrs. Westlake's face before she caught it and wiped it away. "Oliver Pratt was never in my employ," she said quickly. "He was a member of the Davenport staff." Then, as though realizing that it might sound as though she were blaming them, she added, "If there's any fault to be found, it belongs with the head of their security team for allowing him to be hired in the first place." She looked smugly pleased with her conclusion, which neatly deflected all blame away from both families and back onto the hired help.

"Do you think I care who signed the man's paycheck, Meredith? He was in your house. Yours. And he was here tonight. So any way you look at it, *you* put my daughter in harm's way."

"I don't think—"

"No, you didn't, did you? You didn't think to offer an apology. You didn't even think to ask if Thea was all right, which she is, thank God, and no thanks to you or your ridiculous excuses, or about the two people who are on their way to the hospital in who knows what condition. You just thought about yourself and how all of this was going to affect you and your precious political agenda."

"Of course, I'm pleased to hear that Cynthia wasn't seriously harmed," Mrs. Westlake said with stiff dignity. "But I have obligations which you can't possibly understand."

"If they keep you from being a decent human being, Meredith, then I don't want to."

"Well!" Her thin nose pointed to the sky, Mrs. Westlake spun and stalked back toward the building, calling imperiously over her shoulder, "Amelia Ann, let's go. I need to find a way to get you back inside without any of the reporters seeing you like that."

Pale, and looking a little bit in awe of the way Mrs. Fordham had just taken her mother to task, Amelia gave Thea a quick hug, whispering, "I'll call you tomorrow" before hurrying after her mother.

"Wow." Lillian looked just as impressed as Amelia had.

Mrs. Fordham sniffed, sitting next to Thea on the bumper and slipping her arm around her daughter's shoulders. "Nobody messes with my baby." She pressed a kiss to the side of Thea's head, frowning when she flinched. "That's it. You're going to the hospital. Now."

"Okay," Thea agreed meekly. Her head really did hurt. "But, Daddy, could you please go to the police station and check on Doyle? They took him to answer some questions, and he said it was routine and not to worry, but, well, I'm worried." Especially after witnessing Mrs. Westlake's ease at casting blame onto unsuspecting scapegoats.

"Don't worry, sweetheart," her father said, seeming to understand her concern. "I'll make sure nothing happens to him."

"You should take my father with you, Mr. Fordham," Lillian said. "He can get hold of my brother, Peter, and have him liaise between you and the detectives that are questioning Doyle."

"Great idea, Lil," Thea said, feeling relieved. "Thanks."

As her father and Lillian put their heads together to make it happen, Thea leaned into her mother, suddenly exhausted. So much had happened in such a short time, she was still having trouble processing it all. But one thing was remarkably clear. With the threat finally gone, she could finally stop looking over her shoulder and concentrate on her future and the man she knew was absolutely going to be in it.

# CHAPTER 32

**SHE CAME TO HIM** the next day.

Doyle opened the door to Thea's soft knock just as the sun was starting to dip behind the mountains. He'd hoped she'd come but hadn't been certain that she would. Things had been too chaotic at the scene for them to talk, and then she'd gone off to one of the ambulances to be checked over while he'd been sequestered with both the local police and the FBI giving statements and answering questions.

His weapon had been taken as a matter of course for the investigation into Pratt's death, he'd been questioned by five different people from at least three different agencies, and he was pretty sure he'd only escaped detention in a precinct interrogation room by dint of the combined heavyweight influence of Frank Fordham and Rupert Beaumont. And through it all, not a single person would give him any information about Thea, no matter how many times he asked.

Needless to say, his mood had been less than stellar by the time he'd finally returned home.

That had been a few hours after dawn. As he'd predicted, it had been a long night, and it was going to be an even worse day. Even as he'd driven through the gates onto the estate, the reporters had been starting to amass outside. Like locusts, they always knew where the next big meal was. They'd stay there until they'd sucked the marrow from the bones of this story and then swoop off to their next unsuspecting victim.

After checking that Red had already taken care of the extra security the estate would require during the siege and that Thea had been brought home and was currently sleeping, Doyle had stumbled back to his cottage and stood under the pounding showerheads for as long as the hot water had lasted before falling into bed himself.

After several long hours of restless sleep, he'd pulled on a pair of cotton lounging pants and T-shirt and finally sat and let the events of the previous evening wash over him. During his multiple recitations, he'd kept strictly to facts. Nothing personal had been allowed to intrude. He'd had his war face on, and none of his roiling emotions had been acknowledged, much less exposed.

Now, however, he felt his guts twist as he considered just how close things had come to total disaster. Just how close he'd come to losing the best thing that had ever come into his life before he'd even realized it. Oh, he'd known he had feelings for Thea. Affection. Admiration. Lust. But he'd been waiting for that damned light bulb.

Well, he'd gotten it in the moment he saw Pratt fire a gun at her and watched as her body dropped to the ground. If it hadn't been for Simon, he shuddered at what might have been. And what might not have.

So when he opened the door, he didn't say a word. He just opened his arms and let her walk into them. His face gently pressed against the top of her head, he breathed in the scent of her, fresh and clean and warm. *Alive.* He felt her heart beating powerfully against his chest, answering his own. He gave her strength and comfort and received the same back from her ten-fold. This. This was what he wanted, what he saw between Austin and Becca, what he'd wanted for himself. This sense of homecoming, of belonging.

"I thought I lost you," he murmured into her hair.

"You're not getting rid of me that easily."

The reply was obviously meant to be a joke, but Doyle could hear the underlying strain in her tone. He eased her back from his embrace and looked her in the eye. "No, I'm not." Aside from the bruise on her cheek which only emphasized how pale she seemed, there were no outward signs of the ordeal she'd just endured. But he, more than most, knew how easily another kind of damage could lurk just below the surface. "Are you okay? Really?"

"I'm fine. Really," she added, as though she thought he didn't believe her.

Probably because he didn't.

"Your father said you had to have a CT scan done." Because Pratt had slammed her head against a wall. If the bastard wasn't already dead, he'd kill him just for that.

"Then he also must have told you that all of the tests were negative. No concussion. No broken bones. Just some bumps and bruises." She touched a finger to her abused cheek.

That stark reminder of his failure to keep her protected was like a knife in Doyle's gut. "You went through hell last night. I am so damn sorry for that. He should have never been able to get close enough to touch you. I screwed up."

"Are you kidding? You and Simon are the only reason I'm here right now and not chained in some bedroom dungeon, being—" Her voice caught.

Doyle drew her against him again, rocking her gently as she clung to him with every ounce of strength she had. "It's okay." He whispered the words over and over, hoping that eventually they would both be able to believe it. Once her breathing had smoothed out, he asked, "What can I do?"

She pulled back so she could look at him. "Make me feel safe again." Her lips brushed his once, twice. Then she kissed him as though all of the emotions she had bottled up inside of her needed someplace to escape. It was hot and frantic for a moment before it slowed and became something else, something deeper, touching him on a level so far inside that he thought he might go up in flames.

And yet...

He gently broke the kiss. "Are you sure?"

Rather than answer, she took his hand and led him silently to the bedroom. Once they got there, he balked one final time. People reacted to trauma in different ways. Frank had assured him that Pratt hadn't attempted to molest Thea in any way, but clearly the horror of his threats was still a fresh wound. He wanted to make absolutely sure that he was doing the right thing here. For her. For them.

When he stopped moving, Thea turned and gave him a questioning look before reaching up to caress his stubble-covered cheek. "Please, Brennan. I need you."

And there was no way in the world he could deny her. Gently, he removed her clothes, cataloguing and kissing every bruise that marred her body, touching every inch of her skin with quiet reverence as though to reassure himself that she was really safe and whole.

And his.

With gentle lips he kissed her, sliding a hand in slow circles over her breasts, teasing lazily at the rosy tips that tightened and peaked under his questing fingers. She arched under the attention, a small gusty sound indicating her pleasure at his touch. Then she returned the favor, using her nails to do to his nipples what he'd done to hers, making him suck in a sharp breath at the zing that arced from nipple to groin in response.

His hands quested lower, finding her already wet and warm and open for him, putting to rest that final worry. The trauma of the evening hadn't damaged her, hadn't made her fear a man's touch, his touch. She wanted him, needed him, just as he needed her, needed to reassure himself that she was his.

As he slid inside her snug embrace, he looked down at her face, fascinated by the absolute love radiating from her expression. The pace he set was slow, lazy, and meant to show her that this wasn't about sex. This was about connection, a melding of the two into one. As his excitement stoked higher, he fought to keep his pace slow, but eventually he lost the battle and started to stroke more quickly.

He ate the small sounds of pleasure that broke from her lips, until finally he buried his face in the crook of her neck and let out a muffled shout of his own, feeling her contractions around him as she found her climax with him. He breathed her in with every ragged breath he drew and knew this was home.

"I love you."

Thea's hand stilled from where it had been petting along his back, a habit of hers after they made love. Doyle smiled into her neck, knowing he'd caught her off guard. He'd enjoy the moment because he didn't think there'd be many like them.

He pulled back until he could look into her eyes. She looked wary, as though she weren't entirely sure she'd heard him correctly, so he said it again, plainly and clearly. "I love you."

"I love you, too." She said it solemnly, like she was sharing a secret. Or a promise. He kissed her softly to seal the vows.

Finally, she was his.

*   *   *

They dozed for a while and then woke up and made love again, this time more playfully. Doyle didn't tell her he loved her again, but she didn't need him to. She knew he'd meant it. She didn't need to hear it a dozen times a day. All she needed to do was see the look in his eyes and she knew.

After a quick shower, they investigated the contents of his fridge and pulled out the makings for omelets. As he broke eggs into a bowl, he asked, "I'm guessing your parents know you're here."

"Mmhmm." She finished chewing the bite of cheese she'd snitched and added, "After last night, I had to tell them where I was going or they might have freaked when they realized I wasn't anywhere in the house."

"How are you feeling?"

She'd known before Doyle told her that he'd come to the house first thing after he'd gotten back to the estate, and that her father had given him a complete rundown on her prognosis. According to him, only the fact that she'd been out cold from the pain killers the hospital had given her had stopped Doyle from insisting on seeing with his own eyes that she was okay. Evidently, what he hadn't been able to see for himself, he now needed to hear for himself. Again. That was okay, though. He'd managed to soothe away her fears when she'd asked him to. The least she could do was return the favor.

"The headache is gone. Mostly, anyway." She touched the back of her head gingerly. "Like I said, there's no concussion, but I still can't go running for at least a week. And my cheek was only bruised. Although," she added, trying to keep her recitation of injuries as light as possible, "the doctor says I can expect it to turn an alluring shade of green at some point in the near future."

Despite her efforts, there was a flash of molten rage in Doyle's eyes before he buried it behind a teasing smile. "Well, then I guess we'll just have to make sure you get your exercise in other ways that won't jar your pretty head, now won't we?"

Remembering the incredibly tender care he'd taken with her while they'd made love earlier, Thea felt herself blush and heat at the same time. She cleared her throat and tried to redirect the conversation. "Have you checked on Simon and Francine recently? The doctors couldn't tell us much more last night than that they were both stable."

"I called while you were in the shower. They're both doing okay, although they need to run a few more tests on Francine to be sure."

"Did they find out what Oliver did to her?"

"They found a large amount of Rohypnol in her system." Doyle's tone was hard. "He must have gotten close enough to put it in her water glass somehow. She doesn't remember talking to him but memory loss is one of the side effects. That's what makes it such an effective date-rape drug. The victims can't remember anything."

"God." Thea shuddered, suddenly feeling sick. "The champagne."

"What?"

"He handed me a glass of champagne, but I put it down while we were walking. If I hadn't..."

Doyle pulled her into a hard embrace while they both absorbed the implications. If Oliver had managed to drug Thea, she never would have been able to fight him off long enough for help to arrive.

"It didn't happen," Doyle reminded her, kissing her forehead tenderly before going back to his breakfast preparation. "You're safe."

Thea nodded, trying to not think about the what-ifs. Instead, she asked, "Is Francine going to be okay?"

"She should be."

"Good. And what about Simon?"

"He's still sedated, but the prognosis is good." Doyle briskly whisked the eggs as Thea got out a pan and set it on the stove. "Barring infection, he should be released in a couple of days."

"Thank God." She still couldn't get over the fact that Simon had gotten shot because of her. No. *For* her. She and her friends had joked about his overeager attitude and annoyingly strict attention to protocol. Now, when that very thing had most likely saved her life, she felt like an ungrateful ass.

"I owe him," Thea said fervently.

Doyle looked over at her, his expression serious. "So do I."

Their gazes held for a long moment, and Thea could feel her heart start to speed up as the now familiar arousal started to build. Feeling slightly breathless, she turned her attention to the peppers and mushrooms waiting to be chopped.

She resolutely ignored the masculine chuckle he gave as he added seasoning to the eggs and gave them another quick beating. "So, how did Oliver get a gun into the party, anyway? I thought they were supposed to have all that crazy Super Secret Service security."

Doyle's mouth pulled downward. "He took it from Francine. I don't know if he planned it that way, but aside from isolating you from your bodyguard, taking her down was the easiest way for him to get a weapon without having to risk smuggling one in himself. For a twisted bastard, he was pretty damn smart." Thea shuddered, not wanting to remember exactly how twisted he had been.

"Dad had the both of them put in private rooms to try and keep the reporters from bothering them. They wouldn't really try to get into Simon's hospital room for a story, would they? I mean, he just got out of surgery!"

"Sweetheart, some of them would have tried to get into the operating room for a story if they could have found a way." He tested the heat of the pan, took the cutting board from her, and slid the vegetables into the sizzling oil. "Which reminds me, stay away from the gates today."

"I was already warned when I left the house." She groaned. "God, it's like we're under siege by the Mongols."

"Close enough." Stirring the cooking food, he asked, "Have you spoken with Amelia or Lillian?"

"I talked to Lil last night for a minute after we left the hospital. She'd wanted to come and wait with me while Simon—" her voice caught "—while Simon was in surgery, but I told her she should just go home and avoid the circus."

Doyle looked instantly upset. "I'm sorry I wasn't there for you. I wanted to be. But the police—"

"I know," she interrupted quickly, hating that he felt he'd let her down in some way. "You had to give a statement. It's okay. So did I, but Dad convinced them to let me do it at the hospital. I didn't want to leave until I knew Simon was going to be okay." That cold fear that he might die because of her, despite everyone's assurances otherwise, still made her insides a little shaky. She concentrated on shredding the cheese while Doyle poured the eggs into the pan.

"What about Amelia?"

That was going to be a bigger mess than almost everything else combined.

"She said she'd call me today, but when I tried to get ahold of her just before to give her an update, she didn't answer, so I'm guessing she has her phone turned off. I tried the house line, but no one answered there, either."

"The Westlakes and Davenports are probably circling the wagons and doing intensive damage control," he guessed, and Thea thought he was probably right. It was just too bad that it would be Charles that everyone would be trying to insulate from the evening's events. Amelia, as always, would merely be an afterthought.

Thea wanted to get in her car and go see her, make sure she was holding up okay, but she knew that the media presence would be even worse outside the Westlake home than her own. She'd simply have to wait for Mellie to return one of her dozen or so texts, which had all amounted to the same plea: *Call me.*

"I still can't believe it was Oliver." Thea wrapped her arms around herself against a sudden inner chill as the horror of the previous night threatened to break through the walls she had holding it at bay.

Sliding the pan off the burner, Doyle wrapped his arms around her as well, tucking her in tight to his strong, hard body in a protective hug. Thea relished the feeling of safety he provided in addition to the heat he threw off.

"He seemed so nice. So *normal.*" That was the scariest part. "I thought we were, well, not friends, but at least colleagues in trying to give Mellie the wedding she deserved."

"Which just fed into his fantasy." His arms tightened around her when she stiffened. "It wasn't your fault, sweetheart. Nothing you did made him think or act the way he did. He was either a sociopath or just plain nuts, but no matter what, none of this was your fault."

In her brain, she knew that. But her heart was going to take a little more time to convince. "I gave him cookies, damn it." It was a stupid thing to say, but the sense of betrayal was still too immense to put into better words.

Doyle stilled for a second. "Rosa's cookies? The ones with honey drizzled on top?"

"Um…" She struggled to remember. "Maybe. Why? Is it important?"

"Not really. It just explains something." Before she could ask what, he continued, "Kirsten did a quick computer check and matched the postmarks on all the letters to cities recently visited by Senator Davenport and his son."

"And his son's personal assistant."

She felt Doyle nod. "If Pratt didn't leave any kind of journals or other evidence about his plans, at least the police will have something solid to tie Pratt to everything that happened."

Because there was a body in the morgue that couldn't tell them what they wanted to know. Thea hadn't considered the possibility that without those letters, they didn't have a shred of evidence to support their claim that Oliver had been trying to kidnap her other than her word. Suddenly, Doyle's night at the police station took on an ominous undertone.

Panicked, she pulled back so she could see Doyle's face. "Are you going to be in trouble for shooting him? You know that Dad will get his lawyers right on this. If you need—" Her words tumbled to a halt as he pressed his fingers to her lips.

"Relax. I'm not in any trouble. There'll be an investigation because there was a death, but I'm not worried and you shouldn't be, either. It was a justifiable shooting. If they were going to arrest me, they would have done it last night."

Slowly, Thea nodded, the anxiety fading under his assurances. "I'm still sorry you had to be the one to kill him." Because former Marine or not, she knew that taking a life would weigh heavy on his conscience.

"I'm not." The words were flat, but his eyes burned with emotion. Thea wondered at that. Then she remembered the two letters that Doyle had refused to let her read. Whatever they had said, they'd convinced Doyle that Oliver deserved killing. She shuddered slightly, glad she'd never have to find out exactly what had been waiting for her at the house Oliver had arranged to be her prison.

Sitting down at the table with their jointly prepared meal, Thea felt the edginess and hurt slide away, and a strange sense of rightness settled over her. She could see herself doing this every day, sitting down to breakfast with the man she loved, both of them going off to work, and then meeting back over another meal at the end of the day. It was a perfect rhythm. It was the perfect man.

"You're thinking heavy thoughts over there," Doyle chastised, rubbing his bare foot along hers under the table. She grinned.

"Happy thoughts," she corrected. "Definitely happy thoughts."

"About us, I hope."

*Us.* It was silly to get such a rush from that little word, but she couldn't help it. She gave him a sweet smile in reply, and they dug into their food with ravenous appetites. It was as they lingered over their coffee that Doyle oh-so-casually asked, "Do you think you could be comfortable living here?"

The world froze as the implication of that simple question sank in. "With you?"

"No, since you're suddenly Simon's number-one fan, I thought you might like to marry *him*. Of course, with me."

*Marry?*

"Did you just ask me to marry you?"

"No," he replied, scowling.

"Oh." She was confused and not a little mortified.

"When I ask, I'll do it up right with flowers and champagne and a ring in hand."

"I'm sorry. That was presumptuous of me," she stammered. "I didn't mean…"

"Oh, don't get me wrong," Doyle broke in, taking the hands she was wringing together on the tabletop and clasping them firmly in his own. "We *are* getting married. No way are you getting away from me, sweetheart. You're mine."

"I am? We are?" Her head was spinning, but it was a giddy sensation.

"I was just wondering if you would want to live here in the bungalow or if we should start looking for a place of our own closer to town. I know your dad prefers the head of security to live on-site, but if we stay on the north side, I wouldn't be more than ten minutes away if I was needed. He shouldn't object to that."

"Um, maybe?"

"Or if you've decided to accept that job offer from Matrix, we can start looking on the Internet for places out in California," he continued determinedly. "I'm ready to get my security business going, but I haven't committed to anything here yet, lease-wise, so I can set up shop pretty much anywhere we go."

"Doyle…"

"Or we can—"

"Doyle!" She twisted her hands so they were holding his instead of the other way around, leaning forward over the table so she was looking directly into his eyes. "I don't care where we live. As long as I'm with you, I'll be happy."

She watched the truth of that statement sink in, watched the tension seep out of his shoulders, and allowed him to pull her closer until their lips were a whisper apart.

"*Mo chroi, m'anam,*" he murmured. "You are my heart and soul. I love you, Cynthia Fordham."

"And I love you, Brennan Doyle," she replied. They closed the last fraction of space and melted into the kiss, and Thea knew it didn't matter if they lived in a condo in California or a house in Colorado or a double-wide trailer on the moon.

She was already home.

## END

Dear Reader,

I hope you've enjoyed reading Thea and Doyle's story as much I did writing it. Visit me on Facebook or at my website NikaRhone.com to let me know what you thought, and if you have a moment, please consider leaving a review at any of the usual places. Authors thrive on feedback from our readers.

And don't worry about Amelia. She has a happy ending coming her way, and her very own bodyguard to make it happen. He just doesn't know it yet. Keep reading for a sneak peek of their story in the next book of the Boulder Bodyguards series.

# SNEAK PEEK OF BOOK TWO IN THE BOULDER BODYGUARDS SERIES

## BY NIKA RHONE

# CHAPTER 1

**THE PARTY WAS** a raging success.

Everyone who was anyone in the highest rungs of society from all around the Tri-State Area was there, nibbling on imported caviar and drinking over-priced champagne, all the while ensuring that they were seen by everyone they deemed worthy of seeing them, and ignoring those poor insignificants who weren't worth their estimable consideration. Smiles and air kisses were exchanged, handshakes dispensed, and photo opportunities given— discreetly, of course—to the lucky few reporters granted entrée to the first round of gatherings leading up to what was almost guaranteed to be the wedding of the year, if not the decade.

Too bad the only person in attendance *not* impressed by it all was the bride.

In fact, Amelia mused, sipping the too-dry champagne she'd been nursing for the past half hour, she would have paid good money to be just about anyplace else but at the center of the juggernaut that was propelling her toward her fate as Mrs. Charles Wilson Henry Davenport. A fate that, up until tonight, she'd been perfectly happy with.

Or at least she'd convinced herself that she had been.

Because if she was absolutely honest with herself for a moment— something she tried not to do very often these days lest that thin veil of complacency be tragically stripped away—she'd been pushing herself toward this moment with all the enthusiasm of a condemned prisoner heading for the gallows. Or, she reconsidered, glancing at the glittering crowd that moved and seethed around her like a living beast, more aptly to the Coliseum. Because her wedding was all about spectacle, after all. Lots of flash, very little substance.

"Kind of like Charles," she murmured into her glass as she swallowed the last sip.

"What was that, dear?"

*Crap.* Smiling vapidly at the jewel-encrusted woman standing next to her, Amelia said breezily, "I said I should go find Charles. If you'll excuse me, please?" She slipped away without waiting for a reply, a big nasty etiquette *faux pas,* but she honestly didn't care anymore. She knew she should, but she just didn't.

Swapping her empty champagne glass for a full one with one of the roving waiters, Amelia slipped through the crowd, trying to look as though she was moving with purpose, when all the purpose she had was to keep moving. If she didn't, she'd be cornered by whichever of the Davenports' guests was closest when she stopped. Normally not a problem for her, having been drilled in social etiquette practically from birth. She was pretty sure her mother had even read Emily Post to her in the womb. So Amelia knew that she could fake polite interest with the best of them.

But tonight...

Tonight her tolerance for boring chitchat and name dropping one-upmanship was at an all-time low. In fact, her tolerance for everything seemed to be low, quickly thinning to nonexistent. Especially for her fiancé, whom she hadn't seen more than a quick glimpse of since they first stepped foot into the expansive ground floor of his parents' mausoleum of a home and welcomed their first guests.

No, it wasn't a home. It was a showpiece. With its miles of imported marble and strategically placed artwork and antiques, she'd always thought that it more closely resembled a museum than anyplace real human beings would live. All it was missing were the little red ropes to keep the hoi polloi at bay.

Spotting a bright splash of color in the middle of the room, Amelia felt her heart lighten for the first time all evening. Barely even seeing the people she brushed past to get to that beacon of hope—yet another social mark against her but who cared—she only just kept herself from barreling into the arms of her two best friends. Only her mother's voice screeching in her head about decorum reined her in at the last second, leaving her swaying slightly on her high heels.

"You made it." It was a stupid thing to say, and yet she didn't feel awkward for having said it. Not with them. She'd grown up with Thea and Lillian. They'd all seen each other at their best as well as their worst, and they all loved each other anyway.

They loved *her* anyway.

"Like we wouldn't be here for you." A petite cloud of citron and charcoal silk, Lillian Beaumont pulled Amelia into a tight hug of welcome.

After an evening of air kisses and cool, limp finger-touching, Amelia sagged into the embrace with a sense of wild relief, barely noticing when someone plucked the champagne glass from her grasp. A person could only go so long without real human contact before going a little bit crazy. And right now she felt about half a step away from insane.

Reluctantly, she finally withdrew from the embrace, although she did keep a tight hold of her friend's hands as she stepped back to take in the colorful creation she wore. "You look amazing." The swirl of vivid yellows and subdued grays should have overwhelmed Lillian's diminutive five-foot-two height, but the expert cut and the intense energy that emanated from the woman herself made it work for her. "Is that one of Des's?"

"A certified D.F. original." With a dramatic twirl, Lillian showed off what Amelia knew would be another instant hit in their friend's newest entrepreneurial endeavor. It was amazing how much raw talent the man had, and in how many different directions he could fling it.

"It's truly incredible on you," she said honestly. "Des is a genius."

Which was exactly the same thought she'd had when she'd tried on the gown he'd designed for her as a wedding present. The one whose brilliantly tailored cut had highlighted her delicate bone structure rather than making her look like an underfed waif. The one whose soft lavender silk had brightened her pale complexion to a healthy peaches-and-cream, rather than the sickly whiteness of a sun-starved anemic.

The one that was still hanging forlornly in her bedroom closet upstairs after her mother had deemed it unacceptable for the evening's festivities due to its lack of name-brand cachet.

Lillian grinned, unaware of her friend's dejected train of thought. "As he'd say if he were here, 'Thank you, kitten, but did you really expect anything less from the brilliance that is *moi*?'" She ended with a dramatic arm sweep *a la* Desmond.

Laughing softly, because she could picture Des saying it just that way, Amelia next turned to her other best friend, Thea, who was also wearing one of Des's masterpieces. The slightly Baroque-style was offset by the sheer panels of black lace at the sides, keeping the wealth of bronze sequins from overpowering either the gown or the woman wearing it. She looked amazing.

Struggling to bury the renewed disappointment of not wearing her own Des creation, Amelia gave herself up to the hug Thea bestowed on her, reminding herself sternly that there was nothing wrong with the gown she was wearing. Even if it did make her collarbones stand out like chicken wings. And the silver lamé washed her out until she was practically invisible. And the boat neckline made her breasts look almost nonexistent.

God, she hated this dress.

She hated this night.

She hated her life.

Blinking in surprise at the traitorously honest thought that had snuck into her usually well-behaved brain, Amelia stepped back from the hug, totally missing what Thea had said until she realized that her friend was looking at her strangely.

"I'm sorry," Amelia said with a small shake of her head. "My mind must have wandered. What did you say?"

"I asked if you were all right."

"I'm fine." No, she was a big, fat liar, so she quickly added, "Des really outdid himself, T. You look fabulous."

It wasn't just a compliment to deflect Thea's attention, which was a bit too sharp for Amelia's comfort. It was also the truth. Less than a year ago, Thea had been a mess of insecurities and self-doubt. Now, she looked cool. Confident. And crazy in love with the tuxedoed man standing possessively at her side, holding the champagne glass Amelia only now realized she was missing.

Retrieving the glass and accepting a kiss on the cheek in greeting from Thea's fiancé, Amelia had to admit to herself that it wasn't the dress that had given her friend that air of self possession and poise. It was the man. Brennan Doyle had given Thea that and more when he'd finally gotten past his own personal hang-ups and admitted that he was in love with her.

Truly, madly, deeply in love. Nauseatingly so.

Tipping back her glass, Amelia drowned out the spiteful little voice of jealousy with the last of her champagne. She was happy that her friend had found that kind of love. Really she was. Happy, happy, happy.

She just wished she could scrounge up a fraction of that happiness with the man she was set to marry in—God help her—ten days.

"Sweetie, have you had anything to eat tonight?"

Blinking a bit owlishly at Lillian, who was studying her with an expression of concern, Amelia nodded. "We had an early family supper. Duck a l'Orange with shallots and parsnips. They have it every Wednesday. It's one of the chef's specialties."

"Sweetie, you hate duck."

Amelia nodded. "But Charles and his father love it." She foresaw a lot of unhappy duck dinners in her future.

She foresaw a lot of unhappy in her future, period.

Automatically, she raised her glass to her lips, only to be disappointed by its emptiness. "Oh." She stared sadly into the glass, trying to remember when she'd drunk it all and failing. "I need more champagne."

"I think maybe you need to wait a bit on that." Thea plucked the glass from her hand and passed it off to Doyle, who in turn deposited it on a passing tray. He did not exchange it for a full one, Amelia noted with disappointment.

Pasting on her party smile, she said, "Come on, let me show you around. Lil, I think you'll love the master's gallery leading down to the library. There's a wonderful little landscape there that they think might be an unknown Monet. There's a huge debate over how to go about proving the provenance, but even if it's not one of his it's still one of the most beautiful canvases I've ever seen."

She chattered on, hardly aware of what she was saying as she led them through the crowded ballroom and down the wide hallway that connected the more public rooms to the private family area at the back. As she'd hoped, no one else was there. Finally relieved of being the cynosure of the glittering throng her parents and future in-laws considered five hundred of their closest friends and potential campaign donors, her whole body sagged with relief.

And, of course, her friends picked up on it immediately.

"Mellie, honey." Thea put a tentative hand on her arm. "I know you said you were fine, but, sweetie, you really don't look all that fine right now." She chewed her bottom lip, a sure sign that she was anxious about something. "Is it…sweetie, do you want me to go?"

"What?" A shot of pure panic raced through Amelia, straightening her spine faster than one of her mother's disapproving glares. She grabbed both of Thea's arms. "No! You can't go! Why would you want to go?" Her gaze darted between her two friends desperately. "Please, please, don't go."

Horrified to feel tears prickling at the corners of her eyes, Amelia used every bit of willpower she had left to swallow down the emotions that had started to bubble over the usually secure cap she kept on them. It had to have been the champagne. And the stress. And the duck that she'd forced down and had forced its way back up again.

It couldn't possibly be because she was finally realizing what a colossal mess she was about to make of her life. Because even if she did admit it, even if only to herself, the truth was it was much, much too late to do anything about it.

"Why…" Amelia sucked in a breath and managed to smooth the hitch out of her voice. "Why would you ever think I'd want you to leave? I want you here. I *need* you here." Knowing they were going to be in Connecticut for the entire week of parties, dinners, and teas leading up to the wedding had been the one thing keeping Amelia from dissolving into a full-blown panic attack all day.

"I'm sorry, Mellie," Thea said, sounding relieved. "It's just…I know the dragons were giving you a hard time about me being involved in any of the wedding events, and after I found out about the cancellation, I thought maybe you'd decided to try and keep the peace and, you know…distance yourself a little. Which would be perfectly okay if you did," she rushed on when Amelia just stared at her in confusion. "The very last thing I wanted to do is add any more problems to your plate."

"No," Amelia said and then shook her head, although she wasn't certain if she was disagreeing or simply trying to clear her thoughts, which were suddenly spinning in cloudy champagne-tinged spirals in her head. She tried again. "Okay, yes, Mother and Mrs. Davenport were a bit…apprehensive about the press making some sort of reference to last year's incident when they saw you. But, no, I didn't change my mind about having you here."

But she had changed it about having Thea as one of her bridesmaids. Oh, Thea had backed out on her own before Amelia had been put in the awkward position of having to ask, but they'd both known that she would have. Amelia might have had limited success in finding her backbone when it came to dealing with her mother in the past year or so, but she had yet to be able to withstand the combined might of both her mother *and* future mother-in-law.

Duck wasn't the only thing that made her stomach miserable.

The stress of losing her friend from her wedding party, after the terror of almost losing her in a much more real and permanent way to the deranged lunatic who had tried to kidnap her during Amelia's engagement party, would have been enough to give anyone an ulcer. She wasn't there quite yet, but she was close.

Add in the double helping of disapproval and esteem-demolishing remarks bestowed on her daily by the dragons, as the mothers had been so aptly named by her friends, and she figured her stomach would have pretty much eaten its way out of her bellybutton by the Fourth of July.

By habit she reached for one of the rolls of antacids that were always tucked into some pocket or purse or somewhere else handy. Only she didn't have any pockets, and the tiny evening bag she'd chosen was still on her dressing table upstairs, vetoed in much the same way as her beautiful dress had been.

Even as she considered the possibility of a strategic escape upstairs to go pop a few tablets like a drug addict scoring a hit, Lillian held out her hand. "Here you go, sweetie."

"Oh, God, I love you." Ripping open the foil wrapper, Amelia practically inhaled two of the discs. The fruit flavor didn't exactly mix well with champagne, but she didn't care if it tasted like garden dirt. All she wanted was to soothe the gurgling that had erupted in her belly the moment Thea had mentioned leaving.

The familiar motion of chewing had a calming effect, and after a moment she felt her tightened muscles start to loosen. This was good. Her stomach was settling down. Her friends weren't going to abandon her. All was right with her world again.

Well, not all, but enough that she had a shot at making it through the rest of the party without losing control again.

It was only as she was slipping a third insurance tablet into her mouth that the rest of what Thea had said cycled back around and repeated itself. She cocked her head at her friend in confusion.

"What cancellation?"

*   *   *

There were few things Daryl Raintree considered a worse way to spend an evening than working a security detail at a society party.

One of the reasons he'd enjoyed working for the Fordham family for the past six years was that most of the parties they hosted or attended were oriented towards Frank's business. Society held little appeal to them despite their wealth. Unfortunately, there were still times that one of them had to jump into the glittering throng and swim with the diamond-studded barracudas. Like tonight. And where they went, so did he.

Daryl adjusted his stance against the wall just outside the hallway housing more paintings than a wing at the Met, ignoring the sidelong looks he got from passing guests. Even dressed in a tuxedo, he knew he looked exactly like what he was: a bodyguard. At six-foot-four with his father's Sioux heritage stamped plainly on his features, he didn't exactly blend well into this type of crowd the way Doyle could. So instead, he played to type.

With a quiet sigh, Daryl fought the urge to check his watch. It would be hours yet before Thea would want to leave. She'd spent the entire flight from Colorado worrying about Amelia, and judging by their sudden decampment from the ballroom a few minutes ago and the very strained smile of greeting that Amelia had given him as she walked by, it seemed like Thea's fears had been justified. No, they were definitely going to be here awhile. He was just going to have to suck it up.

It was his own fault that he was here, after all. He could have chosen to be placed on the senior Fordhams' detail instead, which wasn't arriving until next week. It was only their daughter Thea that had flown in to do the pre-wedding party train. Ten days of society hell and he'd volunteered for it.

Actually, he'd insisted.

Because he'd been part of the team that had lost sight of Thea nine months earlier, at another party given by the Davenports and Westlakes, and allowed a psychopath to get his hands on her.

It should never have happened. There had been dozens of security personnel in place in and around the banquet hall. Hell, there had been *Secret Service* there. They'd thought they had the situation all buttoned up.

And they'd been dead wrong.

The evening had ended with one of their own wounded, the perp dead, and all of them feeling like they'd royally fucked up.

So when Doyle had told him that Thea was going to be attending not just Amelia's wedding, but all of the varied dinners and parties beforehand, Daryl had known he would be going with them. He owed Thea that. He owed Doyle that.

He owed himself that.

Okay, so maybe it was a sort of self-flagellating penance, because he sure to God hated these things, but he'd sworn that any time Thea was going to be anywhere in the vicinity of either the Westlakes or Davenports, he wasn't taking his eyes off of her for a second.

He didn't much care for the senior Westlakes—the mother was an ice-cold bitch and the father a pompous blowhard—but it was the Davenports he didn't trust. His instincts itched whenever he was around them, and that wasn't just his aversion to society chaffing like a bad rash. Something bad was definitely going to happen.

"Amelia, sweetie, wait!"

Daryl barely had time to straighten from his relaxed pose to alert readiness when a tiny bundle of blonde and silver came stalking out of the hallway Doyle had shepherded the Royal Court into after signaling for Daryl to wait against the wall outside. He ignored Amelia until he saw the other two women come bolting after her, followed by Doyle, who looked annoyed but not concerned. Spotting Daryl, Doyle gave the all-clear signal. Whatever drama was going on wasn't a danger to Thea. Not yet, anyway.

Being half a head taller than most people in the room made it easy for Daryl to follow the three women's progress through the crowd. Amelia Westlake still led the way, looking like the prow of an ice-cutter forging its way through the North Sea, with Thea and Lillian two colorful anchors being dragged in her wake.

It was an odd sight. In all the years he'd known them, he couldn't remember a single other time that he had seen Amelia take the lead on anything the three friends had done. She was the follower, the Princess, the one the other two always fussed over and protected. It was her security call sign that had been picked first back when the girls had been in middle school. The other two had quickly followed. Thea was the Lady, the group's modifier and voice of reason. Lillian was the lead trouble-maker, their Queen Bee. If there was a plot or plan in evidence, she was the one most likely to have thought it up and convinced the other two to join in.

Hence the Royal Court was born.

And while both Lillian and Thea had been known to act out of character a time or two and throw a monkey wrench into the well-oiled machinery of their security details, Amelia was the one least likely to go off script. Her entire life was run by her mother with an efficiency Patton would have envied.

Which was why her sudden change in behavior now was mildly disturbing.

"Do we have a problem?" Daryl asked quietly as he and Doyle followed behind the women.

"Oh, I'd say there's definitely a problem. I'm just not sure whose it is yet."

But it clearly had something to do with Thea. Daryl could tell that by the slight growl that edged the other man's voice, as low and well modulated as it had been. If Daryl was overly-vigilant of Thea because of what had happened the previous year, then Doyle was fanatical. Even a hint of something that might upset her raised his protective hackles. Unfortunately for them both, Thea was not the type of person to sit back and let others take care of her problems for her.

Which was why they were following where the three women led, instead of charging ahead to slay whatever dragons stood in their way.

When the two men caught up to where the women had stopped, Daryl realized he'd been closer to the truth than he'd realized. In front of them were Meredith Westlake and Constance Davenport. Both of these particular dragons were elegantly gowned, stylishly coiffed, and wore identical expressions of distaste and disapproval. Daryl assumed the latter was for the belligerent expression currently gracing Amelia's usually placid features.

Yet another odd sight.

The break from the norm was unsettling, but it also raised his interest. Any problem that could force someone who had spent twenty-three years allowing herself to be molded into the perfect little princess to break form—in public, no less—had to be one hell of a doozy.

Sometimes he really hated it when his instincts were right.

# MORE GREAT READS
# FROM BOOKTROPE

*Acquiring Hearts* **by S. Donahue** (Romance) A whirlwind romance full of emotion, devotion and passion.

*Consumed* **by J.C. Hannigan** (Romance) Jax Walker is a hard man to resist. He's tall, dark, and delicious. Harlow didn't plan on falling for another, with her heart still stuck on Iain. But it's so hard with him gone. And she's been aching since they last touched. Two whole years of silent wondering; of desperate sleepless longing.

*Falling* **by Ryanne Anthony** (Romance) Kimber Forrest felt everyone believed her to be silly and naive when it came to ultimate bad boy Jaxen Malloy. She was determined to prove them all wrong and make him fall for her as much as she was falling for him.

*That's a Promise* **by Victoria Klahr** (Romance) Josie's life has been filled with broken promises and lies. Seth holds half her soul a world away and Blake's lies have torn them apart. In the face of her most recent tragedy, Josie has to decide whether forgiveness is something she can give. But even if that's an option, can she be forgiven?

*Unexpected Chances* **by A.M. Willard** (Romance) Never wanting to love again Tabitha throws herself into work and friends. She needs no one until an unexpected chance meeting has her doubting every decision she had made.

Would you like to read more books like these?
Subscribe to **runawaygoodness.com**, get a free ebook for signing up,
and never pay full price for an ebook again.

Discover more books and learn about our
new approach to publishing at **www.booktrope.com.**